NOVELS BY LAURIE R. KING

MARY RUSSELL NOVELS

The Beekeeper's Apprentice
A Monstrous Regiment of Women
A Letter of Mary
The Moor
O Jerusalem
Justice Hall
The Game
Locked Rooms
The Language of Bees
The God of the Hive
Beekeeping for Beginners: A Short Story
Pirate King
Garment of Shadows

KATE MARTINELLI NOVELS

A Grave Talent
To Play the Fool
With Child
Night Work
The Art of Detection

AND

A Darker Place
Folly
Keeping Watch
Califa's Daughters (as Leigh Richards)
Touchstone
The Bones of Paris

THE BONES
OF PARIS

THE BONES OF PARIS

A NOVEL OF SUSPENSE

LAURIE R. KING

BANTAM BOOKS

NEW YORK

Published in the United States by Bantam Books, an imprint of The Random House Publishing Group, a division of Random House, Inc., New York.

BANTAM BOOKS and the HOUSE colophon are registered trademarks of Random House, Inc.

Library of Congress Cataloging-in-Publication Data

King, Laurie R.
The bones of Paris : a novel of suspense / Laurie R. King.
pages cm
ISBN 978-0-345-53176-6
eBook ISBN 978-0-345-53177-3
1. Paris (France)—Fiction. I. Title.
PS3561.I4813B66 2013
813'.54—dc23 2013010332

Printed in the United States of America on acid-free paper

www.bantamdell.com

2 4 6 8 9 7 5 3 1

First Edition

Book design by Caroline Cunningham

For Robert Difley,

a brother in more than law.

THE BONES
OF PARIS

PREFACE

THE ENVELOPE REACHED Bennett Grey early Wednesday afternoon.

His neighbor Robbie splashed up the muddy drive with it, beaming with eagerness—post was rare here at the farthest reaches of Cornwall, and an oversized, airmailed envelope from Paris was a prize. But Wednesday had been a bad day already, with a headache beating at Grey's skull and shadows dancing at the corners of his eyes. He let his gaze slide over the envelope's surface, and told the lad to leave it on the kitchen table.

There it lay, growling like an angry cat whenever he set foot in the kitchen, while the rain streaked the windows and the day faded to night.

He took a cold supper in the sitting room. He abandoned the dishes in the sink. He called himself a coward and took himself to bed, where he spent the next seven hours feeling the world scrape across his raw nerves.

The raindrops grew smaller, then slowed. As the sky cleared, the full moon pressed against the house, cool light whispering a path along the threads of the bedroom carpet. On the road, the faint sound of farmer Evans' motor came, grew, receded: the hesitant foot on the pedals suggested one drink too many. The odor and feel of his fresh sheets testified to Mrs. Trevalian's distraction on laundry day: the residue came from one rinse rather than two. Out in the yard, a dog-fox hunted: Bennett heard the dig of the big creature's claws into gritty soil, the thump of its landing, the pale squeak of a mouse's death. Waves chewed at the cliffs; air currents climbed and slid down the hills; the grandfather clock in the front room *tick, tick*ed the world towards morning. One of its gears had a flaw that his bones felt whenever the tooth worked its way around. The uneven wear would lead to trouble in another ten or fifteen years—but by then, please God, it would be someone else's problem.

If the envelope had been from Sarah, he'd have forced himself to open the thing, despite the weather, the shadows, and the miasma of dread that clung to the paper like old grease. But it was not Sarah's writing. The letter came from Harris Stuyvesant, a man whose motives Grey had reason to distrust. A man who stirred a whirlwind of emotions: guilt and hate, pity and pain, friendship and the deep ache of unacknowledged responsibilities. A man whose hand had been so tense when printing the address, the nib had caught twice in the fibers.

If that wasn't sufficient warning, the flap had been doubly sealed, its glue reinforced with paper tape. Fear alone would do that, fear that a mere lick of the tongue was not enough to keep the contents from escaping.

The sky was still dark when Bennett Grey left his bed. He dressed, and walked through moonlight to the promontory overlooking the Channel. The slab of stone he climbed onto was the edge of the world, Britain's final bit of land. The infinitesimal shift beneath his boots told him that, sometime in the next century, an added weight such as his would tip the thing into the sea. In the meantime, the rock provided a viewpoint, and a temptation: just lean forward . . .

The eastern horizon grew lighter. The waves below his dangling boot-heels called their Siren song: *You always have a choice.* He could simply bend over and let the sky claim him, let it pull at his garments and cushion him with airy hands for a few moments, then deliver him safely to the rocks, sixty feet below.

There was always a choice.

The sun breached the horizon, flaring the world into a brilliance that thinned, faded, retreated. When the mist had cleared from the water below, Bennett Grey got to his feet and looked straight down at the seething waves.

"Not today, friends."

Back in his kitchen, the sun poured through the windows, beating the dark gremlins into the corners of the room. Still, Grey stirred the fire into life before approaching the table.

He stood in the sunlight with the envelope in one hand and his knife in the other; the blade whispered through the manila paper. Grey slid the contents onto the table. When he lifted the top sheet, a fleeting look downward made him grateful for the reinforcing tape: had Robbie's curiosity got the better of him, the poor lad would have had nightmares for weeks.

Stuyvesant's American script on the cheap French stationery was as tense as his printing on the envelope:

September 16
Hotel Benoit
Rue de Colle, Paris

Bennett,
 Sorry to disturb you, but I need to know if these can be real, and I don't know who else to ask. I'm hoping you tell me they were staged.
 I saw Sarah the other night, she's looking well.

Harris

Grey reread that last sentence: flat, noncommittal, and with a hesitation on the *I*. There was something Harris was not telling him. Something troubling the man.

Grey shook his head at the ill-fated relationship between his sister and his friend, then rested the needle-sharp point of his knife on the topmost photograph to push it away. He repeated the motion three times, moving each picture across his kitchen table with the point of the knife. Four pieced-together images seared onto his mind and soul: the widened eyes; the pull of muscle; the strain in the neck; the texture of the skin. He studied all four, although a glimpse of any one of them would have been enough, for a man with his abilities.

When he had looked, he slid the envelope under the pictures and thrust everything into the stove. He wiped the knife on his trouser-leg, waiting for the flames to catch. He washed his hands with soap. He scrubbed the table and used the steel poker to reduce the ashes to dust.

And then he went to pack a bag.

The pictures were not staged.

The terror was real.

ONE

SEPTEMBER 9–11, 1929

ONE

T HE MORNING EXPLODED.

The room's east windows flared with a hot torment that seared across Harris Stuyvesant's brain, stabbing through his eyes, splintering his thoughts, turning his mouth to old shoe leather: cracked, greasy, foul.

A long way off, miles and miles away, his hand crept across the sticky sheets to the bed-side table, directed by one squinting eye towards the leather straps that stuck in the air like the legs of some dead thing. The hand fumbled, lifted, fumbled again to reverse the watch-face.

Jesus: not yet ten, and already a furnace.

Stuyvesant managed to get his feet to the carpet, waiting out the secondary explosion inside his skull before he rose to stumble a path through discarded clothing to the corner basin. The water was disgustingly warm, but he drank a glass anyway, then bent to let the tap splash over his face and hair. He wrestled with the aspirin bottle for an hour or so, palmed three pills and washed them down with a second glass, then reached out to part the curtains a fraction.

A dizzying panorama of rooftops: tiles and tin, brick and timber, steeples and drying laundry; centuries of chimneypots, with a narrow slice of stone magnificence in the distance. Children's voices and taxi horns competed with a tram rattle from the rue de Rennes and a neighbor's accordion, mournfully wading through a lively tune. His nose filled with the pervasive stink of an unemptied septic tank.

Summer in Paris.

He went back to his seat on the side of the bed, picking up his cigarette case and lighter.

The tap of the Ronson touching wood set off a convulsion in the bed. A hand emerged from the sheets, then a tangled head of brassy blonde hair, followed by blue eyes blinking in outrage.

"Ferme les rideaux putain!"

He wasn't sure if she was calling him a whore, or the curtains, and he didn't think he would be able to shape the question without coffee. Even the French swill that was mostly chicory.

"Doesn't help any to shut them, honey. They're like tissue paper."

"Eh?"

"Nothing," he told her. "I have to go to work."

She understood that, and yanked the covers back over her matted hair. Stuyvesant swiveled around on the bed to rip them off her. "Really," he said. "It's time to rise and shine."

But instead of complaining, or assaulting him with curses, she gave a sinuous writhe to curl against his leg, looking up at him as coquettishly as a person could when her mascara was smeared like something from a German horror film.

"You take me for breakfast, 'Arris?" One soft breast pressed into his knee, two firm fingers walked a path up the inside of his bent thigh.

He smashed the cigarette out against the ash-tray, then bent over the smeared horror-eyes. "I try never to disappoint a lady," he told her.

Be nice if he could remember this one's name.

TWO

A CONVERSATION:
"You knew that Crosby girl, didn't you?"

"Crosby? I don't believe I . . ."

"Peggy? Patricia? There was something about photographs and a scar—this was some time ago."

"Ah, yes: Philippa. What about her?"

"Is she still around?"

"I haven't seen her in months. Why?"

"There was an American asking about her, last night. He claims he was hired by her parents, though he looked a real brute to me. I thought if you were still in touch, you might let her know."

"As I say, it's been months. Did you talk to the fellow?"

"No, but he's around the Quarter if you want him. That girl, Lulu? The one with the light fingers? He's spending time with her."

"Sounds a suitable match."

"Better than the Crosby girl—too naïve for her own good."

"A description fitting half the women in Montparnasse."

"Certainly the Americans. Why on earth do their fathers let them leave the house?"

"Madness."

"I know—they're just asking for trouble. They come to town, sleep with as many boys as they can find, and are shocked as lambs when they get hurt. I suppose that's why so many of them drift away. I can't think how many times someone has said, 'Has anyone seen Daisy?' or Iris or whoever. The girls here seem to make a habit of flitting in and out, and . . ."

The other man nodded.

And in the background, a machine began to tick.

THREE

THIS SEEMED TO be Stuyvesant's day for drunken women. Well, it was Paris; it was 1929. What else could he expect?

Two hours after he'd taken Lulu for breakfast (there: he'd even remembered her name), Harris Stuyvesant rapped on a polished wooden door. The Rive Droite apartment was half as old and ten times as clean as his hotel room across the Seine, and even three flights up from street level, its hallways smelled like money. No septic tanks around here.

He knocked again.

The girl had to be back from the Riviera (or Monte Carlo or wherever she'd spent the summer)—and the building's gorgon of a concierge had spoken on the telephone with someone in apartment 406 before reluctantly permitting him to pass, two minutes ago.

So unless the resident had made a break over the roof tiles . . .

He changed from knuckles to fist and pounded, hard. In response, a long extended grumble welled gradually from within. Locks rattled. The door swung open.

The girl was tall and brown: dark eyes, chestnut hair, sun-tanned skin, dressed in a man's chocolate-colored dressing-gown. The most colorful things about her were two heavily bloodshot eyes, explained by the stale-wine smell oozing from her pores.

Colorful eyes, and vocabulary. Three years ago when he'd come to France, Stuyvesant wouldn't have understood a thing the girl was saying—and even now he missed a few phrases. Those he did get made him blink.

"Yeah, sorry," he interrupted loudly, in English. "I woke you up and you're not happy with me. I need to ask you about Pip Crosby."

"Who?" The accent sounded American, suggesting this was the roommate, but he'd need more than a monosyllable to be sure.

"Pip—Philippa. Crosby."

"Phil?" The red eyes squinted against the brightness, and the wide, dry lips emitted another expletive. Thought appeared to be a challenge, but he caught no flare of guilty panic across her angular features.

"Are you Nancy Berger?"

"Uh."

He took that for an affirmative, and planted one broad hand against the door, pushing gently. "How 'bout I come in and fix you some coffee?" She swayed. He caught her elbow, then hooked his Panama over the coat-rack and walked her inside to a seat, finding a roomy, light-filled apartment, comfortably furnished and clean beneath what appeared to be an exploded suitcase.

He located the kitchen and a coffee percolator, along with a package of grounds that, although stale-smelling, at least wasn't chicory. While the pot gurgled, he snooped through drawers and flipped through a crate of unopened mail. It dated back to June.

When the glass button showed dark, he poured two cups and stirred sugar into both, carrying them out to the next room. The brown girl sat, unblinking, on a bright orange settee, the gap in her robe creating a provocative degree of cleavage (though personally, he preferred freckles to sun-tan). He pushed a cup into her hand, removed a pair of silk undergarments from the chair, and sat down in front of her.

"Drink," he ordered. "It'll help."

Her eyes focused on the cup. She tried to speak, cleared her throat, tried again. "Milk?"

"There isn't any." Her robe kept sagging; in a minute, one side or the other would be unfettered.

She blew across the top, sipped, and croaked, "I don't take sugar." American, yes. She took another swallow.

Soon, she looked more alive and less queasy—and more crucial, her straighter posture restored a degree of closure to her garments. He handed her the note that he'd left with the concierge on Saturday afternoon, which he'd found on the counter under a dusty boot.

"I'm the one who wrote this, Miss Berger," he told her. "Harris Stuyvesant. I've been hired by Pip's—Phil's—mother and uncle to find her. Do you know where she is?"

She shook her head, and kept shaking it back and forth until Stuyvesant sharply repeated the question.

"No," she responded. "Sorry. I don't. She went off with a friend . . . God, months ago."

"Which friend is that?"

"How would I know? I never met him."

"Then how—" Stuyvesant stopped. *First things first,* he told himself. "When did you see her last?"

"March," she said mechanically.

"Any idea when?"

"A couple days after my birthday party."

"When is your birthday?"

"March twelfth."

"So you last saw her around the fourteenth or fifteenth."

"Later." The girl's face contorted with effort. "Maybe the twentieth?"

"But your birthday party was the twelfth."

"My *birthday* is the twelfth. The party was the Sunday after."

Stuyvesant's hands twitched. If she'd been a man, he'd have grabbed her by the collar. If she'd had a collar. "Fine, the twentieth of March. So if you haven't seen Pip since then, why have you been taking money from her every other week?"

She gave him an even blanker look. "Money?"

"Yeah, you know: francs, centimes. There's a standing order transferring money from her Paris bank account to yours."

"You mean the household accounts? Phil's terrible about paying bills. I have to do it for us."

He still saw no spark of alarm or deceit cross her face—although for the umpteenth time, Stuyvesant wished he had the shrewd eyes of his friend Bennett Grey.

"Okay, you last saw her the end of March. What did she say then, about being gone?"

"She had a job. Wait." Her face screwed up as an idea bubbled to the surface like gas in a swamp. "Phil's missing?"

"That's what I've been saying."

"Missing as in, *gone?*"

"Missing as in her mother wants to know where she is."

"Her mother doesn't know?"

"I told you: that is why I am here." He really was going to shake her.

"Who *are* you?"

"Jesus Christ, lady—are you a moron or do you need me to shove you under a cold shower? My name is Stuyvesant. I've been hired by your roommate's uncle to find her. How complicated is that?"

"Why should I tell you anything? You could be anyone."

It actually was a little impressive, that someone in her condition could come up with an original thought. "Is there anyone other than her family who might be looking for her?"

The question was too complex for her addled state, but instead of allowing him to push his way past her conversationally as he had physically, she set her lips together and clammed up.

He smiled, rueful but approving: girls in general were too damned trusting these days. Still, he could've done with this one playing dumb a bit longer. He dug out the letter that had bounced from Nice to Warsaw before catching up with him in Berlin, the week before. She stretched her eyes wide a couple of times, and started to read.

Dear Mr. Stuyvesant,

If I have reached the correct person, I believe you know—or knew—a young woman named Philippa Crosby, Pip to her friends. You would have met her in the company of another young American, Rosalie Perkins, in the south of France last February. It was Rosalie who gave me your name.

I write because we cannot locate Pip, and I wonder if you can help. Rosalie said that you worked as a private investigations agent in Europe, and subsequent inquiries assured me that you are both competent and reliable. I also understand that you are fluent in French, and have spent much of the last few years working in that country.

Philippa is my brother's daughter (he was killed in the War). She moved to Paris sixteen months ago. She was in the habit of writing home every two or three weeks. However, her last letter arrived in early April.

We—that is, Philippa's mother and I—made inquiries in May, but I have recently discovered that our hired agent was, not to mince words, a crook. My sister-in-law, who is not well, was so distraught that she proposed to sail for France herself until I stepped in and said I would find the girl. I am told by colleagues that you might be trusted, as our other investigator could not.

Pip is a very bright girl of twenty-two who, although cherishing the unconventional attitudes of youth, has always demonstrated a level head and a firm degree of responsibility. (Indeed, those qualities are what convinced her mother and me to permit her to travel to Europe in the first place.) It is highly unlike her to simply cease communicating.

I have written to the American Embassy in Paris, and directly to the police, as well as to Pip's own address, but have been frustrated on all counts: by the slowness of the Embassy, the vagueness of the police, and a completely unresponsive roommate. I am told that some of this is due to the widespread August holidays; however, even the building's concierge was unhelpful. In hopes that having a physical representative there will press my urgency on the various fronts, I ask that you consider becoming my agent.

If you are willing to take on this job and are free to do so soon, please cable your reply.

Yours,

Ernest M. Crosby II

Stuyvesant kept his eyes glued on Miss Berger, judging her response to the letter. His own reaction to the thing had been . . . well, a wild mix: a thump of distress at hearing of Pip's troubles—distress tempered by exasperation—followed by a stronger jolt, this one of apprehension. Was Crosby accusing him of something? Then came a queasy surprise—Pip really *had* been young. But his final and humiliating gut response, had been: relief. Because Ernest M. Crosby was offering Stuyvesant an escape from the seedy Berlin hostelry where his last job had stranded him.

So here he was a week later, tracking the eyes of that "completely unresponsive" roommate as they worked their way down the pompous words on the pricey paper. He saw when she reached Crosby's grumble about her—the dry lips half parted in protest—but at the end of it, her reaction again surprised him. She looked up, aghast.

"Jesus. Phil's *missing*!"

The distress on her ravaged face hit him straight in the gut. As if someone told him that a no-care-in-the-world starlet had a dying mother, or that the hard-as-nails prostitute leaving the bar was putting her kid through college.

It's always a shock, when someone cares more about a thing than you do.

He'd liked Pip, sure, but a lot of life had washed over those five days in February. Since taking Crosby's job, he'd thought of Pip mostly as a case—an increasingly frustrating case at that. Suddenly, with a look on Nancy Berger's face, the missing girl blazed into life before his eyes, vivid and gay and in trouble.

He really could've done without it.

"I've spent the last three days asking about her," he told the roommate, "and nobody's seen her for months. I was hoping you might know."

She didn't answer, just went back to the letter, her eyes trailing down the sheet. They caught on something, narrowed, and Stuyvesant didn't need to be Bennett Grey to read this expression.

He gave an internal sigh. Another thing he could've done without:

smart girls who read silly books. A thousand cheap murder mysteries had made the world suspicious of any man who'd been the last person to see someone. Was there any point in trotting out his alibi? He tried picking up where she'd left off. "You were saying that you last saw Pip—Phil—around the twentieth of March. Did she tell you where she was going?"

"This letter says you knew her?"

"Briefly." She waited. He gritted his teeth. "I was working in a bar in Nice—down on the Riviera?—when she and Rosalie came in. Rosalie didn't speak much French and was feeling kind of lost, so I told them to sit and listen to the band for a while and I'd introduce them to a bunch of swell Americans who came in every night. When I got off at midnight, they invited me to join the party. The two girls stayed a few days and moved on to Rome. I haven't heard from her since then."

"What was Phil doing in Nice?"

"Experimenting with the wild life, from what I could see. That's why I thought a few polite American boys would help."

Nancy Berger fixed him with a hard, bloodshot gaze. However, Stuyvesant had yet to meet a girl who could read a lie in his face if he'd had time to prepare. This one seemed satisfied—or if not satisfied, at least willing to suspend judgment. She took another mouthful of coffee.

"Did she say anything about where she was going?" he asked for the third time.

"She told me she had a job. Well, she calls them jobs, even if they don't pay. Which they usually don't—Phil doesn't need to earn a living. You're sure she didn't go off with those Americans?"

"Wasn't she back here after Rome?"

"Yes, of course, stupid of me."

Stuyvesant took out his cigarettes, offered her one.

"I don't, thanks," she said.

"You mind if I do?"

"Help yourself."

"So, what kind of jobs?"

"The usual." His hand twitched again. This time the girl noticed. "I mean, all sorts of things—a little acting, helping out in a hat shop, photographer's assistant, but mostly modeling. In the nude, for artists, you know?"

"But she—" Stuyvesant caught himself, changing it to, "I understand she has a nasty scar. There was a letter after this one," he explained. "With details."

Crosby's follow-up letter had included snapshots, bank information, passport number, and descriptions of the girl, both the mother's—lively eyes; wonderful sense of humor; dozens of friends; loves books, music, daisies, and chocolate—and the uncle's: chipped front tooth; mole on her right knee; broken left arm; a big burn scar across her torso, the last two from a barn fire when she was ten. When he'd read the uncle's description, Stuyvesant had two thoughts: one, it would better suit a coroner than a private investigator; and two, Uncle Crosby didn't suspect that his investigator might have seen that scar for himself.

Nancy nodded. "Yes, she was caught in a fire when she was a child. I gather she was lucky to get out alive. You're certain she's not, I don't know, with some traveling theater troupe? Living with a house full of artists in the South?"

"That's what I'm being paid to find out," he said patiently. "But about those artists: I'd have thought that scar would put modeling out of the question."

"Yes, it was ugly. But some of the artists, they like freaks, you know?"

"You think of your roommate as a freak?"

"*I* don't. But have you seen some of their paintings?"

She had a point. He pulled out his notebook. "Names?"

"Of the artists?"

"Painters, writers, friends, boyfriends. People who hosted parties she went to."

"Oh, for heaven's sake! I couldn't possibly remember—"

"Miss Berger, I'm trying to find your roommate!"

She blinked her swollen eyelids, looking sober for the first time. Sober, rather than knowing. Whatever had happened to Pip Crosby— if anything *had* happened to her—Nancy Berger knew nothing about it.

"Of course. Sorry, I've been gone since May, so . . . You're positive that Phil didn't just go somewhere and her letter got lost?"

He really was going to smack her. "Five months of letters?"

She tugged together the front of the robe as if cold, although the room was anything but. "Names. Tom was one, but that was during the winter. There was a Count, and a Marquise, and a Lady something. English, she was. Phil mentioned a fellow named Louis, and Teddy."

"Surnames?"

"Oh. Well. I'm not sure . . ."

A quarter hour later, Stuyvesant had a page of vaguely recalled names, only two of which included a surname. "And you two lived together for a year," he said irritably.

She turned on him a look of utter misery, and Stuyvesant shut his notebook before those brown eyes could start the waterworks and make him feel even more of a louse. "Look, why don't you get yourself dressed, we'll get some lunch and see if you think of anything else."

The idea appeared about as enticing as having a plantar wart removed, but after a moment she stood and snugged the ties on the robe. "You're right, I can't think without something to eat." She walked away towards the back of the apartment.

"You mind if I have a look at Pip's room?"

Her hand waved in the direction of the door she was passing, and the brown robe slipped out of view.

FOUR

I T WASN'T OFTEN Stuyvesant had to search the bedroom of someone he knew—and yeah, he'd known Pip Crosby pretty much head to toe.

Pip had been February's Lulu, one in a string of mostly blonde, mostly young women who made a man glad to be living in 1920s France. Looking back, he distinctly remembered hesitating—she'd looked about sixteen, sitting in that bar, like a snowdrop in the badlands—but in the end, he hadn't held out for long. Young she might be, but any seduction between them had gone the other way around: Pip Crosby practically tripped him into bed, blinking her big Clara Bow eyes and asking if he knew how to make her a White Lady. Several increasingly off-color jokes later, he had established both her determination to be "fast" and her easy familiarity with the means.

Pip was no virgin, not by a long shot.

It had been brief, ships passing in the night, a distant vice in the darkness (now, there was a line for Cole Porter) until Rosalie had gathered her up and taken her off to Rome, leaving nothing behind but a few days of perfume on his pillow.

A look and a voice, then darkness again and a silence.

He shook his head. *Enough with the regrets,* he scolded himself. *You've got nothing to beat yourself up about. You pushed the two girls at those friendly Ohio boys, if that was what they'd wanted. Pip didn't. If you hadn't slept with her, she'd have gone home with Yves the barman.*

He'd been a little low and she'd been a lot of fun, and that was that until he'd read Uncle Crosby's letter and felt like a complete heel. Why? What was he supposed to do, follow the girl to Rome shaking an admonishing finger at her?

And last week—sure, he'd been temporarily washed up in Berlin, broke and beat-up and ground under the city's heel like the butt-end of a *Zigarette,* but missing persons was a job he was good at. His last such case had been a doozy—and the reason he'd been in Nice to begin with, thawing out after seven snowy weeks looking for a missing heiress. He'd turned south the minute he delivered that sulking, drug-twitching, possibly pregnant young woman to her brother in Le Havre. It had taken all his self-control not to turn her over his knee as well, and he wasn't exactly eager for another case like that one.

But with honest work thin on the ground and a man with expensive stationery offering a hefty per diem, Stuyvesant raised no objections to looking for Pip Crosby. She really had been a pip of a girl, and she really didn't deserve trouble.

Plus, he'd have the satisfaction of helping a desperate mother. What kind of a no-good would scam a sickly war widow, anyway?

He'd scraped together the cost of a telegram and nursed his last deutsche marks and pfennigs until the follow-up letter arrived on Friday. Fortified by Crosby's bank draft, he got his wrist-watch, winter coat, and spare suit out of pawn, then bought a new shirt and drank a bottle of champagne with his multi-course dinner. That night he slept in a bed long enough that his feet didn't stick out the end—alone, true, but knowing that state wouldn't last long where he was headed.

Saturday morning he'd bought a notebook and caught the train for Paris, scrubbed and shaved and solvent. In his first-class compartment— Crosby was covering expenses as well—he opened the thick envelope and pulled out the photograph of a young woman with blonde hair and a familiar grin of Clara Bow mischief.

Three days later, his survey of that blonde's bedroom was interrupted by a voice from the corridor.

"If you open the window, be sure to shut it when you leave. I'm going to have a shower."

A door down the hall closed, the *unresponsive* roommate not waiting for an answer. He let his thoughts dwell for a moment on the shower—no doubt a device with both hot and cold taps—before deciding the brown girl was right: the room was stifling. Paris had yet to realize the summer was over.

He tossed his jacket on the bed, rolling up his shirtsleeves as he crossed the blue-and-brown floral carpet to the velour curtains. Once he wrestled the windows open, he stuck his head out, looking across at an identical apartment block, then down to the tree-shaded length of the boulevard de Sébastopol.

Paris had changed, he decided. This was his seventh—eighth?—trip to the City of Light, and this time around the charm seemed faded, the colors dull, the people edgier than usual. Even the trees looked tired.

Christ, Stuyvesant, quit mooning and do your job. He went back to the doorway and started over.

FIVE

THE LITTLE BEETLES scuttled to the corners when the bone artist pulled open the box. He was impatient at their slowness, but there was no denying, the result was incredibly lovely: the bones they left were more innocent and pure than anything he'd been able to do by hand. Like these ones: freshly cleansed of flesh, they seemed shocked by the caress of cool air.

Some bones resisted their final separation (the tenacity of flesh was extraordinary!), but once reconciled to this strange new apartness, their soft exterior hardened, their color grew rich. Under his very eyes, raw bone took its first steps to becoming silken ivory: magnificent.

When the bones were ready, some would be transformed yet again, Displayed for the connoisseur. These phalanges in the box, for example: they were perfect, untouched by years, by injury, by manual labor.

But it wasn't just perfection that an artist sought. Perfection was commonplace, little more than a foundation—and although the goal of any artist was to shape prosaic syllables into poetry, there were some bones, precious few, that were poems in themselves. Bones that required no artisan's hand to shine in beauty.

Some masterpieces simply blossomed into the light as the calyx of flesh drew back, revealing an elegant and articulate beauty. These thrilling treasures bore the indelible marks of their unique history, inflicted on them while they were still warm and pulsing with blood: the gentle bow caused by a poverty diet; the multiple healed fractures of a woman with a bully husband; the faint, tell-tale cracks of the left wrist, testimony that hope is greater than mere physical agony. Even the detritus of age held a kind of poignant message—but oh, the occasional rare length of bone with a flower of cancer along its clean length, or the swell and kink of a long-healed break: a life's story, carved in mute calcium.

A story like the one his beetles were currently polishing. Broken in its youth and imperfectly set, the wounded ends had laboriously woven a bridge across the gap. The bone was perfect yet flawed; strong, but with a luscious history of pain. What a shame it would be, to leave such a gem buried under flesh.

The artist closed the box, and let the beetles get back to work.

SIX

How many strange bedrooms had Harris Stuyvesant stepped into, hoping for some clue to the person who slept there? Agitators and anarchists, gun-runners and rum-smugglers when he'd worked for the Bureau. Twice there'd been armed men waiting—and once, in a cocaine-smuggler's bedroom, the sound of the closing door had very nearly obscured a tiny *tick* from across the room, where a bomb sat primed and ready on the dresser.

The memory of those distant excitements was almost enough to make Stuyvesant regret telling J. Edgar to take a hike.

Pip Crosby was no bomb-making cocaine-smuggler. Cocaine *user*, maybe—snow was cheap on every corner here in Paris. She hadn't been using the stuff back in February—he couldn't have missed the signs— but if she wasn't off in Antibes or Madrid with some long-haired poet, or with a troupe of traveling actors, migrating Americans, or passing gypsies, then he'd probably dig her out in some dingy corner with an adored pimp, paying for drugs with her body.

The one place he didn't think he'd find her was dead. Drug over-doses had a way of surfacing pretty fast, since a corpse was an inconvenient companion, and it took a lot of work to get rid of one on the sly.

Of course, there was always politics: Europe was full of poor little rich girls who set out to rebel on a family allowance, working their way through Communism and Anarchism and feminism and any ism that might shock Daddy short of actually joining-the-working-class-ism.

In any event, his entrance to Pip's bedroom triggered neither gunshot nor bomb, and his personal feelings about spoiled Americans mustn't get in the way of earning his pay. He sucked in a breath of the oven-like air and let his eyes run passively over the room, waiting for it to tell him its secrets.

Bedrooms were where people dreamed, where they spent a third of their life, where they gave themselves up to the vulnerability of sleep. That one room—its contents and its state—gave away more than the whole rest of the house combined. Tidy or slovenly—or, a tidy surface over ground-in filth? Was it a sterile, business-like place to sleep and store clothing, or filled with mementos of a life fully lived? Open to the house, or walled up against the world, the resident's only safe retreat?

The rest of this particular residence had been furnished by others. Philippa Anne Crosby lived among the foreign furniture in this foreign city for a little more than a year before she wandered away. Pip Crosby had left Boston a good girl (or at least a conventional one) and a year later was picking up strangers in a bar and sharing not just her body, but its damage. Even by Paris standards, it was quick work.

So, Pip, honey: where'd you go after you wrote your mama that chatty letter at the end of March?

Her bedroom was twenty feet square with high ceilings and decorative plaster trim, in a fourth-floor apartment of a block sketched out by old iron-fist Haussmann as he'd brutalized Paris into modern efficiency half a century before. Empty plaster rosebuds showed where gas fixtures had been replaced by electrical lights that looked like gas fixtures. The wall-paper was floral. The furniture reflected the same taste that he'd seen in the rest of the apartment: two narrow beds with padded satin headboards, one of them lightly stained from hair-oil; ornate dressing table with a rococo gilt frame around the mirror and a padded gilt-trimmed chair tucked underneath; a fainting-couch that matched the twin headboards. The curtains were pale blue velour, too heavy for the room.

On top of all that Paris bourgeoisie lay another stamp entirely.

For one thing, the art, mostly paintings, all modern—very modern. A couple were by artists he recognized; they would have been expensive, and Uncle Crosby's letter said nothing about investments in art.

Did Pip have money on the side, or were these gifts from admirers?

Then there were the photographs, nicely framed: street scenes, dramatically positioned monuments, objects on a table, people. There were four, carefully arranged into a diamond, whose subject he couldn't tell: reflections on a pond? A room badly out of focus? In others, startling effects in the developing process seemed to be the main point. Two were moody portraits with more shadow than light: only by putting on his reading glasses could he be sure they were of Pip.

Beside the art and photographs were an odd pair of items—and he couldn't have said why these demanded a closer examination than nude pictures of a twenty-two-year-old girl (with, yes, her scar on display). These were a pair of glass-fronted wooden display boxes, twelve inches on a side and an inch and a half deep, divided into grids with the middle missing: twelve squares framing a larger central square.

The pale wood had a delicate grain and a perfect finish. The glass that covered it was equally flawless, without a hint of ripple. But it wasn't the painstaking workmanship of the containers that drew the eye, it was their contents.

The top row of the first had, from left to right: an old ivory chess rook with a richly elongated blood-red drip descending from its miniature crenellations; the eye and nose from a murky photograph; a glass eye with a chip in the blue iris; and three mismatched and damaged tortoiseshell buttons. The bottom row held: two molars, one marred by cavity and the other with bits of dry flesh clinging to the roots; a small silver-topped vacuum tube; the worn cork from a medicine bottle; and a bloody fingertip that would have been startlingly realistic were it not for hollow tin where bone and flesh should have been. The central square cradled the delicate arches of three cat-sized rib bones; the four squares at the sides all had pieces of old stained-glass windows showing various body parts: a delicate hand and its arm in the two right-side squares; a mouth and an eye with a crack across it on the left.

The other box had a similar mix of *objets diverse*—pieces of photographs, bits of rubbish, bones—with touches of paint to suggest gore. Its center square held what looked like a miniature city-scape: a bleached Manhattan, its skyscrapers made of stubby little white bones that suggested human phalanges but were no doubt the tail-bones of a dog. Two of the "buildings" were topped with pools of gleaming crimson, like rooftop swimming pools brimming with fresh blood.

The boxes were . . . unsettling. One made him think of childhood fears, the other how dangerous loneliness could be: could a boxful of odds and ends provoke such distinct emotions? They were intellectual memento mori overlaid with an almost erotic degree of violence, and his knee-jerk reaction was to take them down and stick them behind the wardrobe. But why? He'd seen modern art a lot weirder, and certainly more graphic.

"The heat's melting your brain, Harris, my boy," he muttered aloud, and walked over to lower his weight onto the gilded chair. The dressing table was dust-free and tidy: silver-handled brush with ivory comb tucked under it to the right, enameled powder box and crystal perfume atomizer on the left, four small silver frames in the center. Three of these depicted a blonde woman, one of them clearly Pip, two others probably meant to be her.

The fourth sketch looked like a three-stemmed martini glass or a tree split by lightning. It had been done on a paper napkin, and on closer examination, he decided it, too, was meant to show a young woman—although the fractured, light-and-dark, vivid-yet-uncertain personality that came to life in those few lines showed a more complex personality than he'd found in Pip. He didn't need to look at the signature, that arrogant, underlined Picasso: no living artist had a cleverer eye, or a wickeder pen, than the little Spanish bantam cock.

He pulled open the dressing table's wide center drawer: hair decorations—pins, feathers, and fabric bandeaux—and a jumble of cosmetics, American and French. The American containers were older, their packaging considerably less elegant.

The top drawer on the right did duty as a filing cabinet, with checkbooks from both an American and a Paris bank, Pip's *identité* papers, and the like. A new-looking address book had less than a dozen listings: the two banks, a hair-dresser's, an English-language bookshop, three first names, and the address and telephone number of the couple who owned this apartment. He wrote down various numbers and pawed through the rest of the drawer, finding nothing of interest.

The presence of her *identité* was troubling; the lack of a passport was both reassuring and suggestive.

The next drawer contained a tin box that had once held Scottish shortbread, now filled with matchbooks. Matchbooks weren't as common here as they were in the States, where bowls of them lay near the cash register of every corner dive and mom-and-pop diner, but even in Paris, nightclubs had taken to handing them out. He recognized most of these: Moulin Rouge, L'Enfer, Bricktop's—the old one, at number 52—Chaumière, Chat Noir. Some he'd been in, but didn't know well—La Lune Rousse, Les Deux Ânes, Le Carillon, Le Boeuf sur le Toit.

Twenty-seven altogether, with no duplicates. He idly thumbed back a cover: it was missing a match. He hadn't noticed any ash-trays in the apartment—he'd used his coffee cup for the cigarette he smoked earlier—so these were probably souvenirs.

The majority bore the names of music halls, bars, *dancings,* and cabarets in the Right Bank Montmartre district, where Paris went to play and to whore. One was from Luna Park, an amusement gardens with a dance hall out west in the Bois de Boulogne. A handful more originated from the boulevards to the east of Montmartre. Only two of them came from Montparnasse on the Left Bank, which since the War had become Paris' American village: Au Caméléon, a superior establishment popular with artists celebrating a big sale, and a new one, La Coupole.

Not exactly the places he'd expect of a Boston girl, even one whose apartment was across the river from what its denizens called the Quarter.

He left the matchbooks strewn over the table-top and went back to the drawer. Beneath the tin box lay half a dozen letters: five from Pip's mother, one from Rosalie. He picked up this one first. The girlish hand-writing gave him nothing of interest—*Thanks for such a lovely time, I hope I can come again next year*—but folded inside were some photographs, beginning with Rosalie along the Quai d'Orsay. Next was the full version of the snapshot he had in his pocket—here, Rosalie occupied the left-hand side of the photograph. She looked even more dowdy than he'd remembered, next to Pip's vivacity.

The next three pictures showed: the girls together at the front of Notre Dame; Pip atop the Eiffel Tower; and the two girls on the beach in Nice.

Then he came to the last picture, and nearly dropped it: Pip, with her arms locked around the neck of a large, bemused-looking man in a smoke-filled bar. She was turned towards the camera with an expression of gamine mischief, head cocked like a film starlet, hair tousled every which way. She'd been drinking some peculiar cocktail made with crème de menthe: she'd kissed him a moment after Rosalie had snapped the picture, bathing his tongue in mint.

He remembered the taste—and the bemusement. Looking back, he seemed to have spent the entire five days of the affair in a state of puzzled enthusiasm. He'd been more than willing to follow along, but even in the whirlwind of music and sun and dancing—and yes, some terrific sex—a corner of his brain had marveled, *Why me?* She'd made him feel young, but then, he'd never thought of himself as middle-aged before meeting Pip.

The door behind him shifted in its frame. The photograph vanished into his pocket, the glasses into his hand. He turned.

"So, are you going to feed me?" the roommate asked.

SEVEN

"WOULD YOU COME in for a minute, Miss Berger?"

Nancy Berger interested Stuyvesant. Not as a woman—three nights of Lulu had sure bled off *that* pressure—but as an unlikely roommate for a girl like Pip. His initial suspicions of her and the bank account shenanigans had faded, but that did not declare her lily-white pure.

Nancy Berger stood in the doorway with damp hair, a scrubbed face, and a crisply ironed skirt and blouse in place of the bathrobe. She no longer smelled of booze. Her chapped-looking lips wore a layer of lipstick, and she'd even managed to do something about the red in her eyes.

Still not to his taste, but at least he didn't feel the urge to throw a tarpaulin over her head.

"Did the room look like this when she was here?" he asked.

"I suppose. Mouette—the cleaner—has been in, but she never puts things away, just dusts around them."

"If Pip—Phil—intended to be gone for long, would she have taken any of this?" Stuyvesant gestured at the dressing–table-top and the open drawers.

The young woman shook her head. "It's like I wrote to her mother back in May, I didn't see anything missing, but Phil and I only share the main rooms. I don't really know her bedroom. She's big on privacy. Obsessed, even."

"In the fifteen months you've lived here, you haven't been in this room once?"

"I told you, I've been away for the last four of those. But yes, of course I've been in, once or twice."

"When was the last time?"

"A few days before I left. I needed—I was looking for some ointment I thought she had. I knew she wouldn't mind if I used some. And her books, I borrowed a few of those—the novels, not the others—and returned them. And a . . . a wrap, once. She'd let me use it before. I put it back the next day."

She was lying, and anyway that was a lot more than once or twice. He let it go for the moment. "Does she smoke?"

"No, neither of us do."

"What drugs does she like?"

"I can't believe we're talking about this."

"So she uses drugs?"

"No. Not as far as I know."

"But she does drink?"

"Sure."

"And collect matchbooks from bars?"

"Does she? Oh yes, I see."

"Are these the sorts of places she goes?"

Nancy reluctantly came inside, looking over his shoulder at the colorful squares, then flicking through them with a short, clean fingernail. "Phil and I used to go out together quite a bit at first, but around Christmas she started to make other friends. It did seem odd that I rarely saw her—you know how tight the Quarter is—but if she goes to these sorts of places, I guess it isn't. I haven't been in Montmartre for ages. Its decadence just feels . . . miserable."

He sat back, physically as well as mentally, to look up at the side of her face. Most people would have assumed that by "these sorts of places" he simply meant nightclubs and cabarets: Nancy Berger had picked up instantly on their geographical similarity.

She reached for the Moulin Rouge, and as Stuyvesant had done, opened the cover. "Good luck, I see."

"Sorry?"

"For some reason, Pip is convinced that if you manage to get your cigarette going with a single match, it's good luck. All I can say is, she must've grown up with some crummy matches."

"I've heard about it being *bad* luck to light three off one match, but not the other way around. She's superstitious, then?" *Something else I didn't notice about her.*

"Madly. Even at first, she was dead serious about things like twisting the stem of an apple to find the first letter of your future husband, or a bird flying through your window meaning someone's going to die, or it being bad luck to open an umbrella indoors. She went a little crackers when I broke a mirror moving in. I thought she was going to throw me out. Or call in the priests to purify the place."

"Why do you say, 'Even at first'?"

She dropped the matchbook and picked up another, squinting to make out the name. "She got more so. She left a dinner party once last winter because there were thirteen. Hey, look." This matchbook, too, had one match torn out.

Stuyvesant thumbed open the one he held, then another.

Every book had but a single gap: Pip's collection of good luck.

And not a one from Nice.

He swept the collection into the tin box and closed it back in the drawer, pulling open the last drawer in case it contained rabbits' feet or horseshoes, but it had only what seemed to be mending—a blouse missing a button, another with a ripped shoulder seam, several stockings—and dust.

He was not finished with the room, but Miss Berger was looking a bit wan, and he thought he'd get more out of her if he fed her.

"Let's go," he said.

He rolled down his sleeves and walked over to retrieve his coat from the bed. When he turned back to the door, his eyes went from the wooden boxes to the diamond quartet of photos, and he stopped dead.

They were not reflections on a pond. They were close-ups of Pip Crosby's terrible scar.

EIGHT

T HE CONCIERGE GAVE them a sour nod as they went past. As Nancy led him along the shaded pavement, she turned to ask, "Are you absolutely—"

"How about we eat, first?" He was getting tired of being asked how sure he was that Pip was gone.

"Yes. You're right. How are you for funds, Mr. Stuyvesant?"

"Pretty flush."

"Then we can have a real meal."

"Maybe not the Ritz."

"They wouldn't let us in, anyway," she said.

Was that a snide glance at my shirt, when she said that? Stuyvesant thought. *A girl who comes to the door in a man's bathrobe?*

She took him to a brasserie near the Louvre, a place where she was clearly known. It was in a cellar, and almost cool compared to the streets outside. To his surprise, her drink order was for a large bottle of mineral water, only including a glass of white wine at his urging.

She was not so abstemious when it came to food. She plucked a roll from the breadbasket the instant it touched the table, smeared it with butter, and attacked it with the enthusiasm of a monk who had just rescinded his vows. She took a second and, buttered knife in action, glanced up.

"Sorry! It's been ages since I ate. I spent the past two days on a series of trains, and since my friends were all in third-class, so was I—with an endless supply of retsina, but none of them thought to include food, and we all ran out of cash."

"Were you in Greece?"

"Yes. Ever been?"

"Not yet."

"Fascinating place. I was helping out in an archaeological dig—the Italians are running it, of course, but they were happy to have a hand."

"Is that what you do? You're an archaeologist?"

"What, a summer's sweat for a handful of broken pottery? No, a friend of mine is in love with a man whose greatest joy is digging stuff out of the ground, and she asked me to go along. It was great fun, though I wished I'd taken a better hat."

"The tan makes you look like you've spent the summer on the beach."

"But not the hands."

She stuck out her free hand, and indeed, though the back was just brown, the front of it showed the hard wear of heavy calluses and half-healed blisters.

Their food came, and she addressed herself to it with considerable focus: one modern girl who didn't simply pick at a lettuce leaf. She was also, now that her mind was coming awake, a deft conversationalist: in between bites she amused him with tales of archaeologists at play; during bites she listened to his adventures in Europe. Light talk: serious eating.

When her plate was empty (though her wine glass remained half-full), she sat back with a purr of contentment.

"Dessert?" he asked.

"I'll explode. Thanks for that. If you hadn't come to my rescue, Mme. Hachette—the concierge—would have found me wasted away, without the energy to crawl out and buy a baguette and some milk." Her face changed, its liveliness draining away. "That joke may have been in poor taste. You think something bad has happened to poor Phil, don't you?"

He cocked an eyebrow. "Read a lot of detective novels, do you?"

"From time to time," she admitted. "All I mean is, it sounds as if Phil has walked away from her life pretty thoroughly."

"Oh, I'm sure to find her living it up on someone's yacht near Antibes, collecting wild stories to tell her grandchildren. But that reminds me—I don't suppose you have her passport? It's not in her desk."

"I haven't seen it. That's good, isn't it? It suggests nobody conked her on the head and dragged her off to a cave or something."

Ladies' novels, too, he guessed. "She wasn't in the habit of carrying her passport with her, then?"

"Heavens, who does that?"

Harris Stuyvesant did that. But then, not everyone lived with the chance of needing to get out of a country fast.

"So in the last weeks before you went off to Greece, what was she doing? Who was she seeing?"

She threw up her hands. "This is the problem. I'm sorry, but by last spring, Phil and I were living at opposite ends of the clock. She'd be out late and sleep late, while I was down in the Quarter before ten most mornings, either at the restaurant or with this Greek student who was teaching me some of the language. Phil and I would mostly leave each other notes: Pick up coffee. The dentist called. Package at Mme. Hachette's."

"What about politics? Was she involved in any radical groups?"

"Phil? Politics? Only if she was hot for one of the men, and she never mentioned anything like that."

"And she showed no signs of drugs."

"To tell you the truth, I'm not sure I would have noticed unless she set the stuff up in the kitchen one morning."

"No money went missing, no strange smells, her behavior didn't change—depressed or manic?"

"You think she was using cocaine?"

"Lots of people do."

"Well, if she did, I didn't see it." She grimaced. "Yachts, drugs; it really doesn't sound like Phil. She had . . . interests. A life. God, you hear about things—of course you do, Paris is like any big city. Bad things happen. But . . . Oh, Phil."

The despair of the last two words was unmistakable, and Stuyvesant jumped to distract her before it could develop—or become contagious.

"Tell me about Phil. Her friends, her life."

"Could we go, please? I'd like to be outside."

Their premature departure earned the disapproval of the waiter, for whom a meal was unfinished if it did not end in a jolt of liquid tar, but Stuyvesant left him a soothing tip and followed Nancy Berger along to the chestnut *allées* of the Tuileries.

He lit a cigarette, waiting for this unexpected young woman to put her thoughts in order.

"Can I have one of those?" she asked.

"Sure—sorry, you said you didn't smoke."

"I don't. Used to, gave it up, except for maybe twice a year when I need one."

She paused to cup her hand around his, steadying the Ronson's flame. She tipped her head back, eyes closed, then let the smoke drift from those wide lips with a disconcertingly . . . *experienced* kind of moan.

"I met Phil when I first came to Paris, a year ago last June. I was staying in a hovel down in the thirteenth arrondissement that was a long way from anywhere, so I mentioned to Sylvia Beach—Shakespeare and Company, you know?—that I was looking for a nicer place to rent, maybe in the fifth or sixth arrondissement. A few days later Sylvia gave me a phone number. It was Phil, who wanted a housemate to share this grand flat she had on the Right Bank. It wasn't the money. She'd only been in Paris a couple of months, and I think she was a bit lonely living there alone. Not exactly where her crowd tended to gather."

"She had a 'crowd,' then? Americans?"

"Sure. And like the rest of us, she spent most of her time down in the Quarter."

"Boyfriends?"

"Naturally. Why come to Paris if you're not interested in sex?" She said it matter-of-factly. "But, I only met a few of them. We agreed early on not to bring men to the apartment unless we were sure the other was away—we'd both had experience with the awkward meeting of roommates and boyfriends. What about you? Did you sleep with her?"

He gave a cough of surprise. "Miss Berger, I'm twice her age."

"She likes older men."

"Does she?"

"Especially artists."

"Well, I'm no artist." They reached the end of the gardens, where a bevy of girls in pleasingly short summer dresses waited to cross the road. "Tell me about the modeling. Was she doing it when you first met?"

"Not at first. Maybe over the summer? Certainly by winter it was a regular thing—I remember her coming back from a sitting half-frozen. After that she started picking jobs based on the efficiency of the artists' heaters."

He chuckled. "Yeah, I've been here in January. You call them jobs, but she had money. You ever ask her why she did it? The modeling?"

"I did, one night before our lives . . . diverged. Somebody'd given me a bottle of really good champagne, and we opened it and talked, like mad. Phil told me she found modeling freeing."

"Freeing? What, posing naked in front of a bunch of artists?"

The smile she gave him held more sadness than humor. "I know, but—you saw her photographs? With the scar? Since she was ten years old, Phil's been taught to see herself as damaged, less than whole. Certainly less than desirable." She paused, frowning. "I wonder if that could be related to her obsession with privacy? Anyway. She found it a revelation that her body might be something others could appreciate, even value. The honesty of modeling was intoxicating. Especially when it came to photographers. You saw the close-ups?"

"I can't imagine having those on my wall."

"I know—waking up to them every morning? The man spent a week taking close-ups of her body, head to toe. I went to the gallery that showed his collection—they were amazing, the textures of her skin— not just the scar, but her . . . well, other parts."

He glanced over: not the faintest hint of a blush. It was on the very tip of his tongue to ask if she modeled, too, but he caught the words and turned them into something else. "She has a lot of art in that room. Can you tell me about the artists? I recognize a few of them, and, of course, the Picasso sketch."

"She was proud of getting that one, cornered him at the Select one night and flirted outrageously until he did a drawing of her. And as I said, she liked—likes—older men. There was one she went on about, eyes like Valentino—and she'd have slept with Picasso except he had a very new young girlfriend. Oh, now *that* was catty of me. Mr.—What was your name again?"

"Call me Harris."

"Harris, of course—sorry, I'm half-dead. Oh, *God,* there I go again!"

He was worried that she would burst into tears then, and he wasn't going to get much more out of her today. "C'mon, I'll walk you back. I need to finish looking through Pip's things, anyway."

She allowed him to turn her in the direction of the apartment. "What a strange job you have. I've never met a private detective before. That I know of."

"I've never met an archaeologist before. Even an amateur one."

"I'm an amateur lots of things."

"Such as what?"

"Linguist. I collect languages."

"How many?"

"I'm fluent in three or four and I can work my way through a marketplace in, I don't know, seven or eight? Maybe ten in a pinch. And chef: I collect cooking techniques. I decided that a grown woman not knowing how to produce a decent meal was foolish, so I came to Paris to learn."

"You're in a cooking school?"

"Informally. I volunteer as an unpaid *plongeuse* and work my way up from scrubbing the pots to stirring them, watching over the chef's shoulder until I can mimic a few of the dishes. Then I start over at another place. I did that three times, and I'd planned my fourth—that brasserie we just ate at—when I came back from Greece. I'm not so sure now that I want another dose of classical French. I'm thinking of changing it to Greek cooking. Maybe Indochinese."

Stuyvesant examined the side of her face. She was tall for a woman, with a strong chin and sharp nose—not pretty, but it suited her. He'd been thinking of her as a student—though she was years older than the standard nineteen-year-old—with a limited budget that had driven her to shared accommodations. However, anyone who could spend a year indulging hobbies and still afford an archaeological summer in Greece had resources.

Unless the resources had been Pip's. But, short of being the best liar he'd ever met, Nancy Berger's reactions didn't fit that theory.

"There's a great Indochinese café tucked in the other side of the Sorbonne," he said.

"The Bambu? Oh, I dream about their lemon grass chicken."

"Or even better, their duck with chilies."

"You're a brave man, Mr. Stuyvesant."

But not brave enough to face the concierge without a qualm. He gave Mme. Hachette a craven tip of the hat and followed on Miss Berger's heels, feeling the dragon's glare scorch the back of his neck.

Upstairs, his companion walked into the sitting room, looked vaguely at the strewn objects from the exploded suitcase, and seemed to sag. When she turned, he realized that she was older still than he'd thought, probably past thirty.

"Dear Lord, I am tired," she announced. "Look. If I leave you with Phil's things, can I trust you not to steal the silver?"

"As if Mme. Hachette would let me walk away with so much as a hairpin. Yes, I'll lock up. And close the window."

"Thanks. Good to meet you," she said.

"Before you go, tell me: what did you go into her bedroom for? It wasn't for any ointment."

She hadn't been embarrassed when talking about naked photographs, but she was now. "I told you, I—"

"Honey, you're a rotten liar."

She sighed. "I am, aren't I? It was a dress. Phil had two or three really special dresses. The kind of garments that take over a woman's entire personality when she puts them on. You become . . . well, you become a person who would wear that kind of a gown. So when I was asked to a very formal occasion, I borrowed one, even though it was too short on me. I had it cleaned afterwards and put it back precisely where I had found it, but if she knew, she'd have a fit. She loved those dresses. She used to . . ."

She stopped, laying a hand over her mouth.

"What is it?"

"I'm talking as if she's dead. Oh, God! Poor kid, she comes to Paris to get away from Boston and what does she end up with? A roommate who's happy to find the apartment empty and a private investigator who's more interested in girls' legs than his job. Jesus, Paris can be a shit of a town."

"What the hell are you talking about?" he protested. "You got no reason to panic like that. Pip's no wide-eyed innocent. She knows how the world works. And she's got enough sense to keep out of dark corners."

"And if she didn't, then she brought it on herself, is that what you mean?"

If she'd been a man, he'd have punched her. "I never said that. I never *thought* that. And lady, I'm doing my damnedest to find her."

Her dark eyes welled up. "I'm so sorry. Oh, God—I seem to have spent the last hour apologizing to you. I'm not usually—it's just—I'm such a useless—oh, why didn't someone at least *notice*?"

He seized her shoulders, forcing her to look up at him.

"Listen. I will find her. No doubt head over heels in love with some handsome young painter."

"It's just, she was so . . . *secretive*. And when she did talk she'd come up with some piece of old wives' hooey and it was just . . . *irritating*. I even asked her if she wanted me to move out, but she sounded surprised and said no, she was happy to have me. Like I say, we might as well have been living in separate houses. Mme. Hachette probably knows more about Phil than I do—*she* could tell you when Phil left, which is more than I can! Oh, I should have pushed it."

"What, moving out?"

"*Talking* to her. If I'd even asked her about her new friends, her strange habits, what she was *doing* . . ."

"Nancy, look: if Pip was so set on privacy, do you think she'd have told you any of that?"

Her teary eyes studied him for the longest time. "Thank you," she said finally.

"For what?"

"For trying to make me feel less of a failure when it comes to friendship." To his surprise, she stepped forward to plant a kiss on his cheek. To his greater surprise, his hand started to come up and hold the back of her head, pressing that generous mouth into his—but he stifled the motion before it started. She wasn't even his type.

Still, she was unexpected. And she might tell him more about Pip Crosby, if he distracted her. Fed her booze. "Would you like to go out with me? Dinner, dancing—the movies, if you like. *Innocents of Paris* is still playing, if you like Maurice Chevalier."

She sniffed, and dug through her pockets for a tissue to blow her nose. Her eyes were red again when she looked up, but dry. "Would this be social, or part of your investigation?"

"What if I said both?"

"Then I suppose yes. But not tonight."

"Tomorrow, then. Seven?"

"Half past."

"I'll wear a shirt with buttons that match," he said.

She gave him that mournful smile. "And I'll wear one of my own dresses."

He watched her go. *Less of a failure when it came to friendship.* Yeah, okay, he might've been a little . . . using towards Pip Crosby, last winter. She'd caught him at a bad time, just after Tim's death, and he'd been feeling so down he hadn't really stopped to think why this pretty young thing would want the likes of him. He'd just let himself be convinced. And then she'd been so damned enthusiastic, and . . .

And maybe *he* should have talked with her a little, too. Asked her about herself. Treated her like a person, not a . . . not a Lulu.

But, really, how was a man to know? Women these days seemed to like being casual, seemed not to want anything but a good time and a good-bye. And in the end, Pip left *him* rather than the other way around. There was no reason to feel any more guilty about her than he did about Lulu.

Other than her youth. And her scar. And the image of a ten-year-old girl falling through the air with flames in her clothes.

Ah, crap. What had started as a quick and cushy job wasn't turning out that way.

He began his bedroom tour, as before, with the photographs on the wall. The first time through, they had struck him as slightly phony, pretentiously arty, like a college freshman with delusions of fame posing his girlfriend for the camera. Reluctantly, now he wondered if they weren't more than that. Not the close-ups of her scar: those were just morbid. But the others . . .

Both of the moody photographs rendered Pip's conventional features dramatic by their severe black and white. In the first, she was lying on a black surface gazing up at the camera lens, hands crossed like a laid-out corpse, hair falling back from her face: expressionless as a mannequin, inscrutable behind heavy makeup. The photograph was disturbing in some indefinable way, and despite the paint and the apparent lack of revelation, seemed more naked than the other one.

In that second picture, a nude Pip was perched on a high stool, right foot coyly tucked onto a rung so the raised knee hid her sex. Her left hand lay on her perfect thigh, while her right arm cradled her breasts, the hand grasping her left biceps. The girl's breasts were every bit as tasty as he remembered, although it took a while to notice them, because the eye found it hard to pull away from the ugly dark scar tissue under the right elbow, broader than a big man's outspread hand. Its surface seemed taut, as if a quick motion would split it right open. The eye was fascinated by it, teased away from the pert breasts and the dark fold between her legs to return to that slick, damaged skin. Even a man whose hand didn't tingle with the memory of (*Go ahead, silly, it doesn't hurt.*) that strangely compelling slickness (*They like the freaks, you know?*)—even that man might take a while (*Yes, Harris, do—*) to raise his eyes to her face. But when he did . . .

What expression *was* that? Stuyvesant dug the uncle's version of Rosalie's snapshot from his pocket, holding it up between the two pictures on the wall. In it, Pip—wearing a lot less makeup and a lot more clothes—sat on the edge of a Roman fountain, leaning against the cropped-away Rosalie. She was pretty enough, and had the pleasing vivacity of youth, but there was mistrust there as well. Whether of the camera, the person behind the camera, or life in general, he could not know.

In the starkly naked portrait, however, that wariness was gone. Pip was all but thrusting herself at the lens, chin high with what Stuyvesant had seen as a defiant assertion of her body. You could feel her pleasure at the idea of rubbing the noses of viewers (most especially her mother and uncle) into the damage, anticipating the gasps of polite horror.

Some fluke of the camera lens gave that adolescent defiance gravitas, making Pip look unexpectedly complex. Like one of those trick drawings—first a goblet, then the silhouette of two faces—he could see her juvenile insolence, but he could also, now, see something else.

Pride. Courage. Beauty, even. Yes, this was a willful rich girl playing the flirt; on the other hand, this was also a young woman who had worked hard to get to a place where she liked herself, damage and all.

People came to Paris because it was cheap, but they also came to reinvent themselves, weaving the city's freedoms—linguistic or racial, artistic or social, and above all, sexual—into a new identity. Here on the banks of the Seine, Pip Crosby was no longer a "good" girl, no longer someone made ugly by a scar. No longer a girl, even.

And now Harris Stuyvesant felt . . . regret. That he hadn't been around to watch. Because whatever it was that brought about that young woman's pride—life in Paris, superstitious rituals, becoming a nude model—he couldn't say it was entirely a bad thing.

Or maybe he was just being a romantic fool.

He left the nude picture on the wall, but worked the other portrait out of its frame, tucking it into his notebook alongside the snapshot.

The contents of the bookshelf provided more by way of confirmation than surprise: half a dozen racy novels, two in English and four in French; twice that number of books on things like Tarot and astrology, again in both languages; and an assortment of new American fiction sent by her mother—each had a brief note and a date inside its cover, from May to Christmas of last year. Nothing political. Casual bookmarks in some of the thicker French tomes, all in the first quarter of their book, suggested that Pip had found them hard going. The book-marks were mostly postcards (Mrs. Crosby from Niagara; Mrs. Crosby from Chicago; a friend—Sally? Susan? The signature was smudged—from the Metropolitan Museum in New York) or ticket receipts: Luna Park, the Folies Bergère, three theaters, and a couple of cinémas. He started to remove them, then changed his mind and wrote down their information, instead.

Not that the cops would ever notice, but if by chance they did come here, they might be unhappy with an American detective who helped himself to evidence.

After he had examined the bottoms of the shelves, he went to the dressing table and did the same. Taking care to make little noise, he removed the drawers, checked behind them, looked at the back of the table and its mirror, and found nothing. He returned the furniture to the original dents in the carpet, and examined the pictures on the wall, taking each down, feeling those with a paper backing.

A small basket on the end of the shelf held a deck of Tarot cards and three Chinese coins with square holes in the middle. The bed-side table held nothing out of the ordinary. The mattress concealed no objects, nor did the carpet.

He took a last glance at the two peculiar boxes with their enigmatic grids of bones and objects, and noticed for the first time faint lines running up the right-hand side of both. He hadn't seen the pattern earlier, but with the sun edging west, the scratching stood out. He tipped his head, and made out four tiny, geometric capitals: DIDI.

He wrote the word down in his notebook. Perhaps she had actually known the artist—if you could call it *art*. Which made him think: Miss Berger hadn't answered his question about the artists Pip sat for. Had her claim of tiredness been a little too conveniently timed?

Christ, he told himself, *you are one suspicious son of a bitch.*

He closed the window, as he'd promised. In the doorway, he turned for a final survey: beds, furniture, drapes; the photographs. Those odd boxes. The sketches, particularly the vivid personality shown by the Spaniard's wicked and perceptive pen. The nude photograph: Jesus.

If she'd given him a look like that back in February—youth or not,

Rosalie or no—he'd have followed her. He'd have dogged her steps all the way to Rome and back.

He tipped his hat to Nancy's closed door, dropped a card with his hotel's number on the table near the phone, and left the apartment. When he had safely negotiated a passage by the gorgon, he checked his watch: 3:40.

Time to see the cops.

But on his way across the Pont au Change—at about the point Victor Hugo had his Inspector Javier throw himself off—Stuyvesant halted to draw the photograph of him and Pip from his breast pocket. He looked at the unlikely pair for some time, a crooked smile softening his features—until his fingers let the scrap of paper go. He watched it dance and drift, down to the water, and away.

No reason to complicate matters. None at all.

NINE

BEGINNING IN ROMAN times, bodies were buried on the Rive Droit near the great north-south road that would one day be divided into the rues Sébastopol, Palais, and Saint-Michel by the Pont au Change and the Pont Saint-Michel. By the twelfth century, Paris had closed in around it, but the Cemetery of the Holy Innocents continued: a field of bones and bodies surrounded by the living. Pits were dug and the city's dead tumbled in by the hundreds. When one pit was full, it was covered over with soil dug from the next. The stench was appalling; the cemetery was the realm of prostitutes and pickpockets; nearby homes looked directly down at putrefying bodies.

A high stone wall was built around it.

Plagues came and went; the level inside the wall rose, until the ground was more bone than soil. The wall's arches and recesses proved a convenient place to stack the pieces of skeleton that came to light with every turn of the shovel: an open-air charnel house surrounded what had once been a churchyard.

Calls were made to evict the cemetery, but it remained, a stinking, dangerous, lucrative sore at the very center of Paris.

In the fifteenth century, frescoes were added to the charnel house archways, darkly humorous images with Death as a reaper, harvesting all mankind yet permitting a last playful dance on the way to the pitted earth. Lady in satin or moneylender with bags of gold; learned cleric or beggar in rags: infant, adolescent, young man, crone: all danced with Death in the end. The Saints-Innocents fresco was the first Danse Macabré; soon, Death's Merry Dance was seen all over Europe, in fresco and carving, wood-print and oil painting.

And the burials went on. For hundreds of years, the dead of Paris were brought to the Cemetery of the Innocents to be turned into clean bone. The stench gagged and infected those living nearby—who were soon added to the numbers. The exposed flesh fed the rats—who carried diseases, that filled the pits, that fed the next generation of rats. The figures on the walls danced with Death, merry and doomed.

Not until Revolution was in the air did the king take official notice of the killing stench and the half-rotted bodies that spilled through the walls. The cemetery was closed to further burials. The bones were used to fill some inconvenient holes underground; the burial field was cleared for the living; barrels of adipocere—corpse-wax—were shoveled up and turned into candles. For, as Charles Dickens would later write:

> The decay of ages, in some of the coffins, leaves but the food for that lamp which is now burning above us . . . and many of the quiet inhabitants of the cemetery become more useful to mankind in death than they ever were in lifetime.

TEN

THE PRÉFECTURE DE Police was on the Île de la Cité, between a one-time madhouse and cells used during the Terror for guillotine-bound prisoners: one did not expect a bushel of laughs from the Préfecture de Police. Stuyvesant adjusted his tie over the offending mismatched button and walked inside.

"Yes, I saw the message you left yesterday. A missing girl. American."

The missing persons *flic* had himself been missing when Stuyvesant came by the previous day, another laggardly return from Paris' August vacances. His name was Doucet, although there was little sweet about him, since he was nearly as tall as Stuyvesant and had a face that had seen nearly the same things in life—certainly his nose had met about as many fists. His English was a shade better than Stuyvesant's French. "Monsieur, do you have an investigator's license?"

Stuyvesant handed over the official document—a meaningless but vital piece of paper that he'd got by doing the occasional job for a Paris detective agency—along with his *carte d'identité*. Doucet sourly studied the documents, then shoved them back across the desk. Next, Stuyvesant gave him a copy of the snapshot—the uncle had sent two—and began reciting the girl's details: physical description; address; work history; date last seen.

"March?" the man interrupted. "Why did the family wait until September?"

"They wrote to the roommate in May. She wrote back saying that Miss Crosby was away for a few days, and then she herself left—she was spending the summer in Greece. By mid-June, Miss Crosby hadn't answered their letters or telephone calls and the concierge just said both girls were away. So they hired an investigator. He turned out to be a crook. They're trying again."

"With you."

"With me."

"Have they reported this man, the 'crook'?"

"I don't think so."

With a sigh, Doucet reached into a drawer and started pulling out forms. Stuyvesant revised his earlier assumption: the man might not be freshly back from holiday. Or if so, it had not been a restful one.

While the detective filled out the forms, Stuyvesant studied the cramped, untidy office. One wall intrigued him. It was covered with photographs: men and women, old and young, dark and light. Some had been pinned up so long, the corners curled; one of a lively brown-haired girl might have gone up yesterday. These, he thought, were the unsolved cases, looking over the man's shoulder.

The *flic* reached the end of the forms, handing over his pen for Stuyvesant's signature. He pinned the photograph to the form.

Stuyvesant cleared his throat: now came the tricky bit. "In fact, the reason her uncle came to me was that I'd met her. Back in February. I was working in Nice when she and a friend—a girl named Rosalie Perkins—passed through on their way to Rome. When Rosalie mentioned me to Miss Crosby's uncle, telling him that I was a private investigator, he thought it might simplify things to have someone who knew her slightly."

Doucet studied him, listening for unrevealed truths. "And was that all you knew her: slightly?"

"Perhaps a little better than that. But," Stuyvesant said pointedly, "she was fine when she and her friend went to Rome, and she made it back to Paris safely. Her roommate saw her, and Pip—Miss Crosby—

wrote home from here at the end of March. And just in case you're interested, I myself was three weeks in Nice after the girls left, then in Warsaw for the remainder of March and all of April, followed by two weeks in Clermont-Ferrand and after that, Germany. I did spend two days here on my way to Germany in mid-June, but I haven't seen Pip Crosby since Nice."

"You lead a most itinerant life, M. Stuyvesant." The phlegmatic comment surprised Stuyvesant a little: he hadn't expected the cop to swallow the story quite that easily.

"I go where work takes me."

"And today your work brings you to Paris, and to me."

"I doubt Miss Crosby is still in Paris, but yes, I've come here to pick up her trail, as it were. And because I believe in working with the police"—*when I have to,* he added mentally—"I've come to share my information and my intentions with you."

"What a responsible attitude. Where do you think she is, your Miss Crosby?"

"Somewhere her mother wouldn't approve of. Which would suggest she's either having such a good time living la vie Bohème that the months got away from her, or she's got herself involved with drugs and everything that goes with it."

"Is there evidence for that?"

"She has some pretty expensive art in her bedroom, that's all. As for travel—"

"What sort of art?" Doucet's face had not changed, but there was an edge to his voice, as if the word had made his interest go sharp.

"I'm no expert, but she has a small Lautrec and a Chagall pastel, and a funny little piece by that Spaniard, what's his name?"

"Picasso?"

"No, although there's a sketch by him, too, on a paper napkin. Miró, that's it."

"You are an art expert."

"Hardly. Museums are good places to get out of the rain."

Doucet gave him a skeptical look. "You were telling me something about her travel, Monsieur?"

"Was I? Oh right, I was saying that her French paperwork is in her room but her passport isn't."

"So if it is a choice between an irresponsible holiday and a life of desperation and crime, towards which of those fates do you lean, Monsieur?"

"To tell you the truth, I think she may be in trouble." Stuyvesant stopped, listening to his own words. *Was* he worried? No, he didn't think so, not really. Still, the cop seemed almost human, and there was always a chance that roping him in with a sob story would kick up a few results. He went on.

"I figured, like you: here's another Yankee Flapper gone off to conquer Europe. But it concerns me that she hasn't written to her mother— which she did regularly, and more than just dutiful picture postcards. Plus that, the only money that's gone out of her bank account since April is a regular draft to cover housekeeping expenses. And although there could be plenty of explanations for that, from a rich boyfriend to a bitter family argument her uncle's too ashamed to admit, until I hear otherwise: yeah, I'd say there's a chance she's in over her head."

"Monsieur?" His English was good, but this phrase was beyond him.

"Sorry. I meant she could be in trouble."

"Politics?"

Stuyvesant liked the way this guy's mind worked. "I thought of that when I found she hadn't been cashing checks. Recent converts to Bolshevism or Anarchism or what-have-you tend to be thrilled about turning their back on the State and its banks. But after five months, I'd have expected somebody to catch on to her bank account and drain it. Plus, there were no political books or pamphlets in her apartment."

"White slavery? Drug dens? Mere prostitution isn't illegal."

"It is if your passport isn't stamped for work," he retorted, then backed down. "Okay, that's stupid, and being locked up for the nefarious use of strange men is downright melodramatic. But you and I both know, bad things do happen to good girls."

The *flic* rubbed his face. "M. Stuyvesant, my office receives an average of nineteen missing persons complaints from America every month. Of those, fifteen reappear in a few weeks, after the love of their lives turns them out for another girl; three have got themselves in trouble and are sailing home to maman; and one is up to no good. I have yet to have one of them show up in a white slave ring, pleasuring foreign potentates.

"However," he said, putting up his hand to interrupt Stuyvesant's protest. "When I received your inquiry this morning, I looked at the case, and see that we received our first report concerning Mlle. Crosby in late May. Our first act was to question hospitals and brothels. Our second was to compare her name to the passenger lists of ships and airplanes. After preliminary inquiries to the telephone number we had been given, we scheduled a visit to her apartment. Before we could do so, my sergeant spoke with a private inquiry agent, who showed him a letter from Mlle. Crosby's family retaining him to look into the matter. The following day the agent telephoned to report that she had been found, and please to take her case off our books."

"But why—? Ah. The crook was milking them."

"'Milking'?"

With a wrench of mental gears, Stuyvesant switched to French. "If your department had found her, that would be the end of his job," he explained. "But if he kept you out of it so he could continue sending reports—and bills—to the family, he could stretch it for months. Milking them—like a cow. The family only figured it out by accident a few weeks ago, when a friend of Crosby's came to Paris and found that the agency address was a bar."

"Yet they did not report this."

"I don't think Mr. Crosby has much faith in foreign police departments."

Doucet sat back, his eyebrows an invitation to talk. So with a mental shrug, Stuyvesant talked. He began with the original letter, handing it to the cop and waiting while he read the three pages. He then described the packet that had followed, with Photostats of her letters home, two copies of the cropped snapshot, and notes of everything the uncle knew, from the dud investigator to a conversation with Pip's travel companion.

This last was a four-page typed document beginning with Rosalie's vehement declaration that Pip was living a squeaky-clean life in the City of Light, that Pip had no sins and no special boy-friend, although many fine and fascinating companions to justify the money to keep her in Paris, and concluding with a list of friends that mostly lacked surnames. At the end, the uncle had attached a note:

> There are things the girl was not telling me, secrets she did not feel she had the right to divulge—this younger generation believes their elders have had no experience with life. She did let slip that my niece had a roommate, an American girl named Nancy Berger whom Pip brought in to "share the rent"—even though I pay it. This suggests that Pip was indulging in a piece of chicanery to supplement her monthly stipend. A disappointing insight into her character, but hardly a major crime.
>
> Nonetheless, having pressed upon this friend of hers that honesty would best serve Pip's welfare, at the end I do not think that the girl's omissions were <u>too</u> dire. If there had been something truly important, something that might explain Pip's disappearance, I believe she would have told me.

Doucet pursed his lips at that underlined *too,* much as Stuyvesant had. As if a situation could be just a little bit dire without having to fret about it.

"And like I said, there were copies of the girl's letters home," Stuyvesant added, having come to the end of his documents. "Twenty-four of them, full of light chat and little information."

From the first letter (written March 3, 1928: Dearest Mama, Your little Pip is in Paris!!) to the last (undated, but with a Paris *oblitération* of March 20, 1929: Chère maman, Spring is coming to la belle cité), the girl's prettily written pages were more full of The Romance of Paris than they were of hard fact. Reading between the lines, however, even someone who hadn't met the girl would suspect an independent young spirit out to create a rich life for herself, an ocean removed from home. A life she didn't think chère maman needed to have too many details about.

"You did not bring the letters?"

"They're at my hotel. Do you want to see them? I'll go get them if you want."

"I have an appointment. Let us meet later. Not here—there's a brasserie on rue Monge, near the entrance to the Arènes de Lutèce. Pink geraniums out front. Six o'clock—no, later. Make it half past."

"I'll bring them."

The two men rose and shook hands under the eyes of those rows of faces—an awful lot of whom seemed to be young, blonde women. Out on the baking street again, Stuyvesant turned to look with bemusement at the Préfecture façade. Not your usual cop, French or otherwise. He had a feeling he'd told the *flic* a lot more than he'd intended to.

Still, it was only 4:30. Plenty of time for a literary excursion.

ELEVEN

Sʏʟᴠɪᴀ Bᴇᴀᴄʜ sᴛᴏᴏᴅ in the doorway of Shakespeare and Company, looking like a wind-blown city sparrow. She was talking to a poet. Stuyvesant knew he was a poet by the hair, not so much cut as pruned—but then, who in Montparnasse wasn't a poet?

The bookseller spotted him approaching down the rue de l'Odéon and waved broadly. "Hello, Mr. Boxer," she cried. "Are you looking for your sparring partner?"

"Who, Hemingway? No. I wouldn't want to be responsible for pummeling the next work of genius out of him."

She turned to the weedy young man with the limp bow tie. "This is Mr. Harris Stuyvesant, the only American in Paris who neither writes nor paints. Although Hemingway says he's an artist in the boxing ring. You sure you haven't taken up bullfighting, too, Harris?"

"I'll leave that to Hem."

"He was in earlier—he's been in Spain working on a bullfighting book."

"Of course he has."

"I'll let him know you're here, too, shall I?"

"Oh, I expect we'll come across each other." Ernest Hemingway was a difficult man to miss in Montparnasse, unless one kept out of the bars entirely.

"We're anticipating much from his new book. I'm hoping for a shipment any day, if you'd like me to save you one?"

"Maybe when I'm not so busy. Actually, it's you I came to see."

"I'm honored. Luis, had we finished?"

The poet gave her a meek tip of the hat and slunk away into the hot sunlight, while Sylvia grasped Stuyvesant's sleeve and pulled him inside. "Harris, it's so good to see you, if for no other reason than you're not about to ask me to publish your poems. How have you been? Would you like a glass of something? Or a cup? I could manage a coffee."

Sylvia Beach was a diminutive American who had come to Paris during the War and stayed. Her *raison d'être ici* was an English-language bookstore that had quickly become the center of the expatriate community in Montparnasse. And as if selling English books in the heart of France wasn't challenge enough, she had added "publisher" to her resumé, taking on the task of publishing an enormous—and enormously controversial—novel by an Irish-born English tutor named Joyce. It was just as well for Sylvia Beach that she thrived on the impossible.

"A glass of something would be great," he told her. "Whatever you have." He could have done with a cold beer, but what she had was wine, red, from a bottle she plucked from the back of the collection. He saluted her with his glass and took a deep swallow. A man knew he was getting old when three nights with a girl like Lulu took out more than it put in. "You're looking very brown and fit."

"Arienne and I are just back from Les Déserts—in Savoy?—and Marseilles, so yes, I'm feeling somewhat restored. It has been a hectic year. And Lord, this heat!" She lit a cigarette and dropped into a chair, looking as if it was the first time she'd been off her feet all day. She sucked in a deep lungful of smoke, and let it out on a sigh of appreciation. "But my dear Harris, what can I do for you?"

He handed her the moody portrait he'd taken from Pip's wall. "Do you recognize her?"

"Yes, she used to drop in from time to time. American, of course. Shy when she first showed up, but that didn't last long. It never does."

"You helped her find a roommate."

"Did I? Oh yes, you're right—the adorable Nancy. Miss Crosby tacked a note up with her telephone number, and I kept my ears open. They seemed a good fit."

Adorable? "When did you last see Pip Crosby?"

"Months ago. She brought me a box of novels her mother had sent."

"Could you narrow it down?"

"Hmm. Must've been after Christmas, since the books had been presents. They were in good condition—I don't think she'd even opened the covers—so I was happy to have them. Oh! Miss Weaver was here and we were talking about *Orlando,* so that would make it late January, maybe early February."

"You haven't seen her since?"

"No— Well, wait, it seems to me I did. But where? Someplace odd." She sat frowning into the smoke, then rumpled her brown hair irritably. "Too much in my head—if something's not related to books, I find it increasingly hard to retrieve."

"Then it's a good thing your job is books."

"I'll think of it. No doubt at three in the morning when my fevered brain is hunting for a distraction from the bills. Why are you looking for her?"

"Oh, I'm just trying to find someone she might have known," he replied vaguely. "What about the photograph: any idea who took it?"

By way of answer, she jabbed an ink-stained forefinger past his shoulder. He turned, then got up for a closer look at the gathered faces. Some of them he'd drunk with, others he'd seen on the streets or in bars. And as he looked them over, he realized that yes, in a number of the photographs, the camera technique stood out. One might even call it artistic in its attention to dark and light, the abrupt contrast of face and background, the way a subject's cast shadow would be used to add dimension to the personality.

"Yeah, I remember now. His name is Ray?"

"Man Ray. A New Yorker like you. He's the only one who photographs the shadows that way."

"One of the Surrealist school, right?"

"It used to be called Dada, but yes."

"Don't they have a hangout up in Montmartre? A drinking hole near the cemetery?"

"Aha! That's it!"

"What's what?"

"Where I saw your girl. It was last winter, and she was sitting in a café with an unlikely group of men that included Man Ray."

"Who else was there?"

"Let me see. Tristan Tzara was one. You know him?"

"The writer."

"The others were artists. Let's see, Tanguey was there, and Chaim Soutine. Oh, and Salvador Dalí."

"That's quite a crew."

"They seemed to be planning something."

"A Surrealistic revolution?"

"No, it was on paper—that's right, they were playing exquisite corpses."

"Sorry?"

"You know, where one person does a drawing and folds the paper, and the next person takes the edges and makes another section of the drawing? It's a parlor game."

"Guess I don't spend enough time in parlors. So what was Pip doing there?"

"Watching, mostly. I only saw them for a minute, so I'm not sure, but she had that slightly confused look you see a lot on the faces of what Alice Toklas calls 'the geniuses' wives.'"

"Was she there with Man Ray?"

"Well, as I remember, she was sitting next to him, but there was a crowd, so she could have come with anyone. And as I said, I was only passing through."

"Where was this? Up in Montmartre?"

"No, it was the Flore. Although if you're looking for Man Ray, I'm pretty sure he does most of his socializing closer to home. He likes the Bateau Ivre."

"So he lives in Montparnasse?"

"Doesn't everyone? His studio is down near Denfert-Rochereau. Hold on— Myrsine?" she called. "Do you know if Man Ray is back in town?"

Her assistant looked up from wrapping a book. "I saw him on the Boul' Mich on Sunday. He has a new assistant, over whom he has lost his head. They say she is to be his model. Une blonde Américaine. Très belle."

"No more Kiki? Well, that's a change."

"Do you have his address—for the studio, that is?" Miss Beach was famously hesitant to give out the addresses of her customers, but a studio might be a different matter.

After consideration, she decided it was. "Yes. Yes, I'll give you the address." She rummaged through the papers on her desk for a pen and a piece of the store's stationery, then handed him the number on rue Campagne Première.

He pursed his lips. "Isn't that across from the Montparnasse cemetery?"

"Yes. Not one of the more cheery cemeteries, I'm afraid."

"Too much business, not enough park."

"Exactly. Oh, Harris, my dear man, if only my poets could turn a phrase like you."

He laughed, and asked her what was new in the book world. They talked for a few minutes, with Sylvia springing up twice to show him new treasures. Guidebooks were a shared passion—although both agreed that few modern guides captured a feeling for the layers of Paris history, built up here, worn thin there. One trip to Paris, doing surveillance on a grifter, he'd spotted her head-down among the second-hand book stalls along the river. To his mind, those stalls were one of the prime temptations of Paris.

"Which reminds me," she said. "Did you know Kiki has written a guide?"

"Kiki can *write?*"

She burst into laughter. "Apparently. And she talked Hemingway into giving her an introduction."

"Should sell a few more copies."

"That's what she figured. A shrewd businesswoman, our Kiki. No doubt I'll carry it, when it's published in English. Oh, and there's this— It made me think of you."

She jumped up and came back with a book, a detective novel by a new writer named Hammett. Stuyvesant had his doubts, but other than his subscription to the store's lending library, buying books was the only way he could pay her for information. He also promised that he'd return for a copy of Hemingway's upcoming hymn to manliness.

She took the novel over to the cash desk to write up his slip. "Will you be with us for a while, this time?"

"Maybe, if I find another job here. Believe it or not, I was thinking the other day that it might be nice to settle down. Keep my books on a shelf rather than in trunks scattered across Europe."

"Here?" She sounded dubious.

"Why? Sylvia, don't tell me you're growing tired of the City of Light?"

"Me? Never! I adore Paris. The problem is, so do an awful lot of others, and the sheer numbers are making things go a bit . . . dark. The party's over, and the sad children and criminals are moving in. The Americans who matter will move on, leaving the rest of us washed up with the other flotsam and jetsam."

"I don't know that having the non-mattering Americans move on would be the end of the world for the locals," he said.

"We Yanks haven't always been kind to Paris, have we? Less 'flotsam' than an occupying army."

"Even armies go home. Still, I can't see this one shifting for a long time. Certainly not until the boom fades and the exchange rate drops."

"Heavens, don't say that. Where would we be without the stock market?"

"Where, indeed?" he agreed, then took his parcel, and his leave. As he passed through the door, another wan poet slipped inside.

Out on the street, the sun was nearing the rooflines, suggesting that the worst of the day's heat might be past. Stuyvesant walked down l'Odeon (dodging a bus-load of tourists) and crossed over into the Luxembourg gardens (giving wide berth to a quartet from the Midwest) in the direction of his hotel. As gardens went, he preferred the Bois de Boulogne—being a Central Park boy, after all—but even these were restful on the eyes. Or they would be, once his countrymen had gone home.

A child with a dripping ice-cream ran across his toes, shrieking wildly. In English.

Yes, Parisians had the right idea when it came to summer: get out. Paris obscured by snow or softened by fog, Paris adrift on fallen blossoms or carpeted in autumn leaves, Paris in the rain, at night, the lights streaking on the pavement—yes. But not Paris with a blast furnace overhead, when five minutes after finishing a beer, a man felt thirsty. Days like this, you kept a close eye on stray dogs, expecting one to come at you with foam-slathered jaws. Days like this, you wondered if winter would ever come again. If a snowdrop would ever bloom in the badlands.

It had been a long summer, in all kinds of ways. He'd begun to feel as tired as Paris, a city worn down by the heat, as used up by foreign invaders as an aging femme de nuit. Maybe even Paris had a limit to her charms. Maybe in another generation, the social and cultural center of the country would shift south, to Lyons, or Marseilles.

And maybe men had been thinking that very thing since the Emperor Julian fell in love with the place, over fifteen hundred years ago.

His thoughts were broken by a loud voice. "Hey, mister, you mind taking our picture?"

"I'spreche kein English," he snarled and pressed on.

TWELVE

THE RUE COLLE was a truncated attempt at a Paris arcade off the rue Vavin. *Colle* meant glue, and the name probably didn't help attract the flaneûrs, particularly when the rue Colle's only shops were a florist's that specialized in funeral wreaths, a stamp-collector who sold pornography, and a nervy Russian gentleman who made beautiful canes.

Halfway down this glass-roofed tunnel with the sticky cobblestones was the Hotel Benoit, more *pension* than hotel: no flower-boxes, no doorman—no sign, even. Stuyvesant had stumbled across the place in 1917, on leave from the Front, when he'd turned his back on the bustle surrounding the Gare du Nord and kept walking, in search of the darkest corner with a bed.

Mme. Benoit was old then, and each time he returned, he found her a fraction smaller, a bit more absent-minded, a little more emphatic in her devotion to Karl Marx. As coy about her age as any Frenchwoman, she had to be in her eighties: her husband had died in La Semaine Sanglante during the Paris Commune. She had watched the Eiffel Tower rise. She cursed the name of Bruno Haussmann and his destruction of Paris with such vehemence, Stuyvesant thought she believed the man still alive. Only the ferocious loyalty of her permanent residents kept her from starvation on the streets—some of the girls had recently instigated a chitty system after Mme. Benoit had failed to charge one month-long guest and charged another three times.

The Hotel Benoit had hard mattresses, thin curtains, a mix of gas and electric lights, and dingy paint. No two pieces of furniture matched. There was no breakfast service, and the nearest hot water was at the Armenian bathhouse around the corner. Still, the rooms were clean, the locks were great, every floor had a toilet and a cold shower, and nobody minded if he stashed a trunk in the cellar between visits. Best of all, if his preferred room was available—and it had been, this time—there was a loose floorboard under the threadbare carpet, for the concealment of cash and a revolver. And being on the top floor, it had three flights of conveniently noisy stairs, plus a window within climbing distance of the rooftops, should the need arise. Some of the permanent residents were ladies with a striking number of male visitors, but they kept it quiet, and most of them were easy enough on the eyes.

He called out a greeting to Madame, whose door stood open as usual, and trudged up the rackety stairs, tugging at his neck-tie and shrugging out of his jacket as he went. He dropped the brown paper-wrapped book on the table, tossed various garments he never wanted to wear again onto the bed, and fetched the thick envelope containing Pip's letters from the bed-side table. He looped his suspenders off his shoulders, checked that the letters were there and nothing else, then retied the fastener.

After a glance at his watch, he dug out his notebook and sat at the table to write down a few brief phrases about the day, enough to help him reconstruct events for his employer when time came to make a report. When he capped the pen, Sylvia's twine-wrapped packet caught his eye. He pulled it open and found *Red Harvest*: "a thrilling detective story." Two pages in, he found himself tipped back in his chair with a grin on his face—not so much at the story, although it was refreshing to find a detective novel that didn't start with arsenic-laced tea in the library, but at the little bookseller who had chosen it. "Poisonville"—hah! Was this how Sylvia saw him?

But it was a fine beginning, and it might have distracted him into reading further had he not been covered with sweat, and aware that he stank. He dropped it back into the brown paper and left it on the table.

Parisians seemed perfectly happy with weekly visits to the bathhouse, but he'd never got used to the ripe smell. Maybe he should change his shirt, for the cop's sake. And if he was going to spend another night trawling the bars into the wee hours (last night's search for information having been cut short when Lulu found him), he couldn't see doing that reeking like he did.

However, he had one clean shirt, and he'd meant to wear it tomorrow, when—thanks to the Crosby check—he was going to his tailor. He didn't like the idea of forcing the guy to breathe *eau de Stuyvesant* in close quarters.

And why bother to change, anyway? If tonight was anything like last night, the damn bars would all be empty.

But sitting on the bed with two-day-old sheets, smelling his own body, the thought of facing the world in this state was suddenly revolting.

He kicked off his shoes, emptied his pockets onto the table, and caught up his soap and towel, walking down the hall to the cold shower. His current employer would have paid for a proper hotel—expenses reimbursed, after all—but he couldn't count on a loose floorboard and convenient rooftop in the Ritz.

Of course, there was nothing to keep him from billing Crosby for the Ritz and pocketing the difference.

This time of day, the tiles were still clean and the tepid water pleasant against his skin. He rubbed himself head to toe with the bar of soap, then propped his arms against the wall and just stood, letting the sputtering stream run over his hair, letting his mind drift over the day. Sylvia's quizzical face, Nancy Berger's flexible mouth. The dragon, Mme. Hachette: looked like a hatchet, too. Doucet the cop: interesting guy. He was looking forward to seeing more of him. A cop with tired eyes that didn't seem to look at the world with complete disgust. Blue eyes, they'd been. Unusual in France. Maybe not as unusual as green—

He jerked upright so abruptly his skull knocked the shower-head sideways, shooting water over the pile of clothing. He slapped off the flow with a curse. The towel was drenched, but he found a dryish corner, then pulled on his slightly damp shorts and undershirt. He peered at his chin in the speckled mirror. Any point in shaving? Not really.

Like he'd said, he would probably be in bed by nine, anyway. With or without Lulu.

Back across the Luxembourg gardens, he crossed boulevard Saint-Michel without being knotted into a tangle of bicycles, then set off across the heart of the Latin Quarter in the direction of the Arènes de Lutèce. *Lutetia* was Rome's name for the city, and the one-time arena was a restful spot in the Quarter—if one ignored the ghostly sounds of lions and dying gladiators.

He spotted the pink geraniums on the rue Monge. Inside the brasserie mingled the clean smells of Pernod, shellfish, and garlic.

No Doucet.

Stuyvesant ordered a beer and stretched out his legs, listening to the conversations around him. A trio of Italians were debating fiercely, hands waving; a young couple sipped wine and flirted with glances and gestures, and occasionally with a caress of shoe-leather amongst the sawdust from the escargot baskets. Two Americans droned on and on about the stock market: how much they'd made, how high it might go.

Jesus, he thought. Would it be entirely a bad thing for the market to drop a little, if it meant that places like this could be returned to the inhabitants of Paris?

"Comment ça va, monsieur?" a voice said at his shoulder.

Stuyvesant rose to shake Doucet's hand. *Sure is tall for a Frenchman,* he thought. *Wonder where he buys his suits?* "Not too bad. Feels like it's going to cool a little. What'll you have?"

The cop was known here, the waiter standing in attendance before Doucet had settled his stiff leg under the table. "Bring me one of those." He gestured at Stuyvesant's half-empty lager.

"How would you feel about an oyster or ten to go with it?"

Doucet's eyes lit up, and he put his head together with the waiter over the types available, now that September was here. Personally, Stuyvesant would just as soon slurp cold mud, but he'd never met a French cop who didn't go all soft at a platter of salty-glop-on-a-shell.

"Thank you for meeting me outside of the office, Monsieur. It is true that I had a meeting, but my sergeant is also somewhat, how do you say, 'by the book.' He disapproves if he thinks I am about to share information with those outside the department."

A share of information had a promising ring to it, but Stuyvesant had seen that bait before, and he knew better than to snap at it too eagerly. "No problem," he said.

"Tell me about your search for Mlle. Crosby, M. Stuyvesant."

"Oh, you know how it goes: you spend days gathering odd pieces before you can start fitting them together. I've found a number of places she isn't, and where she hasn't been seen, and have a few names of people who might have seen her somewhere else." Doucet looked expectant, so Stuyvesant went on, warning himself against the temptation to open up: Doucet wasn't a partner.

"When I got to Paris on Saturday, I headed for Montparnasse, because that's where you look for an American like Pip Crosby. I worked my way through the bars in the Quarter, but nobody seemed to remember her. Sunday things were pretty dead, but last night I shifted up to Saint-Germain. Of course, things haven't picked up yet after the summer, but even so, nobody seems to know her—or if they remember her, they haven't seen her in a long time. Which I thought strange until I saw Pip's—Miss Crosby's—room, and found a bunch of matchbooks from clubs up in Montmartre."

"How is her French?"

"I guess better than I noticed."

"Better than the average American visitor's, would you say?"

"Since the average American visitor can only manage Bonjour, Combien? and Voulez-vous coucher avec moi? then yes. She has French novels on her bookshelf, with tickets to French theaters stuck in as bookmarks."

"I very much hope—" Doucet's hopes were interrupted by the arrival of a square meter of iced oyster bed and another pair of beers. Following several ounces of both, he finished the question. "I hope you did not remove anything from her possessions?"

"You'll be happy to find everything waiting for you, looking just like it did four months ago. As," Stuyvesant said pointedly, "you might have gone to see for yourself."

Doucet was suddenly very interested in the oyster balanced between his fingers.

"M. Stuyvesant, I am given to understand that you are an honest man."

"Who told you that?"

The name he said made Stuyvesant's grin fade. It was not one most Paris cops would have known—or known how to reach.

"What the—what were you doing talking to him?"

"You left your card with my sergeant yesterday, and do you know, these international telephone lines, they are so useful when a strange man comes asking questions. Particularly a strange man who is on the books as having spent a night in a Paris jail. And because I have been in contact with so many Americans over the years, it is not a difficulty to get certain questions answered. The man would appear to know you well."

"And yet he told you I was honest."

"His words were, 'Stuyvesant is an honorable man.'"

Honorable? Hah—tell that to the string of Lulus. Tell it to Pip. "I'm not sure that's the same thing as 'honest.'"

"It is sufficiently close that I am willing to believe that you are not . . . what was your word? A 'crook.'" Doucet chose another oyster, waiting to see if the American would pick up the test he'd set before him.

One of Stuyvesant's problems, these past three years, had been that no agency but the Pinkertons—who wanted his muscles and his English, but not his experience—would hire him without a recommendation from his former boss. And since that boss was Bureau director J. Edgar Hoover, and the two men had not parted on the best of terms, it meant doing without a recommendation.

He wasn't about to explain that history of animosity here—but if Doucet had talked to the man he'd just mentioned, then he'd heard both sides of the story, and was sending out a little feeler: was Stuyvesant honest, or no?

"You're right," Stuyvesant said, reaching for his notebook. "I didn't take anything from Miss Crosby's apartment but information—and, this." He dropped the dramatic photo on the table. "I'd planned on returning it to its frame tomorrow, when I go back."

The detective picked it up by the corner. "Man Ray's work."

"You know him?"

"My district includes Montparnasse, Monsieur. I know all the troublemakers."

"What kind of trouble does he make?"

"None that I know of. But M. Ray moves among the radical out-skirts of the artist community. Surrealists live to shock. They are infatu-ated with crime, the more bizarre and offensive, the better. Dismembered bodies, toilet humor, perverted sex. They have made a hero of the Mar-quis de Sade—as if the abuse of servants and the poor is a noble call-ing."

"Lots of people find the idea of murder entertaining," Stuyvesant commented. "Hell, they'll even put down good money for it, and the more outrageous, the better. The guy who writes those Fantômas stories must be making a fortune, and those'll raise a man's hair."

"Which is why we do not arrest M. Ray and his Surrealist friends. However, we do keep an eye on their activities. Because sooner or later, I believe one of them will decide to make the fantasy real."

Stuyvesant eyed the cop: hadn't they got a little off-track, here? "What's that got to do with Pip Crosby?"

The shells had grown empty, the glass also; before Doucet could respond, the waiter came to clear the table and bring them coffee. When he had gone, Doucet accepted a cigarette, and a light. He twirled the burning end against the tin tray. "Do you know the name Henri Landru, Monsieur?"

Stuyvesant's jerk scattered sugar over the table. "Hey, you're not sug-gesting . . . ? Jesus, just because she's moving with a fast crowd doesn't mean someone has slit her throat."

"So you know the name."

"Sure. You guys sent him to the guillotine six or seven years ago for murdering a bunch of women."

"Ten women and the seventeen-year-old son of his first victim. Landru was a—how do you say?—'most unprepossessing' figure, who took advantage of the state of widows during the War. He wooed them, stole what he could from them, and disposed of their bodies in his kitchen stove. A cold-blooded monster of a man. I worked on the investigation, soon after I was demobilized. Nothing was found of his victims but fragments of bone and the buttons and hooks of their clothing. I attended his trial. The Surrealists made it a cause célèbre, sitting in the court and reveling in every word, making Landru a hero of the unprivileged. I came away from the trial determined that no man would again get away with killing a series of women. Comprenez?"

"I understand." Stuyvesant was glad he hadn't gorged on the oysters: this rapid escalation from drug parties to bodies in a furnace was making him queasy.

"I am not suggesting this is the fate of your young friend, Monsieur."

"I'm really glad to hear that."

"What I am saying is that I have become a believer in the small details of an investigation, and in patterns. Whether a man intends to kill a woman or to take possession of her through the use of drugs, there is a system to his behavior. An interest in those patterns is a large reason why I work in the department of missing persons, that I might be the first to see the traces of a monster.

"Monsieur, a predatory man does not in general snatch his victim off the street. You know this. It is the reason you have been asking in the bars. Once a girl has begun to flirt with that type of person, she is vulnerable."

"Do you have any reason to believe—"

"No. I have seen no such pattern. I have found a marginally higher number of unsolved cases than in previous years, but there can be many explanations for that."

"But if there is a pattern, you think . . . what? It has to do with Surrealism?"

"Monsieur, men kill for many reasons. Anger, fear, even pleasure. I believe that sooner or later, some . . . creature who thinks himself an artist will step past the limits of theory and decide to commit murder as an artistic expression. Will decide not simply to honor Landru and de Sade, but to emulate them. I tell you this, Monsieur, to explain my alarm over the disappearance of a young woman with connections to the art community.

"I have thought about what you told me this afternoon, and I admit, I was wrong, to accept the word of a voice on the telephone. We should have sent a man to see that the young lady was at home. We will change the way we do this."

Stuyvesant stared across the tiny table. An official police detective, admitting a mistake? Impossible.

The *flic* dropped his cigarette and slid his hand into his breast pocket. He held out an unsealed envelope. Something in the way he held the thing made Stuyvesant hesitate.

But he took it, and lifted the flap, seeing the edges of two photographs. *Only two*, he tried to tell himself as he slid a pair of fingers in. Tried.

Two women, one a pretty blonde in her early twenties, standing in the shade of a tree with a wide-brimmed hat in her hand. The other, in her thirties, had dark hair, and sat on a carousel horse looking a bit horsey herself, long of face and teeth. But she was having a good time, and it had been a sunny day. He turned that one over, and read:

Alice Barnes
née 23 April 1905, Chicago, États Unis
vue le 19 juin 1928

And on the back of the younger, prettier girl:

Ruth Ann Palowski
née 2 July 1908, San Francisco, California
vue (?) octobre 1928

"These are two missing women we have confirmed did not go home to Mama," the policeman told him, "and the dates they were last seen here. Mlle. Barnes had been here for three weeks. She spent much of that time in museums and galleries, meeting any number of artists, buying several paintings and sculptures. Mlle. Palowski came to do a course in art at the Sorbonne. She lived in the VI arrondissement for a year, and was an habituée of the Dôme and the Select."

At the center of the Montparnasse art world.

"As I said to you, much of my . . . attention in my job lies in watching for patterns. Several of my missing persons have links to the art world—mostly tenuous, but not with these two women.

"I have begun inquiries into a number of others whose cases are still open, to see if perhaps your Miss Crosby shares any characteristics with them. I hope to God they are with their families." He took the photographs from Stuyvesant and put them back in his breast pocket. "M. Stuyvesant, it is not my habit to bring outsiders into the business of the police department. I do so now because of the other thing your friend said to me."

"He's not exactly a friend."

"This I could tell. In addition to describing you as honorable, he made it quite clear that if I did not wish to have you underfoot, the only way to make you abandon a case would be to jail you or deport you. And even then, he would not bet on my being able to keep you away.

"I am pleased to find that you are not 'milking' Miss Crosby's family by failing to bring your information to the attention of the police. Nonetheless . . ."

He leaned forward across the table, locking onto the American's gaze. "M. Stuyvesant, I will permit you to continue working in my city only if you stay in communication with me. If you withhold information, *any* information that might help me locate these girls, if you try to act the cowboy, I will come down on you with all the weight of the Sûreté Nationale. Do we understand each other?"

"Absolutely. I wouldn't want your Sergeant mad at you."

The weak joke fell on deaf ears. "You may keep that Man Ray photograph, Monsieur. I expect to hear from you regularly."

And he got up abruptly and left, an impressive, untidy, curiously likable cop with a bum leg.

Stuyvesant watched him go, and then signaled the waiter for another drink.

Jesus Christ, he thought. *How'd we go so fast from a girl on a yacht to a maniac killer?*

THIRTEEN

A CONVERSATION:

"You want me to do a danse macabre for you?"

"Just one of the panels. I shall call it 'A *Totentanz* for the Twentieth Century.' You and a selection of eminent modern artists, joining in a Dance of Death around a large, semi-circular room."

"Not very cheerful wallpaper."

"Ah, but you are wrong. A dance is a thing of joy, is it not? Passion and life? A dance and its music celebrate the physical. But would the music be so bright, the dancing so animated, if Death did not stand ready to snatch it away at any moment?"

"That's getting a little philosophical for me."

"Its origins are anything but. The classical Danse Macabrés were frescoes in the round showing Death—a skeleton or decaying body—leading all the world's citizens in his Dance. Pope and prostitute, merchant and monk, plowman and beggerman's child, all join hands with Death in the end."

"Very Breughel."

"Dozens of artists have addressed the theme, from its beginnings at the time of the Black Death. Bosch, of course. There's a book of Holbein woodcuts with captions about each victim, seized by Death and shown the steps of the Dance."

"Death and dancing. Sounds like Montmartre on a Saturday night."

"So are you interested?"

"I don't know much about popes and plowmen."

"Those were the fourteenth century. Ours would see mayors and street-sweepers, movie stars and newspaper boys."

"High-society blondes. Negro trumpet players."

"Precisely."

"Could still have the prostitutes. They probably haven't changed much."

"You may be right."

"Would the thing have to be painted?"

"Painting, collage, photographs. Didi Moreau is looking into the possibility of doing one made from human bones. Each must fit onto a twelve-by-fifteen-foot panel, with the dimensions of the figures life-sized to make the end result more seamless."

"Linking together. Ah—is that why you had us playing 'exquisite corpses'?"

"Precisely."

"And the theme is Death's Dance."

"Yes."

"You care how graphic they are? How realistic?"

"Chaim Soutine is doing a panel along the lines of his carcass paintings."

"Well, that's about as graphic as you can get. In that case, sure, I'd be interested."

"I will have my assistant send you a contract. And may I say, M. Ray, how much I look forward to your panel?"

"It'll be a killer, all right."

FOURTEEN

"C'EST MORTE," STUYVESANT said.

The bartender gave the American one of those wide French nods of shared desolation as he placed the brimming *blonde* on the zinc bar.

"Ira mieux, mon ami," he said, and followed his damp cloth down the long bar to his other thirsty customers.

Harris Stuyvesant looked glumly at the glass. It was ten at night, and he didn't think it was going to get better. Paris was dead. The heat had killed it.

He'd known how it would be before he left Berlin—knew that in August, the city's tailors and hat-makers and butchers all closed their shops to escape the heat. He just hadn't thought that the vacances could stretch this far into September—theaters slow to open, the rich lingering in the south. Even the butchers were still in the mountains, settled on their broad derrières with a glass of vin ordinaire, casting their professional eyes across the grazing moutons while they tried to decide if they could stretch out their vacances until the heat broke down by the Seine.

Ridiculous. Ten days into the new month, and it seemed that only the dirt-poor locals and the ever-naïve tourist wandered the sweltering streets. Pip's friends—those he'd been able to track down from her address book before it grew too late for doorbell-ringing—seemed to be off with all the other scrubbed-face leeches, in Spain playing bullfighter like Hemingway. In the South of France drinking like the Fitzgeralds. In the States raising money like, well, everyone else.

The bartender—"François, call me Frank"—brought his cloth back to Stuyvesant's end of the bar.

"You have not found your Peep," he said, with professional sympathy. Old women and bartenders did love to gossip.

"Nope. Saturday and Sunday here and in the Quarter, yesterday in Saint-Germain, and nothing. I figured I might as well come back here tonight." In a move so well practiced his hand did it without consulting his brain, Stuyvesant slid the snapshot from his breast pocket and snapped it down next to his glass, facing the other man.

Frank had seen it before—he was one of the first Stuyvesant showed it to on Saturday—but still he leaned over to take a closer look at the grinning blonde with the trace of wariness about the eyes.

"Pretty girl," Frank commented. "A . . . friend?"

"Just a job," he lied.

"Her eyes, they are blue, n'est ce pas?"

"Green," Stuyvesant corrected, then immediately reversed himself. "No, you're right—blue. Sorry. Blue eyes, blonde hair, five-six, slim, slightly chipped left upper incisor, speaks pretty good French, did a year of college, likes books, music, daisies, and chocolate." The bartender was unlikely to have seen evidence of the broken arm and the burn scar. Unless he, too, was a painter. Or a coroner.

The two men scowled at the image, Frank searching his memory, Stuyvesant thinking that, since this no longer looked to be a quick job, he'd better have copies made before the photo got any more ragged.

"I thought I'd found a lead," he told the bartender, "but it turned out to be another American girl."

"There are so many," Frank said mournfully. He seemed to like Americans—their dollars, anyway—but Stuyvesant figured the USA's conquest of Paris must be getting annoying. Maybe the early wave was good for a laugh, after the War, but as Sylvia had said, the actual writers

and painters were now outnumbered by hangers-on, common criminals, chronic alcoholics, and open-mouthed rubberneckers. God knows
he found it a damned nuisance, and it wasn't even his city.

He shook his head in a return of sympathy. "If the stock market
keeps on like this, pretty soon somebody'll build a link between the
subway and the Métro."

"That will be the day I retire," Frank said, sounding grim. He raised
his eyes from the picture of the missing girl. "You have been to, you
know . . . ?"

"The morgue? What the hell is it with everyone? She's just missing,
not dead. She's probably gone back to America."

"Some would say that was the same thing, Monsieur."

"Hah, hah."

"Mais non, Monsieur—in fact I meant, have you been to the police?"

"Oh. Well, yes, them, too. And the American Embassy. None of
them were very interested in one more missing Flapper. And last night
I went through Saint-Germain, in case her blood was a little rich for
the likes of Montparnasse. Nothing." He made a mental note to go
back to the Embassy when he had copies of the photo to leave.

A group of Americans came in and Frank went to serve them.
Stuyvesant watched idly, elbow propped on the bar. Three men, one
from Brooklyn, two sounding more like Jersey—painters, judging by
the state of their clothes, the New Yorker maybe a sculptor. Artists
tended to take the first shift in Montparnasse's night-life, finishing
work when the sunlight faded. The Quarter's writers, on the other hand,
were probably just thinking about their breakfast.

This trio were in the midst of some urgent discussion, and Stuyvesant listened with half an ear. Art talk, the older of the two painters—a
man wearing a paint-spattered suit, no neck-tie, and sandals on his
horny-looking feet—declaring vehemently that no matter how much
money they brought in (whatever "they" might be) they weren't art, just
junk in a frame, while the sculptor (corduroy trousers, flax blouse, and a
single heavy turquoise earring that dangled wildly with every gesture)

took the opposite position with equal certainty, blathering on about something called "readymades," although it didn't seem to have much to do with clothing. The third man—shorter, younger, dressed in blue jeans and what looked like a Romanian peasant shirt—nursed his drink for a while before venturing an opinion that the titty displays were certainly intriguing, and did seem to have that disturbing *frisson* of visceral excitement (*Jesus: who talked like that? And sure, naked girls could be artistic, but he wasn't sure how they might be called "junk in a frame."*) that a person felt only in the presence of True Art—

His fellow New Yorker would have none of it, and their voices climbed until Frank touched the sculptor's wrist and suggested, perhaps outside?

They turned to the door, seeming well accustomed to the request. Before they got there, the argument broke off as they stood back to let a pair of women come in. Frank's waiter followed the two, took their order, and came back smiling: they were regulars. One looked familiar, and when the waiter had given the order—white wine and a fancy cocktail—Stuyvesant stopped him.

"Those two who came in? One of them models, for artists, doesn't she?"

"That's not all she does for artists, Monsieur."

Stuyvesant returned his grin, but stayed where he was. No point asking a pair of hard-working girls anything until they'd had their first drink.

Instead, he rotated the picture on the bar, studying the crooked smile and untidy blonde head. As Frank said, there were a lot of American girls here in gay Paree. The crazy exchange rate made it as cheap for women to live here as it did men—nearly as cheap—and although fewer girls might come to experiment with painting or writing, they sure came to experiment. In the process, many of them discovered that girls were every bit as good at having fun as the boys were.

Like Pip Crosby.

He took out the other photo and put on his glasses, comparing the two versions of the girl he'd known. The snapshot that had seemed at first the very image of an expatriate good-time girl seemed to have darkened under the influence of the other photo, as if the character had leaked across the pages.

The Man Ray photo made Pip look older and more mysterious—but then the guy was an artist, a clever one. He could probably make a salt cellar look Deep. The snapshot showed a young girl with wind in her hair. Maybe her smile was a bit . . . knowing, but was there really mistrust in her eyes?

And why the hell did he persist in thinking of them as green? Oh, he knew why, but damn it, Pip Crosby's eyes were blue.

Irritably, he caught up the squares of paper and went back to work.

The models' table had a pair of extra chairs, just in case friends showed up, and they were happy to let him claim one. He said hello, broke the ice for a minute, and before they could begin to wonder if he had something in mind with one (or both) of them, he took out the snapshot.

The older one didn't recognize Pip, but made it clear that she would be pleased to talk about the picture for a while, if the American wished to buy her another drink. He obliged, and when the drinks were on the table the younger one asked to see the picture again. She held it close to her eyes, squinting a little: he'd never yet seen a French woman in glasses.

"Connaissez lui?" he asked.

She shook her head, reluctantly. "I thought perhaps, but no. It is that she looks like a girl who used to come here, oh, two years ago? Three?" She consulted with her friend for a while in rapid-fire French, and while the details may have passed Stuyvesant by, he could tell they were talking about a singer named Mimi who had lived in Paris for a while. Finally, she turned back to Stuyvesant. "The picture made me think of someone, but it is not her."

"Her name was Mimi?"

"We called her that, but I don't think—"

"Elle s'appelait Marie," the older one interrupted.

"Non," the first protested. "Michèle."

"Michèle? Pas du tout. Mais, peût-être Martine?"

The two peppered the air with various names starting with M, but the matter wasn't helped by the surname also beginning with an M. Michelle? Michaud?

He thanked them, and moved on to the next table, and the next.

The place was filling up, and the stink of unwashed bodies was doing battle against the cigarette smoke, and winning. Gratefully, he finished his round of the tables and escaped to the terrace, where the smoke was somewhat diluted.

It took some doing to get the attention of the three artists, now hunched over an iron table under the trees, but they either didn't know Pip, or they were unwilling to detach themselves from the argument to really look at the photograph.

So he went back to the bar and asked Frank to send them a round of drinks. On the waiter's heels, he pulled up a chair and sat.

"Evening, gentlemen," he said. "Mind if I join you?"

The trio had not been warned about Greeks and gifts, because they didn't bother with introductions, just took the full glasses and incorporated their benefactor into the conversation—or, argument. The topic had moved on from displays of women's breasts to a consideration of modern film, although Stuyvesant thought the two might not be unrelated.

He was waiting for a break in the conversation to pull Pip out of his pocket, when a name made his ears twitch.

"—hired Man Ray to do a film of his house-guests, down in Hyères—Provence, you know? Sounds like a piece of junk to me." This was the older New Yorker who had dismissed the "titty displays." A man with a limited critical vocabulary.

"C'mon, that *Sea Star* movie was a work of genius," the Jersey sculptor argued.

"Oh, sure, but basically Ray's just a fashion photographer. If Naoilles wanted art rather than a home movie, he'd have asked Buñuel."

"Who's Noweye?" the younger painter asked.

"Naoilles. Viscount Charles de Naoilles," the sculptor explained. "He and his wife are patrons of the arts."

"Hey, can I get me one of them?"

"You wish."

The critic cut in, "He's mostly interested in film. You need the other one, the guy they call Le Comte—he's newer to the game, and he's got a lot of cash to throw around. But neither of them are just patrons. If you watch 'em closely, they're damned clever. Like that Stein woman—she's got to have a small fortune on her walls by now."

"Yeah, you just wish she'd discovered *you*," the sculptor jeered.

The snort the younger man gave as reaction made the critic's face go red. Stuyvesant interrupted with the Man Ray photo.

None of the three knew Pip, although two of them agreed they'd like to. Stuyvesant left before the discussion grew unbearably raunchy and moved to the next terrace.

One advantage of this tightly-knit American community was that it *was* tight, in both senses. A person found the same faces drinking at the same watering-holes: Coupole, Rotonde, Dôme, the Select, the Jockey, the Dingo, with dozens of smaller places tucked away on the sides—all within convenient staggering distance of that physical and spiritual center of Montparnasse, the Carrefour Vavin. Now a busy intersection, Vavin was originally a rubble heap that Mediaeval students had jokingly dubbed "Mount Parnassus." The sacred home of Greek Muses became the Parisian home for wine, women, and bad poetry—until eighteenth century city planners flattened the mound in the interest of traffic flow, leaving only the name, and the attitudes.

One disadvantage of this tight community was simple numbers. Take the Coupole: on a busy night, two or three thousand people would cram inside. It could take hours to work your way through the upstairs, the downstairs, and the broad terrace, around the bar, the restaurant, and the dance hall. And that was just one place. The Dôme now had a bar tacked onto it, the Americaine, that was nearly as bad, and although people tended to have their favorite haunts, they also migrated from one terrace to the next.

Tonight, Stuyvesant's conversation with the Americans gave him an approach: starting at the Coupole bar, he talked movies, of the artistic variety.

It turned out to be a productive entrée into Montparnasse café society. Everyone had an opinion; every second person was either working on a film or considering it. All had recommendations, pro and con, and if he'd tried to see all the pictures that were mentioned, he would have been staring at silver screens until Christmas.

But certain names cropped up time and again, and certain titles: Clair and Picabia, Buñuel and Dalí, Epstein and Dulac, and above all, Man Ray. "Manifesto of the absurd" was bandied about, and "dreamlike sequences" and "the tyranny of the conscious mind." *Un Chien Andalou* (which was not about a dog, nor was it set in Andalusia); *L'Étoile de Mer* (which was not about sea stars, although it did in fact have a sea star in it, briefly); *La Coquille et le Clergyman* (which had both a shell and a priest, and therefore seemed to be regarded with less respect in this world of sur-reality, just as the "titty display" man was rendered dubious by having actually sold his work).

A couple hours of this, and Stuyvesant was tempted to rise up and overturn the tables—but if he did, the ensuing debate as to the Meaning of his Act might drive him to pound someone's face in. Instead, he rose up and left a number of conversations.

To his mild surprise, he went all night without spotting Lulu. If she'd appeared, he might have forgotten how tired he was after a long day of cops and bluestockings, but that brassy hair did not catch his eye or that strident voice his ear. To be honest, he wasn't entirely unhappy. A quiet night would not go unwelcome, and the bank notes she slipped from his wallet—lifting money rather than asking: Lulu liked to think of herself as an amateur—were beginning to add up.

So he walked along to the pub-like comfort of the Falstaff and let Jimmy pour him a glass of his best Scotch. Jimmy Charters had been a British flyweight boxer, and anyone who put on the gloves was a friend of his. Fortunately, Ernest Hemingway wasn't there.

Jimmy didn't recognize Pip Crosby.

"Want to leave the picture on the bar?" he asked. "See if anyone knows her?"

"I'll do that tomorrow—the photographers have been swamped with rolls of film from vacances."

"Yep, it's rentrée. Things'll pick up now."

"I guess."

"But not *right* now. I'm afraid it's closing time, my friend. Time for you to move on to the Select."

"Nah, I've had enough of plastered Yanks. See you tomorrow, Jimmy."

"Good luck with your girl."

Stuyvesant stood on rue Montparnasse and lit a cigarette, feeling the girl in his breast pocket. Feeling the weight of the day.

"Pip, sweetheart, I'm all fagged out. I'll try again tomorrow."

FIFTEEN

As STUYVESANT CAME to the rue Vavin, he waited for his feet to turn the corner towards the Hotel Benoit. They did not. The night felt soft after the harsh day, and about the last thing he felt like was settling onto that hard, solitary mattress with Sylvia Beach's detective story on his belly and Pip's reproachful snapshot on the desk.

Instead, his feet took him along the boulevard Raspail; up the rue de Rennes; through narrow streets unchanged since students wore doublets. Down the quay to Notre Dame, admiring the massive dance of stone and the reflection of lights and the dark mass of moored barges, then south along that Roman Main Street, the boulevard Saint-Michel (*. . . a new assistant, over whom he has lost his head*), where the perpetual energies of students kept the night at bay.

Farther down, the lights dimmed, and he paused at the feet of the Lion of Belfort to smoke a cigarette. In the daytime, the broad plains of the Place Denfert-Rochereau was a chariot race of taxis and trucks, but at this time of night, he and a rag-and-bone man in a horse-cart were the noble lion's only companions. Old books called this the *Place d'Enfer*, at the *Barrière d'Enfer*: Hell Place, at the Hell Gate. Once upon a time, this was an entrance through the city walls where taxes were paid on incoming goods.

It had another connection to hell, past that of taxation: across the Place lay the entrance to the Paris catacombs.

Practical people, the French. When some long-forgotten quarries collapsed in the late 1700s and sucked buildings and citizens deep into the earth, at around the same time that a huge, stinking cemetery across the river was creating public unrest, the city fathers looked from one problem to the other, and got out their shovels. The quarries were filled with the debris of death; the former cemetery became the wholesale vegetable market of Les Halles. A century later, hell was painted over a second time when Place D'Enfer was changed to Place Denfert-Rochereau, a nice bureaucratic pun employing the name of a war hero.

The catacombs were open to the public sometimes. He'd gone down them one summer's day, mostly to escape the heat, and found cool stillness, the sound of trickling water, and at the bottom of the spiral stairs, an artistic display of former citizens.

Still, it was unsettling to think of the millions upon millions of dead Parisians under his feet. A reminder that the City of Light had shadowy corners. Some of which swallowed pretty girls.

He got up and crushed the cigarette under his heel, grimly amused at the direction of his thoughts. *You, too, huh? Okay, you want macabre— how about a nice wallow through the gravestones?* So Stuyvesant headed up the street to the Montparnasse cemetery, waiting for his somewhat tattered sense of humor to come to his rescue.

The truth was, he wasn't dealing well with rootlessness and solitude. He'd never been further from having that fantasy library full of books. He lived out of a series of trunks scattered across Europe, drank more than he should, smoked more, got into more fistfights than was sensible. He no longer had a family, his only partners were temporary ones, and his friends . . . well, he didn't have many of those, either. Bennett Grey was the only real friend on this side of the Atlantic, and even Bennett was a long way off, wrapped in hermit-like seclusion at the far end of Cornwall.

As for women, well, he wouldn't exactly use the word *honorable*. Maybe that was why he'd taken the job of finding Pip. To make up for a few blots on his record. Good Catholic boy, out for a little redemption.

He used to be a good guy, especially towards women. Just like he used to be cheerful—well, maybe not *cheerful,* exactly, but at least optimistic. Convinced that he would be able to make things come out, in the end.

When he came to the boulevard Edgar Quinet, he paused, considering. To his right stood Man Ray's studio. To his left, just five minutes from here, beckoned Le Sphinx, the best house of prostitution this side of the river—the French being as practical about filling needs as they were about filling holes in the ground. And although he had no pressing urges, the welcome, the voices—just the *company* of Mme. Lemestre's ladies teased at him like a cool breeze. He even had the money for a full night of pampering.

But he turned his back on easy pleasure to cross the boulevard Raspail into the rue Campagne. Man Ray's studio was easy to find: there was a large plaque at the door. It was a beautiful building, ornately tiled and with many tall windows. It was also dark. He continued on his way.

Things *would* come out, in the end. *You'll find Pip,* he told himself as he passed the still-riotous Select. She really would be living with an artist on the Côte d'Azur, as titillated by her scandalous fling with bohemia as she had been by the novelty of sleeping with a middle-aged bouncer. And once he found her (his story went on) he'd also find that she was growing disenchanted with sin. That she was primed and ready to be sent home to Mama, making Ernest M. Crosby happy and generous and eager to shout the virtues of Harris Stuyvesant to a lot of other wealthy American businessmen who needed a man in Paris, or Frankfurt, or Milan.

Still, Stuyvesant had to admit as he flipped the hotel's loud minuterie switch to light the stairs, it was a puzzle, how nobody seemed to know Pip Crosby. It would appear that, despite the efforts of Haussmann and his Napoleon, Paris was still a series of villages. That a man could live his life in Saint-Germain and never meet someone from Clichy—or even from Cluny, at its very elbow.

He stopped as a horrible thought occurred to him: he'd been looking in the Quarter's bars and bistros, but what if she'd gone on the wagon? God, he hoped the girl hadn't come back to Paris and found religion. That was one particular underworld he had no wish to dive into: Raymond Duncan's crew with their dirty feet, home-made sandals, and goats; Madame Blavatsky and her hocus-pocus. As he stood on the stairs, the bulb clicked out.

With a low curse, he took out his Ronson to light his way to the next floor. He used the toilet and came out to find a bald stranger wearing only trousers stepping from his neighbor Anouk's room. The man looked startled; when Stuyvesant murmured a good night, he looked relieved.

Anouk wasn't a professional, but she was certainly a busy amateur.

Inside the stifling room, Stuyvesant stripped down to his shorts, threaded a hanger through his suit, draped the tie over the chair, and tossed the shirt against the door where he'd remember it in the morning. He dropped onto the bed, dry-washing his tired face, then looked across at the table, where he'd left the Hammett novel. Instead, his hand picked up the silver cigarette case.

Nine years ago, it had been an expensive gift for a working girl's salary, made more so by the elaborate engraving. It fit his hand as if designed to be turned over and over like a bar of soap. The tens of thousands of times he had done so had all but worn his initials away.

But the clasp still held. Both of them.

Its hidden compartment had once contained the photograph of the working girl whose present it was: blonde and wind-blown and shining with life, back when Pip Crosby was still in schoolgirl braids. Her name was Helen, and the picture was taken just days before she'd bled to death on a New York street amidst drifts of shattered glass: the Wall Street bomb. September 16, 1920, at 12:01 in the afternoon.

After five and a half years, he'd let the ashes of her picture drift into the Thames River. He'd replaced it with the picture of another girl, also blonde, also shining. This one with green eyes: Sarah Grey.

Who some time after the picture was taken had lost her left hand to another bloody explosion.

He hadn't looked at Sarah's photograph in a while. He had last laid eyes on Sarah herself in May 1926; last heard from her three months later, when her brother Bennett handed him a brief letter with the picture. Three years, two weeks, and a day ago. Not that he was counting or anything.

With Sarah, it had been love. They hadn't yet been to bed together when the bomb happened, but they would have. If Bennett hadn't come between them. Bennett Grey, who of all people should have seen catastrophe approach.

Maybe that niggle of a question was why Stuyvesant never found the time for a trip to Cornwall. For a visit to his only friend on this side of the Atlantic.

In any event, despite Europe's plentiful bed-fillers, and despite having known Sarah for only a handful of days, since her, nothing had really clicked with a woman. He'd never managed to shake Sarah's green eyes, her incongruous deep laugh, the erotic spray of freckles at the neck of her dress.

Wasn't that the way things seemed to work in this modern world? You might not have love, but you could have plenty of sex.

But damn it: if Sarah had wanted to end it, why send him a photograph? Her words had been evasive, but not the picture.

The words had said that she would travel—Rome, Hong Kong. That she needed to accustom herself to a missing limb and the maddening whine in her ear. To stand on her own, and not risk coming to lean upon him.

The picture was another matter. It had been trimmed to fit the silver case—Bennett must have told her about the hidden compartment, damn the man's all-seeing eyes—and although some girls would taunt a fellow with a reminder and a brush-off at the same time, he couldn't believe it of Sarah Grey.

Not that Sarah didn't have good reason to hate him. He'd been slow and he'd been secretive, a deadly combination that cost Sarah her hand, her friend, and her faith in the world. So he'd made no effort to follow her. He'd just made sure that Bennett, hidden away in his stone cottage at the tip-toe of Britain's boot, always knew exactly where Harris Stuyvesant could be found.

A part of him still believed that the picture was a tentative request for patience. That the letter was less dismissal than plea. That both had been meant as signs of her continuing affection. Why else bother to write? But the faces of Helen and Sarah—and, yes, Pip Crosby, along with Maryanne and Danuta and Leisl, even Lulu—had begun to blur together in his memory, and he was beginning to suspect that only Sarah's words mattered: she wanted to stand on her own.

Time for Harris Stuyvesant to do the same.

Time to give up the self-delusion. To admit that for three years, he'd been making every decision based on its proximity to England, arranging his life around a summons that would never come.

Time to set his lighter under Sarah's photograph and let the ashes drift over the Seine. Time to do his best for Pip Crosby, and then go home.

He closed the case and went to push open the window, not expecting much. To his surprise, the air moving over the maze of rooftops seemed to hold a faint promise of coolness. Maybe the heat would break. Maybe Pip's friends would come back from Spain, the butchers return from the contemplation of mountain sheep.

Maybe he could sleep.

SIXTEEN

I T WAS A quick transaction, as those in silent alleyways tend to be. The woman was slightly drunk, slightly annoyed at the inconvenient setting, but happy for the money. Enough for two months' rent, and a bit more.

"Oui," she told the man for a second time. "J'ai fait ce que vous dites, avec son passeporte. Où? À l'intériur d'un livre q'il a acheté, un livre englais. J'ais fixé le papier comme si c'était. C'est tout. Maintenant, où est l'ar—"

Yes, I did as you said, with her passport. Where? Inside a book that he'd bought, an English book. I fixed the wrapping like it was. That's all. Now, where's the mon—

"Pardonne-moi." The apology was swallowed by gunshot, shockingly loud in the residential district. Two gendarmes in the Place Denfert-Rochereau dropped their cigarettes and ran, arriving barely a minute after the noise. There was nothing in the alleyway but a woman with brassy blonde hair, dead on the cobblestones.

SEVENTEEN

THE RISING TEMPERATURE of his fourth-floor room drove Stuyvesant out of bed by eight, Wednesday morning. As he shaved, he avoided looking at his bloodshot eyes, but he did pause to survey his reflection in the spotted mirror inside the armoire.

"Harris my boy, you'll find her today."

Harris my boy was not convinced.

Stuyvesant had to try three places before he found a photographer who would do a rush job on Pip's photo, and then only the knowledge of Uncle Ernest's checkbook kept Stuyvesant from voicing his outrage at the price. He promised to be back in three hours, then walked up to the Rotonde terrace, ordering coffee and tackling the morning's *Figaro*. His French was pretty colloquial by now, but his mastery of the written language lagged somewhat. For example, everyone he knew thought the American stock market boom was just great, but the *Figaro*'s coverage seemed to have an edge of cynicism. He puzzled over it, but decided it was probably just the customary French scorn for anything that didn't begin and end in Paris, and traded the *Figaro* for an abandoned copy of the *Trib*'s Paris Edition.

He read the American football scores while his right ear filled with an argument about the cess-cart an artist had entered into the Autumn Salon and his left ear with a gabfest on the depravity of publishers. Which was fine until the table behind him launched into a discussion in florid French about a shooting that had taken place down in Denfert-Rochereau the night before, and the clash of themes and languages threatened a headache.

He thumbed some coins into the top saucer, settled his Panama at a bit of an angle, and with a wave of the finger to the waiter, he set off into the city.

His first order of business was personal: in Berlin, he'd been down to one summer-weight suit, and that had a mend in its knee. One of his first acts upon cashing the Crosby bank draft the week before had been to wire his Paris tailor and have him start a new one, in a fabric of the tailor's choice.

It wasn't as if a man Stuyvesant's height could buy his suits ready-made, here in France.

As it happened, the tailor's wife had taken ill at the end of July, condemning him to Paris for the vacances. He had apparently been desperate to get out of his house, because to Stuyvesant's amazement, the suit was ready for a fitting.

The plump little man knew his client, and had chosen a light-weight, tightly woven gray wool with the faintest stripe: fashionable but traditional, handsome but practical. The two men studied the reflection in the triple mirror.

"You like, Monsieur?"

"Perfect as always," Stuyvesant told him. There was no denying that new clothes made for a new man.

"It is too wide in the body. Perhaps I could take it in, just a tiny—"

"It's fine."

They had the same argument every time. Stuyvesant only occasionally wore a gun, but he needed his jackets loose, and he'd found this tailor through the Paris detective agency he'd done a couple jobs for. Still, the tailor was a proud man: left to him, a suit's pockets would be sewn up to prevent lumps. Next thing you knew, the guy would be selling his clients handbags.

The tailor shook his head, accepting the great burden.

"Monsieur, I will have this for you by end of day. The shirts, I regret, will not be finished until the end of the week. But you will be pleased with them, the fabric is from a mill that has only recently come back after the War, and the buttons—ah, the buttons, they are spectacular! None of your surface sheen, no. The reflective glint in the shell is deep, giving the finished product a luxurious—"

The man made good suits that lasted, at a price Stuyvesant could afford—and his method of measuring inseams and eyeing the fit of trousers didn't leave a man feeling like he'd been groped. But boy, could he ever talk. Stuyvesant cut him off with a reassurance that the laundry would be back in the afternoon, and with it a new shirt (a little short in the sleeve, granted, and the buttons weren't exactly spectacular).

The tram was crowded, so it took him a couple of streets to notice that he'd boarded the wrong one. He had to back-track to Saint-Michel and wait for another, which when it arrived was mobbed by his fellow would-be passengers. Another day, he might have stood back and taken the next car; today, he used his size to bully his way on board.

Plus that, the tram car was stifling—and, when he got down, he found that some disgusting urchin had left a stain on his trouser leg.

When he reached Man Ray's studio, he was in no mood to appreciate the building's pretty front. He just opened an unlocked door and found himself in the chaos of a high-roofed artist's studio, only with glossy prints and faint chemical smells instead of canvases and turpentine. Photographic prints and paintings hung on the walls, shelves were laden with file-boxes and folders. Everywhere lay a jumble of objects and half-unpacked trunks.

A closer look separated the freshly arrived debris of a summer away from the dusty resident objects waiting for an artistic home: mismatched chess pieces, dried flowers, a topless cigar box holding half a dozen dry wish-bones, a chamber-pot full of old clocks, various tangles of machinery whose purpose Stuyvesant couldn't guess at, and half a dozen articulated wooden models: four of them hands, three right and a left, and two full human figures, complicated wooden skeletons with brass joints. The pair had been posed flat, the bald one pressed between the legs of the one with the blonde wig.

Why did avant-garde artists always have such sophomoric humor?

Not everything in the room was by Man Ray. He recognized a couple of the paintings hanging crookedly on the wall, and damned if there wasn't one of those collage-boxes like Pip had in her bedroom. This one also had a variety of *objets trouvés,* although there weren't any bones, and the closest he saw to painted-on blood was the brilliant red of a tube of lipstick. He puzzled over the little square of face down in the corner, thinking that it looked vaguely familiar, when he realized that the eyebrows had been shaved off and repainted, and knew who it was: Kiki of Montparnasse. Which explained the box's other square of photograph: a nipple.

He smiled, and went on with his perusal. Photographs, letters, uncashed checks, a baby shoe. A folder of sketches for what looked like a painting, showing a line of people dancing to a Negro band: one of the dancers was a skeleton, bones flying in what looked like a Charleston. A chewed dog bone, a bowl brimming with mismatched dice.

The only clear space in the room was a table with a chessboard, arrayed with modernistic shapes ready for action.

Stuyvesant reached the end of the room. He was opening his mouth to call when he heard the sound of footsteps—and when he saw the source, his mouth remained open.

He'd met a lot of blondes who were easy on the eye, but this one put the rest in the shade. She was a stunner, slim and tall, her short hair bleached white by the sun. When she came in, she was frowning beautifully over the stack of envelopes in her hand. She looked up, showing him her perfect face, her aristocratic nose, her very white teeth, and her apprehension. She couldn't have been more than twenty-three; she looked seventeen.

"Oh, Christ, are you here for an appointment?"

"You're American," he blurted.

"Yes. So are you, it sounds like. Maybe you're not on the schedule, then?"

"No. No appointment, that is. I'm looking for Mr. Ray."

"Oh thank God, I was afraid I'd already failed at the task of keeping the schedule, and on my first day here. He'll be in shortly, he's just shaving."

"You're new here?"

"Here, yes. We've been lovers since June," she said, trying for casual. "I don't suppose you see anything that looks like an appointment diary?"

"No, but I'll help you look. My name's Stuyvesant, by the way."

"Lee Miller." She stuck out a strong hand and they shook across the crowded desk.

It was a novel entrée to an illicit search, but Stuyvesant dove in with gusto, stimulated as much by the physical presence of the lover-assistant as by the underhanded way he was making use of her naiveté: "honorable," my ass. "Have you known him long, then?" he asked, surreptitiously noting the return addresses on a stack of mail.

"No, like I said, we met in June, as he was leaving for Biarritz. We're only just back, so I haven't had a chance to look things over. What about this? No, it's a sketchbook."

Stuyvesant moved over to what appeared to be Ray's current projects: multiple prints of negatives, each one with a tiny difference in the blackness of its shadows and the brilliance of its white spaces. A lot of them were of Lee Miller, from early infatuation to ever more intrusive use of the camera lens. He could only hope the girl's parents never saw the nudes. There were other pictures that looked remarkably like the photographs from a police file. One of these was particularly disturbing: had it not been unlikely that a dead person could hold her leg in that languorous position, he'd have been certain that the great thick pool the model was lying in was fresh blood.

Stuyvesant's horrified fascination was cut short by a voice from the stairs.

"Lee, darling one, I need you in the darkroom, if we're going to— Oh, pardon, Monsieur, may I help you?"

"Man, this is Mr. Stuyvesant, and he's not an appointment."

Stuyvesant flipped over the folder's cover and walked forward to stick out his hand.

Man Ray was, as Sylvia Beach had said, an American, maybe twenty years older than the girl, with little of her looks, height, or coloration. Or indeed, her assurance: the photographer's immediate response to finding a man with his lover was to bristle with suspicion and move over beside her.

Oh, she was going to lead this one a merry chase before she was finished with him, Stuyvesant reflected.

But he had business with the fellow, so he turned a shoulder to Miss Miller, blatantly dismissing her from consideration as he held out the photograph.

"I think this is one of yours?" he asked.

The photographer took it. He had the kind of dark, intent eyes some women just got all gooey about, like . . . Like Valentino's?

Oh, Pip, honey—really? This one, too?

"That's the girl with the burn. American, Philippa something. She was interesting."

"Crosby. And how was she interesting?"

The Miller girl had come around to look at Pip's photo; Ray handed it to her. "She wasn't what she seemed. That's rare. With most people, the lens struggles to find something beneath the surface. But this one, who looked like any of a sea of other bright-eyed girls, the minute she sat down you could see her history. Are you following me?"

Stuyvesant put on a puzzled expression: let Ray demonstrate his cleverness.

"It's like—like Lee, here." His hand went around the back of the girl's neck and pulled her face down to his. They kissed, long and hard. A little too long and hard, pressed up against each other. Stuyvesant cleared his throat. Twice. Ray finally pulled away, and spoke over his shoulder to his visitor. "Look at her: those incredible colors in her hair, her eyes; the movement of her; the pulse of life running under her skin and in her every movement.

"But then the camera takes her. Here—" He went to a shelf and plucked off a folder, taking out some pages. "She looks into the lens, and in the stillness, her true self can't help coming to the surface. You can see pain there, can't you?"

And when he said that, Stuyvesant could: the sort of caution that inhabited the eyes of soldiers who had lost a limb, or women who had lost a child. He looked away from her, handing the photographer back his images.

"I guess. But what I'm interested in is Pip Crosby. Her mother hasn't heard from her in a while, and she's concerned. Do you know where she is?"

"No."

"What about you, Miss Miller?"

"I never met her."

"But do you know where she is?"

"How could I, when I don't know her? Mr. Stuyvesant, you sound like a detective or something."

What was it with women and detective stories? We should never have taught them to read. "And you sound like a follower of the Nick Carter tales. Mr. Ray, do you remember when you took her photo?"

"February? Maybe early March. An acquaintance brought her to me, said he needed a photo that he could use on programs and flyers."

"What acquaintance was that?"

"Friend of a friend—you know how things go here. He's in the theater business. Lee, haven't you offered him some coffee?"

"I used the last of it, the canister—"

"Well, for God's sake, go buy some!"

Stuyvesant interposed. "I've had plenty of coffee this morning, thanks. Maybe we could just sit and talk for a couple of minutes?"

Ray looked vaguely around the cluttered studio and waved his hand at the stairway. Lee Miller went first, but Ray inserted himself between Stuyvesant and his radiant young girlfriend.

"I have to say, Mr. Ray, I hear about you all over the place," Stuyvesant said as he followed the artist's scuffed heels. "Tell me, do you regard yourself as a photographer, or as a film-maker?"

"I am a painter. The others are merely exercises to work the eye."

"And pay the bills."

"To some extent," the artist admitted.

"And your photographs, those portraits you do. They put you in touch with a lot of important people, don't they?"

"I suppose that depends on your definition of important. Lee, do something with that."

That was a Spanish shawl matted with white hair, which Lee obediently bundled up and stuck on a shelf, leaving behind an armchair that wouldn't turn Stuyvesant's trousers to fur.

"Brancusi was here," Ray said, as if that explained it. He dropped into a chair and took out cigarettes.

"By important, I suppose I'm thinking of the Surrealists. There's some fascinating work being done there."

It was as effective an entrée into Man Ray's world as Stuyvesant could have found, and it took only regular contributions of *Oh,* and *How fascinating!* to keep Ray on track.

The man did like to hear himself talk. He was also fine with Lee Miller venturing her opinions, so long as they were his.

And what opinions they were. Planned art was a sham, film with plot a travesty. The goal of art was to reflect dream back to reality, and vice versa—to explore the ways in which death and pleasure were one, as were ugliness and beauty, the animal and the divine. Art was improvisation and irrationality, based in the wisdom of the unconscious self, and any *true* artist must declare his mind open to impulse, repudiating the tyranny of structure, of planning, of thought itself. Dreams were truth. Accident was purpose; unconscious expression was the greatest form art could take. The body's urge was the mind's command: bondage was freedom, pain was pleasure, and the gratification of the body was the very essence of art.

Lee Miller sat with her superb legs curled under her, drinking up all this hooey as if it were epic poetry. Stuyvesant couldn't resist tweaking the windbag a bit. "So, the photographs you take could as easily be done by a child with a Kodak, or Miss Miller—or me, even?"

"Of course not. An artist has to see the vision in order to realize it. Like your young woman, Philippa . . . er . . ."

"Crosby."

"Yes. She was brought to me for a simple portrait, but my eyes could see much more in the girl. The snap of the camera lens was itself nothing compared to that vision."

"Who brought her to you?"

Ray studied Lee for a moment, as if considering which part of her to cook first. "I suppose he was her employer, although it seemed to me there was more to it than that. At any rate, he wanted a photograph suitable for publicity, and he'd seen those I did for Paul Poirot and others. However, the reason so many artists come to be consecrated by my camera is because I give them more than a mere photograph. I give them *insight*."

"Um, right. This 'publicity': she's an actress, then?"

"If you call it that. A dive of a place up in Montmartre, amusing in a ghastly sort of way. The Grand-Guignol. Know it?"

Stuyvesant shook his head, although he'd vaguely heard of it. Working-class entertainment—and French, not American. However, one of Pip's bookmarks was a ticket from the Grand-Guignol.

"And your client was the owner of the theater?"

"I don't think he's exactly an owner, although he might be a sort of sleeping partner. He calls himself an 'amateur de la mort.' An amateur of death."

No, thought Stuyvesant, *that's not what it means*. As a Catholic boy, he'd had his Latin beaten into him: *amo, amas, amat. Amateur* meant admirer, or enthusiast.

A *fan* of death.

"So," he said casually. "What's this fellow's name?"

The Théâtre du Grand-Guignol was at the end of a tight little cul-de-sac a couple of streets away from the garish façades of Clichy and the Place Pigalle. *Guignol* was a puppet, also known as Punchinello. Stuyvesant stood before the uninformative closed doors and wondered how a proper theater could make its income off a puppet show, no matter how *grand*.

However, there was no one to ask. Pounding brought no result, although a shopkeeper up the street knew the name Ray had given him—Dominic Charmentier—and said that he'd find the theater open tonight, but the only matinees were on Mondays.

He wondered if Nancy Berger would find a puppet show amusing.

In the meantime, perhaps a visit to a different kind of theater.

EIGHTEEN

THREE HOURS LATER, Harris Stuyvesant stepped out of a cinéma and found Paris changed. The air smelled like explosives; the drone of its traffic was as hostile as wasps. Images from the screen wove themselves into the busy street. Any second now, that old woman with the tiny poodle would melt into the pavement; the pigeons atop the street-sign would explode into a million pieces, their feathers turning into a rain of coins; that trio of *garçonnes* would turn around in unison, stare with their painted eyes, and stalk towards him . . .

There had been three films, or perhaps five—it was hard to know where one stopped and the next began, since there had been no plot and little continuity of character in any of them. The second and third—or perhaps third and fourth—films in the series had been by Man Ray, one of which was announced by the management as a special showing of a film not yet officially released. Ray's had no more plot than any of the others, although the first was disturbing from its opening declaration: *Les dents des femmes sont des objets si charmants*. Women's teeth are such charming objects. The words made him think of the teeth in those boxes of Pip's. The second one, the special one, he found simply confusing.

Still, neither were as bad as the film that opened with a knife apparently slicing open a woman's eyeball and went on to show a group of people on the street, gathered around an amputated hand.

What kind of people would do that? And who the hell would consider it art? He had to agree with Inspector Doucet: arrest all the Surrealists and set them to hard labor for a while, that would rid them of their infatuation with intellectual violence.

They left him feeling . . . unreal. Like waking from a nightmare, or a Mickey Finn. He needed to move—needed the sensation of heels making hard contact with the paving stones, the squint of his eyes against the afternoon sun.

What he'd really like was to drop by the gym and strap on the gloves for a couple good, fast rounds . . .

But he had a date with Nancy Berger. So he shook his head and stepped into the flow of pedestrians—ordinary, irritating, sweating, blessedly real Parisians—and went for a drink instead.

He found Kiki holding court at her usual table at the Dôme. Her face, he suddenly remembered, had been designed by Man Ray: shaved eyebrows, exaggerated paint (blue eye-coloring today) in a feminine version of those Japanese masks. She saw him come in and waved him over, raising her rasping voice in an imperious command for one of the younger men to give up his chair. Stuyvesant shook his head.

"I'm only here for a quick drink, honey, not worth fitting me in. Hey, I hear you've written a book?"

Kiki reached under her chair and pulled one out. "You like to buy one, 'Arris?" Obediently, he peeled off a stack of francs, and asked her to autograph it. She did so, then lifted the book to her mouth to deposit a crimson kiss onto the page next to her signature, following it up with a lingering kiss on his mouth. She drew back with a giggle, and handed him the book.

He dropped into a chair and told the waiter what he wanted, grateful for the reassuring solidity of Kiki's commercial transaction. Too many more of those films and he'd start talking like Man Ray, too. *The wisdom of the unconscious self. The body's urge is the mind's command.*

He'd met a handful of thoroughly nasty criminals who would agree with Mr. Ray: I want it, I take it, and the hell with the rest of you.

Settled by the drink, he paid and strode up Raspail and Vavin to rue Colle. The florist at the entrance was optimistically setting out some bouquets for the evening trade, and Stuyvesant tipped his hat at her greeting—then stopped. What kind of flowers would a girl like Nancy Berger like? Something large and strong?

In the end, he bought a mix of autumn chrysanthemums in yellow and bronze, and had the woman wrap a dark red ribbon around them. He got out his money, then had a thought: Nancy liked to read; she'd borrowed Pip's novels.

"Donnez-moi un autre morceau de cette, s'il-vous plaît," he asked, gesturing at the ribbon.

Upstairs, he laid the flowers and Kiki's book on the table and slid the ribbon under the Hammett story. He flipped it over, crossed it, and flipped it again to tie it off in a rough bow. He'd never get a job at the Bon Marché, but the ribbon looked pretty against the dust jacket. He looked at Kiki's book: would Nancy like that, too? But when he looked inside the cover and saw what Kiki had written, he dropped it back onto Sylvia's brown paper and twine. He didn't know the girl well enough to hand her *that* message.

He took a cold shower, shaved for the second time that day, and climbed into his evening suit, managing to get the tie straight on the third try. He even succeeded in catching a taxi before he'd gone too many blocks.

But as the taxi pulled out into the street, he was hit by the sharp vision of a figure looming up before the hood, a moment from that film with the woman's eyeball. Crossing the Seine a minute later, they passed a knot of people studying something on the ground. For an instant he thought they were prodding at a hand—and on the heels of that vision came the vivid memory of Sarah Grey, sweet face twisted in agony, pale hair plastered with gore, her left arm swathed in blood-soaked cloths . . .

He wrestled open the window and stuck his face to the freshness as they crossed the river. When they reached the Crosby apartment block, Stuyvesant had the taxi wait.

The concierge was impressed neither by his evening suit nor his flowers, but she did telephone to the fourth floor, and gave him permission to go up. He found the door standing ajar and knocked gently before stepping inside.

"Miss Berger?"

Her head came out from her room down the hallway. "Come on in. Have you found out anything? About Phil?"

"Not really. I talked to the cops, I think they're going to get helpful now."

"Good," she said, although there was disappointment in her voice. "I'll just be a minute. There's fixings for drinks in the kitchen. Oh—" Her head re-emerged. "And do call me Nancy."

Another drink or three was a great idea. He didn't bother with mixing anything for the first one, but as it laid hands over his jangled nerves, he made a more formal attempt with the gin and red vermouth, stirring it over some ice and holding it out as he heard her come down the hall.

"Wow," he said.

She smiled, accepting both the glass and the compliment. "You're looking pretty spiffy yourself, Mr. Stuyvesant. Although your enthusiasm tells me I was even more of a mess yesterday than I'd thought."

"No," he protested, although by comparison, she had been. "And call me Harris."

The dress was sleeveless, its waist riding low around her hips. Her arms trim, almost muscular—and, he realized, the tan of her face was unbroken from forehead to wrist and down her chest to the neckline's V. He had a sudden, clear image of Nancy Berger sun-bathing topless under the Grecian sun, and reached hastily for the flowers and book.

"I brought you these," he said.

"How lovely! What fabulous colors. And, a book." She pushed the ribbon aside to see the title.

"I don't know if you read detective novels?" he asked, suddenly unsure of it. "Sylvia Beach said it was good." Although come to think of it, she hadn't, not really.

"Of course I love detective stories, I'm in the middle of an Agatha Christie right now. Do you read them?"

Teacups in the library. "Sure."

"Not much, I guess. Let me just put these in water before we go," she said, stretching for a vase in an upper cabinet.

"Have you thought of anything else?" he asked.

"About Phil?" She turned on the tap.

"Yes."

"No, I have not. And I should warn you that just for tonight, I'm telling myself that Phil's just being a brat. She could be, you know, at times. And although six months is too long for a prank, for tonight, that's what I'm telling myself."

Stuyvesant opened his mouth to defend the missing girl, then closed it; opened his mouth to protest, and finally noticed Nancy's down-turned mouth: her cynicism was as brittle as ice and about as thick as the florist's ribbon. On the third attempt, he found the correct note.

"That's fine, since that dress distracts me quite nicely from my day."

She turned to shoot him a grateful look, raising a taut line of muscle up her throat. "What have you been doing that required distraction from?"

"I've spent the afternoon in the movies."

"Aren't movies usually the distraction?" She set the vase on the counter, reaching deft fingers to the bow on the flowers.

"I was seeing some films made by artists. Surrealists. They were . . . disturbing."

"I believe 'disturbing' is the point. So, no more movies tonight?"

"How do you feel about puppet shows?"

The flowers dropped into the vase, spreading out and looking better than they had in the shop. "Punch and Judy, you mean? Or something more exotic?"

"I have no idea." Juvenile silliness sounded a good antidote to the cinéma; he could still feel the heebie-jeebies creeping across his skin.

"How mysterious! Sounds perfect."

With a swirl of her beaded wrap they were out the door.

The driver was propped against the hood of the car, having a smoke. When Nancy was inside, Stuyvesant turned to the driver. "Do you know the Théâtre du Grand-Guignol?"

The man raised an eyebrow, then cast a glance down at his female passenger before answering. "But of course, Monsieur."

It would appear that adults dressed for a night out were not the usual fares for the puppet theater. But Stuyvesant didn't care what a

Parisian taxi driver thought of his plans, simply told the man that was where he wanted to go, then got in beside Nancy.

The cul-de-sac leading up to the theater was narrow, and the driver stopped on the road outside.

"*This* is where we're going?" Nancy was looking down the alleyway towards the theater, clearly regarding the place as suspect. Stuyvesant, following her gaze, saw that some of the streetlamps appeared to be out, and the tree growing to one side looked like skeletal fingers reaching out of the wall. But surely a puppet theater would not be put in a dangerous neighborhood?

"We don't have to," he said. "No, let's just go get a drink and then we can go dancing. The Coupole—"

"No, no, this is fine, I was just a bit surprised, is all. Pay the man, Harris, and let's go see what's playing."

The Grand-Guignol was not a puppet show. It was nothing like a puppet show, unless the puppets had grown to a nightmare size and their slapstick violence had become terrifyingly real.

Doubts began to stir with his sight of the other patrons: not a child in sight, and few silk dresses. The space was tiny to the point of claustrophobia; the boxes with the slide-up screens at the back looked like confessionals; the pair of angels gazing down on the orchestra made the place seem more like a chapel than a theater.

The Grand-Guignol was not a chapel.

The Grand-Guignol was horror: monstrous, savage, perverse.

Two minutes after the curtains rose, Stuyvesant seized his companion's hand and made to stand up. To his astonishment, she pulled away from him.

"This is—" he started to say, but hisses rose up from all around. He sat down again, speaking into her ear. "This is awful! I'm so sorry, I had no idea it would be . . ."

"Oh, but it's perfect," she exclaimed. He stared at her. "It's so outrageous, it's . . . it's absurd! I mean, no one could possibly take it seriously. It's a joke, Harris. Watch it for a while, you'll see I'm right."

She actually did not want to leave? She was *amused* by this . . . spectacle? What was wrong with her?

Maybe the problem was that Stuyvesant had worked an actual case dealing with cannibalism.

Maybe if he were an innocent, he would find perversion and drawn-out acts of brutality amusing.

He stayed in his chair, appalled and yet fascinated by the convincing violence, the loving work of the stage knife, the weirdly erotic thread of blood down a naked white arm. For the first few minutes, he was intensely aware of the woman at his side, and then she disappeared from his thoughts until the curtain dropped and the lights came up, ending the first act. He'd stopped carrying a flask some years ago, since he no longer lived under Prohibition, but he could have used a belt now.

The interval was brief, far too brief. He braced for another onslaught of depravity, but to his astonishment, what followed was a comedy— rude, yes, but no more so than some of the puppet acts in parks filled with children. Here was the *guignol* side of the name, exaggerated horseplay with human beings as the Punch and Judy. It was a huge relief, after that disturbing start, and he laughed all the harder because of it.

He was surprised when, at the next drop of the curtains, Nancy got to her feet. "Come, Harris, you don't want to see another terror-play."

"What, there's another one?" He jumped up as if the cannibal-villain of the first piece might be after them.

Out in the lobby, she explained. "They alternate, horror and comedy. Like a hot bath followed by a cold plunge. It makes a person feel the contrast all the more."

"How do you know about this? And why didn't you stop me before we went in?"

"I have French friends who brought me—although yes, it was a shock. They claim to have a doctor in attendance because so many people faint, but I think that's just a stunt. And I didn't object because I thought you knew."

"Jesus. No, I didn't. And I'm sorry to inflict that on you."

"My dear man, it takes more than red-colored corn syrup to turn my stomach." A brief shadow passed over her face, but she instantly lifted her chin. "Speaking of which, shall we have dinner?"

He didn't have the heart to pump Nancy Berger about her roommate; still, he couldn't summon much enthusiasm for rare steak, either. "How'd you feel about some jazz and jive first?"

NINETEEN

RICKTOP'S WAS RIGHT around the corner, and Bricktop's was just the thing to blast Surrealist films and stomach-wrenching plays out of a man's mind. As they strolled, Stuyvesant noticed that, although clubs that catered to the Cannes and Biarritz set would stay shuttered for another couple of weeks, the rest of Paris was stirring to life.

Bricktop's was jumping. Even so, the owner spotted him three steps inside the door and leapt down from her perch to greet him. "Harris! I didn't know you were back in town—come here, you big New Yorker, you!"

Belatedly, he wondered if he should have sounded out Nancy on the question of race, because not every American girl would be entirely comfortable with a red-headed black woman seizing her date by the ears and planting a juicy kiss on him, complete with sound effects. When he was free to move, he turned to Nancy, and saw only amusement.

"Bricky, this is Nancy, she's from—where're you from, honey?"

"Southern California," she answered, and offered her hand. "How do you do?"

"Bricky's from Chicago, mostly," he told her.

"This big galoot helping you out?" Bricktop asked.

"Er, no. He's *taking* me out."

"I helped Bricky with a little problem, a couple years ago," he explained. "Now she thinks I'm always on the job."

"'Little problem,' my black ass. He saved my bacon," the cabaret owner declared.

"Just kept it from getting too crisp," he said.

"You looking for a table?"

"I was, but you're busy. We'll sit—"

"Nope, just a minute, we'll give you one." With a wave and a flourish, her staff caused a table to appear, alongside a group Stuyvesant knew from one of his previous times there. In fact, looking around the room, he saw fifteen or twenty familiar faces: typical of the village personality of Paris.

A bottle of champagne attached itself to the table, Bricktop's standard thank-you to Harris Stuyvesant.

Two glasses of iced bubbly helped disperse the heebie-jeebies, and brought up the pink in Nancy's cheeks. He stood up, extended his hand, and said, "I'm not entirely up to date on the latest dances, but I find a waltz and a fox-trot between them cover most songs."

She was a sweet mover, was Nancy Berger, more demanding than any other girl he'd swung around the floor, but when he'd adjusted, he found her strength and quickness appealing. The song ended and quickly launched into the next, and the next. Dancing pushed away a city full of ghosts; dancing made a man thankful for strong legs and healthy lungs; dancing made a man's arms delight at the woman filling them.

When they sat, the champagne in the cooler seemed miraculously to have replenished itself. Two glasses of that went down just as easy.

Bricktop came down from her desk to pull up a chair between them. She had to raise her voice to be heard. "So where you been, Harris?"

"Berlin, and before that Amsterdam."

"Ooh, that Berlin's a hot town. And I hear it's real cheap."

"It is, if you're being paid in dollars." If you're being paid at all, for that matter.

"Ain't that the truth? Never been to Amsterdam."

"It's very tidy, but not much night-life."

"Imagine."

"I wouldn't, if I were you."

"Anything I can do for you, Harris?"

"Other than emptying out your cellar?"

"What, those old things? They were going flat, I'd rather you drink them than me throw them out."

"Sure, Bricky. Well, I've been looking for a guy name of Dominic Charmentier, has something to do with the Grand-Guignol theater. Does he come in?"

"Le Comte? Sure."

Stuyvesant cocked his head. "He the guy who collects art?"

"Le Comte collects all kinds of things. I guess you could call some of them art."

He glanced at Nancy, whose attention was firmly fixed on the band, and drew Pip's photo out of his pocket. "Is this one of the things he's collected?"

Bricktop held the picture out to the light, then handed it back. "She was in with him, but that was months and months ago. What's happened to her?"

"Nothing that I know of, but her mother's looking for her. If this Count comes in, would you point him out to me?"

"Harris, you know I don't put up with any trouble in here."

"No trouble," he said, and made the solemn gesture of turning a key on his lips, becoming aware as he did so that his mouth felt a bit numb. Nothing like bubbly for a fast buzz.

Bricktop patted his arm and turned her attention to Nancy, admiring her dress, asking where she was from and what she did to keep herself busy, looking impressed at the summer in Greece and a stint working as cook aboard a steam yacht the previous year that Nancy hadn't got around to telling Stuyvesant about.

After four minutes, she and Nancy Berger were lifelong friends: there was nobody like Bricktop. After five minutes, a small riot at the next table had her rushing over and cracking wise to defuse the situation. And after six minutes, she was up in front of the room launching into "I Wanna Be Loved by You," throwing a handful of unlikely French words into the lyrics.

"She's a sweetheart," Nancy said.

"That she is," he agreed.

"You and she, you're good friends."

"I've known her for a while."

"Have you slept with her?"

"Nancy! A gentleman never tells."

"Right," she said.

"I promised you dinner. You hungry yet?"

"Yes, but I'm having too good a time here to break off."

More dancing, and somehow the bottle of wine never seemed to run dry. At some point, he found himself discussing the steps of the Black Bottom with his companion, who did not know it, so he dragged Bricktop from her perch to demonstrate. The entire place was soon on the floor doing the step-and-shake of the dance, and the level of energy, which had been high before, now became near to bursting. The place had an end-of-the-world kind of feeling to it, like the pressure of the summer was about to explode into a thundershower.

Stuyvesant and Nancy dropped into their chairs, sweating and infected with the excitement. She leaned forward to speak into his ear. "That Bricktop's quite a teacher."

He swiveled his head to reply. "Personal tutor to the Duke of Wales." Her face was just inches from his. It took no effort at all to let his body sag forward, just a fraction. Her lips tasted of wine and the salt of perspiration, and she was not the one to move away first.

She held out her empty glass, her dark eyes sparkling with amusement.

Something told him he might find out for himself just how far Nancy Berger's tan went.

More champagne, more music, and if it cost Stuyvesant half the Crosby advance, it was worth it. This was the first time he hadn't been working in . . . weeks? Months? He was lit up and he was happy, and going to be happier, and he was just beginning to wonder if it might be time to leave and move on to other things when he realized that Brick-top was bending down to speak in his ear.

"I probably shouldn't tell you this," she said.

"Whassat, sweetheart?"

"Your fellow just came in. Charmentier? Don't you go bothering him, he's here with friends, but I thought you might like to see what he looks like. We've sat them over in the corner."

He half-rose to see past the crowd, and found himself looking straight at Man Ray.

Black widow's peak, downturned mouth, darkly brooding eyes, and the supercilious air of a jaded god. The shining creature to his left might have been a footstool.

The footstool was leaning forward to hear as Ray spoke to the man on his right. A fourth member of the party was missing, having left a wrap across the back of the chair next to Le Comte. Stuyvesant pulled his gaze from the artist to study the collector and patron of the arts.

Dominic Charmentier was a slim, aristocratic-looking Frenchman somewhere in his fifties, although it was hard to tell for sure in the light and the smoke. His pomaded hair might have been blond or white; his skin was unlined. Blue eyes, beaked nose, thin hands, and a wide mouth with a noticeably fuller lower lip. He was listening politely to Man Ray, although his eyes were on Lee Miller.

Stuyvesant couldn't blame him.

"Come on, honey, let's have another dance." Stuyvesant pulled Nancy to her feet.

"I don't think—" she protested, but his arms were already around her.

Running surveillance on a person from a dance floor was tricky, especially since his feet had grown unusually clumsy, but looking past Nancy's shoulder, he could see the party.

Nancy squeaked. "Sorry," Stuyvesant said, and loosened his grip.

"Who are you looking at?"

"Just a guy I thought I recognized." *Just a guy who really rubs me the wrong way. A guy who might have something to do with my missing girl.*

"A friend?"

"Wouldn't say that." Ray seemed to be lecturing the count, his hands sketching shapes in the air, looking impatient when Charmentier did not appear to follow what he was saying. He dashed his cigarette into the tray and pulled out a pen to draw on Bricky's pristine tablecloth.

Le Comte watched; Lee Miller stretched around Ray's shoulder to see; Stuyvesant steered Nancy into one set of dancers, then another. Nancy apologized both times. After a third near-collision she took her hands from his shoulders. "Why don't we just go talk to them?"

"No."

The waiter came with a tray of drinks, placing one before each of the trio and one at the empty chair. Ray dropped his pen and exchanged it for the drink, squinting at the black lines as if to say that he knew the world would consider the sketch a work of genius, but then, he was the only one remotely qualified to actually judge.

It was just too tempting.

"On the other hand," Stuyvesant told Nancy, "why the hell not?"

He dropped his hands from Nancy's body to shoulder his way through the dancers, dimly aware of Nancy's protests and apologies following him across the floor. Dimly aware, too, of an internal voice telling him that this was *such* a bad idea, that Bricky was going to blow her top, that there was always tomorrow . . .

But he'd had too many tomorrows, too many days of heat and frustration, with Berlin and Paris and five nights with Pip looking over his shoulder and *nobody knowing her* and the loathsome films and that gorgeous young woman with the boots of the great photographer resting on her back, and too much drink and not enough food and the club's mad energy—

It was like teasing a burning match over a pool of gasoline. How was it possible to look down your nose at someone standing above you? Something in those bushy eyebrows, it had to be—something that just tempted a man's fist . . .

Not tonight, though. Tonight was just for a verbal jab.

The three seated figures looked up, glasses in mid-air. The music jived on around them, the dancers whirled and stamped, as Stuyvesant fixed his eyes on the dark-eyed artist, swaying slightly (*Jesus, Harris, are you tight?*) as he felt the two pairs of blue eyes from either side of Ray.

"Mr. Ray," he said, "I don't think you were telling me the whole truth this morning."

"No?"

"Monsieur," the other man said. "I believe you should—"

Stuyvesant turned to him. "You're Dominic Charmentier, aren't you? Your friend here, I think he's a liar."

The Frenchman rose, shooting the seated artist a look that was both amused and alarmed. "I'm sure that's not true," he said evenly.

"And I think you're in it with him."

Now the man looked frankly dumbfounded. "Monsieur?"

Stuyvesant leaned forward, his thighs bumping the table, and pronounced the name. "Pip Crosby."

There was a quick flare of—*something* in the Frenchman's face, that three bottles of champagne got in the way of reading. Apprehension? The widening of his eyes, a tiny startled raise of the chin. And that wasn't all: was it pleasure? Guilt? Pride?

"You know her!"

"Of course he knows her." Man Ray was on his feet, too. "I told you that this morning."

"Where is she?" Stuyvesant demanded, directing the question at the artist and the nobleman equally.

"Oh, who the hell cares?" Ray said.

"I care!" It was not Stuyvesant's voice but Nancy's, indignant at his shoulder.

"And who are you?" The artist might as well have said it aloud: *You're nothing but chewing gum on the sole of my shoe.*

Stuyvesant wanted to hit that smug face. He might have done so, but for Nancy hanging on to his left arm and trapping him against the table. Instead, he looked down at the drawing—and was startled to see a skeleton having sex with a voluptuous woman.

With a moment of what felt like clarity, a voice whispered in his ear that there was a better way to knock the artist than on his nose. His right hand picked up the untouched wine glass and dashed it across the ink. Five people went still, watching the ink spread and lose its power, then Ray started around the table towards him.

Childish.

You're drunk.

Leave now.

He turned sharply away, his left hand seizing Nancy's arm and pulling her to one side, his right coming out to straight-arm the truculent little artist out of his way. Man Ray jolted back—directly into Le Comte. The older man staggered, grabbed at the tablecloth, and went down in an explosion of white linen and half-full glasses.

Cries rose up, waiters came running, to tackle the only man still on his feet: Harris Stuyvesant.

The band bleated to a halt. In the silence, the crowd listened to the big, unruly American, cursing and trying to tell the men that he was sorry, he was leaving, he was tanked. Then Bricktop herself was there, furious.

"Yeah, Bricky, I'm sorry, I shouldn't have— Yeah, I'm gone."

The waiters drew back, allowing him to pick himself up from the floor. He winced at a slice of broken glass across his palm as he brushed his evening suit, then wiped more cautiously across his face, blinking against the sting of booze. Nancy was at his side, half supporting him. He allowed his arm to come to a rest across her shoulder.

The trio at the overturned table were on their feet, Lee Miller alternating her concern between Ray and Charmentier, who both declared that they were fine. Into this tableau of disaster rushed the missing fourth member of Le Comte's party, a small woman with short-cropped hair so blonde it was nearly white. She pulled Charmentier's fingers from his face, reassuring herself that his nose was not flat and bloody, then did the same with the photographer. Finally she whirled on the derelict stranger and the dark-haired woman holding him upright.

And froze. Her blazing emerald eyes went wide.

"Harris?"

Sarah Grey.

TWENTY

S ARAH GREY STIRRED sugar into her coffee and tried to decide which hand to wear.

Not the one with the long scarlet fingernails—she hadn't worn that for months. Not only did her right hand have short nails now, but that particular color of enamel was not to be had in all of Paris. Nor the hand she thought of as The Dancer, with the decorative flair of the fingers: it drew more attention than it deflected.

What she'd never been able to get the hands' creator to understand was, a hand should be invisible. In London, she could have worn gloves, but they weren't as popular here, especially not in the hot weather. It wasn't fair. Eleven years after Armistice and the streets were still full of men with empty sleeves, men gimping on artificial legs, men whose faces looked like crumpled blossoms. Nobody looked twice at them. But let a pinned-back sleeve be connected to a small blonde woman, and there came The Look: surprise and pity and the tip-of-the-tongue question, *What happened to*—a question that all but the crudest caught and tucked away.

But not before she saw the impulse.

A realistic hand sticking out of her left sleeve at least saved her from some Looks.

She set down the spoon with a sharp rap and plucked the oldest, most comfortable hand from the macabre display. It was the only one she'd actually asked for, so long ago its paint was chipped and the thumb was cracking. She'd have taken it in for repairs, but conversations with Didi were so . . . unnerving, it was easier to put up with a few dings and nicks.

In this, as in so much of life, attitude was all: if you treated it as a hand rather than a foreign object, people tended not to notice it.

She buckled it on and rolled down her sleeve, then left the house.

It might have been her imagination, but there seemed to be just a hint of October beneath this unending August heat. This would be her fourth autumn here, in a city that she'd intended to pass through on her way to points exotic and faraway, and somehow never left. Her early visits to museums and theaters had given way to work with theaters and artists—no politics, ever again!—as her schoolgirl French grew brisk and Parisian, along with the clothes in her wardrobe. She sometimes studied the stump of her left wrist and wondered at the young woman who used to be whole.

Sarah no longer had any interest in politics, no wish to help anyone, no desire to change the world. She had not even been back to England since her mother's funeral, in the winter of 1927. Most of her friendships had withered. Even Harris Stuyvesant.

She had met the big American just before her life had changed. Within a day of their meeting, she'd found herself thinking about marriage: if not for the bomb, she might be living in New York with a child. If not for the bomb. If not for running from England and all it represented.

Not that she blamed Harris, exactly. She had *meant* to contact him, *intended* to write and tell him . . . what? That she forgave him? What was there to forgive, other than his failure to keep her from an act that she herself had chosen? She tried to write, but with each passing day, it became less possible.

Only her brother remained. She wished Bennett would come to Paris again—he had once, so she was not without hope—but in lieu of actual appearances, he remained a steadfast correspondent. Although even he had changed since . . . That Day. Sometimes it felt as if he was trying to apologize for not protecting her as a big brother should. Still, he remained the most restful person she knew. A person didn't have to *say* things to Bennett. He just knew.

Their mother's death meant an inheritance, not enormous but enough that Sarah didn't have to produce an income. Her first weeks under this luxurious regime, she'd quit her position as assistant to an American millionaire and spent a week wandering the boulevards, where one afternoon she'd happened across a small and charming museum of Renaissance-era arts, entering into a conversation with the director. When she walked out, she found that she had volunteered to help him organize the museum's records—she might look like a scatterbrain, but in fact she both liked to organize and was good at it. She'd spent two months setting the office straight, then moved on to a struggling Rive Droite bookshop where she was a regular customer, helping them renovate their displays and coming up with ways of attracting more traffic. Since then, she had alternated between unpaid labor and actual employment, some of it quite generously paid. The only requirement was that it interested her.

She'd first met Le Comte seventeen months ago, when she was sitting in a frigid gallery around the corner from the Café de Flore. She'd thought this would be a way to learn about the city's artists, and that she did: in no time at all she'd discovered that most of them were children without the innocence, needing constant reassurance as to their genius. There never seemed to be enough air around them, and frankly it was boring. She'd given her notice.

Her last day in the gallery, Le Comte came in out of a sudden rainstorm, a slim, patrician gentleman in a beautiful coat. He tipped his hat politely, revealing pure white hair, and wandered through the gallery, ending up in the side room in front of Didi Moreau's weird little boxes.

"These are intriguing," he said, hearing her come in.

"Yes, aren't they?"

He gave her face a brief glance, then returned his gaze to the collected oddities: thin bones and a lock of pale blonde hair, the photo of a small girl and one small glass eye, brilliantly blue. "You don't care for them."

"Oh, to the contrary, Monsieur. Some of the Displays have a strange beauty and eloquence about them. They inhabit the boundary between a classical interpretation of art and Duchamp's readymades."

"*Objets trouvés,*" he murmured under his breath. "Gifts from the universe."

"I beg your pardon?"

He turned to look at her face-on, giving Sarah a view of money, breeding, and a startling hint of sorrow. "I've never cared for art as an intellectual joke," he told her. "I always suspect the artist of taking my money with one hand while making a rude gesture with the other."

Sarah felt her smile go a bit strained. She told herself not to be so sensitive—and edged her left arm back from his line of sight. "I'm quite certain that Didi Moreau has no such hidden motive."

"Would it be possible to meet the artist?"

"He's something of a hermit, but he is always willing to make an appointment."

She gave Le Comte the artist's telephone number, and sold him four of the Displays. Whether he returned to the gallery or not, she did not know, having moved on to another position.

Over the following months, she'd seen him a few times—with the size of Paris society, it was hard not to encounter the basic set of characters over and over, even one less ubiquitous as Le Comte—but she kept to the edges of the events, and indeed of Paris society as a whole. It was more than a year later that she met him again, at a very swank party at the house of Cole and Linda Porter, near the Place des Invalides. Linda introduced them, and when she was then drawn away to see to some detail, Le Comte cocked his head at Sarah.

"We have met, somewhere."

"I was in a gallery when you bought several of Didi Moreau's Displays."

His eyes flicked briefly, but he caught himself before they could actually reach her hand. "As I recall, you didn't like them much."

"The Displays are fine. It's Didi himself I'm not too crazy about."

"He is an odd one, that is for certain. What are you doing now, if not working in the gallery?"

So she told him, and told him, too, that her time with the old lady whose library had needed cataloging was coming to an end. And he asked about that job, and about some of the others, until after a while she suddenly realized that she had gone on far too long about her not terribly fascinating self.

She gave an embarrassed laugh. "I mustn't monopolize you, Monsieur. I'm sure you have friends here who—"

"One must never disregard a message from the universe."

"Sorry?"

"Mademoiselle, a long and varied life has taught me that key decisions invariably rest on what the thoughtless call coincidence. 'Coincidences' are gifts. If the machinery of the universe presents one with such a gift, one overlooks it at one's peril. But lest you fear you have been cornered by a religious maniac, let me explain.

"My assistant was in an automobile accident, a few weeks ago. I thought I could do without his services until he returned, but we learned recently that it will be several months, and just today I came to the decision that I must hire someone for that interval.

"And now you, a person with the skills I require, stand before me and mention that you are about to be leaving your current employ. Surely you agree that I would be a fool to pass up such a gift from the universe?"

He had probably once been striking, and even in his fifties, those patrician features were handsome, made only more so by the sadness behind his eyes. And because Sarah had spent a year among the skirts of the Paris art world, she knew why.

People called him simply Le Comte, which, in fact, he was: Count Dominic Pierre-Marie Arnaud Christophe de Charmentier—Dominic to his friends and close associates. He and another nobleman, the Viscount Charles de Naoilles, vied informally for who could support the greater number of French artists. But where Naoilles and his wife went in for film, Le Comte had been a patron of modern theater long before he turned his eye to the world of art.

Le Comte's wife had loved theater. Their elder son had enjoyed amateur dramatics. The son had died in 1917 at the age of nineteen, two days before Christmas, shot by a sniper in the trenches. Le Comte's beloved little daughter was said to have been a gifted mimic. She sickened and died a few months after her brother was shot. And on the heels of that tragedy, Le Comte's fourteen-year-old son was killed when a German shell hit a Paris church.

Then the wife committed suicide.

A man does not recover from that series of blows. And indeed, after the War, Le Comte disappeared into his house in the XIV arrondissement. He was not seen for two years.

But he emerged, clearly determined to build some meaning out of the chaos of his life. His first efforts were in a neurological clinic treating soldiers too damaged to function in the world. Oddly enough, he arrived there by art: a painting by Giorgio de Chirico led him to an essay by André Breton, whose wartime work with shell-shock led to the use of "automatic writing" as a therapy. Le Comte became interested. He funded a clinic based on the Breton interpretation of Freud. He bought paintings.

He resumed his interest in the theater.

But his eyes had never lost their melancholy.

"In fact," Sarah told him, "I do understand acting on impulse. My brother once told me that my mind works faster than my brain." Not that her snap decisions always turned out so well. "However, I'm not sure what sorts of 'skills' you need."

"I do not require a typist," he said, seizing the touchy subject without hesitation. "I need a person with brains and imagination. I think I see those."

After that, how could she refuse? They made an appointment for Tuesday morning, and went back to the party.

She spent the next two days casting out gentle feelers for information, and found that in addition to being an art collector, sad-eyed widower, and bereft father, he was from one of France's oldest families and a genuine war hero, an amateur painter, a one-time fencing champion, the half owner of four Rive Droite galleries, an occasional lecturer at the Sorbonne, a personal friend of two out of the last four Presidents of France, and the financial support beneath several foundations for the benefit of injured artists and veterans of war. He was known all over the city; the parties in his family mansion were famous, as was the house itself, from the life-sized garden chessboard to one of the world's most ornate clocks at the mansion's center. His current passion was said to be an odd French theater up near Pigalle, the Théâtre du Grand-Guignol.

She'd heard of the theater, but had never considered it the kind of entertainment she would enjoy. But since Le Comte was one of the backers, she felt she should go, before she accepted any kind of job from him.

She chose a matinee. And sat, stunned motionless, from the curtain's rise to its final drop. Afterwards, she had walked the streets in a fog, so unconscious of her surroundings that it was amazing she hadn't been run down or pick-pocketed.

Because one of the plays had shown—clearly, lovingly, and so graphically the woman sitting beside her had gagged—a man driven to madness, cutting off his own hand.

TWENTY-ONE

S ARAH HAD THOUGHT she was over the bomb—over the worst of
it, anyway. Yes, she still felt a ghostly hand, occasionally reached to
scratch an itch on a missing finger, but there were entire days when a
hand was just a hand, and not the end of a life. She'd lost a limb: she'd
gone on with her life.

But that evening after the Grand-Guignol, it was as if the bomb
were rolling across her all over again, slowly, inexorably, repeatedly.
Without even drugs to muffle the reaction.

All night, in a fever-dream over endless cups of tea, she relived it all,
over and over: Laura's face, a family's destruction, that lovely building
ripped apart and splattered with blood. Her brother, plunged into hell
because of her. Harris Stuyvesant and the death of hope.

Only the bomb itself was a blank: a profound stillness, as if the
world's heart stopped, followed by a wall of noise. There wasn't even
pain: that didn't come until she reached the hospital.

Why even consider a job with this in the background? No. Bury it,
shovel the days and weeks on top. She would *not* keep her appointment
with Dominic Charmentier. She would have nothing more to do with
the Grand-Guignol or its owners.

And yet . . .

When the sun rose, she bathed and dressed, intending to take a
tram as far as she could go in the opposite direction. Maybe a train. She

hadn't been to Chartres in a while; the rose window would be a joy. And yet her feet carried her north: past the tram stops, away from the Gare Montparnasse, to the river and beyond.

In the end, she was only slightly late for her appointment with Le Comte, in a café around the corner from the theater. He rose. She simply stood in the doorway, unable either to enter or to flee, so after a moment he came forward, gently shepherding her to the chair across from him. If he felt her trembling, he said nothing, merely poured her coffee and laid a fragrant brioche before her.

She could not meet his eyes. She felt as if she'd uncovered something nasty about a friend. She opened her mouth to tell him that she had decided not to accept his job, but he spoke first.

"You went to the theater, I imagine."

"I didn't like it."

"One is not meant to like it. One is meant to respond to it."

"It was . . . awful."

"The Grand-Guignol is not me," he said, simply.

She did not answer.

"Let me tell you how I came to be involved. Like many of my countrymen, I lost loved ones in the War. Like many of us, my reaction was to push it away, believing that to speak of it would grant it authority. It was not until a friend introduced me to the work of a neurological clinic treating shell-shocked soldiers that I began to understand: the only way to overcome one's fears is to confront them. The clinic aimed at bringing the dark things to light.

"We French, as you English, have survived a time of unparalleled horror. Our impulse is to deny it, to paint a pretty stage set of normality and tell ourselves, again and again, that this is the real world.

"But the horror behind the painted set invariably leaks through. The effort of maintaining it, of convincing ourselves every day that this is life and it is lovely undermines our balance, eats at any faint trace of happiness.

"The only way is to face it."

He might have been talking about Sarah's life, rather than his own.

He told her about finding the theater, how offended he was—and yet how drawn he was, too, both for what was on the stage, and what was in the audience. How those in the seats seemed lighter when they left, as relieved as if they had survived an actual ordeal. How he talked to doctors, psychiatrists, soldiers—and learned how a play could be a catharsis, freeing those who had spent far too long bottling up their natural impulses. How a theater might bring in people for an illicit thrill, but in the end, perform an act of psychological cleansing far greater than any priestly confession.

By bringing the dark things to light.

The Grand-Guignol had opened in 1897. Many assumed its appeal would shrivel after the real-life horrors of the Front, he told Sarah, but it had not. Plays that immersed an audience in stark terror followed by wild laughter opened a door. They invited the audience to believe that their own fears were as ephemeral as what took place onstage.

And if she thought this cerebral view contrary to the visceral reaction of the audience, he said, it was not: as Freud would explain, the analysis of a mental aberration and the experiences of the sufferer were two sides of treatment's coin.

His voice was soothing, gently pulling her from her state of prolonged shock. She picked up her cup, took a swallow of the cold chicory-flavored liquid, and lifted her gaze.

His eyes crinkled and he sat back. "I see you begin to understand. As I told you the other night, what I require is an assistant with both ability and imagination. There is considerable responsibility. The hours are erratic. You would be dealing with everyone from dukes to dustmen. And although when I request that something be done, I expect my instructions to be followed promptly and to the letter, I also would ask that you contribute your own thoughts concerning the projects you undertake. My assistant is, to some degree, a partner."

"Just what does this 'assistant' job entail?" she asked.

"Ah," Le Comte said, "now, there is the question. When is a job not a job? When is a theater not a theater?"

He reached into his vest pocket to draw out a silver lump about two inches across: a skull. With a touch, the top of the skull came open, revealing a watch-face.

"The death-watch," he told her. "A joke, of course, but also a serious and beautifully made timepiece. My tailor despairs, because there is no way to wear it that does not wreak havoc on the waistcoat. But I carry it for two reasons. First, it amuses me. But equally important, this particular watch is purported to have belonged to the Marquis de Sade—a 'fact' known by many. Every time I draw it out to check the time, those around me experience that brief quiver of fascination we all have at the forbidden."

He tucked the timepiece away.

"It represents what I try to contribute to the Grand-Guignol." He spoke in more detail about the history of the theater, the changes he has made after becoming involved half a dozen years ago.

She found she was leaning forward on her elbows, interested at last. Le Comte pointed out that, as the Opéra sold the voices on its stage and the Folies Bergère sold its dancers' legs, the Grand-Guignol sold its atmosphere. "Our audiences are not fools, they know it is not real violence and bloodshed taking place before them, but we go to enormous trouble to make them suspect it *could* be—just as my watch *could* have been in de Sade's pocket when he performed his atrocities.

"We accomplish this in two ways: verisimilitude, and the wider stage.

"As you have seen, we pay meticulous attention to detail. The blood looks real, the motions of violence are closely choreographed, the mutilations look extraordinarily realistic.

"But the workings of the stage—the believable effects, the intensity of the actors, the subtle effects of lighting and sound—are only a part of our impact. Reality and fiction blur at the Grand-Guignol, every step along the way: anticipation rises and builds, becoming nearly intolerable as a patron gets off the Métro, walks down the ill-lit alley, enters a former convent sacked in the Terror, passes the house doctor who stands ready to treat the faint of heart.

"But the performance begins even before that patron leaves his front door. Rumors of darkness pervade the theater: the actors are unstable, the directors and owners untrustworthy, bitter feuds are written up in the newspapers. Even the format of the plays—one is immersed in unbearable, claustrophobic madness, and a moment later plunged into light comedy, only to have the stage darken and terror creep in again—makes one doubt one's very sanity.

"Between the staged effects and the real-world knowledge, people who come to the Grand-Guignol are already half-convinced that one day, those in control of the plays may lose their hold, and permit a murder to become real. That a fake knife or vial of poison may be replaced by a real one. You heard giggles during the performance, did you not?"

"Yes," she admitted.

"Those were the high-pitched laughs of fear, not of relief. We consider it the highest applause when a Guignoleur cannot help calling out a warning as a man creeps across the stage with a knife.

"Max Maurey, the theater's last owner, established the idea that a performance is never limited to what happens onstage. He made publicity stunts central to the world of Guignol. Some of those feuds are, frankly, inventions. When a murder is discovered, we volunteer comments to the *Figaro* and *Petit Journal*. When a Surrealist makes a film with dramatically mangled bodies, one of us will write a prominent review.

"And as you might imagine, when a theater presents such disturbing fare as ours, the owners are suspected of their own dark doings—and so much the better. When unsavory acts are suspected of one of us—myself, Jouvin the owner, Zibell the director—it contributes to the effect. When I am at the opera, I want those in the boxes around me to wonder if my ring conceals poison or my stick a dagger."

Sarah couldn't help chuckling, at the arch to his eyebrow, the faint quirk to his lips. "How very Dada!"

"Truth told through lies—the Surrealists are discovering what the Grand-Guignol has known for years: when art is indistinguishable from real life, it comes alive. And when it lives, it changes the viewer."

"But what if you're, I don't know, out at night with mud on your trousers? Aren't you afraid someone would report you for burying a corpse in the Bois de Boulogne?"

"Excellent! Precisely the kind of suggestion I expect from my assistant. Though it would be the Parc Montsouris."

"You don't live here in Montmartre?"

"My family home is near the Place Denfert-Rochereau. It is but two minutes' stroll from the public entrance to the Paris Catacombs," he added with a twinkle.

"How convenient. Still, I'd think the constant act rather, well, all-consuming."

"Mlle. Grey, I am a mediocre painter, a bad musician, a worse actor. The Grand-Guignol is my art, and my craft. Most of all, it is my service to the mental and emotional well-being of the city. A part of that performance takes place on what one might call the larger stage: Paris itself."

"So, what do you need an assistant for?"

"To ensure that the machine runs smoothly—on stage or, more often, off."

"I can imagine that would be a problem. One hitch and the dramatic climax becomes a farce."

"You are absolutely right," he said intently. "The Guignol is a precise tool, as exacting and specific as the torture instrument of a Mediaeval Inquisitor."

And just as the hair on the back of her neck began to rise, his features rearranged themselves into a boyish grin.

Le Comte was a troubling man, and a troubled one. The smooth, easy surface of the aristocrat was his public face, along with the illusionist's act of delight in wickedness, but the more Sarah knew him, the more she felt the well of despair underlying it all.

A man who sought to find meaning in personal devastation.

A goal Sarah Grey could understand, more than most.

In any event, she'd been hired in May. Since then she had supervised a script, hired two actors, put together and distributed half a dozen flyers, helped actors rehearse, edited three short plays, found a source of taxidermied bats, and bought a thousand cows' eyes swimming in formaldehyde inside decorative glass urns. She had arranged for the purchase of a car, overseen three elaborate parties, and hired a group of

Satan-worshippers to perform a Black Mass. She had drawn up contracts with several artists for panels to make up a danse macabre in the Charmentier mansion. She fed rumors into conversations like a stoker feeding a firebox. She soothed the engineers who built machines for Le Comte's beloved stage effects—everyone else hated the complicated devices, which always threatened to fail at key moments, but as far as her boss was concerned, the more complex the better, in effects or plots. She no longer flinched at the terrible screams of the actresses; and although she was not inured to the effects and she closed her ears to the more repulsive perversions, she could sit through a show with a degree of grim humor. In the process, she learned a dozen ways to kill a person.

She had taken the job as an impulse; she had been surprised by how satisfying it was. Not that it was easy. Le Comte was demanding, and empathy was a tool he rarely chose to employ. But as the summer went on, she began to see the good that he did—for Paris, and for her. A prolonged assault of fictional horrors could indeed be as cathartic to the soul as a dose of foul-tasting medicine was to the body: she saw it not only in the faces of the audience as they left, but in the undeniable fact that she was sleeping better than she had for years.

She had spent the hot summer in a state not unlike that of the Grand-Guignol audience, veering between sheer delight and skin-crawling dread: Le Comte definitely participated in all aspects of his adopted theater.

It took a while to catch the correct note of his style, that banter-with-an-edge he used for the press, the sense of *This is a joke . . . isn't it?* that permeated his most outré remarks. At least once a week she decided he had gone too far, that he was too . . . disquieting to be around anymore. Then the next morning he would say something that reduced her to helpless laughter, and she would be captivated anew by his outrageous imagination.

Two weeks ago, as the August vacances were coming to an end, he decided to bring Africa to the Grand-Guignol. A writer was ordered to begin a play on voodoo; the stage crew puzzled over a bit of trick machinery, to unfold at a key moment; the makeup crew investigated various kinds of blackface; some Nigerians were located, and actors dispatched to consider their gestures and stances. In the meantime, groundwork was laid for the external play: Le Comte bid prominently at an auction of African masks; a few days later, he was seen to buy a Matisse à l'Afrique, followed by a Picasso. He did the rounds of the jazz clubs, befriending musicians around Josephine Baker and Bricktop.

As the play took shape, he was struck by another idea: the Grand-Guignol was limited by its size, but the world was full of cinema houses. Why not adapt the stage production for the screen?

As it turned out, one of the artists doing a panel for the Charmentier danse macabre was a photographer who was interested in film. Tonight, Le Comte was entertaining this ugly little American and his young lover-assistant, a woman so stupefyingly magnificent she made Sarah want to wear one of those all-over Arab robes. Le Comte needed Sarah there, and she would not be able to return home before evening: hence her early-morning conundrum over which hand to wear.

The long day wore on. Sheaves of drawings were produced. The gorgeous lover turned out to actually know nearly as much about photography as Man Ray himself, leaving Sarah feeling like a mouse in the corner. The mismatched quartet settled down for dinner. Long before they reached Bricktop's, three hours later, Sarah wasn't sure if she felt more scorn or despair at the dark-eyed photographer's bombast.

Bricktop's small club was crowded, as usual. When they were shown to their table, Sarah excused herself to use the lavatory, desperate to permit her aching face to lose its polite smile for a few minutes. She touched up her powder; she *tsk*ed at a new chip in her hand. She renewed her lipstick, straightened her stocking seams, glanced through her incomprehensible notes.

She delayed as long as she could.

She stepped back into the ferocious noise of the club just as a big man in a cheap evening suit assaulted her employer and his artist, then half-collapsed against a female companion.

Reassuring herself that Le Comte and Ray were not hurt, Sarah whirled to confront the assailant—and stopped, more shocked than any macabre play had left her.

Sandy hair, pugnacious jaw, crooked nose, dots of shrapnel along his cheekbone. A look of astonishment dawning in those cynical blue eyes.

Harris Stuyvesant.

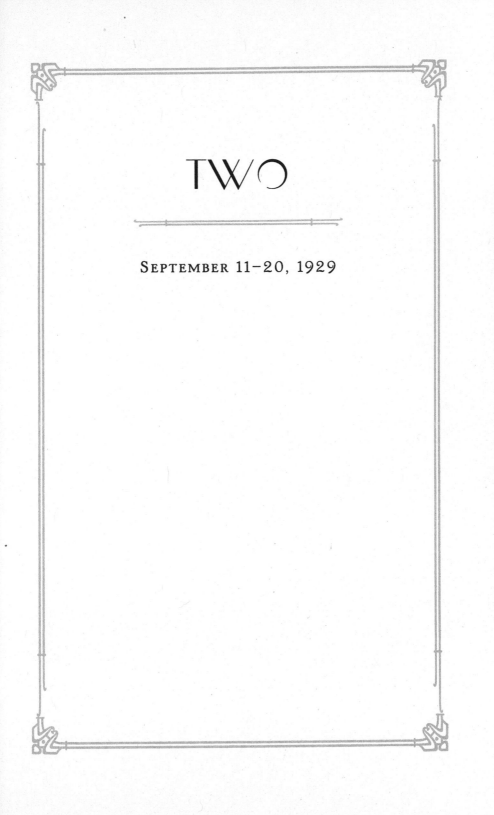

TWO

SEPTEMBER 11–20, 1929

TWENTY-TWO

A LETTER:

Dearest Sarah, sister mine,

I send you a photograph-pin and a story, both for your amusement.

The photograph comes via an itinerant photographer who just <u>happened</u> to be passing through the village yesterday, my usual day of the week to walk up to the shops for fresh milk and the London papers. He had arrived early that morning in an ancient Morris converted into a mobile studio, a display of Autochrome photos on its sides to tempt the peasants into spending their hard-earned shillings for the glories of a colour portrait to hang on Grandmama's parlour wall. And, for those with fewer resources or less time, he also had a clever device that snaps a picture and instantly manufactures it onto a round button with a pin on the back—I suppose for young lovers wishing to decorate their lapel with the object of their affections? Or perhaps for a farmer proud of his prize hog.

Autochromes, to judge by the man's display, require long exposure, resulting in a satisfying solemnity on the faces of his victims. The button camera, on the other hand, is but a snapshot, with the button itself emerging from the device in under a minute.

This, as you might guess, is a more useful means by which to capture the image of a reluctant passer-by, a man willing to take but the most fleeting of looks into a camera lens, a man who is rarely to be found in the more customary hunting grounds of the genus <u>photographus</u> <u>itinerantus.</u>

I will say, the Project are nothing if not creative in their efforts: this man clearly knew his business, and was prepared to spend his morning taking photographs of grubby urchins and farmers' simpering daughters in order to get a chance at me. I might almost have thought him a genuine member of his profession had I not been forced by the placement of his wheeled studio to edge between it and the grocer's bins.

Close-up, I could not fail to notice the singular lack of wear on his coat shoulder from carrying the long tripod of a portrait camera, and the relative lack of chemical stains on his skin, and the slight deliberation of his fingers when performing actions that should have been automatic, and the lack of a dark tan that one expects on a man who spends his summer following the traveling fun-fairs and seaside crowds. That, and the depths of foreboding in his eyes: God only knows what they told him about me.

I took pity on the poor fellow and did not instantly slip away, but freely granted him the button-snapshot. If I were a good man, I would have played along and posed for one of his Autochromes, that you might admire my green eyes, orange neck-tie, straw-coloured hair (straw-textured, too, if truth be known, after a long summer) and the pretty red bruise on my forehead from where Robbie tried to show me how to play rounders with a rock on Sunday. But I am not a good man (a claim I know you will refute with sisterly indignation), so I made the photographer work for his picture of the Hermit of Land's End, thus giving you nothing but a button to attach to your pinafore or garden-smock.

This is by way of an answer to your recent question, if the

Watchers are leaving me alone: not as much as I might wish, but without the intrusiveness I might fear.

I hope your time in the country has darkened your freckles and brought a bounce to your step, little Sarah. I look forward to meeting this Comte of yours. I was thinking that I might be able to prise myself out of Cornwall again next year. January or February perhaps—yes, the weather will be abysmal, but since no-one travels then, I might be able to face the ferry without being tempted to commit murder. Or suicide.

Keep well, and give your blacksmith my respects.

Your loving—

Bennett

TWENTY-THREE

THE LIGHT HAD that kind of knife's-point brilliance to it that made a fellow bleed over his sins of the night before. Stuyvesant washed down a palmful of aspirin he'd bummed from the Dôme's maître d', and waited for the coffee to do its work.

You absolute mutt, he berated himself. *You drunken bonehead. The first time you see Sarah Grey, you're standing there stinking of gin with her two friends at your feet.*

Was there any chance last night of finding out where she lived?

No.

Was there any chance she'd want to see him, ever?

The very slimmest.

But a thread was better than nothing, even if it meant crawling on his belly across Paris to find her.

He managed to choke down a couple of eggs, and the aspirin helped, both with the headache and the bruises he'd got from Bricky's waiters.

Next stop: the flower shop, totting up a hefty bill.

After that: pick up the new suit, and hope it helped make him look like a grown-up and not a brawling adolescent.

Now to throw himself at Bricky's feet and hope he hadn't permanently blotted his copybook with her.

Look on the bright side, he mused as his taxi grumbled across the river. *At least you didn't end up in jail this time.*

He arrived at Bricktop's on the heels of his floral apology: ten dozen multi-colored roses, making the entranceway a glory of color and scent, and although Bricky was clearly steamed, he thought he saw a teensy crack under the very edge of her indignation. He summoned all his Yankee charm, got on the knees of his new suit, and swore he would not rise until she had forgiven him.

But she was harder than that. He was left with no way out, no choice but the ultimate weapon: the truth.

He rose from his knees and took her down the street to a sleepy terrace café where they would not be overheard, and he told her all about it. Almost all.

At the end of it, she eyed him, then: "You feel bad, that you treated this Crosby girl like a dog."

"Bricky, when I was a kid, there were good girls and bad girls, and you could tell them apart. Now, it's . . ." He stopped. Bricktop went cold when she got angry, and she'd started out plenty cool enough. *Shut up, Harris.* "Yeah, Pip Crosby was a sweet thing and I treated her like crap. I guess I am trying to make up for it, a little. Sending her back to her mother where she belongs."

The hardness relented a degree. "And you think they know where your young lady's gone? Mr. Ray and Le Comte?"

One of the things he hadn't told her was how everyone else looked at Pip and saw doom. "I don't know, Bricky. I just feel like Ray knows *something* about Pip Crosby. And 'something' is more than I've found anywhere else."

"When you find her, will you just bundle her up and send her home?"

"Not if she's healthy and happy," he said obligingly. "I just need to be sure. So, what do you know about those two?"

Bricky knew something about everyone in Paris, and she was happy to share. She seemed less fond of Mr. Ray than she was of Le Comte, although she admitted that she didn't really know either of them, since they weren't part of the Bricktop "set." Still, it took her half an hour to run through what gossip she'd heard.

"Okay, well, thanks for that, Bricky. War hero, huh? Pretty stupid way to introduce myself. I'll hunt them down and tell them I'm sorry."

"And you promise not to punch Mr. Ray again?"

He leaned across the table to give her a kiss. "Bricky, I'll kiss *him* if it makes you feel better."

"Only if he asks you to. But you've got a pile of apologies to make, Harris."

"I've already sent him and Miss Miller flowers with a pretty note. I sent Nancy flowers, a note, and a petit bleu as well. And I'd apologize to Le Comte, too, if you want to tell me where he lives."

"That's easy. He's got a mansion a couple streets from Denfert-Rochereau. I'd guess anyone down there could point it out to you. Although—she reached out for his wrist and moved it to see the watch-face—couple times I was down there, I saw him having coffee at a place just around the corner. You know, the same street as Raspail but a different name? Down towards the park? Anyway, you might want to walk past there first. Might save you cooling your heels on his doorstep all morning."

"Bless you, Bricky. Am I forgiven?"

"Yeah, I guess you can come back to the club. But if there's a next time, that's it for you at Bricktop's. I'm not running any boxing gym."

He walked up to the Métro and rode through the clattering darkness to Place Denfert-Rochereau—formerly Place D'Enfer, Hell Place. He was little short of astonished to come up into the air and, first, find Bricktop's vaguely described café, and second, spot Dominic Charmentier sitting on the shady terrace with a newspaper.

He was equally surprised at the mix of feelings welling up at the sight of the small, tidy aristocrat.

The man was a hero, according to Bricky's gossip—and sure, *hero* was a cheap word, but Le Comte had been given two medals, one of them for dragging three common soldiers out of danger. Which meant that he'd chosen to be at the Front, since the automatic posting for his kind was well to the rear. And although the man had come through in one piece, the poor bastard had lost a lot. He'd even done all kinds of Good Works since then.

Last night Stuyvesant had been more than ready to condemn the man because of his apparent friendship with Man Ray—and, because he was close to Sarah Grey when he, Harris Stuyvesant, was not. But today? Sober and leaning up against the Métro entrance with the sun dappling through the trees and a sidewalk musician crooning an old song? He could not decide if the fellow's standoffish attitude was arrogant superiority, or the reserve of a much-wounded man.

Not that any of it mattered. The guy was his only lead to Sarah Grey.

As if Le Comte felt the emotion coming across the street at him, he glanced up from his paper, saw nothing of interest, and returned to the news. The waiter brought a coffee; Le Comte reached for it without acknowledging the man. He sipped, put the cup down, turned a page.

Harris Stuyvesant settled his shoulders in his suit, and stepped into the sun.

TWENTY-FOUR

DOMINIC CHARMENTIER RATTLED the morning paper, waiting for Sarah Grey's friend to work up the courage to cross the street. In general, Americans were an entertaining lot, what with their boundless energy and complete lack of subtlety—although like any Parisian, there were times when he viewed the *Yanqui* invasion with as little enthusiasm as he would a herd of bison loosed in the Trocadéro.

This one he wasn't so sanguine about. The fellow's meaty fist could have done some real damage, if he hadn't been too drunk to aim. But as Bonaparte had advised, one did not interrupt an enemy embarked on error, and that one across the street, all unknowing, was heading in precisely that direction.

Still, Charmentier didn't intend to sit here drinking coffee forever. If Mlle. Grey's friend didn't make his move soon, he would end up chasing his quarry down the street, and start the match points down.

A small article on African art caught his eye. He read it with care, aware of the man lurking in the shadows around the Métro station, and took out his silver pencil to write down the gallery address in his pocket notebook. He turned the page, and waited for another headline to come to his attention.

Ah: at last, the rough American was summoning his nerve. Le Comte watched his approach around the edge of the paper, and when the man stood before his table, he let the paper subside. His eye traveled up the man's oversized form, pausing at the slight meander to the stitching, the ill fit of the jacket, before he met that bloodshot gaze. "Mr. Stuyvesant, good morning. I wondered if you intended to join me."

"Don't mind if I do." The chair scraped disagreeably on the paving stones, although the scraper seemed oblivious of the winces of everyone in earshot.

When the good-looking young waiter was standing by their table, Le Comte ordered another coffee. "This time, please bring it while it is still hot. And for my friend here . . . ?"

"Coffee's fine."

The lad scooted away.

The opening *coulé*—testing of swords—was finished, Le Comte thought in amusement: now, *en garde.*

"I have to apologize for last night," the American said.

"I would think so."

"Yeah, I'm sorry. I was drunk and stupid. I'm glad I didn't hurt you."

"Oh, small chance of that, Mr. Stuyvesant, but it is good of you to seek me out to tell me. I trust you will do the same with M. Ray?"

"I'll try, though I'm not sure he'll take an apology. He's a little . . . snooty."

"Snooty? As in, looking down one's nose?"

"Yeah, sorry. Your English is excellent."

"Thank you. Your French is quite intelligible." Le Comte saw the big man twitch at the nick of this verbal épée, but he hid a smile. "Why do so few Americans bother to learn the language? People like that Stein woman—you know her? She has been here for years, yet can scarcely order a cup of coffee."

"Yeah, Paris takes its time to welcome outsiders, doesn't it?"

Le Comte felt his eyebrows rise. Was that a bland insult? Could there be more to this oversized Yankee Doodle than fists and cheap tailoring? "Perhaps I can make up for the general . . . 'snootiness' . . . of my fellow countrymen."

"That's big of you. Tell me how you know Pip Crosby?"

"*Do* I know her?"

"Ray said you do. You took her to him to be photographed. You gave her presents. You went to Bricktop's with her."

"Ah, you mean Philippa. Yes, certainly I knew her."

"'Knew.' Is she dead, then?" The man pounced on the word as if tricking a confession out of a criminal.

"My good sir, I hope not. But I understood that she returned home some months ago. Did she not?"

"No. And apparently the last person anyone saw her with was you."

He could hear the bluff in the American's accusation. Did the big man lack the skill to conceal it, or had he not bothered to try? "How extraordinary. When was that?"

"End of March, first part of April. My witness wasn't clear on the dates."

"I think you may find that your witness is unclear on a number of facts. Miss Crosby did accompany me to Luna Park on the—" He stopped to flip open the notebook on the table, consulting the calendar in the front. "The twenty-second of March. Not quite 'the end.'"

"How can you be sure of the date?"

"Monsieur, I would only go to Luna Park on a Friday, when prices are raised to keep out *la racaille*. And it could not have been the twenty-ninth: that was Good Friday. The outing was to be a treat for Philippa, and to distract her from my news, which was that I did not wish to see her anymore."

"You broke up with her?"

"Monsieur, there was nothing to break. She was an amiable companion for several months. But she had begun to demand commitments and services I was not willing to indulge her in."

"She wanted you to marry her?" Again, the blunt and triumphant pounce. It began to grow irritating.

"There was never any question of that, M. Stuyvesant," he replied. "No, Philippa wished me to invest in her as a film actress."

"What was wrong with that?"

"The girl was attractive enough, but she lacked the plastic features and intensity required for motion pictures."

"Or for the stage?"

"On the stage she was adequate for certain roles, those that allowed her to flaunt her . . . what might be called exhibitionist tendencies. But I could see that she would never be a success. Philippa stood on the stage to show off. A real actress stands before an audience to pull them in."

"Therapeutic for her, would you say?"

Bon Dieu—a second surprise! "That is a subtle analysis, M. Stuyvesant."

"And here you thought I was just another pretty face. So you like things that are fresh and shiny and damaged, eh, M. Charmentier?"

Le Comte stiffened at the bite of this unexpected opponent's blade, retreating a fraction. "'Fresh, shiny, and damaged.' What a provocative trio of adjectives."

"Hits you where you live, eh?"

At that, Le Comte laughed. "Ah, j'adore l'anglais Américaine! Mr. Stuyvesant, your three adjectives capture the very essence of modern art. Who cares if something old and tired comes to harm? Damage only matters when it shows."

"Like Miss Crosby's scar."

Reactions honed half a lifetime ago drove Le Comte's response: never show damage; lean hard into your riposte. "True—and an analogy for life itself, once you consider that caressing the tissue of her scar caused Philippa the most exquisite pleasure."

The swordsman felt the brief satisfaction of a touché, as the man's clenched jaw betrayed a fisted hand beneath the table—ah, but this was foolishness. The pointless bristling of a young dog.

He sat back, raising a hand. "Monsieur, please forgive my crudeness. I think she may have been your friend, and you appear to be asking if I harmed Miss Crosby in some manner. I assure you, she was brimming with life and loveliness when I last saw her."

The American hesitated only briefly before changing his line of attack. "What do you know about Pip's relationship with the art world? She has a number of expensive pieces in her room, along with a sketch by Picasso and photos by Man Ray. How'd she come to have all those?"

"Some of them I may have given her, although I do not remember anything by Picasso. The Ray photographs I commissioned in hopes that we could use them for promotional flyers in the theater, although in the end they were more artistic than commercial. She may have bought the others. Or stolen them, for all I know."

"Did she steal anything from you?"

"Not that I am aware of."

"Then it's not very polite to call her a thief."

"No, I should not have done that. Curious, how short-tempered one becomes under attack. Are we nearly finished, Mr. Stuyvesant? I have a full day, with a long night ahead of me."

"I need to talk with your secretary."

"Who, Mme. Chrétienne?"

"No, Sarah Grey."

Finally! "The divine Miss Grey, is it? She is my assistant, not my secretary."

"Okay, I need to talk with your assistant."

"About what?"

"About . . . I just need to talk with her. Look, I can understand you don't want to give me her address, but I ought to warn you, I'm a really persistent sort of a guy. And Paris isn't *that* big a place."

"Very well."

The American blinked. "You'll give me her address?"

"No. That would not be the act of a responsible employer. However, I will provide an opportunity for you to speak with her, in a public venue."

"That'll do," the man said, although it was clear that he regarded it as a mere wedge beneath the door.

"Come to my house tonight. There's a party. Formal, but not without its entertainment. I think you might enjoy it."

Stuyvesant watched the slim, white-haired man glide away down the street. It was like boxing a featherweight: once you managed to connect, boy, you could knock him for a loop, but your opponent was quick and could blood you a dozen times in between.

Three places, the man had flinched, just a little: one at the snide remark about the aloofness of Paris society, when Stuyvesant let him know he wasn't going to just stand there with his guard down. Second was when he'd repeated Nancy's idea: that Pip Crosby's exhibitionism might be in some way therapeutic. Was Le Comte's surprise because he'd never thought of Pip as complicated, or because he didn't expect the idea from a big-fisted American?

But there was no doubt: Stuyvesant's personal dig had got at the man, just for a second. Did he like fresh and damaged goods? Stuyvesant couldn't tell—but Le Comte hadn't liked the accusation, and he'd come back fast with that spiteful reference to sexual conquest.

Come to think of it, there'd been another bit of fancy footwork later on, when the man had introduced the possibility that Pip was a thief. What was that for? It felt like another attempt to distract, but away from what inadvertent revelation? The Picasso sketch? Man Ray's photos? The pieces she'd been given, or bought? He'd have to think about that.

He also wondered if there was something a bit off about that Luna Park date. Almost as if Le Comte had remembered the date very well, but pretended he did not.

Between one thing and another, tonight's party promised not to be dull.

Stuyvesant stretched out his arm to look at the gray sleeve. Why did he get the feeling that Charmentier had looked down his nose at this spiffy new suit?

Dominic Charmentier walked away from the café under iron control: never show an injury.

He hadn't fenced for years, and the surge of old instincts had been startling. That clash of swords across a linen tablecloth called to mind an unauthorized contest he and his fellow students had once held to pit the quick flexibility of the épée against the heft of the sabre. The lighter weapon had won then, too—but only just.

You are out of practice, he scolded himself. *Your reactions are old and slow.* Perhaps it was not a good idea, to permit an opponent too much freedom of movement across a dueling piste.

TWENTY-FIVE

Stuyvesant hadn't written down the names in Pip's sad little collection of good-luck matchbooks, but he remembered enough of them to make a beginning. Many of the places were open both day and night and, in Montmartre as in Montparnasse, this could mean two completely different clientèles. But maybe Pip had taken her lunches there, too . . .

She hadn't.

Twelve bars, six cafés, and five of the friends in her address book, all with the same answer: no one had seen Pip Crosby since March.

By five o'clock, both cafés and bars were at an ebb. He hadn't eaten since breakfast. If he stopped to think about the information he'd been gathering, he would want to throw himself into the river—or into a bottle. And if he was going to Le Comte's party, he'd need to get some food into his stomach first.

So he took the Métro back across the river and went to the Dôme for a belated lunch. Kiki was there again, her painted-on eyebrows heavy today, and uneven, with the lids an odd yellow-green. She waved a flirtatious hand, and although Stuyvesant had planned on eating a sandwich at the counter, he decided he could do with something more substantial. And certainly she would offer a welcome distraction from thought.

He kissed her cheek, and this time let her order an admirer to give up his chair. Not until he sat did he realize how tired he was.

His drink came faster than his food, but he refused a second: tonight, facing Sarah Grey, was no time to get sloppy. When his *steak frites* came, he ate quickly, listening with half an ear to the conversation around him.

It was the talk of modern Montparnasse: the hangers-on, the painters who rarely finished a canvas, the writers whose only publishing history was in one of the small literary journals that paid in copies. Five years ago, this table might still have held economic failures, but it would have been bristling with creativity. All these boys could do was snipe at their betters and complain of their tight-fisted parents.

Halfway through his steak, the talk circled around to Man Ray, which might have surprised him—most women considered former paramours a sensitive topic—had he not known Kiki. Instead, he wouldn't be surprised if she'd brought it up herself, for a chance to declaim her complete lack of interest, her pity for the American replacement, and her detailed predictions of abuse and *catastrophe*.

"You wait," she told her fervent audience. "M. Ray, il a des mauvaises habitudes. In no time at all, l'Américaine will bear the scars of his depravity."

Stuyvesant wondered where she had picked up that particular English phrase, since her English tended towards the monosyllabic and inadvertently spoonerist. But the distressed exclamations of the young men made her preen, and he smiled as he ran the last of the frites through the juice on his plate.

Kiki saw his expression, and bristled. "Est-çe que tu ris de moi, M. 'Arris?"

"No, no," he protested. "I wasn't laughing at you, I was thinking of something else. I'm very sorry, Kiki mon amour." He'd seen Kiki assault a man with a wine bottle, and although she wasn't that boozed up now, she still had a quick temper.

But her feathers went down slowly, and only after she had informed everyone in hearing what a terrible man M. Ray was, and that any girl with less fortitude than Kiki of Montparnasse was at a grave risk of coming to harm.

"You should watch that, Kiki," he warned as he signaled the waiter for l'addition. "Ray could sue you for defamation of character."

"Is it defamation if it is true?" she shouted. "He comes here, he sleeps with the beautiful women, he takes the pictures and gets rich, he says rude things about the French—yes, he does! And if he does some wicked thing, pouf! He is l'artiste, he is expected to make the bad comportement, to make dark things with women, and no one has a soupçonne que lui."

"Oh, come on, Kiki, what is there to suspect the man of?" he chided, counting out money into the saucer. "Having the ego of an elephant? When Man Ray is long forgotten, Paris will still be singing the praises of Kiki of Montparnasse."

She didn't know whether to be offended or pleased, but Stuyvesant took advantage of her silence to get to his feet. He bent, kissing her cheek again. "Sweetheart, you are the queen."

That, she understood. She glowed in pleasure, while around her the courtiers seized her discarded accusations to play with them.

"—dark photographs, I know what she means."

"—really disgusting thing to Maisie the other night, when all she wanted was to have him take a snapshot with her own camera."

"—suppose he had anything to do with that girl who went missing?"

"Girls go missing all the time. Boys, too."

"Yes, but—"

"—about Lulu, poor thing? She was only in here the other night."

Stuyvesant's head snapped around, finding himself staring down at one of Kiki's young artists with scarcely enough facial hair for a mustache. "*What* did you say?"

The boy's eyes went wide, and Stuyvesant forced his shoulders to relax, pasting a smile on his mouth. "Sorry, didn't mean to startle you. I just heard you say something about Lulu, wondered what she was up to."

"She was shot."

The crowded terrace became very silent and still, although no one but Stuyvesant appeared to notice: waiters in slow motion delivered trays; mouths gaped open, then drew shut. Exactly the sensation that followed the *zip* of an unexpected bullet overhead: an infinitely heavy dive for cover, muffled shouts, lethargic return of fire . . .

He blinked, and the activity around him started up again. He might as well have been sitting in the dark theater watching characters poke at an amputated hand.

He cleared his throat. "Shot."

"Yes. She's dead, poor thing. On Tuesday night."

"But I just—"With a huge effort, Stuyvesant caught the words back.

The boy nodded. "I know, she was just in here the other night, so happy and alive. What will her little boy do now?"

"She . . . she had a child?"

"Two. Hard to imagine a woman like that as a mother, isn't it?"

A bearded Jesus in a faded pink beret spoke up. "So irresponsible. The kiddies were left alone half the time."

"No," a third boy objected. "They all lived with the grandmother, so whenever she got arrested or stayed the night with someone, the kids barely noticed."

"Sounds like you knew her really well," the pink beret mocked.

"We were modeling together, one day, and we got to talking. She was sweet, really."

"She was a whore, or as good as."

The sparse mustache objected before Stuyvesant had to. "Hey, don't insult a poor dead woman."

Kiki had permitted the conversation to go on without her long enough. "She picked up the wrong man, it sounds like."

"Hey, we ought to start up a donation, don't you think?"The mustached boy glanced at his companions, who nodded their agreement. "Shall we put you down for a contribution, Mr. . . . ?"

He stood up and pushed his way out of the café, onto the street, away from the crowds. In the rue Vavin, he leaned up against a wall and lit a cigarette with shaking hands.

Jesus Christ: shot. Lulu! Hours after he'd last bedded her, she was dead in . . . where? A bar? Someone's bedroom? Why hadn't he asked?

He hadn't asked because he didn't want anyone to see he cared. Didn't want anyone to put together a dead Lulu with an interested American. He'd met her on Saturday night at the Coupole, one of hundreds of drinkers, and they'd gone back to the hotel. Sunday they spent together, in and out of bed. Monday they might have been seen, but it was late when they'd met at the Coupole (after putting her kids to bed? Oh, Christ) and they hadn't stayed there long.

There was no way he could go to the police. And in any event, why? He was a cop himself—near enough—and he was certain that nothing had happened during his hours with Lulu that would give any hint of her killer: she'd mentioned no names, said hello to no friends, told him no secrets. Going to the *flics* would just waste their time.

Besides which, even if they didn't lock him up while they thought things over, the French had a bad habit of throwing troublesome foreigners out of the country. You disrupt the neighbors, you're invited to leave. You go to the wrong political demonstration, sign the wrong manifesto, you're shown the door.

And he couldn't leave France, not yet. Not only because he hadn't found Pip Crosby, but he was also on the brink of seeing Sarah Grey. He'd waited three years: he wasn't going to leave her with the image of him drunkenly leaning on Nancy Berger.

He stood away from the wall, dropped his cigarette to the street. Best to act as if nothing had happened. Go to your party, work your case. If accused with having spent three nights with the woman (Would they believe he had no idea of her last name?), he'd have to put on a look of shock at the news: Lulu? *Dead?*

Easy enough: just remember how he'd felt on the Dôme terrace.

He put back his shoulders and walked down rue Vavin, turning into little rue Colle and tipping his hat at the flower seller.

His confident plan lasted precisely three steps inside the hotel's entranceway.

"M. Stuyvesant!"

"Bonjour, Mme. Benoit."

"La police était ici."

How often could a man have the breath knocked out of him before his lungs ceased to work? Stuyvesant's raised foot came down, very slowly.

The police. Were here. Looking for that *wrong man* Lulu had picked up? Take a deep breath: be casual, even if the words squeak a little. "Oui? Je travaille avec un Inspecteur Doucet—c'était lui?" I'm working with Doucet, was it him?

"Non, c'était le gendarme du quartier."

Shit. The local cop. But that was good, wasn't it? If they were after him for Lulu, they'd have sent more muscle than a single gendarme. Maybe Bricky had reported him for the fight. Shit again—he'd be out of the country on the next boat.

Do not panic. Take a breath.

"Vraiment? Huh. Que voulait-il?"

"Des documents volés."

Stolen documents? Why would a local cop be looking for stolen documents in his hotel room? But Mme. Benoit didn't know, and she wasn't about to throw his things onto the street because of some cop. If anything, the pointless accusation endeared him to her Parisian heart.

And it had been pointless. She'd shown the guy into Stuyvesant's room herself, kept her eye pinned on him lest he steal something—or plant it. And when he'd found nothing, she'd locked the door again and escorted him out onto the rue Colle. The triumph of la Révolution beamed from her wrinkled face.

Stuyvesant summoned the appropriate enthusiasm. "Mon héroïne!" He seized her gnarled hand to kiss the age-spotted skin, causing her to titter like a girl.

"Vous êtes si charmeur, Monsieur!"

"I save my charms for you, Madame."

"Oh? Et la jeune fille blonde que j'ai vu dans l'escalier le mardi?" She shook a finger at him, and although it had been Monday, not Tuesday, that Lulu had last come up the stairs, he did not want to distress the old woman by pointing out her failing memory.

"Elle n'est seulement un substitute pour vous, Madame."

She slapped his head, then surprised him by putting her hands against his ears and pulling him down for a kiss on his cheek, so soft it felt like being kissed by a cloud.

He forced his feet up the stairs at a more carefree pace than he felt. In his room, he closed the door, turned the lock, set his back against it—and let the bewilderment take him.

Sure enough, the room had been searched: rumpled bedding, a drawer slightly ajar, wardrobe door hanging open, Kiki's book to one side of the brown paper where he'd left it.

At least the *flic* hadn't looked under the carpet. Hadn't found the loose floorboard, the lock picks, the revolver.

He pulled out the hard little desk chair and sat down. After a while, he opened the drawer where he kept the bottle, and took a swallow, then another.

Jesus. First Lulu, then this.

Tuesday night, the kid had told him. Down in Denfert-Rochereau, where a big American had been sitting and smoking a cigarette for any insomniac resident.

Had anyone heard him come in that night? Yeah—that bald guy, coming out of Anouk's for a piss. She probably didn't even know his name.

Why was it a person only had alibis for when he didn't need them?

Lulu wasn't the first person he knew to die violently, but he didn't think he'd ever been sleeping with one a few hours beforehand. "Ferme les rideaux putain!" she'd grumbled at him. Shut the whoring curtains? Shut the curtains, whore? He couldn't ask her now—and what was he doing wondering about that?

God he was tired. Two mornings ago, she'd told him to shut the curtains and curled up against his knee, inviting him back between the sheets. And two nights ago somebody had set a gun to her head— or maybe not her head. How could he know? Did it matter?

He had to stop thinking about it. Nothing to do with him, and nothing he could do about it, anyway. He had enough of a job searching for a twenty-two-year-old American, without stopping to hunt down the killer of a brass-blonde Parisienne in her thirties, or forties. That was for the cops. His only responsibility was to make sure they didn't put him in the frame for it.

And bless Mme. Benoit in all her crusty Commune-ism. He should buy her something extravagant. Wait a few days first, then buy it. Did she like chocolates?

What the hell had the search been about? What documents could Harris Stuyvesant have other than his own *identité*? Or had Mme. Benoit got that wrong, too? Maybe Doucet had sent a *flic* down for something—any other letters from Uncle Crosby perhaps—and the cop had misunderstood the order? Or the concierge had misunderstood the message?

It made no sense.

Worst of all, he couldn't think how he should respond. Would an innocent man phone up Doucet and shout at him? Would he howl in the street? Shrug and go about his way?

He didn't know. It had been too long since Harris Stuyvesant had been an innocent man.

TWENTY-SIX

T HE BONES OF Paris are beautiful.

At the end of the eighteenth century, two events coincided to make them so. In 1774, a long stretch of the rue d'Enfer simply opened from below, tugging in paving stones, houses, and residents, leaving a gaping chasm. A commission was ordered. The Inspector General of Mines mapped out hundreds of kilometers of abandoned mines and quarries, dating back to Roman times, where the limestone marrow had been extracted from the earth to shape the city's magnificent buildings.

While the work of mapping and reinforcing was under way, disease and stench from the literally bulging cemetery of Saints-Innocents, north of the Seine, were becoming intolerable, adding their unease to the spirit of revolution in the air. Further burials were forbidden. The cemetery's Danse Macabré mural—oldest in Europe, built over a plague pit—had long since vanished, but now the Innocents' skeletons began their own dance across Paris: at night, by cartfuls, accompanied by the clop of hooves and the somber chants of priests. It took two years to empty the cemetery and pack the bones into the city's one-time quarries.

A generation later, the Inspector General of Quarries found the rude tangle an offense to sensibilities, and ordered them tidied. Vast underground hallways were transformed into works of art: walls of tibias, mosaics of femurs, neat façades of gleaming skulls. And lest a visitor miss the point, its entrance at the Place D'Enfer bore a warning:

ARRETE! C'EST ICI L'EMPIRE DE LA MORT

Stop! Here lies the empire of death.

Yes, the bones of Paris are beautiful, indeed.

TWENTY-SEVEN

"Wow," said Stuyvesant.

A century and a half ago, one of the Charmentier family had stripped twenty or thirty kilometers of stone from under the ground to build himself a house: two hundred meters of stone wall; a gateway a little smaller than the Arc de Triomphe; the mansion itself forty feet high with gargoyles over the windows, half a dozen balconies, windows gleaming with silken drapes and rich furniture, the gleam of crystal chandeliers . . .

Almost made a man forget to be nervous about a gendarme's tap on his shoulder.

A car debouched a sleek couple, she wearing enough diamonds to buy a small South American country. The man nodded, the woman gave Stuyvesant the kind of look a lady might bestow on a street-sweeper, and they set off across the acre of cobbles. Stuyvesant adjusted his tie, and followed.

Inside the gates, a broad cobblestone yard surrounded a circle of grass with waist-high hedges and a fountain. More lawn and hedges circled the sides of the yard, disappearing around the *hôtel particulier* itself.

The mansion's entrance was flanked by torches—actual fire, not gas replicas. As he approached, he saw how odd the entrance was. But, he'd seen the place before, hadn't he? No, that was its twin brother: a Montmartre café called "L'Enfer"—Hell—with a gigantic fanged mouth surrounding its entrance and scenes from a Mediaeval descent into hell dripping both from the three-story façade and from the interior ceiling.

A lot of hells in his life, at the moment.

This one proved both less permanent, being of plaster and canvas rather than stone, and more disturbing. He didn't remember the one up on Pigalle being quite so . . . emphatic. Maybe it was the eyes? There, they had stared off over a person's head, but here the focus was clear. Or it could be the mouth: the Café L'Enfer's hell-mouth surrounded the delivery door, allowing the customer to slip in a few feet to one side, but here, it was the entrance. There was even a lower lip, with sharp teeth one had to step over, and a sinuous forked tongue waiting to slurp a victim within.

Then there was the trio of doormen, two of them animate: on the left, a slim yellow-haired demon with a long tail looped over his left arm used a trident to urge partygoers inside. On the right, an enormously tall figure draped in black leaned on the handle of a scythe, his face invisible under the shadow of his hood, the *Do come in* gesture of his hand as much threat as promise.

The third doorman was a fully articulated skeleton dressed only in a silk hat and bow tie. He didn't do a whole lot of gesturing.

The diamond-woman hesitated, an understandable response, until Death stretched out one long arm to her; she giggled as her escort hurried her in past the jabbing trident. When the figure made to do the same with Stuyvesant, the big American held up a warning finger. The long arm paused, then drew back, allowing him to enter unmolested.

The entrance hall was vast, dim, and almost unpopulated, apart from the family portraits hanging on the walls, many of whom had that same disdainful nose. Instead, light and noise poured down the monumental stairway directly ahead of him, a structure that had taken a regiment of men a couple of years to complete, what with the carvings and plaster, the curlicues of wrought iron, the square meters of gilding—and, anticlimactically, the velvet rope across the bottom.

Another demonic butler gestured him towards a splash of light around the side of the stairs where, like a Kodak Brownie strapped to a dinosaur, a snug elevator waited.

The lift was unattended; its doorway juddered shut to carry the middle-aged couple upwards. Stuyvesant anticipated some further bit of theatricality—a corpse dropping from the roof perhaps, or water rising up their legs. But in a minute the shaft echoed with the sounds of the door opening, with no further shrieks. Down it came, the door drawing wide in invitation.

To arrive on the second floor without some jolt of adrenaline was almost a disappointment.

The lift gates opened at the top of the stairs. Through a pair of doors lay a kind of upstairs entrance hall with a domed ceiling topped with four windows, dark with the night. The room was a perfect square, its floor an expanse of glossy black-and-white tiles, the walls heavily marbled black-and-white travertine. Mirrors threw the room back and forth into infinity, including the glossy black double doors into the center of each wall. One set opened onto the stairs, and hence the lift. The two across the room were shut, as were those to the left, but those to his right spilled a blaze of electric lights and a whole lot of noise.

He gave his hat and overcoat to a cadaverous butler dressed entirely in black, and walked out into the tile. In addition to the mirrors at the centers, each corner had a statue: two white marble figures, man and woman, and the same in black. However, it was the center of the room that dominated, with an impressive piece of machinery half again as tall as he was. He walked slowly around the thing.

It was a clock, he decided. Or maybe four clocks put together, since each side had its own face. Before him was a timepiece with an ornate bronze face, its hands pointing, correctly, to 8:16. A complex set of decorative wheels around the outer edges overlapped to further inform him that it was Thursday, 12 September, 1929. The next face, to the left, was of mottled silver resembling the full moon. Its main dial appeared to indicate the moon's phase, at present slightly more than halfway towards full; there was another dial as well, marked with hundreds of small lines but no explanation. The face after that was of inky black enamel set with scores of tiny diamond chips, over which a glossy black hand set with larger diamonds pointed to a circle of what Stuyvesant was pretty sure were the signs of the zodiac. There were two other dials, of inscrutable purpose.

The fourth side, facing the noisy ballroom, was golden. One of its dials was a clock like the first side, but showing 24-hour time, now 20:17. Its two other circles had pointing hands, but again, Stuyvesant had no clue what they were trying to tell him.

On the top of all four faces stood Death with a scythe, ready to sweep it at a small hanging bell, to chime the hours.

The bell was in the shape of a human skull.

While he lingered around the clock, the elevator had gone down for another set of guests, a family group of one portly man, his dowdy wife, and their about-to-be-portly young son. The three swept past him with no glance at the clock or its admirer.

Stuyvesant pulled himself away from the contraption and was turning to follow them towards the open doorway, when a familiar shape caught his eye. He walked over the black-and-white tiles to the wall beside the stairway doors: yet another of those boxes like he'd seen in Pip's bedroom and Man Ray's studio. This one seemed linked to the clock at his back: one of the squares was packed with tiny springs, another held an elegant brass cog. The piece of face in this box, occupying the lower right corner, was the photograph of an eye wearing a jeweler's loupe, a man in his fifties or sixties. Here, the large center box held a rather ominous-looking device that was probably a caliper, but could as easily have belonged to an Inquisitor.

The doors led to a ballroom larger than the dance floor of most Paris nightclubs. It was slightly below the level of the black-and-white tiles, and started with a bedroom-sized platform surrounded by an ornately carved marble balustrade, with three steps leading down, left and right. There were similar raised areas at either end of the wall of windows opposite, with a potted palm on the right-hand one and a string quartet playing on the left. He could barely hear the music, partly because of the distance, but mostly because the crowd was paying them about as much attention as they were the potted palm. The din was impressive.

The sea of heads was framed by a spectacular view: the wall was mostly glass, with a lighted formal garden below and the city stretching out beyond. The edges of the garden had the sort of tall, thin trees that made him think of Italy, but the center was a checkerboard, dark and white like the tiles in the entranceway.

All it needed were life-sized chessmen, he thought.

He leaned on the balustrade to survey the crowd, hoping to spot Sarah Grey. As often when one walked into a wall of party noise, the mass of people was mildly repellent. He seemed to be the only solitary being in sight. As he stood there, he became aware of the hair along the back of his neck, and the sense of vulnerability that urged him to put his shoulders to the wall.

His eyes narrowed, searching for the source of his hackles' raising. It was nothing obvious, and the blatant game played by the building's exterior was absent here: no hell-mouths, no imps crouched on the blazing electric chandeliers, no dead-faced wraiths circulating with trays of champagne. But there was something. And whatever it was, it was having the same effect on the others.

High voices, nervy eyes, frozen smiles: there was fear in this room, but he couldn't find the source. That suggested the fear came from some insider knowledge, something these people knew and refused to acknowledge. It reminded him of a party he'd been to, working undercover at the Bureau, where glancing looks and too-bright conversation had swirled around a crime boss with a dangerously short temper. But when he located Charmentier, standing near the fireplace with a glass in his hand, the glances and brightness seemed no greater there than across the room.

If Charmentier was a threat, his guests did not know it—and looking at him, neither did he. Le Comte looked like a man who had produced an abundant banquet although he'd have been happy with dry toast. Like a man whose pleasures were always tinged with the bittersweet.

Stuyvesant couldn't help resenting that look, just a little. Here was a guy as rich as Croesus, with half of Paris ready to answer the snap of his finger, and the best he could manage was a faint smile and a picturesque air of melancholy. Half the people in the room would give a major body part to take their host's place for a few nights. Including certain private investigators, who'd had to beg to be put in touch with an old friend, who would go home to a cold-water hotel room, where he'd go to sleep with one ear open in case the local cops decided to drop in for another senseless search and—

He hadn't realized how tightly he was focused on his host by the fireplace until a hand touched his sleeve. He whirled, then dropped his raised fist in a hurry. "Sarah! Jesus, sorry, I didn't hear you coming."

"Obviously. Mr. Stuyvesant, are you quite all right?"

Mr. Stuyvesant, he noted with a pang. He told his body to relax, made himself lean one hip against the hand-rail, put an easy smile on his face. "Yeah, I'm fine, it's been a funny kind of a week. Hey, I'm really sorry about last night, I just hadn't realized how much bubbly Bricky's guys had been pouring into my glass. I hope your . . . friends are all right?"

"Mr. Ray is merely an acquaintance, although he said last night that he was fine. As for my employer, he, too, is unhurt."

"I hunted him down this morning, to apologize—well, you'll know that, I guess, since I'm here. I wasn't sure if he actually was okay, or just being manly about it."

"Oh, I think he'd leave those games to you, Mr. Stuyvesant."

"Ouch. You really must be mad at me."

Her face shifted, becoming ever so slightly embarrassed. "One doesn't like to see one's friends brawling in public."

"Especially when your boss is the victim of that friend's idiocy."

Her smile was unwilling, but it was there. In return, he gave her his very best grin. "It's great to see you, Sarah—you're looking peachy. What're you up to? How's your brother?"

She was not looking peachy, she was looking thin and modern, but his ready acceptance of being demoted to *friend* took her tension down a few notches. "I'm very well, thank you. I live here now—'here' in Paris, not 'here' in Montparnasse—and I'm finding it very much to my taste. As for Bennett, he's doing pretty well, considering. I had a letter from him this morning, along with a picture of him that had been pressed into a sort of brooch. Whimsical, you know? But he seemed to think it had been taken by an agent of that group, spying on him."

"The so-called 'Truth Project'? I'm sorry to hear that."

"Of course, he is more than a little paranoid about them, so it could have been just a stray photographer. In any event, his letter sounded more amused than disturbed."

Sarah's brother Bennett was, for lack of a better term, a human lie-detector. Twelve years ago, a bomb on the Western Front had stripped the man of any normal psychic defenses, rendering him excruciatingly sensitive to the world around him. The dissonance of lies, those every-day deceptions of human interaction, caused not just mental distress, but physical pain—Stuyvesant had heard his friend keen with agony at a lie. Grey walked through life as if he'd been flayed raw. The government was thrilled; their interest in his abilities had nearly killed him.

"Surely they can see that he's better left alone?"

"Yes, except he's no longer such a complete hermit. He even came to see me in the spring."

"Your brother comes to Paris?"

"Just once, so far. It's partly why I live down in Vaugirard—you know it? A quiet suburb with market-gardens. It's inconvenient, but I thought he might find it less trying than the center of town. My neighbors—villagers, really—have seen so much shell-shock, they didn't find his twitches anything out of the ordinary. Bennett developed quite a friendship with the farrier, when he was here."

"Now, there's a picture." Grey was not much taller than Sarah, with the same pale hair and emerald eyes. From a distance, he could be an adolescent boy—about as far from a blacksmith's build as one could get.

"It is a bit Mutt and Jeff," she agreed.

"I imagine the blacksmith is a placid sort of a person?"

"Bennett says that the man could wheedle purrs from a bull."

Stuyvesant laughed. "I miss your brother," he said, unthinking.

"You could go and see him."

"Yeah."

"I know, Cornwall is a long way from anywhere. Well, perhaps he'll come to Paris, one time you're here. Why *are* you here, anyway? Are you working? Back with . . . ?"

"The Bureau? No, I'm long quit of them. I went independent. At the moment I'm looking for a girl. Her mother and uncle haven't heard from her in too long, so I said I'd help."

"Oh dear. Would I know her?"

"Pip Crosby? Philippa, her name is. American, blonde, blue eyes, about your height, twenty-two years old. Has a flat just off the boulevard de Sébastopol, and seems to have spent more of her time on the Right Bank than I'd have expected."

"Is that the person you were asking Dominic about? Does she have some connection with him?"

"One or two links cropped up, I wanted to ask him about them. Which I did, this morning."

"And?"

"Sarah, I can't tell you about an investigation."

"Was that girl you were with last night helping you 'investigate'?" He looked at her in surprise, and was pleased to see her blush, just a little. "None of my business," she said briskly. "No, I don't think I ever met your Miss Crosby. Or if I did, she's faded into fifty other young blonde Americans."

"Tell me about Dominic Charmentier, then."

"Why should I?"

"Because he's an interesting character."

"He works hard to be."

He might have interpreted the dry words as scorn, but there was a trace of admiration in her tone of voice. "How do you mean?"

She reached for her little evening bag, but Stuyvesant got there first, popping open his silver cigarette case. Was her faint hesitation because she wondered if it held her photo?

She said nothing, merely pried out a cylinder with her fingernail and allowed him to light it for her.

"I don't suppose you've been to the Grand-Guignol?" She turned her back on the crowd, propping her slimmed-down backside against the railing.

"I have, in fact."

"So you'll have seen how much of the performance is offstage. The spooky theater, its house doctor, the setting. But have you any idea of the role management plays? As a sort of sub-stratum to the enterprise?"

"Probably not."

"Everyone you see here tonight has been specifically chosen because of his or her influence in Paris society. There are two newspaper owners, with three of their editors and seven journalists, half a dozen fashion designers, the Maires of three arrondissements, five factory owners, the directors or owners of all the major department stores, a few Comtes and Vicomtes, a couple of Barons, and more chevaliers than I can recall. This is in addition to the writers and artists—I don't even try to keep track of those, since none of them reply to an RSVP, and when they arrive they have uninvited friends."

"Like me."

"Oh, you were invited. Le Comte gave me your name this morning."

"What's the point? Of gathering all these movers and shakers together?"

"Ask me that at the end of the evening," she said.

"Ah. Do I take it we have a surprise in store for us?"

"I couldn't say."

The smile that replied to his laughter was a prize, but he wasn't about to push it. "So tell me about your boss and the . . . sub-stratum."

She glanced at her wrist-watch. "Better if I show you. Come."

They stood shoulder to shoulder while a trio of languid women with too much makeup came slinking through the heavy doors. Stuyvesant's fingers felt the impulse to reach out for her hand, but he stifled it, and let her move in front of him into the black-and-white foyer. There she kicked away the props from the double doors, allowing them to drift shut. When they had done so, she pointed at them, although she herself turned to face the big clock.

Obediently, Stuyvesant looked at the doors. The carving was ornate, although the light here was not strong enough to . . . Wait. Was that . . . ?

Yes. This side of the door—panels, frame, even its brass fittings—

was one solid mass of writhing bodies, intertwined legs and arms punctuated by the twin smoothness of buttocks and breasts. When the door stood open, the frieze that might startle a Parisian sophisticate would be all but invisible—although even then, the door latch on the plain side now bore a suspicious resemblance to a male member.

"Well," he said. Was she blushing again? Impossible to tell in this light.

"Yes, I know," she said. "Although I think this is just his private joke. Come and see the rest."

The door was the celebration, albeit somewhat twisted, of lively lust. "The rest" was its opposite.

The rest was death.

TWENTY-EIGHT

Harris Stuyvesant stood in front of a wall of tortured faces and wondered what the hell to say. Sarah's tour of the house had showed him everything from mummies to a set of Renaissance silver spoons engraved with skulls to a chandelier made out of bones. A drawing room was decorated with African death-masks coated in pale clay to imitate bone, Mediaeval depictions of the tortures of hell, South American pottery of priests removing hearts, and pieces of modern art on a theme of death (Harlequin on his death-bed; a wild man with a descending knife; mourners surrounding a dying man in a claustrophobic room). One wall of the library was covered with a painting by a Bosch imitator that lovingly explored the many ways human beings can inflict torture and death. The shelves on either side of it held volumes concerning the extermination of witches, illustrated anatomy books, and medical tomes describing procedures far worse than the illness they were intended to heal. Behind glass was an unpublished manuscript from the Marquis de Sade, rescued from his son's flames by a servant.

But of all the Baroque horrors in Charmentier's living theater of the macabre, this wall of faces in a small side-salon was the worst.

"What the hell are these?"

"Strangely enough, they are the work of a well-meaning woman. During the War, an American sculptress came to Paris to make prosthetic masks for soldiers with terrible facial injuries. She made them out of copper, meticulously detailed. The masks made it possible for the men to walk the streets without causing children to scream. These are the molds she worked from, showing the men's true faces, beneath their masks."

"Jesus," he said. And a minute later, "God, those poor bastards."

There were dozens of the stark plaster heads. All showed grotesque perversions of the human visage: faces shattered and crudely glued together, skin grown over missing noses and craters like moss over fallen rock. With their closed eyelids, they looked like death-masks. Having fought beside them, Stuyvesant was in no doubt that every one of those men would have preferred a clean death.

"What is Charmentier doing with them?"

"He bought them when the studio was closed, after Miss Ladd moved back to America."

"They should have been smashed to dust. But what I meant was, why does your boss collect all this?"

"I know, as if his life hasn't been dark enough. I sometimes wonder if by putting it 'out there' to look at, he doesn't have it inside him quite so much. Oh, that doesn't make a lot of sense, does it?"

"Yes, in a way. Although it could also be that he just likes the creepy stuff."

She glanced at her watch rather than open an argument. "We need to get back to the party."

"Are we waiting for something?"

"With Dominic, we generally are."

"A surprise?"

"One that even you won't guess," she said, sounding smug.

He opened a door, and they were back in the tiled entryway where the great clock ticked off the age of the universe.

"That's quite a device," Stuyvesant commented.

"Isn't it, though? There's some terribly sad story about it, that the poor clockmaker who built it committed suicide when it was finished, knowing he would never build anything greater."

"Really?"

"It's probably not true. A lot of the stories about Dominic are sheer fiction—do you know, I overheard a story about him at a party last week that I'd made up myself!"

"Why would you do that?"

"It's part of the act, dear boy. The more people imagine him as a wicked, debauched creature, the more they flock into the Grand-Guignol."

"Doesn't strike me as a very comfortable way to live."

"I suppose someone with a notorious name has to choose either to fight against the common belief, or just decide to go with it."

"How do you mean?"

"Oh, the usual thing. The French adore their nobles, but the aristocrats are the first to feel the guillotine. There's all kinds of titillating stories about the nobility: droit de seigneur, cellars full of pretty girls, corruption and perversion. The Charmentiers may have had a few unpleasant characters in their family tree—Dominic thinks there was syphilis in a couple of the generations, and you know what that does to the brain—but no more than any others. You know about the garden chessboard?"

"I noticed there was one."

"That's a good example of the stories. People will tell you that one of Dominic's ancestors built that garden feature just before the Terror, when the Vicomte and some close friends used to play with human pieces—except when the pieces were captured, they'd actually be impaled, or decapitated."

"Eighteenth-century gladiators," Stuyvesant commented.

"Ridiculous, of course. But that's what I mean, all sorts of mad stories circulate around the aristocracy here. Dominic welcomes them—they all feed back into the Grand-Guignol. He and Man Ray are talking about doing a film in the garden. You know Man's an ardent chess player?"

"I saw the chessboards in his studio. I take it the film will involve decapitations?"

"Probably."

"Is that what he was sketching for Le Comte on the tablecloth last night?"

"No, that was something else."

"Can I ask you, what do you think of him? Ray, that is?"

"He's a pompous ass, but he's madly talented. Why?"

"Oh, just an argument a friend and I were having."

"What kind— Oh," she said with a glance at her watch. "I must go."

"What's behind that door?" he asked, pointing across the entrance-way. He'd been through three of the doorways: the grand stairway, the ballroom, and the private residence. This pair remained shut.

Sarah glanced across the tile where he was pointing. "I suppose it's more of the residence. Come on."

The ballroom had been full before. Now the guests were shoulder-to-shoulder, and the level of what Stuyvesant had taken for fear had risen with the noise. It had to be merely anticipation, these people knowing Charmentier and his Guignol theatrics. Still, it raised his hackles, feeling like anxiety rather than eagerness. He bent his head to Sarah, at his side on the raised entranceway.

"What's giving everyone the heebie-jeebies?"

To his astonishment, she gave him a grin that shot a jolt of familiarity down his spine: the Sarah Grey of old, alive with mischief. "You caught it! I should have known you would. Harris, you wouldn't believe how much time I spend producing effects that no one notices. Except you, and—well, I'd guess it's the policeman in you."

"Been a while since I was any kind of a cop. And what are you talking about?"

"The effect. So: how would you go about frightening a crowd of educated, well-to-do people—especially if they're anticipating it? What subtle influences can one inflict on them to slide under their guards? Look, and tell me what you—what you perceive."

Her hesitation gave him a clue. He studied the room, blanking out the cacophony of high-pitched conversations. "Is it something to do with the lights?"

"Very good. Yes, it's partly the lights. We tried them with a bluer tint, but that made everything look like the bottom of a swimming pool. With this, they just make people look slightly ill. What else?"

"Maybe, the music? It's hard to hear under all the shouting."

"You're close. It's a wave of vibration being piped in from all four corners of the room. If everyone were to stop talking, you'd hear it, a noise almost too low for the ears, but it gets on your nerves like nothing in the world. And there's a third thing."

He listened, he looked, but in the end had to shake his head. "I don't see it."

"That's the really dreadful one—and I had nothing to do with it. There's a smell. Can you catch it? Probably not now, with all the perfume and smoke, but even if the room were empty you might not notice it. Consciously, that is. Dominic says that the mind has dark little pockets that react to certain kinds of odors. One of those is a dead body."

"Your boss planted a *corpse* here? For a *party*?"

"Harris! Of course not, what do you think of me?"

"Sorry. Overreacting. Like I say, it's been a tough week." He emptied the glass, wished he had another, and gave her his best deprecating smile. "So if not a body, how did he do it?"

"He replaced some of the soil around his palms with earth from a graveyard. Which frankly I thought a bit silly, but it's his house."

But no Great War soldier would ever call that reaction silly. The smell brought an instant and bone-deep revulsion, and although graveyard soil might in fact be too dilute, he wouldn't use the word *silly* anywhere in its vicinity.

He fought the impulse to lift his handkerchief to his nose.

Sarah gave her watch another quick look, but they appeared to have some time left before whatever surprise was scheduled, because she plucked a graceful flute of champagne from a passing tray and took a deep swallow. A reward for her labors, or fortification against what was to come? He shifted, in order to see her better, and she glanced up, eyebrows arched in a question.

"I just wondered if you were bracing yourself against whatever bit of theater is on its way."

"Oh no," she replied. "I've become fairly hardened to it all. Just a long day, is all."

"Nearly over."

"Not quite. I have to go somewhere with Dominic after this."

"What, the Select? Even Bricktop's will have shut by the time this lot takes off."

"No, not a bar. He has a pet . . . artist he promised to go see."

"Doesn't sound like one of your favorite people."

"Oh, he's all right. I should be grateful, really. He made this hand for me. And half a dozen others. He's just . . . even for Montparnasse he's an odd egg."

"I cannot imagine what it takes to be considered odd for Montparnasse. Two heads? Drives around in a cart hitched to a unicorn?"

"Perhaps not *that* odd. It's . . . Well . . . You know how some people simply rub you the wrong way, and you can never say why? He's just . . . strange. He lives like a hermit, in this house that seems to have more cellar than upstairs, and rarely goes out except for Sunday morning Mass. He has no social graces, although I try to tell myself that it's not his fault his eyes are bad and he has to stand right up close to one, or that his hands are cold and he *will* insist on touching—"

She broke off, with an uncomfortable laugh. He said nothing. After a sip at her glass and a survey of the room, she resumed. "As you can tell, I am not fond of the man. But it's part of my job to deal with him, and there's no doubt he's a remarkable artist. Those are his— Oh, you probably can't see them in this light. If you get a chance, make your way over and look at that collection between the two big portraits."

Stuyvesant followed where she was indicating. On the side wall between a pair of larger-than-life paintings of two people so ugly they might be called grotesque were eight or ten small, square shapes. He didn't have to fight his way across the crowded room to know what they were.

"The boxes."

"Oh, you saw them?"

"Not those particular ones, no. But there were two similar ones in the bedroom of the girl I'm looking for. Signed DIDI."

"That's right, he calls himself Didi, although I'm not sure why. His name is Hyacinthe—Hyacinthe Moreau. He got started as a taxidermist, and made prosthetic hands during the War, but the last few years, some of the influential names in the art world have taken him on—including Dominic—and his Displays are becoming enormously popular. One never knows what will catch on."

Stuyvesant felt a click, somewhere in the depths of his memory. Sarah kept talking (. . . *thanks to Dominic that his pieces are selling so well, which means Didi now has all the time in the world to play with his Displays. That's what he calls it, "playing"—unfortunate how that always brings to mind the image of a small child playing with the contents of its nappies. Oh, that's awful of me—you won't say anything to—*) but his mind stood empty, waiting for the connection.

The word *display.* In a bar: a conversation, recently overheard. In English—Americans? Artists, he thought—and with that came the flood of recognition: Those three artists, Tuesday night in Frank's bar: Didi, not titty. *The Didi Displays . . . that disturbing* frisson *of visceral excitement . . .*

He blinked, and cut into what she was saying. "I'd like to meet him."

"Who, Didi? You wouldn't like him."

"Still. Where does he live?"

"He won't see you. He never sees anyone."

"Except you and Charmentier."

"Well, Dominic is his patron, and . . . Oh. You want me to introduce you."

"Will you?"

"No!"

"Please? Sarah, there's a girl missing. I wouldn't ask this of you if I didn't think it might help."

The green eyes glared. He thought she was going to walk away. Then they wavered, and looked instead at the half-empty glass in her hand. "Damn," she began, "and I hadn't meant to—"

But he never heard the end of the sentence, and Sarah never tasted the end of the drink, because her hand jerked along with everyone else's when the piercing, full-throated scream of a woman in terror sliced through the tumult of the room, reducing it to oaths and squeals and the sound of breaking glass.

TWENTY-NINE

S ILENCE FELL, HEAVY and absolute. Before anyone could even cough, a tight spotlight flared into life. It illuminated two of the astonished musicians, staring out over the crowd. The light jerked. It flitted crazily across the room, pausing on first one small group of frightened faces, than another. One of its apparently random jerks brought it to the fireplace where Charmentier stood, his head turned now to look at the far right corner, at a small dais that duplicated the quartet's platform. As if in obedience, the light flew across to that corner.

Besides its palm tree stood a woman. Tall, buxom, dressed in an ivory evening gown. The jewels in her pale hair threw light as only real diamonds could. Behind her was a velvety black background from which sparked similar diamond reflections. The woman stood very still, one arm stretched to point up, her lips slightly parted from that prodigious scream.

The tiny sound of approval Sarah made snapped Stuyvesant from his shock: here was the production she had been waiting for—had herself planned, in fact, judging by the sound. That it had taken her unawares only proved the effectiveness of the woman's voice.

A ripple of murmurs passed through the crowd as they realized that their host had pulled off another of his anticipated coups de théâtre. But before the sound could mount, the woman spoke.

"Mesdames et messieurs," she began in formal cadence, "je suis la pleine lune, qui monte le ciel de nuit." I am the full moon, mounting the night sky, Stuyvesant began translating to himself, but after that he started to lose words, and the sense of what she was saying. Something about the coming equinox, Africa, and some kind of alignment—her French vocabulary was either very colloquial, or very formal. Then she used the word *sanglant*: bloody. In a flash, the spotlight went crimson. Her gown, her hair, and her sparkling jewels turned to blood, causing another ripple of reaction through the audience.

Her voice climbed, the words coming faster as she spoke of blood and cleansing. He thought it was blood as a cleansing thing, rather than cleaning off the blood, but what with the speed and the way this damned language tended to drop off all the endings, he couldn't be sure. Whatever it was seemed to get her all worked up, and he wasn't especially surprised (having so recently sat in the Grand-Guignol itself) when she reached up her sleeve and drew out an impressive knife. She spent a while caressing it, kissing it, reciting what sounded like a poem about blood. She then held it high. Throwing back her head like an eager lover, she plunged the dagger into her breast. With a strangled cough that brought up the hair on the back of his neck, she collapsed.

The light jerked away as if the man at the controls had fallen off his chair in shock. And then the red filter was snatched away, and the long white beam traveled across the ceiling, descending, timidly seeking the terrible sight of the full-moon lady, collapsed and *ensanglantée*. The stripe found the wall and became a circle; the diamond-stars of the backdrop sparked back in response.

But when the beam touched the stage, all it revealed were bones: bones, and a drift of ancient satin, and the harsh bright-red glitter of the necklace that lay at the chin of the woman's grinning skull.

Long after the applause had died away, after the guests, relieved at last by a climax to the evening's tensions, turned with renewed vigor to drink and food, after the talk had caused the chandeliers to vibrate and the ears to ache, the party began to die away at last. Stuyvesant lingered, spending time with the Displays, standing at the window and gazing down at the grass-and-marble checkerboard in the garden, stubbornly keeping watch over the small, exhausted woman he cared too much about. All the time, Le Comte, with Sarah at his elbow, said long and friendly good-byes to his guests. When the crowd had thinned to the last twenty or so, the big American joined them.

He thrust out his hand. "Congratulations. That was quite a show."

"I am glad you enjoyed it," the Frenchman answered.

"Thanks again for inviting me. And your house is, well, magnificent."

"For that you should thank several generations of my family."

"I admit I didn't quite catch everything the moon lady was saying. Something about a bloody equinox?"

"More or less."

"Was there a point to it?"

Sarah answered him. "The theater is about to debut a new play about Africa, with elements of the full moon. You know, the idea of lunacy being tied to the moon? This was by way of introducing the play."

"Ah, I see. Get everyone talking."

"That's the idea."

"But what was all that she was saying?"

"Harris," Sarah broke in, "M. Charmentier needs to say good-night to his other guests."

"Oh, of course. Well, thanks for inviting me, it was fun."

"You must come again," he said politely.

But Stuyvesant deliberately misunderstood. "Oh, are you having another of these shindigs? I'd love to join."

"*Pardon.*" Charmentier frowned. "'Shindig'?"

"Soirée. Party, you know?"

Sometimes, the act of bumpkin could be a tool to disarm. Other times, it achieved the opposite, stirring interest. With Charmentier, it was the latter. He tipped his aristocratic head, hearing the crass attempt at manipulation, and seemed amused.

"Miss Grey, do we have room for one more for our event next week?"

"I think we could manage."

"Send M. Stuyvesant an invitation, would you please?"

"Certainly." She put her hand on the American's arm, to gently urge him away, but Charmentier was not finished.

"Oh wait, I nearly forgot," the Frenchman said, although it appeared to be less a matter of remembering than of deciding. He slid his hand into his pocket. "I saw this on the street, Mr. Stuyvesant. It made me think of you."

In the center of the slim palm lay a newly minted ten-centime piece. One half of it was gleaming and perfect, the other appeared to have been run over by a metal cart-wheel heavy with grit. Stuyvesant took it, running his thumb over the deeply scored surface as if to smooth it: fresh, shiny, damaged.

"You just happened to find this," Stuyvesant said. "After our discussion about just this manner of damage."

"Such things often come to those whose eyes are open."

"Hell of a coincidence."

"There may be a hell, M. Stuyvesant, but there is no coincidence. Objects are given when one requires them."

Bennett Grey would know if this was deception: Stuyvesant couldn't tell. "Or one makes them, and pretends."

"Why would I wish to do that?"

"To appear omniscient, I'd guess. To show you have God in your pocket."

Sarah was following this incomprehensible duel with increasing unease. Before the room could explode in flames, or violence, she again took the American's arm, firmly this time.

"Harris, come along now, it's getting late and the other guests will be wanting their beds."

Charmentier's eyes moved over to his assistant's face, and he smiled. "You look tired, my dear. You did fine work tonight. Go home now, have a glass of wine with your beau. I'll say good-bye to my guests and go see Didi on my own."

She only made a token protest before thanking him and pulling Stuyvesant away, turning on him in vexation.

"What was that all about?"

"Just something he and I were talking about this morning. How you never seem to see fresh coins anymore."

She didn't believe him, but Stuyvesant didn't care, because the Frenchman's words were ringing in his ears. *Your beau.* Charmentier's mistake warmed his heart—and not only because it showed that Le Comte could be wrong.

"Hey, Sarah, I know it's late, but like the man said, how about you and me—"

She wasn't listening. Stuyvesant turned, and saw the man coming down the steps against the stream.

"Well," Stuyvesant commented, "it's fashionable to arrive late, but this is a little extreme."

When the figure rounded the bottom of the stairs and turned towards them, he recognized Stuyvesant, raising his hand in a brief gesture. Sarah took a step towards the late-comer, but Stuyvesant caught her hand for a last, urgent remark—taking care to keep his manner light, even teasing. "Nice to be called your beau."

She shot a glance at the approaching man. "Harris, I—I'm sorry. I should have told you this earlier. Dominic wasn't talking about you. Harris, I . . ."

But the late-comer was there. He needed a shave and had bruised-looking circles under his eyes, but his face relaxed as he approached. Sarah waited until he was standing beside her. Until he had bent down to give her raised cheek an affectionate kiss. Until he'd held out his hand to Stuyvesant, looking puzzled. She took a breath.

"Harris, this is Émile Doucet. My . . . fiancé."

THIRTY

A CLOCK COUNTS OFF the seconds of a human life.
There is satisfaction, one *tick* carrying the echoes of a countless number yet to come.

There is disquiet, one *tick* taking a person ever closer to cessation: when measured by Time, we are but a swing of the pendulum.

Olivier Lambert was a clockmaker. He began as a locksmith, with a small shop on the Rive Droite, where he might have continued building locks and answering late-night summonses to let keyless people into their houses, except that one day, a Danish locksmith-turned-clockmaker named Jens Olsen happened in. The two men fell to talking; the conversation grew into friendship. Over a series of amiable nights and mornings, Olsen told Lambert of fabulous clocks that measured not only the day, but the eons. During his months in Paris, he taught Lambert many of the clockmaker's skills.

When Olsen left Paris, Lambert closed his shop for a pilgrimage to Strasburg and Prague. He studied the great cathedral clocks and talked his way into their intricately calibrated works. His sketchbooks filled.

Back in Paris, he started to build: astronomical clocks measuring seconds, minutes, years; clocks that parsed the phases of the moon and positions of the stars; mechanisms that knew their way to eclipses and breathed in and out with the motions of the tides.

In 1913, a wealthy Parisian nobleman—home on leave from the

Front's carnage and desperate for a promise of the future—hired Lambert to make the greatest clock of his career.

It would have a central drive stem, from which grew four faces. It could be as ornately worked as the clockmaker wished, money being even less of an object for the aristocrat than it was for Lambert.

He spent twelve years building his masterpiece. His workshop was a room in this employer's Paris mansion. There he made his tools, cut the gears, experimented with metals, engraved the faces. Whatever he asked for—gold, precious stones, experts in champlevé and basse-taille enamel—he received. During the War, progress was slow, but each time the nobleman came home on leave, he would spend long hours studying the mechanism taking form at the very center of the house. And each time he went back to the Front, he urged Lambert to continue his work.

The war ended, the clock grew, until in the autumn of 1925, it was finished at last. Just in time for the nobleman's fiftieth birthday. A party was planned.

As Lambert took apart his workshop and packed away his tools, he fretted over what future there might be for a fifty-nine-year-old clockmaker who had held one job in the past dozen years. There had been some communication—a wealthy Englishman with a derelict clock that needed rebuilding—but Olivier Lambert did not want merely to repair a mechanism, not when his mind was bubbling with new ideas.

On the night of the party, he wound Le Comte's clock and stood by as his employer set it to ticking, to the cheers of his gathered friends. Later, in the wee hours of December 22, for the last time Olivier Lambert ran his hands over the magnificent four-faced clock that had been his life for all those years.

His drowned body surfaced a week later, in Le Havre.

THIRTY-ONE

THE HOUSE OF Hyacinthe Moreau was at first sight unexpected. Having seen Didi's work, Stuyvesant wouldn't have been surprised by a haunted mansion with shuttered windows, or a garret above a mortuary. An *appartement* in the catacombs, maybe.

Instead, Sarah led him to a neat, two-story house set back from a tree-lined street in the XIII arrondissement. Looking over the stone wall, he saw what looked like the home of a bank teller with a buxom wife and three very average children—or it would have, had the paint been fresher and the tiny front garden better tended. As it was, the rose-bushes that had originally lined the walk now reached thorny fingers towards the iron gate, catching at the clothing as one entered. And as they picked their way through the garden, Stuyvesant saw the cracks in the window trim.

"You suppose Sleeping Beauty lives here?" he asked.

Sarah's reply was an exclamation, at the branch of stickers attaching itself to her sleeve. He went to rescue her, but she pulled away with a jerk.

She was either impatient or frightened, and had been since she met him at the Métro stop ten minutes before. Of course, he had been late: not only did it take Mme. Benoit some time to wake him for the phone call, since he'd spent most of the night shooting awake at every creak of the stairs, but he'd also been delayed by having to hunt through her stack of morning papers before he found even a small piece about a shooting near Denfert-Rochereau: three lines. That's all Lulu got.

Still, he thought the problem was less his tardiness than her disclosure about Émile Doucet.

He kept quiet. Time enough to talk when they were finished with the maker of hands.

They ran the rose-bush gauntlet without bloodshed. The door knocker assured him that they were at Moreau's house and not Snow White's: it was a metal gargoyle with a movable upper jaw. Sarah plucked the maxilla gingerly from its rest and let it fall. They listened to the echoes die away. After a minute, she repeated the act. Nothing.

"You sure he's home?"

"The note said ten o'clock," she replied. "Oh, and I should warn you about the smell—it's from what he calls his 'corruption boxes.' Part of the taxidermy process."

Great, thought Stuyvesant: *another source of eye-watering summer stink*. He raised his fist to the door, but before he could pound, it clicked, and opened. A tiny house-maid all in black looked through the gap, like a child with a pinched face. She nodded at Sarah and sniffed at him, saying in a stuffed-sounding voice, "Bonjour, Mademoiselle."

"Bonjour, Madame Jory. Nous avons un rendez-vous avec M. Moreau," Sarah said in fluid French. We have an appointment with Monsieur Moreau.

"Vraiment?" The woman's thin eyebrows rose.

Sarah dug the note out of her handbag and gave it to the maid, who snuffed again, read it closely, and returned it with what might have been a shake of the head.

"Il semblerait donc," she agreed: so it would seem. "Venez avec moi."

Had her initial reaction not told them that guests were unexpected here, her failure to take their coats confirmed it. She just led them across a foyer that looked like an illustration for The Classic French Home, knocked on a closed door, opened it without waiting for an answer, and put her head inside to shout, "Monsieur, vos visiteurs sont ici."

Then she stood back with a long, drawn-out sniff—a nasal condition, he decided, rather than an expression of disapproval. By the musky smell that welled from the doorway, a blocked nose might be a requirement for employment here.

The stairs inside were narrow, steep, and uncarpeted, lit by a small bulb dangling from a wire overhead. Stuyvesant had seen entrances to servants' quarters that were less enticing, and there was no question here of "ladies first." He tried each step before committing his weight to it, tense with the anticipation of attack.

He reached the bottom without incident, and emerged from the tunnel of stairs into a low-ceilinged room. An odor of damp was inevitable, given the basement setting, but this was far worse. The place smelled as if rats had died in the walls.

The cellar's occupant was nowhere in sight. This was definitely his lair: in one corner was a stack of the wooden frames he used for his Displays, empty and glassless. A work table had boxes in progress: one was filled with the skulls of what could only be birds, fragile and delicate, displayed against a background of color—even in the dim light one could see colors from cardinal red to peacock blue. Another held the pelt (if that was the word) of a hummingbird behind an impossibly tiny, needle-beaked skull. The room's only other furnishing was a cheaply built chest of drawers some three feet high and two wide.

Stepping forward to examine the three boxes brought a passageway into view. There he found another work-room, and following that, a third. The place was a labyrinth. And it would appear that many, if not all, of the pieces on the walls were unfinished, since few had glass over the contents, and each room had a cabinet of drawers. Opening a few, Stuyvesant discovered objects similar to those of the nearby boxes. And bones: many, many bones.

A man's echoing voice broke the damp stillness. Stuyvesant turned, but Sarah was not behind him, and he realized in a panic that the labyrinth had more than one way around. He hurried towards the voice— two voices now—but came to a dead end. Backtracking, he found another room without an exit . . . until finally he rounded a corner, to be met by the sight of Sarah and a very peculiar little man, framed against a wall of amputated hands.

The sight set him back on his heels—but they were not human taxidermy, they were prosthetic limbs, kith and kin to the wall of plaster faces in Charmentier's house. *Christ,* he thought, *what next: a wall of buttocks?*

There must have been a hundred of them, in all colors and sizes, ranging in extent from a glove to a full sleeve: here, a cluster of various attitudes of hand for a long-fingered man, ending at the wrist; there, a row of five arms that were fitted just below the armpit, their elbows bent at five slightly different angles. A surprising number were for women, their fingers posed for everything from a near-hook to open and relaxed.

He blinked, and looked at Sarah. The little man was holding her hand. Not with affection—and definitely not on her part, since she was looking at the fellow like she had his pesky rose-bushes. But even he had an attitude less of a lover than of a palm-reader.

In any case, she was in no immediate threat. Stuyvesant cleared his throat to cover his alarm. "The place is a maze," he said. "I couldn't see where you'd gone."

"Harris, this is Hyacinthe Moreau. As you can see, he is among other things a maker of prosthetic hands. Didi, this is an old friend, Harris Stuyvesant."

Reluctantly, it seemed, the creature of the cellars let go of Sarah and permitted Stuyvesant's hand to wrap around his. It was a fragile thing, its fingers as bird-like as the bones he used. The rest of the man was similar: narrow shoulders, thin wrists, and a nose like a beak. His blue eyes were so pale they looked white, set in pasty skin that might never have been introduced to sunlight.

The artist winced at having his hand shaken, and retrieved his fingers with an air of having to count them. He returned his attention to Sarah.

Stuyvesant was amused to see her tuck her own extremity away, then fail to notice Moreau's attempts at retaking it.

"My dear Mlle. Grey, you must permit me to touch up your hand," the night-dweller protested in a reedy voice. "It is a thing of such loveliness, attached to a lovely lady, to permit it to grow worn is a great pity."

"Didi, you have better things to do than fuss with my tin hand,"

Sarah replied with a satisfactory firmness. "I brought Mr. Stuyvesant here to talk to you about a girl he's looking for, whom he thinks you might know."

"A girl?"

Stuyvesant caught himself before he could respond with, *Yes, girls— you know, prettier than boys and with bumps under their shirts?* Instead, he took out a copy of Pip's snapshot. The thin fingers closed on it like the appendages of some wall-climbing lizard, and Moreau bent over the photo. Myopic, but no glasses. Vain?

"Mlle. Crosby," he said.

"That's right. You know her?"

"I cannot say I know her. I have met her. Briefly, once."

"How did that come about?"

"She came with one of my . . . friends."

"Which friend?"

"Just . . . a friend."

Sarah broke in. "Was it Le Comte?"

"A kind man. He brings me many useful gifts."

"What sorts of things are those?"

Reluctantly, the pale gaze left Sarah to look—briefly—at her companion before continuing down the room to the work table. "He knows what I like, what I need, to make my art. And he goes everywhere in the city. When he notices a promising object, he takes possession of it, and brings it to me."

Stuyvesant took it as an invitation to step across to the table and look into the small crate that sat on top. Inside were a tiny bird's nest with three half eggshells, a once-white infant shoe, a tangle of half a dozen delicate rib-bones, and two washed-leather bags like the one he'd kept his marbles in as a boy. The first one contained, remarkably enough, marbles, although new-looking and a lot fancier than those he'd kneeled over, forty years before. The larger bag held shards of broken glass. He fished one out and held it to the light. An eye looked back at him, part of the face from an old stained glass window. With that piece were two more eyes, some fingers, and a large toe with a sandal-strap across it.

Moreau had stood at his elbow while he went through the box, un-willing to protest but clearly anticipating disaster from clumsy hands. When Stuyvesant had returned everything to its place, the artist pulled the crate over and picked out one of the rib-bones, smoothing it under his fingers to reassure himself that it had not been harmed by the American brute. Moving the box revealed another crate with a simi-larly odd assortment of objects: a cigar box containing a large handful of pulled teeth, most of them pitted with decay; a stuffed mouse, sitting up on its haunches with its forepaws lifted, something in the process of taxidermy having caused the creature's face to twist as if in agony; a ladies' brooch about two inches high, intricately woven from some black thread-like material. It took him a moment to recognize it as a memento mori, made from the hair of a beloved dead person. He let it drop to the table, causing Moreau to hiss in protest.

"So, Charmentier brings you things," Stuyvesant said, unconsciously wiping his fingers on his coat-front as he moved on down the table. "And you put them into your boxes." He bent over a trio of buff-colored stones. Two of them were just stones; the third was amber containing a fossilized insect.

"Many people bring me gifts. Neighbors, shopkeepers—I keep a box for their offerings, near my gate. Artists—the artists have been so generous. Duchamp gave me a box of shells, Picasso the sketch of a mask, Foujita—you know Foujita?—he brought me these." The Japa-nese Surrealist's gift was a bundle of used chopsticks. "Man Ray brought me some fascinating spoiled negatives last week. I'm trying to work out how to mount them in a Display with a light behind them."

Moreau held up a strip of exposed film to the electric bulb, admiring the tiny images. When he laid it down again, Stuyvesant picked it up, and after a minute realized the similarity to the photograph in Ray's studio: a nude woman with skin draped like a taut garment over her hip-bones, lying in a puddle of thick liquid that looked like blood. These showed her from different angles, and the film had been overex-posed in the processing, but there was no doubt they were from the same session.

"Do you have a lot of pictures like this?" he asked the box-maker.

His question was rewarded by a flick of those odd pale eyes—the briefest flick—off to the left, in the direction of an open doorway. Stuyvesant did nothing to indicate he had noticed the look.

"I . . . well, any number of things. The teeth: I have been working a lot with teeth, of late. The coins on the shelf were from him. They're Roman. From the time of Julian, he says."

Sarah spoke up. "Dominic is a devoté of found objects. He tried to explain it to me, that the universe comes together in a moment of revelation to present a person with some key object. The attentive see it, but most people just walk right past, oblivious."

"He said something like that last night, about the coin."

"It's like a religion with him. 'Being aware of the world's machinery,' he calls it."

"What about this? How is this rock part of the world's machinery?" Stuyvesant picked up a lumpy rock some three inches long that looked just like a bit of dog's dropping.

Moreau answered him. "Coprolite. I was telling Le Comte about my idea for a box concerning permanence, and the very next day, he brought me that. It made the ideas just flower. The ugly side of permanence. Permanence as corruption and decay."

"Why? What is it?"

"Fossilized dung."

The American set the object down. *I really have to stop picking things up.*

Moreau returned to his previous concern over Sarah's hand, and Stuyvesant heartlessly abandoned her to the artist's disquieting attentions to make a further circuit of the rooms.

They were, he decided, one of the artist's boxes writ large, a number of smaller rooms surrounding the main workshop with the hands on the wall. Each held boxes in various stages of completion, from bare wood through everything but the glass covering. He suspected that the contents of the rooms were linked in Moreau's mind, although it was impossible to connect them into any kind of theme: one room had bones, but also a dozen woven baskets containing nails and snips of wire. In another, all the contents were circular, from coins to tiles to the decorative ends of stick-pins. A third room had a lot of bird-related objects—skeletons, feathers, and broken eggshells—but also contained a sheaf of photographs showing opera singers, moving-picture actresses, young children of both sexes, and apparently random shots of streets, many of them blurred as if a camera's shutter had gone off accidentally. They could easily have been the work of Man Ray, but none were of Pip Crosby.

Sarah's voice in the next room had taken on the strangled accents of desperation—Moreau seemed to be exhorting her to pull off her hand, that he might examine it—and even though Stuyvesant was not finished, he laid down the photos and went to her rescue. He had seen what he needed—or rather, he had seen what he was not permitted.

Moreau's guilty glance had been in the direction of a sturdy set of shelves that almost looked as if they were mounted against a wall. Almost.

"Thank you, M. Moreau," he said, heartily plunging his own grip between the man and Sarah. "I have to say, your Displays have that . . . how could I put it? That *frisson* of visceral excitement that a person only encounters in the presence of True Art. If I happen to find any exciting objects, I'll be sure to keep you in mind. C'mon, Sarah, let's leave the man to his work."

And before Moreau could object, Stuyvesant retrieved the photograph of Pip Crosby which the artist had quietly tucked in beneath the others: he wasn't about to leave the girl with this weird man. He then herded his accomplice back the way they had come, through the rooms and up the stairs to the startlingly bright entranceway.

At the gate, he spotted a box with a hinged top, mounted against the wall. Gingerly, he lifted the top, then leaned forward to see what was inside: a dead rat with one black ear. He dropped the lid and trotted to catch up with Sarah, already halfway down the block.

As he drew near, her steps slowed, and she shot Stuyvesant a glance under the brim of her cloche. "Thank you for coming to my rescue."

"No, thank *you*, for distracting him so I could have a look around. What a lunatic!"

"And what on earth was that you said, about a *frisson* of excitement?"

"*Visceral* excitement, don't forget the visceral. Some artists were talking in the bar the other day, must have been about Moreau's boxes."

"Ah, that explains it. I could hardly keep a straight face when you came out with that, it was so unlike you."

"What, you don't think I have an appreciation for art?"

"I know you do, but not for Didi's sort of contraptions."

"I will admit, they have a way of getting under your skin. Which I guess is what those guys were trying to say, but—Jesus. Fossilized crap? I can see why the neighbors put a rat in his box."

"The rat is a gift, not a comment. That's how Didi will view it, anyway."

"What does he do with dead rats?"

"Puts them in one of his corruption boxes. I suppose I should have shown them to you, but really, I can't bear thinking about them. There's a kind of beetle that eats flesh, and he has a bunch of them that he uses to clean the bones."

"Inside his house? That's . . . disgusting."

"I know. And something even more disturbing? Do you know what he said to me, the first time I met him? I came to see if he could make me a hand, and he'd been examining my wrist, making a mold, and doing sketches of my right hand for comparison. He said, 'I regret I do not have your bones.' At the time, I thought he meant there was some way he could rebuild my hands around the bones."

"He didn't?"

"I think he just wanted the bones. He buys . . . bits from the hospital, when— Oh, really, that's enough. I can't talk about it. Do you think it's too early for a drink?"

But again Harris Stuyvesant was not listening to her. Harris Stuyvesant was staring off into the Paris street, his eyes seeing a box full of beetles.

If you had a body on your hands, and you wanted its bones . . .

He shook himself. *Jesus Christ, Harris, your imagination is going berserk around all these artsy types.*

THIRTY-TWO

I T WAS NEVER too early for a drink in Paris, although the tables were mostly empty. He pulled out a chair for Sarah well away from the only other customers, an elderly couple with matching glasses of wine and a tiny quivering dog on the woman's lap. When they had ordered, he offered Sarah his silver case, and lit their cigarettes.

She closed her eyes and tipped her face to the sun.

The contrast with Nancy Berger's gesture three days earlier was striking—Sarah Grey wasn't about to give a public moan of pleasure—but more than contrast, Stuyvesant was hit by a memory. The first time he'd seen Sarah was also in sunlight, the bright spring sunshine of an English garden in bloom: pale hair blazing, a tilt of mischief to her head, laughter in her eyes. A sight guaranteed to lift a man's heart. Even a man not already inclined towards small, curvy, golden-haired women.

"So, Harris, what have you been up to all this time?"

Waiting for you. "Like I said, doing odd jobs for odd people. Right now I'm looking for Pip Crosby."

"Without much success."

"Unfortunately. Although at least it brought me to you."

The feeble joke made her turn away from the sun; made her sit forward to scrape cigarette ash into the little tray. Made her raise her defenses against him.

He'd known since he saw her at Bricktop's on Wednesday. He'd seen it last night, and it had been standing in front of him for the past hour. No, be honest: it had been in front of him for three years, in Sarah's absence and Bennett's silence.

This was not the sunlit young woman he'd fallen in love with. That Sarah was gone.

The Sarah Grey before him was someone else entirely, her personality as radically transformed as her poor body. He'd tried—he was still trying, like mad—to cling to that vision of Sarah, the shining, carefree, blaze of a girl; trying to look past the thin face and guarded eyes to the exuberance that had captured his soul.

And he failed.

Because her eyes? He'd seen that look before, in soldiers coming back from the Front; in the victims of violence; in those whose trust had been betrayed.

Sarah Grey had walked through dark places, alone. A part of her would forever remain in darkness.

Oh, God. If he'd moved faster, in April 1926. Just a little faster . . .

"Harris, you look unhappy. What's wrong?"

He studied her face, and saw both fear of what he was going to say, and the determination to let him say it. Courage like that took a man's heart and wrung it out.

So he smiled, and he lied. "There's nothing wrong, honey. I just was thinking, I feel like I ought to introduce myself."

Whatever she saw in his face gave her pause. After a moment, she set her defenses aside along with her cigarette, to extend her hand across the table.

"How d'you do," she said in a posh accent. "My name is Sarah Grey."

At the touch of her, that warm little paw in his, feelings threatened to spill back, but he forced them down. "Harris Stuyvesant, at your service."

"Are you an American, sir?"

"Sure as shootin', ma'am. And you like Americans."

"I did, once upon a time. These days, I know rather too many of them to be impressed by a mere accident of nationality."

"How sensible of you."

"I am a sensible person, Mr. Stuyvesant."

It was a warning. He smiled. "I can see that."

After a moment, she returned his smile, and if it lacked the wattage of a spring day in an English garden, it was nonetheless real.

Peace, declared and accepted.

The glasses arrived, and he watched as she grabbed hers and put half of it down her throat. "You really don't like that little man, do you?"

"I loathe him. Although as I said, his lack of social graces is hardly reason enough to shun him."

"It's a lot more than bad manners and standing too close. If I were you—if I were any woman—I'd take care never to be alone with him."

"Oh, Harris, you can't think . . ."

"I can. I do."

"But my dear man, the fellow is an absolute invertebrate. Even I could knock him cold."

"So long as you didn't accept a drink from him first."

Her green eyes went wide. "You really believe . . . ? I couldn't imagine . . . Well, actually I sort of could imagine. How awful of me. But you may be right. Although I'm not sure how I'd explain to Dominic that I can't make any more deliveries to his pet artist."

"Tell him your fiancé objects."

"Ah," she said. "Yes. About that . . ."

"Are you actually engaged? You don't have a ring."

"I'm going to marry him," she said firmly.

"I take it he doesn't know? About me?"

"He does now, more or less. I hated to do it, because he has something that's taking up all his time at the moment, but he had to know. Look, Harris—"

"I'm happy for you, really. Even though I'd love to rip out his guts and decorate the Pont Neuf with them."

She chose to see only the joke, and let her eyes give him a low-wattage sparkle.

"So, tell me about your cop," he said. "How'd you meet?"

He took great care to keep his face polite, interested. That of a friend, not of a man. With no trace of the dreams inhabited by green eyes, the string of noncommittal affairs, the three years of sticking close to London . . .

Friends.

And whatever else she saw in his face, whatever memories she had or suspected in him, she did see the friendship.

"Coincidentally, he was doing what you are now: looking for a missing girl. But then, that's his job, missing persons."

"When was that?"

"Almost exactly a year ago," she said. She'd been sitting with a book in the Jardin des Plantes when Doucet came through the park with the photograph of a pretty, pale-haired girl. The conversation had quickly wandered from his missing girl to her book, and her nationality, then to the weather (Sarah being, after all, British). Before long they found themselves at a table with cups in front of them, followed somewhat later by a second table, with glasses. The next day there was a visit to the girls' school where she was working, and the following day, he enlisted her help in a tour of Montparnasse cafés, and after that . . .

He'd been clever, Stuyvesant had to give Doucet that. He'd seen at once that although Sarah would instantly reject a romantic advance, she might be cajoled into helping him. And once under her guard, he could work on her softer side.

The sympathy in his face may have slipped, just a little, after several minutes of besotted conversation, because Sarah stopped. "Oh, Harris, you don't care for all that! What about you? Has it really been three years of odd jobs?"

"Hasn't your brother mentioned what I've been up to?"

"Not in a while. I thought you said you hadn't seen him?"

Stuyvesant made a mental note to slap Bennett Grey around a little, next time he was in arm's reach. "I haven't, but I send him a lot of picture postcards."

"If they're color pictures, the neighbor lad probably steals them."

"Robbie? You may be right. But I've been around. A job here, a job there. Driver for an American movie director looking for a castle. Bodyguard. Three or four missing persons. *Plongeur*—dishwasher—in a high-class restaurant. Doorman in a house of ill repute. That one was . . . different."

"I'll bet! Were the girls all beautiful and pampered? Or, ill-treated and searching for a patron?"

"Sarah Grey, you are reading all the wrong sorts of novels. The girls were perfectly nice and well behaved."

She didn't believe him. It took some doing to convince her that the girls had been surprisingly conservative, even prim, outside of their bedrooms. (He, personally, having had no experience of the interior of those bedrooms. Of course not.) Talk and drinks brought color to her face. It was all very amiable.

And if there was a grinding sound deep in the breast of Harris Stuyvesant, a noise that came from suppressing the impulse to pull her head forward and kiss her hard, he took care to keep it well concealed.

She gave her wrist-watch a glance, and exclaimed at the passage of time. "I need to go pretty soon. I have a thousand things to do before next week."

"What's next week?"

"The full moon event in the catacombs. Dominic's calling it a Danse Macabré, although there may not be enough room for dancing. Have you already forgotten the invitation you forced him to make?"

"I doubt I could force that man to do anything, and yes, I do re-member. Although I don't remember anyone mentioning catacombs. Why there?"

"Because it's Dominic."

"Okay. But if it's a full moon event, why hold it underground?"

"I know, and with the equinox only five days later."

"And Christmas just around the corner."

That lovely chortle, twisting his heart. "Not entirely a non-sequitur, in fact. But it's what he wanted, so it's what I'll do. I should warn you, it's formal."

"Not the usual collection of Montparnasse bums, then?"

"A few. Those who can be trusted not to wear corduroy and sandals."

"Are there any?"

"Absolutely. Haven't you ever seen Djuna Barnes in full plumage? And Man Ray's new girl, she's something."

"Lee Miller."

"You've met her?"

"*Something*'s the word."

"The sort of girl who makes me feel short and dumpy."

"Never that."

"Thank you, Mr. Stuyvesant."

"What about Didi Moreau? Is he coming?"

"Lord, no. Not even Dominic can make him a reasonable party guest."

"You know, it's funny, I'd never heard of Moreau before I got here, but this week I've seen those Displays of his all over. Even Pip had a couple."

"That's what happens when you have a patron like Le Comte."

"They've known each other long?"

"No, in fact I put the two of them together, a year and a half ago."

"Quick work."

"Didi's a disturbing personality, but his work is solid. Profound, even."

"I'll take your word for it. What about your brother—what does he make of your new crew?"

"Bennett's visit was before I started working for Le Comte. Are you asking if my big brother has vetted my boss?"

"Nah, I'm just curious what he made of them all. He's a clever man, your brother."

"When it comes to weeding out the disreputable, you mean."

"Not too sure about that—he seems to like me okay, which doesn't say much for his judgment."

She laughed, then glanced at his suit. "Harris, perhaps I shouldn't say anything, not knowing your financial situation, but if you have a smidge extra cash, you might see that your dinner jacket is up to snuff."

"I may not be grand enough for your crowd, eh?"

"They're not my crowd, and it only matters if you want to blend in. And, maybe your shoes . . ."

He stood up before he could say something asinine. "I'll see what I can do. Thanks for taking me to see that very odd egg."

She assembled her handbag, adjusted her hat, got to her feet. "You will remember, Dominic feels protective about him?"

"When I rob his house," Stuyvesant vowed, "your boss will never find out."

"Harris! You're not going to rob the poor fellow!"

"Wouldn't think of it," he said, adding silently: *Not today, anyway.*

He offered her his right arm. She hesitated. He looked down—and remembered. "Oh, Jesus. Sorry, other side."

"No, that's okay," she said, and threaded her left arm through his right elbow.

He couldn't help glancing at the hollow metal fingers resting on his sleeve. The paint was worn at the tips, the thumb dented and bent a fraction outward with an impending crack at its base. He impulsively reached his hand over to cover it, although whether to warm it or to conceal it, he couldn't have said. He squeezed her arm into his side, feeling the straps that covered her flesh-and-blood forearm.

"It really is all right," she said. "It was hard at first, of course, but now it's mostly frustration, when I can't figure out how to do something with it. I may actually go back to a hook and just ignore the stares. At least I'd be free of Didi."

He stopped moving, but she tightened her arm to keep him from facing her.

"Harris, I need you to be my friend about this. Please, *please* don't act like Bennett. Every time he looks at my hand he goes all tragic, as if he'd set the bomb. I was not a child, remember. *I* made a choice; *I* watched a friend die; *I* live with the consequences. Not you. Not Bennett. Don't try to take that away."

His left arm gathered her in, until she was leaning against his chest with his chin on her cloche.

He understood. To believe she'd caused a friend's death was hard enough; to think she'd done so through a well-intentioned accident— that would be intolerable.

But he also knew the truth. Sarah Grey was guilty of nothing but loyalty and friendship and the passionate commitment to a cause she believed in. That it was the men in her life who bore the blame: her would-be lover, Harris Stuyvesant, who had failed at his job; her brother, Bennett, who had made a choice that threw her to the fire.

Pedestrians flowed around them, and he felt her small body breathing against him. Eventually, she stirred. Reluctantly, he let her go.

THIRTY-THREE

AN INTERNAL CONVERSATION, translated from the French: Where did I put those charming little vertebrae the boy brought me? So neat and tiny—ah, here, in the box labeled *hypodermic needles*. Who knew a man who cleans the floors in hospitals could be so useful?

Yes, these are sweet, but they're little more than cartilage. They lack the beauty of bone.

True. What if I paint them? Or—dye them? Yes, for a tightly-packed rainbow Display. I shall have to find out how to dye cartilage. Make a note.

What about the skull that odd American brought you?

Pity he cracked it so, removing it.

Clumsy fool.

Aren't most of them? But in any event, it's too large for a Display. I wonder how old it is? Such a lovely feel. Like silk.

What if you built a Display without glass, to permit touch as well? Would there be enough to fill all thirteen squares?

Perhaps if I use the fine saw, and mark it with care . . .

On the other hand, what if you turn to another form?

Such as what?

Dream something up! Something larger, grander. Your mind has been dwelling on taxidermy, lately. Begin there.

It is true, that the tight limitations of the Displays frames can be as satisfying as bondage, but they can also be simply restricting.

Also, one is forced to wonder about any art form as critically and commercially successful as the Displays.

Taxidermy, you say?

You have been longing to try human skin. Decent-sized pieces of it, that is.

True. Even those scraps—talk about silk!

Imagine an entire person—no: imagine a tableau of people. Cured by you, arranged by you, set in place by you, for all eternity. Museums would kill for them.

Museums would never show them.

Collectors. There are always private collectors to appreciate you.

I don't know. Still . . . human skin is the ultimate technical challenge. The stretch of the stuff. The subtleties of position, and limb, and facial structure.

A lot more intriguing than rabbits!

I like rabbits. And where would I find a . . . subject? The hospital might notice if its cleaner walked out with an entire body.

And what kind of a body could you expect? Old, battered, abandoned.

Hideous. I'd as well work with Mme. Jory.

But there are others.

Are there?

I can think of one or two.

The hair . . .

Yes!

Magnificent. But is it permitted?

You are an artist. You are Didi Moreau. All things are permitted.

THIRTY-FOUR

To COMPENSATE FOR having been granted an entire morning in the company of Sarah Grey, the afternoon would require two confrontations of him.

One of them he'd set an appointment with, at four o'clock in the Préfecture office on the Île de la Cité. The other had avoided him since the fiasco at Bricktop's two days ago, responding neither to his flowers nor his petit bleus, hanging up when she heard his voice on the telephone.

Time to risk the wrath of the guardian dragon.

He went armed—not with his revolver, although he was sorely tempted to take that reinforcement, but with flowers, wine, and a large box of expensive chocolates.

Madame Hachette scowled when he handed her the flowers, and her eyes lingered only briefly on the wine he set on her table, but when he finally brought out the chocolates—all the while having plied her with running conversation and a string of humorous apologies that was less self-deprecation than outright self-abnegation—her fingers twitched. She did not reach for them, not yet, but she was definitely softening.

Before she could crack, their complex negotiations were interrupted by a voice drifting down the stairway. "Oh, for heaven's sake, Harris, stop groveling and come up!"

Mme. Hachette caused the offerings to vanish from her table, and he bolted for the stairs in relief.

Up on the fourth floor, Nancy stood in the doorway and watched him come up the stairs. "I don't see any chocolates for me."

"I'll buy you a chocolate store. Along with the flower stall next door."

"Which will turn my nose red and my backside wide. Never mind, come in. Anything on Phil?"

"A lot on her, but no clear signs yet. I'm sorry."

"Her mother must be frantic. But, you're doing your best."

Stuyvesant hoped that was true.

Despite Nancy's protestations, the flowers he had sent her stood in the sitting room, dwarfing the low table in front of the sofa and making it impossible to see the fireplace, or anyone in the chairs opposite.

"Hmm," he said. "The florist was a bit more . . . emphatic than I'd intended."

"I did wonder where they found a bowl big enough."

He bent to peer under the laden branches. "I think it may be a horse trough."

"The neighbor across the way has already asked for it. Her baby needs a bathtub."

"The rest of the family could fit in there as well."

"In any event, it was a very clear message."

"Is my apology accepted?"

"Apology? For what?"

He straightened in surprise, then saw the mockery in her dark eyes. "I shall try not to make a habit out of fisticuffs in a bar."

"You do know that a person can be arrested for fistfights here?"

"I am indeed aware of that fact."

"And the woman?"

He nearly said, *Which woman?* That would have been a bad mistake. "She's an old friend I haven't seen for years."

"A good friend?"

"Used to be pretty good. Now I'm closer to her brother."

She studied his face, searching for the lie she could feel in him. "Are you going to see her again?"

"I saw her this morning. She knows some people that Pip was involved with. She could be helpful."

"Do you mean Man Ray?"

"Not specifically," he lied. "It's a kind of tangled knot of connections, both social and professional. It may take me a while to sort it out."

"And she'll need to help you?"

"Her name is Sarah. Sarah Grey. You'd like her. But yes, I expect I'll see her again, for one reason or another."

"If one of the other reasons turns into—"

"It won't," he interrupted.

"If it does. You'll tell me?"

"Nancy, she's engaged. To a cop."

"Oh. Well, fine. But I won't do with two-timing."

"I wouldn't ask you. Now, is there any chance of coffee?"

"Not wine?"

He nearly blurted out that he'd had about six glasses already with Sarah. "I need to prove my sobriety to you."

"Dull, but noble," she muttered, turning towards the kitchen.

"Would you rather have it outside? Now the heat's broken, coffee in the sun isn't a repulsive idea."

"What a romantic offer: something not actively repulsive."

Stuyvesant walked across the Pont Neuf later that afternoon with a lift in his step. Not that he was all that sure what he felt about Nancy Berger, and not that he'd budged her from her conviction that something awful had happened to Pip, but at least she'd forgiven him for his behavior at Bricktop's. She'd even agreed to go out with him again—although not until Sunday.

In the meantime, the sun was bright and the air was no longer stifling. There were boats on the Seine and rows of fishermen along the bank, a fringe of long cane poles.

In a minute, the buildings closed around him. As he came closer to the police offices, his mood closed in as well. Doucet was fine for a cop, but the memory of that possessive kiss planted on Sarah's cheek would take some getting past.

But he'd need to push it away, now. He really couldn't do with getting himself arrested for decking a policeman.

When he saw Doucet, however, he had less of an urge to punch the man than to bring him a drink, or maybe tuck him into bed for twelve hours.

"You look like hell," he told the man half-obscured by a desk laden with files.

The bloodshot eyes squinted up, wondering what Harris Stuyvesant was doing in his doorway. Or maybe just wondering who it was.

"We had an appointment," Stuyvesant reminded him.

Doucet eased back in his chair and dry-washed his unshaven face. "Merde. What else have I forgotten today?"

"What's up?" He was getting a bad feeling about this.

"A nightmare. I feel as if I've stepped in a hornets' nest, and they're all pouring out at me."

"Is this related to Pip Crosby?"

Doucet's chair screeched back, nearly tipping over, and the *flic* snatched his coat from the hook. "I need some air."

"You need a drink."

"I wouldn't stop at one."

The Frenchman exploded out of the door as if demons nipped his heels. A pair of *flics* on their way inside looked after him in alarm, and were not reassured by Stuyvesant's eloquent shrug. He trotted behind the fleeing Doucet out of the Préfecture de Police and through the Palais de Justice, watching Doucet step into the Pont Neuf traffic as if it were three in the morning. Horns blared and brakes squealed as the oblivious cop plunged through the traffic, leaving Stuyvesant to slip through the resulting snarled knots of cars, collecting a series of curses all his own.

Doucet only stopped when he ran out of land. He stood at the prow of the Île de la Cité, facing the setting sun. Stuyvesant slowed as he saw that the man was not about to throw himself off, and caught his breath. After a minute, he took out his cigarette case.

Half an inch of tobacco later, he remarked, "The Vert-Galant used to be a separate island. Called the 'Île aux Treilles,' because of all the grape trellises. But you probably know that."

Another half inch. "You sure you don't want a drink?"

"The very reason I took the position in the missing persons department," Doucet moaned. "The very reason."

If he doesn't spill it pretty soon, I'll be forced to beat it out of him. "You have another Henri Landru on your hands?"

Doucet shuddered. Hardened cop, ex-soldier, and he shuddered. Then he reached for the cigarette case with uncertain hands. "We investigate, M. Stuyvesant. I swear on my soul we investigate all our cases. And because . . . because of Landru, I am on guard for any faint trace of a pattern. But in a city of this size, people vanish. They travel, they have accidents. Some are matched with bodies in the morgue." He turned his head to the American. "I swear to you, I never take my task lightly."

"I believe you. How many?"

"I don't know. Dozens perhaps. We've only worked our way back to the beginning of last year."

Stuyvesant's gut lurched. "I . . . No, I don't believe it. You'd have noticed."

"Would I?"

"Yeah." Stuyvesant dropped his cigarette and crushed it out. "Yes. You're a good cop, Doucet. Quit beating yourself up over this and let's get to work."

The Frenchman went rigid. "What the hell do you think I've been doing? I've barely left the office in three days!"

"Then it's high time you have someone else's eyes look at the problem," Stuyvesant snapped back. "And for God's sake, let's get you something to eat."

He thought the cop was going to hit him. Then Doucet's broad shoulders dropped as if his strings had been cut. "You're right. You'd think I'd never worked on a major case before."

Stuyvesant physically turned the man around and pushed him towards the nearest brasserie. "Didn't Sarah tell you? I'm always right."

"Yes, she said that she knew you."

There was so little tension in the statement, Stuyvesant had to wonder just what Sarah had told him. That she and Harris Stuyvesant were just old friends? Because if so, if Sarah was hiding what Stuyvesant had once meant to her, then—

Stop it, Harris. This isn't the time. Take the poor bastard's mind off things for five minutes, and let him catch his breath.

"Did Sarah tell you how we met?"

"Your former colleague told me, on the telephone. You were hunting a terrorist."

"That's right. Three years ago. I was still with the Bureau then, more or less, and a roundabout set of connections led me to her brother. He'd been invited— Say, is this place okay? Want to tell the man what you want? Nothing to drink?"

Stuyvesant waited for his companion to make his lunch order, then immediately plunged back into his narrative, keeping the man's thoughts away from that list of names.

"Bennett had been invited to a country house-party where my suspect was going to be, and said I could tag along and meet him. Have you met Sarah's brother?"

"He was here briefly, in April. Nice fellow."

Nice? Doucet couldn't know much about Sarah's brother. *Interesting* would mean he had some clue about Bennett Grey's odd gifts. *Unfortunate, distressed,* or *poor bloody bastard* would have made it clear—but if Sarah Grey hadn't told him, Harris Stuyvesant certainly was not about to. "He is, very nice."

"Shy, wouldn't you say?"

No, I wouldn't. "He had a bad war."

Doucet's lips compressed in sympathy, and Stuyvesant went on with his story. When the food came, the *flic*'s reaction made it clear that he had been neglecting more than sleep. Stuyvesant kept talking, avoiding all mention of bombs but otherwise drawing out the story of Bennett and the General Strike. At last, there was color in the man's face. When the empty plate had been exchanged for cups of coffee, Stuyvesant lit him a cigarette and finally let the Inspector talk.

"Since speaking with you on Tuesday, my Sergeant and I have reviewed every unsolved missing person report back to January 1928. Every one."

"Lot of work," Stuyvesant commented, with feeling. The older the case, the more digging required.

"In the past two days, we have located roughly half of those reported missing. Some were alive and no one bothered to let us know. Others were dead, but again, we weren't told. Drowned Parisians who only come to light when they hit salt water are a constant source of irritation for the Le Havre police."

Stuyvesant cocked an eyebrow, but there was no jest in Doucet's face.

"We have got the list down to forty-seven names."

"*Forty-seven?* Sweet Jesus. Did any of them have connections to Pip Crosby?"

"We're working on it."

"Lived in her neighborhood, went to her bars, worked for the same—"

"I know my job," Doucet snarled.

"Yeah. Sorry. Can I ask, how many of them are blonde women?"

"It would not appear that a larger proportion of missing persons have been blonde women," he replied with care. Neither man said the name both were thinking.

"May I see that list of names?" Stuyvesant asked.

Doucet looked around for the waiter. He did not let the American pay l'addition.

The list was, in fact, a ringed notebook bulging with anguish and loss. Daughters reported missing by their mothers; mothers who walked away from their children; fathers whose loss drove a family out onto the streets. Many were so poor, the person reporting their absence had nothing to show but the name: no picture, not even a birth certificate. At the other extreme was the fiancée of an Indian prince, last seen here with the prince's English secretary.

The first two pages of the ring binder were the actual list, a running tally of contents that had been amended whenever names were added or crossed out.

There were a lot of amendations.

The tally pages contained: the names; the person's age, sex, and hair color; his or her home address, including the arrondissement; the place where they were last seen; and their date of disappearance. They were organized according to those dates.

The two names Doucet had already given him, Alice Barnes and Ruth Ann Palowski, appeared halfway down the first page: June and October, 1928. Two women and a man came between them. At the top, Stuyvesant read:

> 3 jan 28—Katrine Aguillard—f—brn—19—Fr—12 rue Charlotte
>   (XVII)—inc
> 13 fev 28—Lotte Richter—f—blonde—German—inc (XIII)—Pigalle

The *inc* he figured meant inconnu: unknown. Working his way along the line, this meant that Katrine Aguillard, a nineteen-year-old French brunette whose home was on rue Charlotte in the XVII arrondissement, had disappeared on January 3, 1928, from an unknown location. The following month, Lotte Richter, a German blonde who had been staying somewhere in the XIII arrondissement, had disappeared from the Pigalle district.

There were mostly women. Brunettes outnumbered blondes, plus assorted grays, blacks, red-head, and one bald (Daniel La Plante, a sixty-four-year-old shoe-shiner). Their homes tended to be in the outer arrondissements; their places of disappearance tended to cluster in Montmartre and Montparnasse. They were mostly between twenty and forty-five.

Behind the brief cover pages were the details of each case, copied in what he came to know as four different hands. Some of the case notes went on for two or three pages, and these often had photographs of varying quality attached. Others were brief, saying in effect little more than: this person seems to have vanished, and nobody knows why.

The youngest person on the list was six years old.

As he read, he tried to sort out the relevant information—but what was it? The only men who'd brought a twitch to his mental fishing line were Man Ray, Didi Moreau, and Dominic Charmentier. However, Paris was a large pond full of would-be criminals swimming in the depths. It was too early to limit his pool of suspects.

Anyway, what *was* he suspecting the men of? If he wasn't ready to assume that Pip Crosby was . . . that *something dire* had happened to Pip, what did that leave? Dirty films? White slavery? Anarchist plots?

He watched for patterns—any patterns. Was that art? Margot Jourdain, a nineteen-year-old brunette from the VI arrondissement, had gone to a party in Montmartre on March 22, 1928, told her friends that she was going to talk to a man about a theater job, and not been seen again. Luc Tolbert (brown hair; twenty-eight years; resident of Orleans; last seen August 12, 1929 at Luna Park) was in Paris visiting a sister who worked as a shop girl, but supplemented her income with work as an artists' model. Raoul Bellamy (brown; twenty-one; home in the V arrondissement; last seen March 1, 1929, in a bar a quarter mile from the lair of Didi Moreau) had recently played a small role in a modern film. And so on.

He was using a coarse net to strain for minnows: the chances of catching anything was minuscule. But he read and he thought, and when he turned the last page, he looked over at Doucet.

Who had been quietly snoring into his desk blotter for the last ninety minutes.

His interior dialogue over whether to wake the man was rendered moot by the noisy entrance of the sergeant who occupied the desk outside Doucet's office door.

"Inspecteur, I'm—" the man was saying, until he simultaneously realized that the Inspector was snoozing and that there was a stranger in their midst.

Doucet snapped upright, holding a paper. "Yes, Fortier, what is it?"

The alert effect was a bit spoiled by the small note stuck to his left cheek. Fortier—Doucet's by-the-books Sergeant by reputation, a thin, Caspar Milquetoast–looking fellow in person—shot a surprisingly belligerent glance at the intruder. Doucet said, "Don't worry about M. Stuyvesant, he's helping us with our inquiries."

In America, the explanation would have been shorthand for, "This guy is one step from being in handcuffs," but clearly in France the words were taken at face value. Fortier glowered, then told Doucet, "I'm off home for a few hours, my parents are here for dinner, but I'll be back afterwards."

"No, take the night off, we'll start again in the morning."

"You sure? I'll be fine after a break."

"Yes, I'm sure. It's better to come at it tomorrow with a fresh mind. Go."

The baleful glance Fortier shot at Stuyvesant was no doubt intended as a threat, although it looked more like petulance. Still, the man left before l'Inspecteur could change his mind.

"I was about to go, myself," Stuyvesant told Doucet.

"Have you found anything?"

His immediate impulse was to deny any iota of interest, to keep any and all cards up close to his mismatched buttons. But Doucet had let him in, giving him free access to all kinds of information that he had no right to. He owed Doucet honesty in return—although maybe not complete honesty. He rubbed his tired eyes.

"Nothing I can be sure of, but there are a couple of things I'd like to follow up, if you don't mind." *Or even if you do.* "I've been looking at Pip Crosby's possessions and talking to her roommate and friends. That took me in two directions: the American photographer Man Ray, who you know, and one of your home-grown nut-jobs, Didi Moreau. In my conversations with both men, one name came up. Sorry to say this, but that was Dominic Charmentier. Sarah's boss."

Then he shut his mouth and waited for the questions.

They came, fast and furious. Are you suggesting Le Comte might in any way be involved in something unsavory? *Le Comte de Charmentier?*

Is there any scrap of actual evidence that makes you suspect him? Evidence beyond a macabre house décor? And what on earth prompted you to take Sarah to see this crétin Didi Moreau?

Twice, other cops stuck their heads in to see what was going on; both times Doucet ordered them out. Stuyvesant kept his patience in check, reminding himself that his opinions had been bound to alarm Doucet.

Eventually, Doucet got to the stage of ordering Stuyvesant to have nothing more to do with the case, with Dominic Charmentier, or with Sarah Grey.

"I can't leave Sarah vulnerable," Stuyvesant protested.

"She is not vulnerable! And in any event, considering Le Comte's association with Moreau and Ray, she will no longer be working for him."

It was tempting, really tempting, to loose a few verbal lightning-bolts of his own and damn the consequences. Because if he'd wanted to drive a wedge between Sarah and this man, here it was, a wedge as big and sharp as he could ask for.

But Stuyvesant pushed all his masculine impulse into a box and shut the top, settling for a mild but devastating question. "What's Sarah going to do when you order her to quit her job?"

"What?" Doucet, who had been on his feet for the last minute, now peered across his desk at the American.

"When you try and tell her she can have nothing more to do with Charmentier."

"She will resign, of course!"

"You may not know her as well as you think. Did she ever tell you how she lost her hand?"

"Of course."

"Did she say that she was there because she refused to leave? That she'd decided she was morally obliged to join in an act of public outrage by committing suicide?"

Doucet's jaw dropped.

"Yeah, I didn't think she did. The Sarah I knew didn't take well to being ordered about."

Slowly, the angry gaze turned inward. Doucet sat down. Stuyvesant lit two cigarettes, and half-rose to hand one to the cop.

Two men, smoking tobacco while reflecting on the impossibility of women.

"She will not like it," Doucet said at last.

"Nope."

"But she must be warned."

"She won't like that much, either."

"She is a sensible woman. She can be made to see the possibility of danger."

"She's a woman who has made some terrible mistakes in judgment, and who won't want to hear that she's making another one. She'll fight you on it."

"But she must be told," Doucet said, sadly.

Stuyvesant crushed his half-smoked cigarette in the tray and got to his feet. "Better you than me, buddy," he told the detective, and let himself out of the man's office.

He'd intended to ask about the gendarme's search of his room, but feared the question might push the man over the edge when it came to irksome Americans.

To his relief, when he got back to his hotel, the cops weren't waiting and the room hadn't been searched again.

It had probably been a mistake: they'd been looking for another big, sandy-headed American.

Yeah, he should be so lucky.

THIRTY-FIVE

I T WAS FRIDAY the 13 in Montparnasse, and darkness was settling in. For the first time, the air felt actually cool: things would be wild tonight.

Stuyvesant sat at his hotel desk, enjoying the fresh air through the window while he wrote up his case-notes for the last couple of days. When he had done so, he frowned, trying to imagine how he was going to justify all that wandering around to the man with the checkbook.

Maybe Sylvia Beach had a pet writer who could turn his notes into a pretty story for Uncle Crosby. He tossed the notebook onto the chipped desk and stretched the kinks from his neck. With all of Montparnasse at his feet, unlimited funds in his pocket, and the Quarter looking to return to life at last, Harris Stuyvesant sat, feeling glum.

He'd spent the last week in and out of Paris bars and cafés, with nothing to show for it. The Paris he'd flirted with on previous trips, the Paris for which he'd played hard to get, the Paris he believed he would return to, once he had his feet under him—why did he feel that he'd missed his chance?

He stood up with a screech of the chair's legs. *Come on, Harris,* he chided. *People always insist yesterday was better, yesterday was when the sun shone brighter and the drinks were stronger and the girls were all eager to please. It's how you show your superiority over the other Tom, Dick, and Johnny-come-latelies.*

He pulled open the door to the wooden wardrobe and looked at what lay there. He'd had the stored trunk brought up from Mme. Benoit's cellar, so he had his fedora again. Evening wear tonight, or just the dark suit? The suit showed wear in daylight, but with the new Berlin shirt and a silk neck-tie, it would be more adaptable than the evening suit and bow tie. And cheaper to clean if someone threw up on him.

He left the revolver and lock picks under the floorboard, and although he was tempted to slip the brass knuckles into his pocket, he decided against them, too.

Brawling was just too hard on the trousers.

He settled his hat and strolled down the rue Vavin to Raspail, turning south. Nearing the crossroads of the boulevard Montparnasse, a blind man—a blind and deaf man—would have known something was up: not even eight o'clock, and the corner had the air of a joint where last drinks had just been called, loosing a manic surge towards the bars.

Two spindly-legged girls in ridiculously tall heels clattered by, their high-pitched and overlapping conversation, more giggle than words, evidence of a visit to the snow dealer that afternoon. Seconds later, two pale youths in ill-fitting suits went by in the other direction, discussing the pawnshop value of the rings that covered their every finger. In their wake came a trio of femmes de nuit with the bodies of twenty-year-olds and the eyes of raddled old refugees.

Stuyvesant paused at the corner to survey the Times Square of Montparnasse village. Cafés that a few years before had been a bar and six tables of ardent conversation under the chestnuts were now a teeming throng of frantic drinkers, with dozens of tables jammed from window to pavement's edge, all of them far too noisy for anything resembling a conversation. The chestnuts were dying of alcohol poisoning. The entire street throbbed and heaved, from the depths of the zinc bars to the solid lines of taxis plying the roads. *As if you'd dressed a heaving mass of maggots in black suits and silk dresses,* Stuyvesant thought, and felt a powerful impulse to turn back to the Hotel Benoit and spend the night with a book.

Instead, he pushed through the stream of clean, earnest, wistful onlookers—the wide-eyed school-teachers from Ohio, the hopeful college graduates from Detroit—and crossed the street to the Dôme.

The Dôme was the most American of the American-driven cafés on the boulevard Montparnasse. Every second shouting mouth bore a New York accent, and the rest were from Chicago or Jersey. He pushed his way back, keeping a firm grip on his wallet, until he found a table where he could see the place.

He greeted the harried waiter by pressing five American dollars into his hand, a guarantee of brisk service from that point forward. He ordered a drink, and dinner, and asked if the fellow had seen Man Ray that night.

No, he hadn't. But that tip would guarantee that if Ray appeared, he'd know about it in two minutes flat.

He drank a boilermaker and ate his way through the platter of duck and frites, watching the crowd. In the hour he sat there, he saw three men go off with femmes de nuit (one of them looking an awful lot like an homme de nuit), one small packet exchanged for money, one flat envelope exchanged for money, and a lot of women putting on their makeup at the table. A pick-pocket worked his way through the room—twice, the second time returning the wallets to their purses and pockets, no doubt somewhat emptier than they'd been at the start of the evening. Stuyvesant caught the man's eye and gave him a small salute: you had to admire professionalism.

The only time he intervened was when a slicked-down dandy with sharp eyes dribbled something into the drink of his date, a scrub-faced Midwestern farm-girl in a new Paris dress. That time, he signaled the waiter and pointed out the imminent mugging, and watched with satisfaction while the man in the long apron drove the solitary *apache* out of the room, then propped the girl up in a corner until she came around.

That alone earned the waiter another five bucks, even though he never did report the arrival of M. Ray.

By ten o'clock, things were beginning to grow truly hot. The noise level made the windows seem to bulge outward; the room's thick smoke made a person think the kitchen was on fire.

A regular night at the Dôme.

Stuyvesant paid, resumed his hat, and started threading his way out of the café. Halfway across the room, he looked back, and saw his table already occupied by two pairs of elbows. It was as if he had never been.

Kiki was at her table under the trees, her husky laugh cutting through even that night's racket. She saw him, and waved; he tipped his hat, and went on.

Tonight, he was fishing, trolling a lure up and down the boulevard Montparnasse. In and out of the Coupole and Rotonde, dipping through the Select and the Falstaff, wandering as far up as the Deux Magots, then down to the Closerie des Lilas. He drank and he listened and he prodded the conversation, and drank some more, but the whisky might have been water, and sometimes, the fish just weren't biting.

He learned nothing, about no one.

Four hours after he'd left the Dôme, he came back to the Carrefour Vavin. By then, the Dôme and Rotonde were closed, their tables stacked and dark, but the Select was going strong. The wild revels had changed, giving way to an air of drunken desperation that made Stuyvesant want to keep his back to the wall. As he approached the door, he noticed the same *apache* go past, surveying the crowd for another potential victim: Stuyvesant wondered if the slick little villain was responsible for some of the names on Doucet's list. Near the door, one of the Canadians— McAlpin? McAlmon, that was it—was snarling at a pretty young man whose drinks he was paying for. His humor was vicious, excoriating, but the boy, who looked like he needed a square meal and a pair of shoes, kept a fixed smile on his face through the abuse.

And, of course, it was the kind of night that Hemingway should appear, beery and blustery and ready to take on all comers, be it in words or in arm-wrestling. From the look of him, he was nearing the open obscenity stage where he sought out the homosexuals for his mocking. Stuyvesant moved around the other side of the crowded room, and there he saw the person he'd been looking for all night.

Man Ray sat pontificating to a table, the spectacular Miller woman draped against his left side. Judging by the exaggerated gesticulations and the way he nearly stubbed his cigarette into a nearby sleeve, the photographer was well oiled. Two of his younger companions were as intent on his words as his lover was, the three of them bent forward over a table buried deep in glasses and ash-trays, their shiny-faced enthusiasm testifying to the newness of their Montparnasse experience. A couple of old-timers Stuyvesant recognized—a writer of grim fiction and a painter of unintelligible canvases—were sitting back in their chairs, catching every third word in the din but preserving the requisite display of apathy.

Then there was Kiki. The queen of Montparnasse sat two tables away from Ray, back turned, blatantly draped around another painter, her nonchalance betrayed by an occasional swivel in her chair to glare at the oblivious Lee Miller. Her eyes condemned the girl to the torments of a fiery hell.

And here he'd been concerned about Man Ray's intentions.

Lee Miller saw him and waved for him to join them. The gesture interrupted Ray, who paused, saw whom she had issued an invitation to, and scowled.

Stuyvesant gave an ostentatious look at his watch, made an exaggerated visual scan of the crowd, and with a shrug, wound his way through the hectic room towards them.

It was a mistake, one that he only woke to a couple of hours later. Ray spent the time flaunting his mistress, flaunting his genius, freely admitting his fascination with death, agreeing that he knew Didi Moreau and Le Comte and pretty much everyone in the Quarter. Stuyvesant could have flat-out accused him of committing murder in the center of the rue Montparnasse and the man would only have laughed and said, "Sure!"

If Stuyvesant had been able to get drunk, he might have dived into a good old-fashioned brawl and the hell with the effects on his trousers, or his police record. But it was one of those nights when the more he drank, the more sober he felt.

And so he tipped his hat to Madame Select, and walked away— away from the artists, away from the café, away from Montparnasse and all its smug, loud-mouthed, pretentious temporary citizens.

It was one of those velvet nights—or early mornings—when the sky seemed to look down and shake its head in affectionate disdain. *You are small*, it said, *but still I enjoy you.* At the river, he sat and lit a cigarette, the flare setting off a minor upheaval from the dark recesses of the bridge. A figure emerged—male? female? human?—and thrust out a rag-covered extremity. He gave it the lit cigarette, and it retreated to its den, requiring no more interaction from him than that.

He reached into his pocket for another cigarette, but instead of the silver case, his hand came out with the snapshot of Pip Crosby. He turned it towards the light from a nearby streetlamp, and looked at the girl.

Jesus, what a long day it had been. A long week. His skin crawled with drink and disgust and exhaustion, his mind presenting him with a series of stark, clear words and vivid images. Nancy's despair over Pip, and her unvoiced accusation. Doucet's bleary eyes; his ring binder swollen with dates and faces and loss. The flash of . . . *something* across Le Comte's face the other night in Bricktop's. Moreau's Displays and Man Ray's women. Lulu dead on the street—sweet, cheerful Lulu, shy about her missing tooth, not at all shy about filching the odd small note, a woman whose murder was too inconsequential for the papers. The invasion of his room.

The Quarter used to be fun, lively. Now its corners seemed to crawl with menace.

And on top of it all, he couldn't even get tanked. Instead, here he sat, as clear-headed as a new morn.

He looked at the photograph as if he'd never seen Pip before. Looked at the cheerful grin and saw it for what it was: a brave mask hiding the blonde child who screamed away from flames; the broken arm and the long agony of the burn—first the pain and then the scar. The controlling uncle, the sickly mother, and the defiant creation of a new life and a new person: Phil Crosby. Spirited, resolute, answering to no one but herself.

He wished he'd known her.

The week began to leak past him like a failing dam—a dam he'd been fighting to sustain, a dam holding back a massive burden of cold, dark images and grim thoughts and the bitter assumptions of others. A dam that finally gave way.

He held on to Pip's photo as the wave broke over him. When it passed, he was still on the bench, still holding the snapshot, with tears in his eyes and conviction in his mind.

I failed you, honey.

He wasn't looking for Pip Crosby.

He was looking for her body.

THIRTY-SIX

S UNDAY MORNING DAWNED clear, the autumn-tinted leaves still
full against the blue. Church bells clanged, here and there across
the town, pulling the scrubbed and penitent from their rest.

Also the scrubbed and unrepentant, such as Harris Stuyvesant, who
was tucked into the recessed and overgrown entranceway of an empty
house across from Didi Moreau's misleading bourgeois façade, grimly
waiting.

Moreau did not emerge in time for the 8:00 mass, nor the 9:00. At
10:05 the door opened and the bird-man stepped out, tie crooked and
a smudge of something pale on one knee, but clearly intent on church.
Stuyvesant waited for the maid to follow.

Five minutes passed, then ten, with no sign of her. He had just decided to take his chances with the house when the door came open
again. She bent over to check that the door was locked, then scurried
off in the opposite direction from her employer.

Maid and master attended different churches.

Stuyvesant crossed the narrow street and ducked inside Moreau's
gate, calling down a pious blessing upon all negligent gardeners. And a
minute later, upon all unconcerned builders, who installed door locks
that permitted an investigator easy entrance.

Inside the foyer he drew on a pair of silk gloves and listened to the
silent house. The spotless entranceway was an old-fashioned setting for

an artist claimed by the avant-garde, cluttered with floral art and mirrors over faded Morris wallpaper, the floor green-and-white tile. There was even a small decorative table beside the door with a polished tray, as if someone might leave a calling card.

Did Parisians leave calling cards? Other than dead rats at the gate?

The door to the rest of the house stood open, although he imagined it would be shut in the winter. Standing there, he heard no conversation, no shift of floorboards, no running water from within. The house was empty.

Friday's visit had shown him nothing of the house, since the door immediately to his right had taken him to Moreau's basement lair. The door had a twin on the other side of the foyer. When he opened it, he found a coat-cupboard with a pair of rubber shoes and seven antique umbrellas.

Three strides took him across the tiles to where the hallway carpet began. It was old and showed wear down the center, but the colors were still bright.

To his astonishment, the rooms opening off the hallway were every bit as out-of-date as the entranceway. Heavy furniture, a massive fireplace in every room, velvet curtains, cart-loads of polished knick-knacks. The only indication this wasn't 1870 was that the lights were electric.

Could it be a joke, he wondered as he studied the porcelain lavatory pull painted with forget-me-nots? One of the modern artists—Duchamp?—had signed a urinal and entered it in a show. Still, creating a house-sized joke seemed elaborate even for a Surrealist. More likely the place was what it appeared: the artist's childhood home as he had inherited it, intact and undisturbed down to the final aspidistra.

No wonder the maid had hurried off to church. A life spent caring for a Victorian mausoleum and its basement-dwelling master would make even a strong woman—even one without a sense of smell—crave spiritual reassurance.

He retraced his steps to the foyer, and studied the door's mechanism, which seemed to be the only twentieth century element in the place. To his surprise, it was not locked. The hinges made no sound, although the wooden stairs did creak a little. He flicked on his penlight, moving slowly downward, making only the noises of a house settling into the day.

At the bottom of the stairs, he turned off the light to listen. Not that he expected Didi Moreau to have a friend here, but search habits were hard to break.

He was about to turn the light on again when he stopped, then stopped breathing: some tiny noise, a skin-crawling texture of sound, little more than a faint whisper of breeze over a wheat field. When he took a few steps towards Moreau's workshop, the sound disappeared. Back at the stairs, it returned.

Aware of a stir of hair up his spine, Stuyvesant flicked on the light again, and searched out its source.

The stairs were open-backed and made of wood. In the space underneath, side by side, were two sturdy wooden crates with hinged tops. The smell alone told him what these were: Didi Moreau's corruption boxes.

His unwilling fingers reached out to work the latch and raise the lid. Below was a layer of fine screen. He pointed the beam down.

A million tiny creatures fled, pouring off the lump of gore towards the corners of the box. The red mass had no hair, just muscle, sinew, bone, and a long, naked tail. The noise had been the susurration of tiny jaws, ceaselessly gnawing flesh from the neighbor's gift.

He lowered and latched the top, checked the other box—the same setup, only the bone here appeared to be the skull of a small goat—and then stepped back.

His quiet cough of laughter didn't quite cover a shudder.

He began with a circuit through the labyrinth, following his path of two days before, to make sure the cellar was empty. He noticed small changes: a box that had been on the wall then was now on a table with several of its compartments emptied. Two others that were hanging had been given their glass coverings, with the name DIDI now carved into the frames. The small crate of Dominic Charmentier's whatnot that Stuyvesant had pawed through—Le Comte's gifts from the universe— had been emptied. Some of its contents were arranged on the nearby shelves, although the bird's nest was missing, and the infant's shoe was already incorporated into a Display, given pride of place in the center. And in a room of animal parts, a rat's skin was stretched on a frame: it had one black ear.

When he was satisfied that the cellar was uninhabited, Stuyvesant returned to the room with the hands.

When asked about prized photographs, the artist had betrayed himself with a glance at this room's dimmest corner. The shelves, Stuyvesant now found, stood not against the wall as they had appeared, but a short distance away, creating a narrow passageway, pitch-black and smelling of damp. The penlight showed a featureless passage ending in a turn. There was probably a door at the far end.

He looked all over for a key, but found nothing. With a sigh at the relative sizes of his body and the secret passage, he threaded his broad shoulders inside, shuffling his feet sideways a few inches at a time.

He didn't quite get stuck, although the turn gave him a few bad seconds, and made him glad he hadn't worn his new suit. Once around the corner, his light showed him a very old door set with—yes—a very new lock. He swore under his breath.

He managed to retrieve the picks from his trousers pocket without dropping them, but after wasting several minutes attempting to manipulate them one-handed, he decided that wasn't going to work. He tried working the mechanism blind, his hands jammed down in front of him as if using a ridiculously snug pissoir, but in the end, the only way he could get at the thing was to balance on his right foot and tilt his entire body into an angle, like a gymnast glued into the beginning of a cartwheel.

He balanced on his right foot, torn between the terror of a disastrous tumble and the knowledge that he looked absolutely ridiculous. He was shaking from strain by the time the lock gave, sweating freely despite the cool stones. When at last he staggered through the hidden door, he stood bent, hands on knees. God, he needed a cigarette. Did Moreau smoke? He didn't think so. Would the man be able to notice a little tobacco over the stink? Yes, probably.

He rubbed his hands together to shake off the desire, and the ten-

228 LAURIE R. KING

sion, then cast his light around him. He was in a little stone cupboard an arm's width across. A bulb hung from the ceiling, its wire tacked down the wall to a switch. He thumbed it on, dropping the penlight into his pocket.

Some men filled their strongboxes with money; others hid pornography. Didi Moreau's most guarded treasure appeared to be the latter—although Stuyvesant was soon to suspect it was both.

The artist's store-room contained what could only be called "death pornography." Half a dozen stilettos, their grips lovingly polished, brown stains covering their blades. Three shrunken heads, eyelids stitched shut. A gold-and-ruby poison-ring, its lethal needle sticking out from the lower edge. A dozen pretty little bottles with sealed glass stoppers, in each of which floated a naked eyeball. A decorative inlaid box containing swatches of soft leather, in hues from eggshell to ebony: all the colors of the human race.

Then he opened one of two file-boxes on a shelf, and found the photographs.

If they'd been openly pinned to the walls in Moreau's workshop, or stuck on a shelf outside, Stuyvesant would have paid them no mind. But twenty-three envelopes containing pieces of photographs, hidden away with twelve eyeballs and a box of dubious leather squares? Sure, that leather could have been very cleverly treated deerskin, and everyone knew that shrunken heads more often than not came from monkeys. But no artisan had ever made a glass eye that realistic.

So he hitched up the knees of his trousers and squatted down, laying the pieces from one of the envelopes onto the floor. There were twelve, roughly torn squares that fit together like a puzzle: a line of three made hair and the top crescent of forehead. With the next row's continuation of the hair-line came a left eye and an ear. The eye was stretched wide, staring at something below the camera lens. He sorted through the remaining pieces for the other eye, but found only a shadow and the stone wall behind her: the right side of her face was turned away from the camera.

He laid the other two corners down, and the strained neck that joined them. More slowly, he used the three that remained to fill in the woman's face: the left margin with stone, hair, and the side of her mouth; stone, neck, jaw, and throat on the right. Oddly reluctant, he stretched out his arm to lay down the final piece.

Torn into twelve pieces was the photograph of a woman in her thirties with brown hair and gray-looking teeth.

It was hard to tell if she was pretty. Her hair was collar-length and hadn't seen a comb in days. Her lipstick was smeared like a clown's—but there was nothing in the least comical about her expression.

Yeah, he could see why Moreau had kept this envelope hidden.

The picture looked overdone, staged: an actress feigning either madness, or an insane degree of terror. Her expression would go with the sounds he'd heard at the Grand-Guignol, that high-pitched, hair-raising cry of terror from the depths of the actresses' lungs. Mock fright that scraped the nerves with its realism.

But why would Moreau lock away a staged act of terror?

The fractured woman on the floor stared upwards as Stuyvesant made a quick survey of the other envelopes.

They appeared to be various poses of four different women—none of them, thank God, Pip Crosby.

Seven envelopes contained versions of the first woman: older than the others, her gray hair a matted tangle; in one of the pictures, her mouth was so wide-stretched a person could count her missing teeth. Five of the envelopes contained pieces of a blonde with the beginnings of dark roots; she had good teeth, plucked eyebrows, and dark eyes. There were also five of another brunette, a girl with faint freckles, strong white teeth, and small gold loops in her ears.

One of the envelopes had a segment missing; another had two gaps.

The blonde was the only one wearing full makeup, although the girl with the earrings had also begun her ordeal with lipstick. On all three, the makeup was smeared across their face by sweat and tears.

None of them looked much like an actress. And in any event, what actress would agree to such unflattering poses?

All the photographs were either close-ups or had been cropped to the immediate area around the head. One of them, the gray-haired woman, revealed a slice of collar under her chin. All were taken either indoors or at night outside, using flash powder that turned the faces into masks. All showed stone in the background, and when he compared them, he found it was the same wall.

The twenty-three shots were all different, but as far as he could see, only the young brunette had a version fully facing the camera. In most, the women had their heads turned to their right, as if they were pulling away from something to their left.

In none was there any hint of what that might be.

Twenty-three photographs: mesmerizing, extreme, impossible to believe. Equally impossible to dismiss.

He jerked, at five brisk taps coming from over his head. Then silence. He waited a moment, and when nothing else came, he returned the photographs to their box and reached for the other one.

No more photos, thank God, only letters, six of them. The first one said:

Cette photo être utilisé dans une Affichage. Comme avant, ne pas utiliser plus de deux morceaux.

This photograph is to be used in a Display. As before, do not use more than two pieces. The other five were similar, each having to do with a Display. All were typed. All seemed to be orders for custom pieces incorporating the photographs and, in two cases, other items: an earring and a tube of lipstick. Whether Didi's client had sent him the photographs and souvenirs, or had chosen from those provided by the artist, was not clear.

He was startled from his reading by water gushing through pipes nearby. He glanced at his watch, and cursed. That series of taps—it was the clack of the maid's Sunday shoes across the foyer tile. Moreau would not be far behind.

He started to close up the box, and then stopped. His first impulse was to leave everything untouched; his next, to take it all. So he compromised. He removed one letter and one photograph of each woman. He stirred the envelopes around, hoping that Moreau would not discover his loss, and returned the boxes to their positions.

Penlight in hand, overhead light off, he fitted himself back into the nightmare passageway. Getting the door locked was a tiny bit easier than opening it had been, and he sidled down the stonework, hoping he wasn't leaving too many betraying threads behind.

Back in the room with the display of hands, he could hear clearly the sounds from overhead. The kitchen, he thought: she was preparing lunch—water running, a clatter of pans.

He headed for the stairs—then froze. Voices came from ahead. He hadn't heard the door, or footsteps, but one of them was Moreau. He and a woman exchanged words, although he couldn't make them out. *Go eat your lunch, Didi,* he urged.

But the doorknob at the top of the stairs rattled and Stuyvesant moved fast. Before the door was fully open, he was under the stairs with the corruption boxes, flashlight in his pocket. From his other pocket he drew a long black mask: if he had to hit Moreau and run for it, at least he could keep his face from being seen.

Lights went on above the stairway; feet descended the creaking wooden steps; the tiny legs and jaws of hungry beetles stirred ceaselessly in the corruption boxes against his knees, making his gorge rise. He watched: polished shoes; Sunday trousers; jacket; then the man's head, moving off into the labyrinth. Silence fell. And stayed. Stuyvesant's pulse, which had begun to quiet, rose again. Should he head for the door now, while the man was out of sight? Would Moreau visit his safe-room? Would he see . . . ?

"Monsieur!" came the woman's voice, so immediately above him that Stuyvesant cracked his head on the wall. "Do you wish that I put the roast back into the oven?"

"No, no. I'll be there in a moment." The woman's shoes clacked away again—and Stuyvesant realized that they had not retreated earlier, but lingered at the top of the stairs. Perhaps a reminder to lunch was a regular part of their Sunday routine.

If he'd made a break for it, he'd have come face to face with her.

He wondered if she would need to make a second call, but in a minute, footsteps crunched along the gritty floor and—thank God—up the stairs. Stuyvesant narrowed his eyes against a betraying gleam, but the

artist was studying something in his hands and passed upwards, oblivious. The light went off, the door closed—did not lock—and after four
steps on the tile surface, the carpet absorbed the artist's heels.

Stuyvesant blew out a breath and lunged out from under the stairs,
away from those damned, whispering boxes. Once the motions overhead had localized to the dining room, he crept up the steps to ease the
door open a crack. When a distant clatter came from the kitchen, he
slid through the door, across the tiles, and outside.

No hue and cry was raised in his wake.

He did not stop at the first café he came to, but he did stop soon. He
threw the first drink down and was halfway through the second before
the heebie-jeebies began to leave his skin. He took the stolen envelopes
from his pocket, lining them up on the table.

Real distress, or expert pretense? If he'd seen these in another place
and time, he would be convinced that the faces grimaced in genuine
agony, the sweat was from true pain and terror. But in 1929 Paris, clever
people with twisted ideas about artistic expression were thick on the
ground, and he was willing to admit that some of them had the skill to
pull one over on Harris Stuyvesant.

He did know one man who could say for sure. But, had he any right
to place that burden on an already fragile spirit?

THIRTY-SEVEN

S TUYVESANT HESITATED OUTSIDE Nancy's door to straighten his tie, as if that might settle his thoughts as well. *You hid the photographs under the floor,* he told himself. *Now hide them from your face.*

There was no way he would go on a date with those things in his pocket. What if she—

The door opened.

"Just one minute late," he greeted her.

"Three, by my clock," she replied. She stepped back so he could enter.

"Then your clock's wrong," he declared stoutly. He turned to close the door, saying, "And on a Sunday, you never know whether the trams are running or not, so I ought to get credit for—"

Her mouth interrupted his. As he turned back to the room, his arms were abruptly filled with warm and muscular femininity, face raised to his in a kiss, and the stifled words exploded into fireworks of internal dispute: *How tall she is and oh, my, not a speck of hesitation about her and—Sarah, what about Sarah, I ought to—but Sarah was surely beyond the hand-holding stage with that cop of hers and—no, Nancy isn't about to—at least she may not intend to—not quite yet, anyway—*

Delicious. And worthy of focus.

The burst of conflict faded, the envelopes faded, as the taste of her demanded his attention, his full attention. The taste of her, and the languid demands of her mouth, and the full awareness that the body pressing against his knew exactly what it was doing, and precisely what it wanted. His arms gathered her to him, and the days of frustration and revulsion and fear and uncertainty came together in a push, and he bent towards her and in a minute, it was going—

She pulled away; his arms tightened. Her hands came up to push against his chest, and although he felt as though his body was being pulled inside-out, he let her draw back.

There was mischief on her face, but arousal in her eyes.

After a minute, he cleared his throat. "Well, that was certainly . . . unexpected."

"I wanted to get it out of the way. Otherwise we'd both be dwelling on it all afternoon: will we, won't we, when? Now we've kissed, we can relax and move on."

He thought it was too bad that *moving on* did not mean *into the bedroom*, but he had to agree, it made for a considerable shift in how he looked at the next few hours: less stress, greater anticipation.

Nancy Berger was really something.

They began on the river, a view of the city Stuyvesant had only before glimpsed. Nancy led him to the rail of the steamer, callously elbowing aside a family of awe-struck Midwesterners, and taking care to speak only French around them lest they attach themselves to their fellow countrymen.

"Any news?"

It was a question Stuyvesant had spent the weekend dreading, the question that turned disappointment into accusation: Why haven't you found her? What have you been doing?

What could he say? *I think you're right: Pip Crosby is dead?*

Because once he started telling her what he'd been doing, where did he stop? He might tell her about Le Comte's party, but how could he not then talk about Sarah? He could confide his problems, but how to explain Lulu? He could talk about Man Ray and Didi Moreau, but what could he begin to say about Doucet's frankly terrifying list of the disappeared?

"I have three—" he started, then realized even that route was impossible: I have three men who might have murdered her? He cleared his throat.

"I have three men who might know where she's gone, but I hope you understand, honey, I can't go into the details until I'm sure."

She stared across the river, looking as if he had not spoken. Looking as if she was listening to the hesitation and not the words. She sighed, then changed the subject.

"I'll bet you've never played the tourist."

"I'm sorry, Nancy. I will tell you, just not yet."

"I understand. So have you? Played the tourist in Paris?"

He propped his elbows next to hers on the railing. "Not since the War."

"You were here? With the American forces?"

"For a few months."

"Where?"

Her brother, it turned out, had volunteered about the same time Stuyvesant had, and had spent time in the same part of the Front. But when she showed him a photograph, fading and worn, he did not know the face—at least, no more than he knew the faces of any stranger in a familiar uniform.

"He died?"

"It took a while, but yes, the War killed him eventually."

"In France? Or did they ship him home?" He settled one arm back across her shoulders.

"Oh, he sailed home. And he stayed there for five years, before he came back to Paris and put a gun to his head."

"Sounds like you were close."

"Ned was my twin."

His arm gave an involuntary contraction. They stood, watching the city scroll past, and the four envelopes under his floorboards crept back into Stuyvesant's mind.

"The police came on Thursday," she said. "To look at Phil's room."

Thursday was the day the gendarme had tossed his own room.

"Good. Was it Doucet?"

"A skinny little guy with a turned-in mouth?"

"Sergeant Fortier. Did he find anything?"

"Not that he told me."

"So, where are we going?" he asked, after they had traveled a while downstream.

"Several places I like," she replied. "I hope you're wearing comfortable shoes."

Stuyvesant later figured they covered ten miles that day. The steamer let them off at Suresnes. They walked to the American cemetery to leave flowers on her brother's grave, before setting off in a lazy circle through the Parc de Saint-Cloud and across the bridge into the Bois du Boulogne. There they wandered aimlessly, talking all the while, holding hands from time to time, pausing three times in quiet corners to neck.

She'd decided to find another apartment, she told him. She didn't have to say, *Because Phil is still there.*

Late in the afternoon, they allowed themselves to be pulled along by a drift of crowds heading towards Luna Park. At the entrance, Nancy turned to him.

"Do you skate?"

"What?" he said absently. Looking up at the cheerful sign, he'd had a vision of Pip Crosby, going for a last outing with Charmentier, her . . . what? Friend? Mentor? Employer?

Murderer?

"Harris?"

Why the hell had he imagined that she might be off in the sun—

"Are you all right?"

—or that he'd be able to step in and be the hero, sending her back to her mother and Uncle Crosby, to laugh with them about *That time in Paris when we thought*—

"Harris!"

He made an enormous effort, and was back with Nancy. "It's not exactly the time of year for skating."

"What is the matter with you?"

"Nothing."

"You're thinking about Phil, aren't you?"

He blew out a breath, and admitted, "I was thinking about her mother and her uncle, yeah."

She watched a man, a woman, and a little girl with ringlets go into the rink. "We lost two soldiers in my parents' building, during the War. The son of a family upstairs was killed outright. The son of another family downstairs was declared missing in action. You'd think they would have an easier time of it, since they at least could hope, but in fact, it was far worse for them, not knowing."

"Like a wound that doesn't heal."

"Not finding Phil would devastate her mother," she agreed.

"And the uncle. He seems close to her."

"Maybe a little too close."

"What do you mean?"

"Just, something Phil said once, that her uncle would control what kind of tooth-paste she used if he could."

"That's what you meant when you told me she came here to get away from Boston?"

"Did I say that? It's probably true. She missed her mother. It made her sad when her mother couldn't travel." She straightened her back and turned to him. "Look, if Phil's going to join us, I'd rather go home. Being here with her is just too jarring."

She was right: it wasn't fair—to Nancy. With an apology to Pip, he reached for Nancy's hand and gave her a smile as bright as the sky.

"Nope, I'm okay. Let's enjoy the sunshine while we can. Speaking of sunshine, isn't it awfully warm for skating? How do they keep the ice going?"

"It's roller skating!"

"Really? Oh, it's been a long time since—"

He allowed her to lead him into the cacophonous rink, strapping on a pair of too-small skates and teetering around the edges before his body remembered. And then Nancy was famished, and they handed back the skates and walked on quivering legs to a sort of biergarten that had fewer howling infants than most of the surrounding cafés. Once restored, they gravitated to the rides: a roller-coaster where Nancy shrieked along with the Paris shop girls, a spinning tea-cup where Nancy laughed as freely as the children, and a carousel where Nancy claimed a golden lion and Stuyvesant stood at her side. He bought her a pair of red balloons, he won her a doll at the shooting gallery, he let her crash into him all along the undulating floor of the dodgem cars. When night fell and the smaller children were taken away, they moved to the dance hall, which Nancy pronounced "magnificently bourgeois," donning an air of Edwardian dignity entirely at odds with her clothing.

And all the while, he was mourning Pip Crosby. The previous day, he'd been in a rage, maddened by failure and wanting to hold his gun to someone's head—anyone's head. He'd spent the day walking, and by the end, he was no longer angry, he was simply sad, and grimly determined.

So today, while he laughed at Nancy's antics with a bean-bag toss, he was also feeling the loss of a Clara Bow grin. When Nancy misjudged a kiss on the carousel, the crack of their meeting teeth evoked a memory of a similar mishap with Pip. And when they closed out the park at midnight and claimed two seats on the crowded tram, he was saying good-bye to Philippa Anne Crosby.

His feet ached pleasantly. Nancy fell asleep on his shoulder, beret tipped over one ear, the surviving red balloon bobbing over her head. He woke her when they changed lines, and woke her again when they disembarked, tucking her arm in his, and walking her to her door, up her stairs, into her front room.

She blinked at the familiar surroundings, then sat with a *thump* onto the settee. He lowered his bulk down beside her, physically tired but far from sleep. Unlike Nancy, whose eyes were again drooping.

It was clear as day that the entertainments were over, even without the ghost of Pip Crosby looking over their shoulders.

She leaned against him, inviting him to wrap his arms around her.

"I have an appointment in the morning," she murmured. "A rental agency."

"I'll go in a minute."

"I don't want you to. I mean, I do, but . . ."

"Sweetheart, I'll see you tomorrow. Dinner, right?"

She turned her face to his, and although it was touch-and-go for a few minutes as to whether their choice would stand, when she began to sag, he sat back, pulling her into his shoulder. She nestled into him with a sigh, a sweet little noise of contentment that twisted his heart into a complicated knot.

The building was silent, not a sound of water in the pipes or a shift of settling walls.

"I had a brother, too," he said into the stillness. "His name was Tim. Great kid. Bright as can be. Everyone loved him. He used to follow me everywhere, when we were boys. And when I enlisted, so did he, even though he was underage. When I went back to the Bureau, he followed me there, too. Until one day he got caught up in a riot, one I might've stopped but didn't. He fell, and somebody kicked him, hard. Came out with a head injury that took about as long to kill him as your brother's did."

She did not react.

"I wasn't there when he died. It didn't involve a gun, but it's hard to go home, to look his widow in the eye. I send her money. Hope that's enough."

Nancy slumped against him, completely slack. Just as well. He smiled, kissed the top of her head, then stood and slid his arms underneath her.

She jerked awake, startled, before throwing her arms around his neck and allowing him to carry her to her room. He set her down. She stood, obedient as a child, while he turned back the covers and pushed her gently onto the edge. He took off her shoes, lifted her legs to the bed, and tucked the covers around her.

When he kissed her forehead, her eyes were closed, but she smiled.

He stood in the doorway for a while, listening to her breathing.

Unresponsive roommate, my ass.

He closed her door, and opened the next. Fortier had removed some of Pip's letters, her checkbook, some papers. But he had shown no interest in the art on the walls.

In five minutes, he let himself out of the apartment. When he came to the river, he turned left, following the quay to the Île St. Louis. He crossed over onto the little island, wandering through its silence until the Pont Saint-Louis took him to the Île de la Cité. Past the magnificence of Notre Dame, around the Palais de Justice, and across the road to the small park at its prow, the Vert-Galant. Voices came from a moored barge; lights from the shore danced along the placidly flowing water.

He took out his cigarette case, but this time, his fingers sought out the hidden latch. He felt it give, worked his fingernail under the slick paper inside.

He slid the case away, then took out the Ronson.

By its light, he saw Sarah's face. She studied him as the flames crept up from the corner, gazed out from the blackening paper.

And then she was gone. He dropped the burning ash, letting the light breeze carry it out onto the water.

One good-bye to Pip; another good-bye to Sarah Grey.

Time to start anew.

THIRTY-EIGHT

A CONVERSATION:
"Lee, where's my revolver?"

"You have a *revolver*?"

"Sure. Have you seen it?"

"Why do you have a revolver?"

"You never know when you might want to shoot someone."

"Who is there to shoot? You think the Germans are coming back?"

"Not for a while. But there's always me. Or you."

"Yes, sweetheart, I saw your *Suicide* picture. It wasn't very funny."

"It wasn't meant to be funny."

"Well, it wasn't beautiful, either. Please, Man, get rid of the gun."

"Why? Revolvers are beautiful things."

"With all the drunks who come here, I'd think a loaded weapon was the last thing you'd want lying around."

"Clearly it isn't lying around, or you'd have seen it."

"If I find it, I'm not going to give it to you."

"Yes, you will."

"I'll throw it in the river."

"You do and I'll beat you."

"Please, Man."

"What, are you afraid I'll shoot you with it?"

"More likely yourself."

"Don't worry, honey. If I shoot you, I'll take a fantastic picture of your dead body. You'll be famous forever."

"What if you shoot yourself?"

"Then I'll make sure you get blamed for it. You'll still be famous."

"Only if there's a camera around."

"There is that. Okay, I'll make sure there is."

THIRTY-NINE

L ATE MONDAY MORNING, at a table stacked with half a dozen coffee saucers, Stuyvesant crumpled up yet another sheet of paper. His
notebook was up to date, the week's letter to Uncle Crosby written, but
this last writing job was a killer.

He'd spent an hour that morning, cursing his clumsy fingers
and Mme. Benoit's glue pot, piecing together the four photographs—
all but one, unfortunately, missing a segment. The results were a little
distorted, and the youngest girl had a gap where her eye should have
been, but they would be recognizable.

Their emotion was all too recognizable.

How could he possibly inflict these photographs on Bennett Grey?
Sarah seemed to think her brother as shaky as ever. It astounded
Stuyvesant that the poor bastard hadn't walked into the ocean long
before this. And if he did send them, what could he say? *A friend of
mine may be dead, but I have no proof?* Or, *I think a brave little fool named
Pip is dead, which is easier than thinking of her alive? Oh and by the way,
I have these awful pictures I want you to look at—which may not even have
anything to do with my case?*

Stuyvesant had to know if the pictures were real. If they were fakes,
Grey would simply look at them and laugh. If they weren't, well, it
would be a lousy thing to do to a man like him.

But Stuyvesant had to know. And Bennett was the only one who could tell him.

In the end, he decided not to give Grey any details. There was no need to write him about missing blondes, or suspicions about the men surrounding Sarah, or the complexities that had cropped up in Stuyvesant's relationship with her. Just ask the man if the photos were fakes, and let it go at that.

> Bennett,
>   Sorry to disturb you, but I need to know if these can be real, and I don't know who else to ask. I'm hoping you tell me they were staged.
>   I saw Sarah the other night, she's looking well.
>
> Harris

But all those unsaid facts didn't make the morning any easier. As soon as he had a page he could live with, he put it with the photographs into the envelope he'd bought, all the time trying to decide if he was being irresponsible, if he should in fact tell Grey what was going on . . .

The shoddy post office pen stubbed twice into the rough manila, but at last he had the thing addressed, securely sealed, and in the post.

The instant he handed it over, he wanted to snatch it back.

"I want to start by asking you a favor," Stuyvesant began. "Let me have my say before you jump in. Okay?"

It's not like you have any proof, he told himself for the tenth time. If he did, he'd have handed it over, even if that meant revealing the Moreau break-in.

But the pictures weren't proof, of anything. He'd have to point the cop at Moreau without them.

Doucet tipped back in his chair, hands folded over his vest.

"First off, I've decided to look at Pip Crosby not as a missing person, but as a murder victim. You don't—"

Doucet's chair legs thumped to the floor. "Why? What have you learned?"

"Nothing. Not in the sense of evidence. There's just an accumulation of facts that . . . Well, okay, it's a feeling. That if she was out there, I'd have heard. But like I was saying, *you* don't have to look at it that way. In fact, I'd rather you didn't, since if you pass the case on to your homicide team, I'll be out in the cold.

"Secondly, I'm going to figure Pip is one of a series of murders. Why and who I don't know—like I said, this is how I'm looking at them, and I'm just trying to include you in my thoughts.

"There are three names that have come up time and again in relation to Pip Crosby. Those are Man Ray, Didi Moreau, and Dominic Charmen—"

"Oh, Monsieur, you cannot be serious about—"

"You said you wouldn't interrupt."

Doucet raised his hands and sat back again, all but saying aloud how little interest he had in Le Comte.

"I'll start with the American, Man Ray. He knew Pip Crosby. He took photographs of her. He has pictures with models looking like the victims in brutal murders, and he makes the kind of motion pictures you wouldn't let your mother go to, although I'm hardly an impartial judge of that kind of shock-art. But both those things mean that he knows actors, and he hires models. He's friends with Moreau, who uses human bones in his Displays. Ray brings Moreau objects. He likes damaged women. His current one looks like she could be Pip Crosby's sister."

What he couldn't say: Man Ray knows well how to use the kind of flash used in those horror-photographs.

"Then there's Didi Moreau. An extremely odd egg, lives in a kind of mausoleum—hasn't changed so much as an antimacassar since his mother died. He has an equally ghoulish imagination and a basement workshop full of bones and body parts. He's trained in taxidermy, and has boxes filled with carrion beetles that he drops rats and you-name-it into. They're too small for a person, but he has both the skills and the tools for taking apart a larger subject. And beyond that, he's—he's cold, I guess is how I'd describe it. As if his Displays are the most important thing in the world, and everything else—every*one* else—is only there to provide him with raw material.

"But using his personality as a reason to suspect him runs up against the problem that it works the other way, too. He's clever enough to do away with a number of people, but doing it without getting caught? That might be more or less accidental." Personally, he could see Moreau absent-mindedly letting bodies pile up in his sitting room. Perhaps if the maid was in charge of disposal—but that was too far-fetched. He went on, since he could mention none of Moreau's hidden possessions.

"Then there's Dominic Char—yes, I'm sorry—Charmentier. Le Comte. He's worked with both Moreau and Ray, he brings Moreau boxes of whatnot. If Moreau sees the rest of the world as being there to bring him raw material, Charmentier sees the world as being there to serve him. And sure, that's something that goes along with having fifteen generations of money, but it's also a thing that I've seen in the kind of killers who find morality an inconvenience. You're a cop, Doucet. You know what I'm talking about."

Doucet gave a noncommittal bob to his head.

"Look at the man's house," Stuyvesant argued. "Have you seen it? The room with the plaster faces?"

"Sarah told me about it."

"What kind of a person would collect those things? I know the man has paid a heavy price for his country, and he talks about the Grand-Guignol as some kind of psychotherapy for the world, but it seems to me his collection takes things a little far. Those faces, they make you wonder."

"Plaster masks are a long way from murder."

"But still, if your face had been destroyed, would you want your image decorating someone's wall?"

"There's nothing new about the aristocracy's lack of sensitivity," Doucet pointed out. "Both our countries had revolutions because of it."

"It's not just lack of sensitivity. He . . . sometimes he's like a walking version of that theater, doing things that are just hair-raising."

"May I respond now?"

"Go ahead."

"Le Comte is a war hero, from a prominent Parisian family. He single-handedly supports a number of organizations for the indigent, the wounded—and the families of policemen killed in the line of duty. He lectures at the Sorbonne, he is personal friends with half the politicians in France, and if nothing else, he would be recognized wherever he went. I am no particular friend of his class, but this man has earned the right to a quirky hobby like the Théâtre du Grand-Guignol."

"Don't you think those could be a clever devil hiding his tracks?"

"M. Stuyvesant, listen to yourself. Do you have any proof for these accusations? Any evidence? Anything other than your dislike for the aristocracy?" The sharp edge to Doucet's voice was not simply the impatience of a policeman, it was personal. And Stuyvesant knew where it came from: a yellow-haired, one-handed Englishwoman demanded that Doucet act; his job as a cop made action impossible.

"Not a bit. Yet."

Doucet shook his head. "M. Stuyvesant, if you wish to remain in France, I strongly suggest that you do not pursue your baseless suspicions."

"Okay, how about Moreau?"

"Why him, and not M. Ray?"

"You should be looking at both of them. But Moreau gives me the creeps. He . . . I didn't like the way he tried to get Sarah to take off her hand."

Doucet grimaced. "He did make the thing. She'd have to take it off for him to look at it, wouldn't she?"

"I know. It's just . . . He seemed more interested in the stump than in the hand itself. And then there's this."

He took from his pocket the object that he'd removed from Pip's bedroom late last night, wrapped in a clean-enough handkerchief. He laid it on Doucet's desk, folding back the linen. "I got this from one of those Didi Moreau boxes that Pip Crosby had on her bedroom wall. I'm no expert, but that looks to me like a human finger."

Doucet picked it up between thumb and forefinger, holding it to the light like a speculating gemcutter. "You could be right. But what of it? It's no crime to possess human bones."

"No, but how you get them can be another matter. You know those carrion beetles? Well, this bone seems really . . . fresh."

Doucet placed the object back on the handkerchief with the same distaste Stuyvesant had felt at the fossilized feces. However: "His neighbors might not like it, but I would doubt that it's against the law to feed your beetles pieces of human being. If, for example, you got them from a hospital."

"And if you cut them from the person against their will?"

"It's just a bone," the cop said. "No indications of violence."

"Inspector Doucet, I don't have the keenest imagination in Paris, but I have no trouble seeing Moreau as a guy who would happily amputate a hand to get at the bones."

The two men looked at each other, then looked away.

Stuyvesant was tempted to ask how Sarah had reacted at being told to steer clear of her boss. However, he didn't think a direct question would be a great idea.

"How's Sarah?"

"Fine," Doucet said automatically. "Busy. Le Comte is having a party Wednesday—the night of the full moon."

"I know, he invited me."

"He did?"

"Yeah. Why?"

"Oh, nothing. It's just that, I understand the venue is small and the invitation list . . . equally so."

"Too exclusive for the likes of me, you mean?"

"No, I'm sure you are . . ."

"Sarah was there. I think he asked me because he knew I was a friend of hers."

The *flic* slapped shut the file on his desk. "Anyway. She's very busy planning it. I'm thinking of taking her off for a few days, after she's finished."

Stuyvesant's internal smile faded at this deft reversal of claims. "Good plan," he said politely. "She does have a tendency to work too hard." Then he caught himself: one-upmanship was a stupid game to play with this man. He slumped back against the chair. "Sorry, I'm being petty. I like Sarah a lot. I'm glad she's happy."

Doucet eyed him with mistrust, but after a minute, he took out his cigarettes. "I will look into the lives of Moreau and this American photographer. If I take the police pathologist along with me to Moreau's house, it could save some time. As for M. Ray, it might be simpler to have his visa revoked."

"Sending him back to New York, free to carry on?"

"If he is, in fact, guilty of anything."

"As you say."

Doucet tapped at his cigarette a few times. "My responsibility is to Paris, not New York. Still, I would not wish that on my conscience. He may stay, for the present."

"And you suggest we don't even look at Charmentier?"

"If I did see any evidence that he should be investigated," Doucet said reluctantly, "I would do so. Even though my superiors would not make it easy for me."

"On the other hand," Stuyvesant supplied, "who'd be surprised if a blunt American were to stumble into Charmentier, here and there?"

Doucet fixed him with a long, hard gaze, which Stuyvesant moved to deflect.

"I take it you haven't talked Sarah into quitting?"

"She refuses to consider it until after the party."

"So she is vulnerable."

"In any number of ways."

"You know my history, Doucet. You know I'm good at what I do."

"When you are not stumbling drunk in a night-club."

Ouch. "That was before I knew what was involved," he pointed out. "*Who* was involved."

"There can be no more such mistakes."

"No."

"And you will inform me immediately, if you turn up any pertinent information."

"Yes."

Both men stood. Stuyvesant waited, to see if Doucet would put out a hand, but the cop had one more thing on his mind. "Monsieur, you are aware that the police disapprove of civilians carrying hand-guns?"

"Yeah, I'm aware of that."

Doucet listened and looked for the hidden meaning, and found it. The two men exchanged a firm clasp, and Stuyvesant left.

He dodged across the Pont Neuf to the pointed end of the Île de la Cité, where he leaned on the rail, watching a fisherman put together his long pole.

He was glad for a declaration of truce, between him and the cop. But Doucet was right, there could be no more slips. Any careless word or gesture could put Sarah in danger. Any failure of attention could let a key fact slip away—and put Sarah in danger.

Exactly as he and Bennett between them had done, three years ago.

FORTY

Twenty minutes later, Harris Stuyvesant was standing in an art gallery.

At least, it was supposed to be an art gallery. Sarah had given him the address, saying there were several Didi Displays on the walls, but the place looked more like a junk dealer's.

A nicked and dust-impregnated elephant's foot umbrella stand with a spray of peacock's feathers in it, one of which was splattered with something he hoped was only brown paint. Three stuffed finches with jeweled eyes, threaded onto the sort of metal skewer used by Turkish restaurants. A boot—just a plain old boot with mended laces, but displayed inside an ornate gilt frame more suited to a Renaissance painting. On a long display shelf stood a skeleton, but of what? After a closer look, he decided the object included the remains of three or four different animals, pieced together to create an impossible creature: the skull of a small crocodile and front feet of some paddling creature, its back feet had the blunt nails of a dog, and it all came to an end in a long prehensile tail of some kind of monkey.

As he wandered through the exhibits, the room's original odor—surprisingly fresh and citrusy, as if someone was making lemonade in a back room—gave way to the smell of damp earth, although there was no sign of a garden, or even an open window. He gave a mental shrug, walked on—then jerked to attention as the next breath plunged him into the icy panic of the trenches.

The bespectacled organism who had greeted his entrance sniggered. "Monsieur, do not be concerned, it is not a gas attack, merely the Odorama."

Stuyvesant stared, first at him, then at the direction of his pointing finger. Indeed, the terrifying smell was already fading, and it did seem to emanate from a peculiar contraption in the corner.

A bicycle wheel, ticking gently clockwise, its spokes mounted with fifteen perfume atomizers. As he watched, one of the bulbs edged into the noon position, where a miniature set of paddles waited, and a ridged trigger wire. The bulb pressed the trigger, and the paddles snapped down, releasing a puff of scent.

Banana.

"Un opéra d'odeur," the man explained, then translated in heavily accented English: "A symphony of scent."

"Un polyphonie de puanteur," Stuyvesant commented. The man giggled.

"Yes, Monsieur, the odors of life are not always pleasant."

The current one was cloyingly sweet, as if he'd stuck his head into a vat of candy floss. He moved away, before it could change to rotting corpses or dog shit.

"I'm interested in Didi Moreau," he told the man.

"Are we not all? This piece is by Le Didi." The gallery owner made a proud gesture at the skewered songbirds. "And this here." His hand displayed the glories of the unnatural skeleton. "And in the next room, we have more."

The adjoining room contained several Moreau boxes, and as he studied them, Stuyvesant had to admit that they did contain that artistic je ne sais quoi, a sensation that insinuated itself into the viewer's mind and touched off a note of response. One of the boxes, for example, focused on a childhood day at the beach: sand, a square of faded postcard, a doll-sized beach umbrella. One of the squares was empty, although its sides and back were painted; after a while, he decided that its pink was the exact color of sunburn. The pain of nostalgia, he guessed.

"Would Monsieur care to see some of Didi's . . . older work?"

The man might have been offering dirty postcards. Stuyvesant summoned the appropriate enthusiasm, and waited while the man unlocked a door.

He looked around the room in surprise. "This is taxidermy."

"Yes, Monsieur, much as I enjoy the Displays, I find it a pity that Didi has moved on from his Tableaux. We are fortunate to have a few."

Stuyvesant could see why the door was kept locked, even in Paris.

The Victorians had been big on taxidermy tableaux, dressing up thirty stuffed mice, for example, like a classroom of schoolchildren, or arranging elaborately dressed kittens into a formal wedding. They also had a peculiar fondness for freaks: two-headed sheep, puppies with an extra pair of legs coming from their shoulder blades.

Moreau's work might have given even Victorians pause.

A bloody murder scene in an old-fashioned kitchen, enacted by red squirrels; a battlefield littered by dozens of tiny uniformed white mice, sprawled in death or advancing with bayonets fixed; a Mediaeval torture conducted by two lizards on a ginger kitten stretched on a miniature rack.

Any impulse to black laughter died at the sight of the room's other pieces.

Somehow, rape, sodomy, and mass orgies lost any amusement value when the contorted figures were all six inches high and covered by baby-soft fur.

Stuyvesant cleared his throat. "As you say, these are certainly . . . unique. Surrealists must find them, er, viscerally exciting."

The man clapped his hands in the thrill of finding a kindred spirit. "Precisely! Oh, Monsieur, I will admit that I have great hopes for these. Monsieur Didi was here just the other day, in conversation with another artist, discussing how the Tableaux might be used in a film."

Stuyvesant turned, seeing his own face in the man's thick glasses. "Oh yes? And who might that be?"

"Monsieur Man Ray. Do you know him? A genius, his film on . . ."

Stuyvesant let the man run on. But as he studied the frozen twist of the features on the tortured kitten, he could not help seeing the agony in the pieced-together photographs.

With a group of artists whose highest ambition was the outrageous and the offensive, who was to say where they drew the line? When the most basic tenet of a man's philosophy was that society's mores and values were there to be smashed and pissed upon, why not extend that to human life?

So what if a girl's mother and uncle were in an agony of uncertainty? So what if a little boy went to bed without his mother's brassy blonde head bending down to kiss him good-night? What did that matter—so long as the great God Art prevailed over the City of Light?

Forty minutes after walking away from the de Sade orgy of hamsters, Stuyvesant stepped inside the Théâtre du Grand-Guignol.

The audience was different from the previous week. A lot more women, for one thing, their nervous laughter dominating the room even before the curtain rose.

No, not nervous: anticipatory. They knew what was coming, he decided, and were looking forward to it. And, he saw, many of those in the confessional-like boxes had men at their sides, with a great deal of physical contact going on, even with the lights still up.

The lights dimmed, and he braced himself, calling to mind what both Nancy and Sarah had told him: the shock was deliberate, the emotional equivalent of a Scandinavian sauna and icy bath.

It was a different play from the one he'd seen with Nancy the week before, although it had much the same effect: relentlessly horrific, startlingly realistic, utterly disturbing. This one had an unexpectedly Amazonian edge to it, with two women trapping a handsome young—

Stuyvesant jumped when something touched his leg. He stared at his neighbor, but her eyes were fixed on the stage. He looked down, and indeed, it was her slim hand, resting above his knee. Could she possibly be unaware . . . ?

Then the hand moved, and he was in no doubt. The fingers slid gently down the inner side of his leg, then traced a circle up again, then down.

Each time, they traveled a fraction of an inch closer to his fly. Another minute, two at the most, and things would have got out of hand.

He peeled up her fingers and returned her arm to her lap, sitting back amused, if physically uncomfortable.

The play ended, the shift was made to comedy, with the exaggerated relief of too-loud laughter. But after the short-lived farce they were back in the land of horror, with a doctor performing surgery on an un-anesthetized and well-endowed young woman, tying her wrists to the table, performing an examination that closely resembled a dance of the seven veils, hunching over her fainting body like one of the art gallery's taxidermy figures . . .

And again, the hand came to rest on his leg.

This time, he removed it before it could start its progress in the di-rection of his crotch. He placed it firmly on her skirt, pushing it down in a command.

But as his hand withdrew, she grabbed it, pulling firmly.

He let her.

He was curious, to see how far she might go. Excited, too—even a man long past adolescence had his fantasies—but mostly curious. Not for long: when a girl takes a man's hand, tucks it under the edge of her skirt, and eases her knees apart—well, there's not much doubt about what she has in mind.

He was tempted, if for no other reason than it was an experience he was unlikely to have too many times in life. But in the end, before he could learn just how little she was wearing, he pulled his hand away and leaned over against her ear.

"Désolé, chèrie, but you chose the wrong sort of man for this."

A professional would have picked up on the catch in his breathing, to say nothing of his shifting to get comfortable, and known he was no pansy. But this one just whipped both hands down to tug at her skirt, then stared fixedly at the stage until the end of the play.

When the lights rose, so did she, pushing her way down the row of seats without looking back.

Too bad, really. It had sure helped take his mind off the stuff on the stage.

In the end, there were seven brief plays, beginning and ending with darkness. The gasps and cries of the audience began to sound more like something you'd hear in a bedroom, and indeed, when the lights came up and the attendees spilled out onto rue Chaptal, the coy glances and flushed cheeks more closely resembled the glances of incautious lovers than the appreciation of playgoers.

He'd been to a brothel one time that had a woman happy to push things, a little further than usual. As it turned out, his preference lay elsewhere, but it had been enlightening to see how a touch of pain could spice things up.

This was something, he reflected, that Sarah Grey would not understand.

But Nancy Berger might.

FORTY-ONE

DESPITE A DAY spent with artistic murder and mutilation, Stuyvesant had a lift to his step as he rounded the corner onto the rue Vavin.

Maybe the Grand-Guignol had a point: nothing like a dose of adrenaline and quease to make a man appreciate life's promises. He was looking forward to a cool shower. He was looking forward to Nancy. He'd even managed to push the worries about Pip and Lulu and a list of vanished women out of his mind for a few minutes at a time—he found himself humming a tune, one of the Cole Porter songs he and Nancy had danced to at Bricktop's: "Let's Do It. Let's Fall in Love."

"Even educated fleas do it," he sang under his breath, trotting up the steps.

"Monsieur!" came a voice through the perpetually open door just inside the building's entrance.

"Bonsoir, Mme. Benoit," he replied. The old Communite widow was standing just inside her door, so he stepped right up and took her in his arms, dipping and twirling her cautiously around her cluttered sitting room. "Birds do it, bees do it," he sang.

She giggled like a schoolgirl and batted at his chest until he let her go. "Monsieur, I am too old for such things."

"I've seen your boyfriends, Mme. Benoit. You're never too old for love. What can I do for you?"

"Un petit-bleu," she said, patting her hair back into place and giving a lift of the chin to the small table by the door.

Reluctantly, he picked it up. Like a telegram, a petit-bleu was never good news.

It wasn't. It contained an apology from Nancy: she had a visitor tonight. Maybe later in the week?

He felt his mood deflate like a leaky balloon.

He'd been holding tonight in front of his nose all day, a carrot to get him through the letter to Grey, the conversation with Doucet, the gallery—to say nothing of those damned plays. If he'd known the day was going to end with another frustration, he'd have let that lady play a little more than whoopee on his leg.

Christ. He needed a drink.

"I need a drink, Jimmy."

The Falstaff was where you went when you wanted a safe drunk. The one-time prizefighter knew how to keep things from getting out of hand without calling the cops, especially when it came to his occasional sparring partners—Charters was small, but quick despite his years out of the ring.

He poured Stuyvesant a generous whisky, then left his hand on the glass as he studied his customer.

"I'll give you a drink, but that isn't what you need."

"You don't think so?"

"You look like you need to hit something."

"Are you going to let me have that?"

The barman took his hand away, and Stuyvesant let the booze sear its way down.

But Jimmy was right. Harris Stuyvesant needed to hit someone. If he hung around the Quarter tonight, he'd end up brawling—and risk a very uncomfortable conversation with Sarah's cop fiancé.

God, what if it's Hemingway I take a swing at? Be just my luck to walk into him and end up lacing on the gloves. And it's damned hard work, climbing into a ring with that bastard: can't let him see you pulling your punches,

but if you knock him out, you'd never hear the end of it. So touchy, you'd swear
he was five foot rather than six.

He threw some money on the zinc bar, waved his thanks at Jimmy, and took himself down to one of the French gyms to bash the hell out of a bag, first, and a couple of guys, after.

When he went back to the hotel, he was aching pleasantly from fist to knees, and had great hopes for the temptations of his hard bed. He stripped, climbed between the sheets, and switched off the lights. But as the darkness settled in, the room seemed to fill with reproachful ghosts.

FORTY-TWO

MONDAY'S AGGRAVATIONS PROVED nothing compared to Tuesday's.

Doucet told him that he'd found no incriminating evidence in Didi Moreau's house: none. Moreau claimed the finger bones had been left in the offerings box at the gate; that he didn't even know they were fingers.

Doucet hadn't found the safe-room; Stuyvesant didn't dare tell him about it.

He loitered on the street outside Man Ray's studio for two hours before Ray and Lee Miller came out and walked north along Boulevard Raspail to lunch at the Coupole. He settled down across the street at the Rotonde, and thought all was going well until the Miller woman gave him a little wave of the fingers, looking amused.

Since he'd been spotted, Stuyvesant retreated, going back down Raspail to a photographic supply shop he had noticed a few streets over from the Ray studio. He found that, yes, M. Ray shopped there, and that M. Ray was a regular customer of magnesium powder, being a devoté of flash-photography. Stuyvesant then worked the conversation around to the woman Ray had taken up with, agreeing with the shopkeeper that Mme. Miller was indeed une pêche, but he wondered—just wondered—if perhaps M. Ray was taking advantage of her innocence . . .

The man's chattiness ceased; in thirty seconds, Stuyvesant was out on the street.

He then went to see if Dominic Charmentier might be taking a long breakfast at his customary café. He wasn't sure if he planned on talking with him or just pounding him one, but in either case, he did not get the chance. Rounding the corner, he saw the man standing farther down the street, his hand raised to summon a taxi.

At his side was Sarah Grey; she was laughing as he helped her into the cab.

Which left Nancy Berger. Stuyvesant went back and forth over how best to approach her before finally deciding that showing up at her door while she was occupied with her damned visitor carried too great a risk of rejection, so he telephoned instead.

At the start of the call she sounded cross; at the end, she had gone coy. She still wouldn't see him.

And to top the day off, he was stalking past the crowded Dôme terrace on his way to a less-populated brasserie, when what should he hear but the commanding tones of Ernest Hemingway, demanding that Stuyvesant join his coterie.

The cocky writer spent the whole evening crowing about his financial security and pecking verbally at Harris Stuyvesant.

And as he left the bar, the skies opened, turning Harris Stuyvesant's new suit and Panama hat to sodden burlap.

FORTY-THREE

WEDNESDAY WAS NO better.

In the morning, it rained. Why had he ever complained about the summer?

In the afternoon, he received a letter from Pip's mother that was so determinedly chipper it made him want to put his gun to his head.

And why the hell hadn't he heard from Bennett Grey?

FORTY-FOUR

A CONVERSATION:
"I don't suppose there's been any reaction from Cornwall?"
"Captain Grey? No, sir."
"I hope it wasn't a mistake, letting him have that letter."
"Sir, I don't understand why we didn't open it first."
"He'd have known."
"Sir, we could have done it so he'd have been unaware."
"Anyone else, maybe, but not Grey. Nobody believes how much he sees."
"Even if that were the case, sir, what would it matter?"
"Because we need him, damn it—and we need him friendly, which he wouldn't be if he suspected interference. We're lucky he didn't raise holy hell last week over that bloody photographer of yours."
"You honestly think he spotted him, sir?"
"I know he did. Just like he'd spot it if anyone but the postman touched that bloody letter. He'd have known in a flash. You think I'm exaggerating."
"Sir, I—"
"Never mind. Just follow your orders, and keep everyone away from him except the men with the binoculars. He knows about them, he puts up with them, but that's it."

"If you say so, sir."

"A bloody pain, is what he is. Any rate, I'm off, wake me if the little prick does anything."

"Sleep well, sir."

"Not bloody likely!"

FORTY-FIVE

WEDNESDAY EVENING, THE full moon began to push through clouds above the City of Light. It nosed into the city's dark corners, danced on the Seine, played with the spires of stone and steel. Caused the blood to stir in reply.

Harris Stuyvesant bathed and shaved and dressed with care, making up for the shortcomings of his evening suit by impeccable grooming. He checked his nails and teeth, retied his bow tie, buffed his polished shoes, and looked at the man standing in the mirror.

With luck, no one would mistake him for one of the waiters.

He walked. Down through Montparnasse, heels clicking on the pavement, through the swirls of pedestrians feeling the moon in their bones, he thought about women.

Nancy Berger, who had stepped away from him.

Sarah Grey, who had not—or, not entirely.

Pip Crosby, who had disappeared from life. Poor scarred girl, turning a pretty face to the world, putting on a brave front, always aware—every instant, she must've been—of the slick, burned skin that tugged at her side.

And Lulu. *Jesus: how can you* still *not know her last name?* All he knew about her was that she'd been warm and spontaneous and fun, exactly what he'd needed after the failures of Berlin. And that now she was dead, leaving two small children and a mother behind.

Pip and Lulu: two women with nothing in common except taking one look at his sorry face and responding with bounce and willingness. He had spent days with both of them and never bothered to look under the surface. Never noticed any unhappiness either might have. Given only fleeting thought to how much trouble they'd been through.

And the other thing they had in common: both were dead. Probably. But why? Lulu might have picked up the wrong man, or crossed one somehow, but what about Pip? If her death was tied to those insane Displays, then how? Even Moreau wasn't nutty enough to kill a girl in order to harvest her bones.

Was he?

Not many would be.

Unless . . . could the process itself be the goal? What if the corruption of death was not the means of the art, but the ends: the art itself?

If an amputated hand could be tossed onto the pavement for actors to prod, if a signed urinal or a line of tacks glued on an iron were considered art, when a ballet film opened with rooftop artillery and boxing gloves, who was to say that there weren't deranged art lovers out there who considered a rotting body the ultimate in avant-garde creativity?

If so, he'd like the chance to make the artist into an artwork of his own.

He walked under the brilliant moon towards the Place D'Enfer, aware of the bones of Paris beneath his feet. Across from the Métro station he turned east, passing the café where he had jousted with Le Comte, and in a minute entered the man's gates.

The hell-mouth façade and the flaming torches were gone, leaving behind a classical Paris town house attended by mere uniformed footmen—one of whom Stuyvesant recognized by his yellow hair as the tailed demon with the trident.

No one threatened to sweep him inside with a scythe or a bony arm.

Inside the door, six attractive women wearing black evening dresses waited, only their lack of jewels and bare hands suggesting that they were not guests who'd made the faux pas of shopping at the same couturier. One of them took his hat, the next his coat, and a third ushered him to a door opposite the little elevator that had taken guests upwards for the other party.

Inside the door was a narrow but brightly-lit spiral stairway, circling upwards to the right and down to the left: stairs that explained the fourth door in the room with the clock. Another young lady stood two steps above the landing, gesturing for him to descend.

Well, Sarah had said there would be catacombs.

He started down the worn stone steps. They were similar to those he'd seen in the public catacombs. Personally, he'd found the sewers up near the Place de la Concorde a more admirable civic effort. And if it was philosophizing a person was after—well, there was nothing like a well-polished, twenty-foot-wide sewer mains to encourage reflections on mortality.

But evidently, Dominic Charmentier was a man for the catacombs, not the sewers. He seemed even to have his own entrance. Had young Dominic grown up in this house, with the bones of six million fellow citizens beneath his feet?

Well below. He'd forgotten how deep the quarries were. These steps just kept winding down, and down, until the rhythm of descent became disorienting. The electric lights strung on the outside curve, one bulb every four steps, occasionally dimmed, but they did not quite go out. And if they did, as one of Charmentier's tricks, he had his lighter in his pocket.

He went on. He was far from alone—voices of other guests echoed along the stairway, along with bursts of crowd noises and music from below as an unseen door opened, then drifted shut—but all he saw was an endless series of stone steps unreeling ahead of him, a hand-rail to his right, and the string of lights above it.

He must have descended two hundred steps before one tread did not give way to another. When he reached the bottom, the abrupt cessation of *step-step-step* made him stumble.

The pair of black-gowned girls waiting at an open set of doors showed neither surprise nor alarm at his entrance: no doubt they had stood there all night watching guests reach the bottom on uncertain feet. He gave the nearest a smile, passed through the doorway . . .

The smile faded as he saw what lay beyond.

Bones. Off to the left in an inexorable curve, and to the right with a sharper turn half-hidden by a decorative chest-high locker, he was in a world of bones, polished and lovingly arranged. The nearest were femurs, the large double-knobs of their lower ends forming the background, with a double-chevron of lines made of face-forward skulls alternating with lengthwise tibias. The wall behind him was also bones, only here the chevron had been softened into a wave, with the portions above and below the undulations filled with the blunt upper ends of ten thousand tibias; the middle section was made of either pelvises or shoulder blades, arranged to emphasize the up-and-down of the wave.

Here lies the empire of the dead.

The art of death. He wondered how the people whose bones these were would have reacted, had you told them where they would end up.

Suddenly, chaotic life invaded the ossuary quiet. The attendant of the inner door laid hands on a worn brass handle and pulled the massive block of time-blackened wood open, allowing the cacophony of a party to wash across the placid bones. He settled his shoulders inside his suit, and gave a last glance down the corridor before obediently stepping through.

It was a cavern, half again as long as it was wide. Its ceiling, as much as fifteen feet in the center, rested on stone pillars left behind by quarrymen. Other bits of stone, waist-height, protruded from the walls holding tall church candles on them, adding an unexpected honey aroma to the smells of perfume and gin and cigarettes. The room was already crowded, despite his early arrival, with a hundred or so people happily enjoying the unusual venue.

As he stepped into the artificial cave, a full glass was pressed into his hand and a series of things hit his eye: the moon, the fog, and the Lord of Death.

The moon was full and somewhat larger than life, painted on the roof of the cave along with a velvety black sky and an expanse of stars. The fog covered the floor of the cavern, a weird, low-lying mist that swirled around the ankles of the partygoers. As a knot of guests on the other side of the room unraveled and moved away, he traced the phenomenon to its source: a broad silver tureen atop a waist-high protrusion of stone, boiling over like an untended pot, except cold and insubstantial.

But it was the walls that made him stand with his glass untasted, jaw dropped.

The walls on either side of the door were covered with tapestries: floor to ceiling, snugly fitted together, thick enough to soften the din of conversation. The colors were slightly faded, but the images clear: groups of life-sized figures in Renaissance clothes moved through streets, gardens, and grand rooms, dancing. Here was a panel of peasants kicking up their heels under some trees at the side of a wheat field; there was a gilded room with lords and ladies in a stately pavane; next came what looked like a dance class of children. Leaps and slow glides, embracing or separated, they danced—and with them, in every panel, danced a skeleton holding either a musical instrument or a scythe.

Halfway around the room, the tapestries changed, giving way to startlingly modern panels of the same size and theme: dancers with Death. As Stuyvesant approached, he realized that they were all by different artists, a few of whom he recognized. The first panel, for example, could only be Matisse, and he thought he could pick out a Magritte and one by the Italian de Chirico, but many of them were strangers to him, and few of the panels were signed.

He worked his way around the room, oblivious to the crowd behind him. The farther he went from the entrance, the less complete the walls were, with several panels little more than sketches. But all showed people dancing with Death, and most of them were linked in some fashion—an arm from one painter's dancer held a drink in the next painter's panel; a skeleton's trombone turned into the lines of a feather boa when it crossed the border.

At the far end of the cavern, Stuyvesant looked at his glass, which somehow had become empty. This room was going to be incredible when it was finished.

Four panels from the room's entrance, the tapestry's biggest skeleton stretched from floor to ceiling, raising a scythe nearly his height. That was where the fog-emitting pot stood, and beside it Dominic Charmentier, Le Comte watched with a little smile as a group of women eddied forward, exclaiming at the cold steam, trying to scoop it up in their diamond-ringed hands. Above his shoulder, Stuyvesant noticed for the first time, the reddened clouds of the tapestry had been disturbed to insert the face of a clock, its hands decorative like those far, far upstairs.

A voice came from near Stuyvesant's shoulder.

"That's called dry ice—isn't it extraordinary?"

He turned: Sarah Grey, wearing a dark red gown with a high neck and elbow-length black gloves, a red-and-black bandeau with a diamond pin in it encircling her pale hair. Unfortunately, at her side was Émile Doucet. Stuyvesant nodded at the cop and told Sarah, "You look drop-dead gorgeous." At her reaction, he added, "And you look even prettier when you blush."

That made her go pinker yet, and she laughed, that gorgeous, incongruously deep sound that caused Doucet to drop her arm abruptly and head for a nearby platter of iced sea-creatures. "Oh, Harris, that suave American sweet-talk. You look very handsome yourself."

"That's what my tailor tells me."

"In a completely unbiased opinion, I'm sure. Have you decided not to risk the punch?"

Was she looking at his fist, or his glass? "Which punch is that?"

"The source of the fog."

"Ah—a drink. Is that where it's coming from? I thought I was seeing things."

"Terribly *Hound of the Baskervilles,* isn't it? Dominic heard of this American company that manufactures the stuff, and had me send for one of their contraptions. I'm told it's only carbon dioxide, but it burns like the dickens if you touch it, and it reacts violently to water—or, as you see, fruity punch. Great fun—it bubbles like a witch's cauldron and belches out that smoke."

"You sure it's not poisonous?"

"Wouldn't that be a coup for the Grand-Guignol—killing off half the arts patrons of France? No, I'm assured that so long as no one eats it, and there's decent ventilation, there's no risk. Although the company sent along a helpful list of symptoms to watch out for."

"What are those?"

"Increased pulse, reduced sight and hearing, shortness of breath, drowsiness."

He cocked his eye at the crowd around them. "In other words, the same symptoms as we're all going to be feeling, anyway."

"Yes, it's probably a good thing we have a limited supply. Harris," she said, "have you met Cole Porter? Cole, this is an old friend of mine, Harris Stuyvesant. He's from New York."

"We have met, haven't we?" Porter said, offering his hand.

"Last year," Stuyvesant agreed. "At Bricktop's."

"That's right, the man with the Lindy Hop. He doesn't look like it, but this friend of yours can really dance," he told Sarah.

"I remember. Pardon me, I have to see what Dominic wants."

As she moved across the room, her fiancé abandoned the oysters to drop in behind her. Stuyvesant's eyes followed them—and with that shift in perspective, the room fell into place: for a moment, that shiny-headed fellow and the dyed-blonde who might have been his daughter (but probably wasn't) merged into the tapestry behind them. Three regal ladies, one of them with a lorgnette to her eye, continued the line of dancers in the paintings on either side; one of the gyrating tapestry peasants danced face to face with a slim young man in a faultless evening suit.

Stuyvesant blinked and looked at his glass.

"Powerful stuff, isn't it?" a voice asked. Cole Porter, eyeing Stuyvesant over the top of his own drink.

"You got that right," Stuyvesant said. "Jeez. These walls are really something."

"The first time you've seen them, too?"

"Yep."

"Do you live here in Paris, Mr. Stuyvesant?"

"No, just passing through. Looking for a girl."

"Of course you are. Anyone in particular?"

He took out Pip's snapshot, and heard the familiar refrain: vaguely familiar, *haven't seen her in a while*. "What's she done, that you're looking for her?" the composer asked.

"She's gone missing. I'm an investigator—I was hired to find her."

"Hope you're not looking for me, too." Porter's flip tone was jarring, but Stuyvesant put away the photograph and returned the man's light jest.

"Why, are you missing?"

"I'm in New York at the moment, working hard on a play."

"I see."

"Supposed to be," Porter added, "only there's nothing but interruptions over there, so I told everyone I was going upstate to work, then got on a ship for Paris. Before we docked, I'd finished most of what I needed to do. I'll go back next week, with nobody the wiser."

"I promise not to tell."

"Besides, I didn't want to miss the chance to see this place. I've seen Le Comte's famous clock several times, but it's rarer to be offered a view of his infamous tapestries. They're something, aren't they?"

"Why 'infamous'?"

"Oh, the usual melodramatic tripe, putting out the eyes of a painter after he's done your portrait, cutting off the fingers of weavers when they've finished a masterpiece. You know, stories that send a trickle up a person's spine. Makes me almost wish I wrote songs like that."

"You heard *The Threepenny Opera*? Now, there's one for the dark songs."

"Brecht and Weill, right? In Berlin?"

"Yeah. Everyone in it's a criminal. Even the hero's named Mackie the Knife, and he's a murderer and rapist."

"Not quite what I need for *Fifty Million Frenchmen*, but thanks for the tip."

However, before Stuyvesant could deliver his other suggestion—*a distant vice in the darkness*—the composer was pounced upon by an American heiress wearing more pearls than clothing, who called everyone in earshot "darling."

He slipped into a gap around the punch table, accepting a cup of the pink liquid foaming with fog, and stifled the urge to cough.

The crowd grew, and dancing began in the center of the space—the quartet dove into a flurry of notes that it took Stuyvesant a minute to recognize as a jazz variation on the Saint-Saëns *Danse Macabre*. The figures on the walls shifted with the shadows, seeming to dance. It became difficult to move. Stuyvesant took up a position at the side of a stone pillar, to be out of the way but also to keep an eye on Dominic Charmentier. The man did not himself dance, but he circulated, dipping into one conversation after another, summoning drinks trays, moving on.

Twice, he saw one of the girls in black bring Charmentier a fresh drink, on a separate tray.

The third time, he looked around for Sarah, spotted Doucet, and looked down, finding her bent head-to-head with a bird of a woman. He migrated across the floor towards her, earning Doucet's disapproval but Sarah's smile.

She introduced him to the small woman, a clothing designer called Coco, and asked him if he was having a good time.

"Just great, thanks. Say, what's your boss drinking?"

"Dominic? It's probably apple juice. Why?"

"Doesn't he drink?"

"No. Why do you ask?"

"Your boss is an odd duck," he said mildly.

She fixed him with a look. "Harris, I'd appreciate it if you'd keep your questions to yourself when it comes to Dominic. It doesn't make my job any easier."

His eyes met Doucet's, as disapproving as hers. When Sarah turned to shout a bit more at the bird-like woman, Doucet moved to speak in Stuyvesant's ear.

"She's right, you know. Your obsession with M. Charmentier wears at his patience."

"My obsession with M. Charmentier may solve a murder."

"M. Stuyvesant, do not make Sarah's life any more difficult for her."

"Me? You're the one ignoring—"

Even in the tumult, their voices attracted Sarah's disapproval. "Boys, if you can't play nicely together you'll have to leave the party!" Her scolding was only mock on the surface. She waited, and when neither of her self-appointed escorts would retreat, she pointed a commanding finger, first past Stuyvesant's left shoulder, then past Doucet's right: the two men exchanged a glance, then turned on their heels and plunged into opposite parts of the crowd.

She was not the only person to find Stuyvesant's questions irritating. This was the cream of Paris society, from both Right and Left Banks: any gathering that combined Josephine Baker (in a surprisingly demure gown) and Natalie Barney (in a man's evening wear), an ex-President of the Banque de France, and three of the fourteen painting members of the Académie des Beaux-Arts was a party to be reckoned with. And although he managed to slip questions about Pip into conversations with a couple dozen people—"Hey, come to think of it, I don't suppose you've seen this girl?"—soon Sarah appeared in front of him and told him that she could see it was a mistake to invite him, and if he didn't stop, she would have him escorted out.

Which wouldn't have been so bad if Doucet hadn't been at her shoulder at the time.

In any event, people were getting too tipsy to focus, so he left the picture in his pocket and went out onto the marginally clearer space in the center of the cavern that had become the dance floor, where he could keep an eye on Dominic Charmentier.

Midnight approached. The tumult grew. Charmentier kept drinking his apple juice, his smile growing ever more condescending. Doucet shadowed Sarah, but after she snapped at him like a mother dog with a half-grown puppy, he did so from a distance.

The band played on. The dance got wilder. Dust sifted down from time to time, but the pillars held and the artificial moon stayed attached to its ceiling.

Around half past eleven, he stood quenching his thirst in the perimeter of the room when Sarah appeared at his elbow. Looking around, he found Doucet a dozen or so feet away, watching with a sour expression.

Stuyvesant bent over Sarah to bellow, "You've put together a great party!"

"I'm glad you're having fun," she replied. Her short hair had gone curly in the rising humidity, her face glowed with warmth.

"I was trying to decide how much of your boss's weird interests came from growing up in a house with bones in the cellar."

Her face tightened, but she answered. "I've heard him wonder the same thing, himself."

"Amazing how beautiful they are, those bones in his hallway."

She glanced sideways, and decided that he was merely making conversation, not conducting an interrogation. "I know. Have you taken the public catacombs tour?"

"A long time ago. It made me a fan of cremation."

She laughed, that low-pitched chortle that did such compelling things to the base of his spine, but before the conversation could develop, one of the black-gowned girls came up to Sarah and spoke in her ear.

"Sorry, I'm needed," she told him, and dove into the crush.

With a hard look in Stuyvesant's direction, the cop followed.

He wasn't sure how it happened. It was shortly after midnight, following plenty of both alcohol and irritation, when he looked over the crowd and saw Doucet, leaning forward and giving Sarah orders.

That's how it looked, anyway. And the man's big hand on Sarah's arm looked like the hand of a bully.

Without thinking, Stuyvesant slammed his glass onto the nearest flat surface and pushed across the room towards them.

Closer, he could tell that she was both tired and annoyed. Doucet was not so much grabbing her arm as he was holding it to keep from being jostled apart, but Stuyvesant saw her mood and the hand, and common sense gave way to his overactive sense of chivalry.

"You two look like you're having an argument," he said in loud joviality. Well, he had to speak loudly, over the noise and the crowd, but his voice was stronger than he'd intended.

They both frowned at him. And all three then spoke at once.

"She proposes to make her way home alone," was from Doucet.

"Maybe you should take your hand off her," was Stuyvesant.

"I do not require a man to take care of me," Sarah announced. Which would in fact do for either of the men looming over her.

She looked from one to the other. "If either of you imagine that this show of possessiveness is— Oh, for God's sake, would you both just leave me alone!" And with that, she burrowed into invisibility among the shoulders.

The two men faced each other, hackles bristling, then as one, turned away.

For the next quarter of an hour, Stuyvesant pursued the red-and-black bandeau on the yellow head, but she seemed to have an instinct for pursuit, and disappeared behind one back or another. He finally saw her standing beside Cole Porter, checking the watch strapped over her black glove. As Stuyvesant moved forward, a sound came. A chime.

A swell of reaction moved across the floor, people cutting off their conversation and turning to orient themselves to the moon overhead. By some trick of lighting, its earlier glow had increased ten-fold, with the flecks of stars sparkling like diamonds. The clock sounded twelve times—no, thirteen—and into the silence that followed, the voice of Dominic Charmentier penetrated the chamber, in elegant rolling French.

"Mesdames and messieurs, thirteen chimes mark the true moment of the full moon, a gift to us from the heavens. Ladies, will you all please turn to the man who happens to be on your right, and greet him most warmly."

Stuyvesant had no female to his immediate left, but watching Sarah, he saw her turn to the man on her right and give his cheek a quick peck. It was Cole Porter.

She'd known the stroke of the clock was coming. She knew, and had deliberately positioned herself not beside her fiancé, nor her former lover, but next to one of the few men in the place whose affections she was in no danger of stirring.

When Stuyvesant left, a while later, Doucet was still lingering in the background. From the cold set of Sarah's face, Stuyvesant did not think her fiancé was going to be seeing her home.

FORTY-SIX

A CONVERSATION:
"Yes?"

"Sorry to wake you, sir, but you wanted to know if Captain Grey—"

"Tell me."

"It's nothing, sir, just that he left his house and walked to that look-out rock he sits on. I wouldn't have rung if—"

"I take it he hasn't stepped off the cliff yet?"

"I, er, that is, sir, do you want me to inquire?"

"Of course not. Let me know if he does."

"But sir, why would he?"

"That bloody photographer is why! You keep playing clever buggers with Grey, you're going to push him off that cliff."

"Yes, sir. Sorry, sir. Would you like—"

"I'd like to finish my night's sleep, if it's all the same with you."

"Yes, sir. I won't disturb you—"

"Yes you will. If Grey does anything but walk back to his house, I want to know, no matter what time it is."

"Yes, sir."

"I'm surrounded by idiots."

"Yes, sir."

FORTY-SEVEN

ON THURSDAY MORNING, the autumn sun rose.

Paris woke, flung open her shutters, downed her chicory-laced coffee, and set about the eternal business of business.

Harris Stuyvesant snored on.

So did Man Ray and Lee Miller.

Inspector Émile Doucet swore at his Sergeant, Fortier, who told those who worked nearby to watch out, l'Inspecteur had a sore head.

Didi Moreau went into his overgrown garden to find his donation box stuffed with old shoes, which he examined, then carried down the stairs to his workshop.

Dominic Charmentier stirred his coffee and considered the nature of gifts from the universe.

Sarah Grey's housekeeper, come to begin the day's tidying, frowned when she found that her employer's bed had not been slept in the night before. Mlle. Grey usually let her know, if she would not be coming home.

And across the Channel, Bennett Grey's emerald eyes winced away from the sight of four pieced-together faces, out of an envelope mailed in Paris.

FORTY-EIGHT

Thursday morning, it took the combined efforts of the Dôme kitchen and the bathhouse around the corner to restore Harris Stuyvesant to a state where he could even consider a conversation with Inspector Doucet. Having been fed, boiled, pummeled, and shaved within an inch of his life, he settled his fedora on his new haircut and stepped back into the sunlight.

He felt almost human.

On his way to the Île de la Cité, he stuck his head in at the hotel. Non, Mme. Benoit reported, nothing had arrived for him. *Damn.* He should've written to Bennett on Sunday instead of going skating with Nancy. Surely the Post & Telegraph reached as far as Cornwall?

No way around it: time for Doucet.

The *flic* was Stuyvesant's only source of information and protection within the force. He'd been a fool to antagonize him. But arriving at the Préfecture, he was pleased to find Doucet in even worse shape than he'd been.

Stuyvesant's immediate impulse was to say something clever like, *Looks like Sarah led you on a merry chase last night.* Fortunately, his brain caught his tongue, and turned the words to, "Bonjour." He stuck out his hand for shaking, dropped into the chair, took out his cigarette case, got one going, and set the case and lighter on the desk in front of Doucet.

"I may be getting too old for parties like that," he said.

After a minute, Doucet's face relaxed a notch. He picked up the case, opened it, used the lighter.

"What are you going to do about Sarah?" Stuyvesant asked. *You*, not *we*, seemed only politic.

"I have a man on her home. The only person who has gone in or out was her housekeeper."

"It won't be easy to keep her under surveillance without her noticing."

"I very much hope it will not be for long."

"Can you tell me what you have in mind?"

"I'm going to take Moreau's house apart."

Stuyvesant put on a thoughtful frown. "When Sarah and I were there, talking to Moreau in the room with all the hands—you know the one I mean?—he gave a sort of meaningful glance at that bookshelf in the corner. It occurred to me there might be some kind of hidden panel behind it. Did you happen to look back there?"

"No." Doucet's expression was eloquent with disbelief, but Stuyvesant's face gave nothing away. Nor did he tell the big cop to take a can of grease.

"Well, you might. And what about Man Ray and Charmentier?"

"Sergeant Fortier has gone to speak with Mr. Ray. But my juge d'instruction has specifically forbidden me to investigate Le Comte."

Two men who didn't trust each other when it came to a woman could nonetheless hold a long and eloquent silent conversation about other matters. Stuyvesant leaned forward to flick off a length of ash. "Well, I may be seeing Charmentier myself." He held his breath: perhaps offering Doucet a tool his superiors didn't control would make up for the stupidity of the night before.

"I must forbid you from harassing him," Doucet said, in a voice so forceless, he might have been sounding out words on a page.

Stuyvesant smiled. "I wouldn't think of it. What about the missing persons list?"

Doucet, as relieved as his visitor to have negotiated the trickier bits without ending up in a shouting match, tapped the page he had been scowling at when Stuyvesant came in.

"We have removed sixteen more names."

"That's some good work."

"Seven were accidental deaths and four died of natural causes, all of them far from home—Scotland, Germany, America. Three were fleeing arrest warrants that we didn't know about, and two are a mother and daughter who left at the same time funds went missing from the bank where the father worked. Rumor has them in Mexico."

"Which leaves, what? Thirty?"

"Thirty-one."

"Can I see?" Stuyvesant threaded his fingers together to keep them from grabbing the file.

"A private investigator is not permitted access to an official police investigation," Doucet said, in that same forceless voice. He stood up. "I must take my lunch now. I generally am away one hour. I don't expect to see you here when I return."

Stuyvesant was in Doucet's warmed seat before the door clicked shut, uncapping his pen.

There was a lot of new information: dates, home, family, education, jobs, physical descriptions. Where a photograph had been added, he noted any distinctive characteristics—hair color, eyes, moles, scars. He hesitated over the men, of whom there were five, but in the end included cursory notes on them as well. Given the time limit, he did not pause much to think about what he was reading, merely winnowed as much information as he could from each pinned-together report before turning to the next.

Fifty-eight minutes later, he finished recording the sketchy facts of the last missing person in the file (Gabriella Faulon, black hair, crooked eyebrows, small mole on the side of her nose, arrested in 1924 for public drunkenness, married, no children, last seen on Tuesday at the Musée Grévin—the wax museum—on the boulevard Montmartre). He flipped her records shut, put the other thirty cases on top of her, straightened them a little, and closed the file.

He stretched the kinks out of his neck. This was just the kind of slog he hated, paperwork and cold recorded facts—the thing he missed least about his former job under J. Edgar Hoover. Give him a suspect to grill, any day. But he knew how to handle information, and he did it scrupulously, even though his only pleasure was in the finishing.

He passed Doucet on the stairs, exchanging a polite nod.

FORTY-NINE

S TUYVESANT HEADED FOR what was becoming his usual place for
reflection, the little pointy park of the Vert-Galant. He gave the
bronze Henri le Grand a tip of the hat and settled onto a bench, to let
his mind chew on the list. Instead, his thoughts went sideways, to a pair
of women.

He wished to hell women were as easy to understand as rum-runners
and anarchists. He'd thought Nancy was interested—more than interested, very nearly promised to him. Was there something about his kiss
that put her off? Halitosis? Or was the visitor she'd been entertaining
the past three days an old lover whose return pushed Harris Stuyvesant
to the side?

Enough. Turn to something you might be able to understand.

Thirty-one names, men and women who had walked away, or been
carried, from their lives—one of whom was Pip Crosby. (The child on
the original list had been located: her father was awaiting trial.) They
began on January 3, 1928, when young Katrine Aguillard was now
known to have set off to visit a friend in Rouen without telling her
parents, and ended last Tuesday or Wednesday with Gabriella Faulon,
whose drunken female housemate noticed she wasn't in her room near
the Place Pigalle, then took three days to report Gabriella's absence to
the police.

Five men, twenty-six women, mostly French, predominantly Parisian, scattered across the city, more or less evenly distributed over the twenty-one months covered by the list. Many of them had some connection with the art world—but then, who in Paris did not? He began to flip at random back and forth through his notes, hoping his eyes would happen across a pattern his brain was overlooking.

The dates? Half were vague, and some told nothing but the day a disappearance had been reported. Lotte Richter, for example, a blonde woman from Hamburg, was reported missing after a birthday holiday in Paris, when a surprisingly conscientious hotelier brought her belongings to the Lost Property Office in March. He could only say that she had been there on February 13, when she'd paid him.

What about hair color? Eleven brown, ten blonde, six black (one of those with a question mark), two gray, and one each red and bald. That seemed like a lot of blondes to him, considering how rare it was in France, but then he was bound to be a bit wary of threats to blonde women. Did it make any difference if the blonde hair was bleached?

How about nationalities, then? Seventeen French, five Americans, three Germans, two each for England and Italy (the Italians were a pair of women, from the same town, who disappeared the same day, leaving an unpaid hotel bill and two suitcases of clothing) and one each for Poland and Spain. The Germans were Lotte Richter, Clara Klein, and Elsa Werner; blonde, blonde, and brunette; Hamburg, Frankfurt, and a village near Berlin. That all three women had dates in the first seven months of 1928—February 13(?), March 26, and July 21 or thereabouts—might be significant, or a statistical anomaly.

What about the five men—did they have anything in common? Four had gone missing in 1928. Daniel La Plante and a man known only as Joseph (disappeared May 14 and early November, respectively) were older than the others, and worked as a shoe-shiner and a beggar. Marc Dupont (blonde; September 20; born and lived in Montmartre) was twenty-two years old and worked as a waiter and occasional actor. Eduardo Torres, a swarthy, handsome, nineteen-year-old native of Valencia, was believed to be working in Paris as late as November: his family reported him missing in January after he failed to make it home for Christmas. The only man gone missing this year, on March 1, was

Raoul Bellamy, a medical student at the Sorbonne, born in Brittany, who supplemented his family's stipend by the occasional modeling job.

Five men and twenty-six women. The numbers could mean that women were more vulnerable, or that their absence was reported more often. And, there were a lot of arrests on the lists, mostly for petty theft and drunkenness. And . . .

He slapped the notebook shut and dropped his head into his hands.

How did he expect to make a pattern out of a million unrelated facts? People simply vanished, for all kinds of reasons. He'd taken a job searching for an American girl, and this was where he'd ended up—searching for some kind of madman killer? It was a waste of Ernest Crosby's money. An honest man would go straight to the Post Office and cable the man to admit he was a failure: that he'd let Pip Crosby walk away from him in Nice, and she'd met somebody bad, and she had died.

He was crap as an investigator, and he had no business hanging on here in Europe. Pack your bags, sail home. Get a job in a garage, tinkering with engines.

But God damn it, sometimes there *was* a pattern. Doucet suspected one here, and Doucet was no flighty fantasist.

Take the cop's personal bug-bear, Henri Landru. Landru picked off well-to-do widows for their money. Had anyone happened to notice earlier that each woman replied to lonely hearts notices, lives could have been saved. Or the American known as H. H. Holmes, who'd spent eight years treating an unknown number of women and men—thirty? eighty? hundreds?—as a natural resource, taking pleasure in their torture and cashing in on their wills, their possessions, and even their remains, stripping the flesh from their bodies and selling the skeletons to medical schools. If anyone along the way had asked some questions—insurance agents, the medical school, hotel employees—he'd have been hanged years—and lives—earlier.

At the Bureau, mere mention of the name could silence a room.

But it wasn't always about money. Men killed for the thrill of it. Or to prove they could—look at Leopold and Loeb, a pair of rich kids who'd committed murder as an intellectual challenge. They made Jack the Ripper almost comprehensible: the London monster at least seemed to have been driven by some twisted kind of sexual gratification. And Stuyvesant had heard of a Frenchman who preyed on shepherds, murdering them in the fields, doing terrible things to them first. Insanity didn't always come from a raving lunatic: if it did, the Ripper would have been caught—and if he'd possessed H. H. Holmes' means of rendering the bodies down, London's prostitutes might still be quietly disappearing.

Disappearing like Pip Crosby, and Alice Barnes, and Ruth Palowski. Holes in the world. Lulu's family could at least hold a funeral.

He forced his mind back to the list. What about those points of contact with art and film? Working in a Montparnasse café, taking the odd modeling job, acting a tiny part in a commercial film. One woman was the cleaner in a cinéma.

He did not know what the numbers would be for a random sampling of Parisians, but he suspected you could find that pretty much everyone had some kind of a link to art.

In any event, there was no clear arrow pointing at Man Ray's studio, at Le Comte's grim theater, or at Didi Moreau's disgusting projects.

There was no reason at all, really, to think that the people on this list were related in any way, including their deaths. They certainly hadn't all been dragged off to be sex slaves. His imagination had been fired by personal matters, and he was wasting his time pursuing monsters under the bed.

Stuyvesant sat, head in hand, feeling the last few days taking over his bones. It wasn't even 5:00 p.m.: if he went to bed now, he'd be staring at the ceiling at three in the morning. He had nothing new to tell Doucet. He couldn't face Sarah. And Nancy evidently wanted nothing to do with him.

All he could do was go bash something.

FIFTY

A CONVERSATION:

"Sir, a report's come in that Bennett Grey has left his house."

"This isn't his usual day for the village."

"Not the village, sir. Captain Grey was seen cycling towards Penzance half an hour ago. With a valise."

"What, he's *traveling*? Oh, Christ."

"Sir, do you want—"

"No, I do not want you to pick him up. We may find he's just gone to buy himself a pair of rubber boots."

"Sir, that letter the other day—"

"The one you lot wanted to open."

"Yes, sir. Do we even know who it was from?"

"Harris Stuyvesant."

"Sir?"

"Before your time. American. Used to work for their Bureau of Investigation. He was the one responsible for—well, everything, come to that. The Bunsen affair."

"Oh. *Oh* . . ."

"Yes: oh."

"And you think Captain Grey is going to see him?"

"Possibly. They're friends. Sort of. The American writes him chatty postcards every few months."

"Coded?"

"I doubt it. He's the kind who wouldn't bother."

"So, sir, your orders? Concerning Captain Grey?"

"Keep an eye on him. A discreet eye, damn it."

"And if he gets on a train?"

"Then tell me where he's going. We'll decide what to do after that."

"Yes, sir."

"God, what a pain in the arse that man can be."

"Sir?"

"Nothing! Go on, get out of here. Christ."

FIFTY-ONE

THE PUNISHMENT OF the boxing ring was a satisfying counterpart to an afternoon bent over scraps of paper. He'd happened to arrive at the same time as another amateur of about his height but ten years younger and a lot fitter, and it was hard work to keep the guy from wiping the mat with the visiting American. When it was over, and both men were bruised and grinning, he slapped the fellow's shoulder and took him and half a dozen of his *bons amis* out for a drink or two, which turned into three.

He arrived back at Mme. Benoit's a little before ten o'clock, nice and sore and tired, looking forward to the hard mattress. His first stop was at the toilet—street-side pissoirs got pretty rank by this hour—and the minuterie was still on when he came out. He pushed open his door—and heard something rustle on the floor.

A petit bleu.

Thursday 3:00

Dear Harris, my visitor has left, can you come over for dinner? Bring a clean shirt for the morning.

I've moved to the rue Suger in the VI, look for the place with the orange door—sorry, not yet sure what the phone number is.

Nancy

He gave out a cough somewhere between outrage and laughter. He didn't know if she was working hard to be provocative or if this was just the down-to-earth approach of a modern girl, but it had to be the most remarkable seduction he'd ever been a part of.

The only blunter propositions he'd ever heard had been standing on a street corner with a price tag attached.

Who did she think he was? Sure, sex was cheap in the Jazz Age, especially in Paris, but why would she think he'd be so eager to jump into a bed still warm from another man?

Except . . . he was. If anything, a good-girl façade over a whore's lax virtue was every red-blooded boy's dream. Then again, he wasn't. Sex with Nancy Berger promised to be a muscular romp, and yet a part of him, that romantic softie he kept well hidden, was sorry she hadn't at least pretended at the lovey-dovey.

He was half tempted to set the Ronson to the edge of the petit bleu. Or crawl into bed and claim Mme. Benoit hadn't delivered it until morning.

Wasn't it supposed to be the girl who played hard to get?

Life could be damned confusing sometimes.

He liked Nancy. He liked her a lot. He was, he realized as he stood looking at her words, disappointed as much as anything, that she would think a blatant offer was all he wanted from her.

So, she would be another Lulu—not, he caught himself instantly, that she was going to die in an alley. Nancy would be one of the string of mostly-blonde, mostly-young women he'd bedded. The string of women who weren't Sarah.

Why should he feel the least bit disappointed in that?

He glanced at his watch, and snugged up his neck-tie. She'd probably be awake. Maybe not, depending on how much energy she'd spent on her "visitor," but it would only cost him a few minutes to find out.

He put on his coat, and went back downstairs.

He did not, as she'd suggested, take a spare shirt. He didn't even take his overcoat. He didn't expect to be gone long.

———

He found the orange door, and banged on it, his fist as implacable as his expression. A light went on in the transom overhead, and after a rattle of locks, Nancy was beaming out at him.

She was dressed for bed, although not perhaps for seduction, since she wore neither makeup nor silk. At least she wasn't wearing the ugly brown dressing-gown she'd had on that first day.

"You dear man!" she said. "Come in, I'd given you up."

"Hi, Nancy."

"Come in, the upstairs neighbors complain if they hear talking after nine p.m."

He stepped inside. She shut the door, and stepped into his arms. A minute later, she leaned back.

"Harris, what's the matter?"

"What's the matter? Nothing's the matter. Can I have a drink?" He supposed he should be grateful she'd had a bath, so he didn't smell the other man.

"You want a drink?"

"Don't you?"

"I thought— No, let's have one, by all means. Come in. Isn't this a nice little hole-in-the-wall? Sylvia helped me again, it belongs to an American writer who's gone home to his wife while she's having a baby."

He saw the drinks cabinet and walked over to it, his back to her as he looked through the bottles. "You said you thought. What did you think?"

"Just that you might be a bit more . . . eager."

She sounded disappointed. Jesus, was the woman a nymphomaniac? "I guess I'm enough older than you to have certain expectations about women, and it still comes as a surprise, sometimes, the . . . attitudes of modern girls."

She'd sat down on a settee, and now looked at him across the low table. "Would you mind translating that little speech for me?"

"I just . . ." He looked into his glass, swirling the liquid. "You had someone else here until very recently. As soon as he was gone you snapped your fingers for me. I don't mind, you understand. It just takes me a minute to . . . get into gear."

She gaped, as if he'd been talking in one of the few languages she didn't know. "What makes you think I had someone here?"

"You told me yourself. Your visitor."

"My—" Her astonishment changed to—could that be a look of outrage? Why? She'd been pretty blunt herself. "You thought— And you—?"

Her reaction was baffling. Even more so when the bunched eyebrows of outrage began to twitch. In a moment, she lost control of her face, and gave a snort, followed by a coughing sound. She fell back against the settee and let loose with an unladylike bellow of helpless laughter.

"What the hell?" he asked. "Nancy, what—?" But his every word only made her whoop. "Nancy, for Christ sake!"

"Oh, Harris," she cried, "you dear innocent man, have you *honestly* had no idea what I was talking about?"

"What, when you sent me your note? You said you had—"

"Women have a 'visitor' every month, you poor idiot."

His stunned expression reduced her to choking paroxysms.

After a while, he went to sit down beside her. And began to chuckle.

Soon, breathless roars of laughter gave way to the breathlessness of his mouth on hers.

And in the morning, he wore his previous day's shirt.

FIFTY-TWO

THE AUTUMN MORNING was honey-sweet, as the two of them walked down the rue Suger with linked hands. They drank café au lait in the shadow of Notre Dame, fed each other bits of croissant. Stuyvesant walked Nancy back to the orange door, where he brushed her swollen lips with lingering kisses good-bye.

The streets were filled with happy people. Concierges swept their sidewalks, beautiful women opened their shutters and leaned out, a fruit vendor piled an artful pyramid of radiant apples. As he crossed out of the Luxembourg Gardens, bicycles whirred merrily and a trio of young men perceived how he had spent the night, smiling their approval. The street-sweeper on the rue Vavin tipped his hat and greeted Stuyvesant's coin with a burst of Italian song. The bouquets in the florist's beamed as he passed.

He was humming the same Cole Porter song under his breath as he trotted up the fourth-floor stairway and spotted his door standing open. "Bonjour, Yvette! Ça va bien?" he called to the maid as he came through—and stopped dead. "Bennett! What are you doing here? And . . ." He looked from Bennett Grey to the man at the window, and the blood drained from his scalp.

Doucet turned, but Bennett Grey spoke first.

"Harris, what have you done with Sarah?"

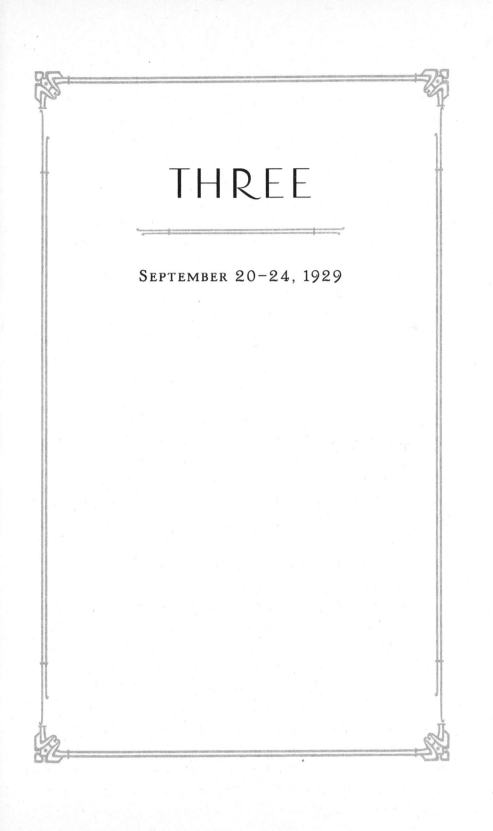

THREE

SEPTEMBER 20–24, 1929

FIFTY-THREE

TWENTY-SIX INTERMINABLE HOURS after Bennett Grey had dropped the four photographs onto burning coals, he closed the door to Sarah's Paris house. The trip over had been hell. The faces haunted him as he bicycled to Penzance, waited for the train, crossed southern England. He half hoped that the Truth Project's spies would simply arrest him and save him from any further involvement with Harris Stuyvesant's problems, but they kept their distance.

London was a cacophony, the train to Dover a seething mass of men and women trying to hide their loathing of each other and of the crying children. He changed compartments twice before finding one with neighbors who might not shred his nerves—only to be joined at the last minute by a solitary woman whose darting eyes and knotted fingers made him want to scream.

He spent the journey in the corridor, humming hard, in an attempt to keep from going as mad as that poor woman.

On the ferry, he took to open air.

At the Gare du Nord, with a headache setting fire to his skull, he had the foul luck to encounter a series of young men—men who had been children ten years ago when half of France twitched with shell-shock. An older porteur would have treated him gently, knowing too well the tediousness of a weeping man. An older douane official might not have been so . . . officious. Bennett Grey held on to his failing control, answering their questions—*Why only one small valise? Where have you come from? What is your business in Paris?*—as tears crept down his face.

At last, the young official looked up and noticed his state. With a grimace of disgust, he thrust the passport back over the desk and waved his permission to close the disrupted valise, leaving Grey to follow the porter off to the taxi ranks.

He kept his eyes tightly shut as they drove across Paris, humming tunelessly all the time. He dropped the house key twice before it turned.

He stood with his back against the inside of Sarah's door for a long time.

He liked Sarah's house. It was a place where his sister had found balance and a degree of happiness, and he could feel it in everything from the lay of the sofa cushions to the flowers in her back garden. He even approved of her choice of man, a person as like Harris Stuyvesant as she could find, without the shared burdens.

She wasn't home. Not that he'd expected her to be, since he hadn't stopped to send a cable. Nor was her housekeeper in, and that was a gift: the woman did love to talk, and if he had to deal with one more human being this morning, he would collapse.

Stuyvesant's problems could wait.

Tea helped: he was English, after all, so tea helped—even though the milk was distinctly foreign, along with the water, and the kettle, and the smell of the gas in the hob. Sarah said she couldn't tell that the milk came from French cows, but he could. The very air was different here, so of course he could taste a change in water.

At least the tea on his palate and the cup against his lips were English: he had brought both of those on his earlier, less hurried, visit.

Also the biscuits, from Fortnum & Mason's. The combination soothed his nerves and his stomach, allowing him to consider something more substantial to accompany his second cup of tea. Toast?

But the bread in the bin was three days old. Four, even. It was Sarah's usual kind, from the baker up the road, but his fingers read its dryness, his nose evaluated its stale aroma. The only reason Sarah would have bread more than two days old was if she intended to cook something calling for dry bread—and there would be a fresh one beside it in the bread-bin. She had not been here yesterday morning, to buy bread.

Absently, his tongue reflected on the after-taste of the milk. Even a year ago, he would have noticed its age in an instant, but the incremental fading of his sensitivities over the years had continued. It was not as diminished as he made out during his compulsory sessions with the Truth Project's technicians, but any degree of dulling was a gift. Five years ago, a prolonged assault like the journey here would have seen him carried off the train on a stretcher.

But today, he could stand in Sarah's French kitchen and feel the welcome, letting his skin reassemble itself, letting his nerves embrace the calm.

Were it not for that faint note of disquiet *(Why not pour out the milk before going away?)* he might even be nursing a little candle-flicker of happiness.

His hands went about their task: take the knife from the drawer, carve away the dried end, slice a piece, light the grill, slide it in. When both sides were uniformly brown, he spread it with butter (French) and jam (strawberry—made in June by his neighbor in Cornwall) and took it to the table.

That he was able to eat it—most of it—and wash it down with the slightly stewed tea proved that he wasn't worried about his sister. Not really.

Sarah was busy. She didn't know he was coming. She was a grown woman with a demanding job. After that party she'd put together for Le Comte, she'd probably gone off for a lighthearted weekend with friends.

But fear was contagious. Four tormented women and the stress in Harris Stuyvesant's pen threw an uneasy light on his sister's absence. His imagination kept presenting Sarah's black-and-white face, stretched towards the right, contorted by a rictus of terror.

He abandoned the toast for the telephone.

The housekeeper lived two doors down from a grocer's, whose number Sarah kept in the front of her Paris directory. Six long minutes later, the woman was on the line, telling Grey that yes, Mlle. Grey appeared to have gone away, but no, she hadn't left a message, which was unlike her—although didn't Monsieur think it marvelous that the young lady had a gentleman?

He listened to the stream of words exclaiming that Mademoiselle hadn't let her know that Monsieur would be coming and she hoped his *voyage* had been *confortable* and she would be instantly over to make up his bed and bring him some—

He placed the receiver back in the cradle, walked over to slide the bolt on the door, and went upstairs to his sister's bedroom. Just a quick look before going, headache or no, to hunt down Harris Stuyvesant.

He ignored the sound of the key, the rattle of the door handle, the insistent tapping of the thwarted housekeeper. Twenty minutes later, none the wiser as to Sarah's whereabouts, he was putting on his coat when a very different pounding came on the door, with a man's voice demanding that he open up.

Doucet's panic blew through two inches of wood like artillery fire.

"She took nothing." Grey sat in Stuyvesant's chair, face drawn, fingers knotted together. Doucet stood across the room with his shoulder planted on the window frame, as if needing an anchor to keep him from coming for Stuyvesant. "Her trunks were there, her valises, her passport, and *identité*. Everything, including her everyday hand."

"She can't have gone home after Le Comte's party." Doucet's voice made Grey flinch: calm and deliberate on the surface, boiling with strain beneath. "When the men I had watching the house said no one went through her door but the housekeeper, I thought Sarah was enjoying a quiet day at home. Then late this morning, the man on duty telephoned to say that a small blond foreigner let himself in with a key, after which the housekeeper could not get in. I went to see what was going on."

"Where did those photos come from?" Bennett asked Stuyvesant.

"What photos?" Doucet asked.

Stuyvesant overrode both questions. "Why didn't you put a man on her earlier?" he demanded. "I'd have taken her home myself, if I knew."

"She was angry. At both of us," he added, before Stuyvesant could. He turned to Sarah's brother. "At the party Wednesday night, your friend here and I were being . . . difficult."

Grey instantly grasped his meaning. "You were being males. And you imagined Sarah would be amused by two men fighting over her?"

"There was no fight," Stuyvesant protested. "A mild ruffling of feathers, maybe. But yeah, she was tired and this was an important event for her. Like Doucet says, she wasn't happy about it."

Doucet resumed. "I said I'd wait and see her home, but she told me to leave, that she would make her own way and telephone me in a day or two. And"—he cut Stuyvesant off—"yes, I did wait outside of Le Comte's front gates. But when two a.m. came and went and she hadn't appeared, I could either ring the bell and ask if she was still there, or leave. I left."

"Yeah, well, I guess I'd have done the same," Stuyvesant admitted.

"It didn't occur to you that she might use a back door?" Grey asked.

"Of course! I had a gendarme watching the back. At six in the morning, he went off duty. I sent his replacement to her home instead."

"So either she's still in Charmentier's house," Stuyvesant said, "or she left by another way."

"My sister is no fool. And she knows you both well. She might have figured that she was being watched."

"So where would she go?" Doucet asked. "In her evening dress, without so much as a toothbrush?"

"With a guest-list like that, she could be anywhere," Stuyvesant said.

"Someplace welcoming?" Grey suggested. "With someone not apt to crow over her like a rooster?"

His companions winced.

"Bricktop was there," Stuyvesant told him. "They know each other. Cole Porter. And I saw her talking with one of the Academy guys."

"'Guys'?" Doucet asked. "I saw three members of l'Académie."

"Um, Provost?"

"Prévost?"

"That's it."

"I'll contact him. She also spent some time with Josephine Baker," Doucet offered.

Stuyvesant spoke up. "And she had a long conversation with Natalie Barney."

An awkward silence fell, as the three men considered the possibility of Sarah Grey seeking shelter from the most notorious lesbian in Paris.

"No," her brother said, more in protest than conviction.

"What was that about photographs?" Doucet was finished with the distraction.

"Sorry," Grey murmured.

"My fault for not warning you," Stuyvesant told him.

"Monsieur—"

"Let me ask you something first. You made a raid on Moreau's house yesterday? Did you find anything in his secret room?"

"You know about the room? You said—"

"I know what I said. Did you find anything?"

"Three of those hideous shrunken heads they sell at the circus."

"Nothing else? No eyeballs, no letters?"

"Eyeballs? Monsieur, we found nothing, only the heads. Now, I think—"

"Yeah, yeah, the photos. Just—don't arrest me until this is all over, okay?"

FIFTY-FOUR

S TUYVESANT GLANCED TOWARDS the bottle on the table, and decided it was too early.

"Okay. I broke into Didi Moreau's house. Sunday morning, when he and his maid were at church. I found the room behind the bookshelves, had the devil's own time getting in. You didn't go back there yourself, did you?"

"Fortier."

"Figures. The passage is a dozen feet around a corner and maybe ten inches deep," he explained to Grey. "I didn't have a Fortier, so I shoved my way in, and yes, I found those shrunken heads, but with them were a dozen little bottles containing human eyeballs, some leather from what looked like human skin, half a dozen letters regarding specially commissioned boxes—no signature, no identifying name or address—and twenty-three different photographs of four separate women. They had all been carefully torn into twelve pieces, but I took one of each woman and pieced them together. The women looked . . . tortured."

The word spread across the room like frigid oil, and Stuyvesant changed his mind about the drink. He took a healthy swallow, passing it over to Grey. Doucet looked at it askance, but he, too, took a gulp before handing it back.

"Now, we're dealing with men who know everything there is to know about faking realistic effects—not just Moreau, who does taxidermy, but Man Ray for one, Le Comte for another. Er, have you two been to the Grand-Guignol?" He was surprised when both men nodded. "With Sarah?" Both men shook their heads, emphatically.

"She wasn't working for Le Comte yet, when I was here," Bennett said.

"So you went on your own?"

"Grand-Guignol embraces the darkness in men's souls. I was interested in the theory behind it. Lancing infected psychological wounds."

"I don't know how you could stand it."

"What, honest fakery? I have no problem with that. I'll admit that the audience reactions were less straightforward. People like to hide their pleasures. But for most of them, it was a game, and they were happy with the rules, and they left the theater less burdened than they had gone in."

Doucet looked puzzled, but Stuyvesant went on. "Anyway, I found pictures in Moreau's room, taken at night—or at least in the dark, with a flash—of a series of very frightened women. They didn't *look* like actresses made up and pretending, but as I said, there are theater people involved. So I decided to send the photos to a man who could tell for sure. My friend Bennett Grey.

"Sarah hasn't told you about her brother, I could see that when I asked you about him. You know I met Bennett three years ago when I went to England in search of a bomber. What you don't know is that Bennett has a . . . talent. He knows the truth. Give him a roomful of identical Rembrandts, he'll point directly at the genuine one. Tell him a long story with three true things in it, he'll pick them out. Have fifty men march down the street in unison, he knows which trained with the British Army and which with the French, who was wounded, how long they'd spent at the Front. Don't even *think* of going up against him in poker.

"All of which means that if I sent Bennett the photographs, he could tell me whether the emotion on the faces was real, or realistic."

The cop was outraged. "You acquired evidence illegally, then you sent it to a *friend* to guess if it was genuine? Evidence that I might otherwise have found and used in a *trial*?"

Stuyvesant raised his voice, too. "There's no 'guessing' involved. And do I need to point out that this 'evidence' would have disappeared, too, if it was up to you?"

"Monsieur Stuyvesant, you cannot expect me to—"

"Try him," the American snapped.

"Pardon?"

"Test him. You'll see. What this man can do is astonishing."

Doucet looked ready to walk out—either that or get out the hand-cuffs.

Bennett Grey spoke. "Shall I explain?"

"Monsieur, I—"

"It's not as simple as Harris puts it. And it's not a parlor trick. I wish it were. It started when I was blown up, in the trenches."

Respect for a fellow soldier, and Grey's even voice, cooled Doucet's anger.

"Literally blown up. An artillery shell went off under my feet. It should have killed me. It did kill me. And when my heart started beating again, I was newly born, with absolutely none of the mental defenses adults have spent their lives building.

"Have you ever wondered why a newborn shrieks? It's the overwhelming assault on all his senses. That shell made me into an infant again, with everything around me vast and new and absolutely shattering. As if all my senses were going full blast, pouring in the world, every tiny detail of sight and touch and smell screaming at me simultaneously, with no way to protect myself.

"To some extent, I grew skin—it's still growing, in fact. Not long ago, I'd have jumped off the ferry into the Channel rather than continue the trip I made yesterday. But even now, the thing that brings the most . . . trouble is discord. A man who feels one way and acts another is like fingernails down a chalkboard. If he's lying to me, it's uncomfortable. If he's lying to himself, it is an agony.

"And despite what Harris tells you, there are times when I am blind.

He knows this all too well. Religious fanatics, the quietly mad, the honestly deluded: if the belief goes all the way down, if a man truly believes his own lies, there is no discord, and I am as without defenses as any other man."

Doucet studied the small man, hesitating to brand his potential brother-in-law a liar. Or a lunatic.

"Try him," Stuyvesant urged, then to Grey added, "Sorry, but I think you'll need to."

"I understand."

Doucet looked bewildered. "You want me to . . . ?"

"Try and lie to him," Stuyvesant finished. "Tell us, are you engaged to Sarah Grey?"

"Yes," Doucet replied.

"No," Bennett said.

Stuyvesant smiled.

"Well, not formally," Doucet admitted. "But we have an understanding. And if we're asking pointed questions, what about you? M. Stuyvesant, are you in love with Sarah?"

The smile faded.

"Yes," Bennett said. "And no. He's not sure."

"Maybe we should do this with something more . . . impersonal," Stuyvesant suggested.

"Do you have those photographs?" Doucet asked Grey.

"I burned them."

"You *what*?"

"I needed them gone. In any event, can you imagine what your customs officers would have done with me if they'd found them?"

"Nom de Dieu! Those were evidence—perhaps the only evidence out of that room, and—"

"Not the only."

Grey's placid phrase cut Doucet short; he followed the small man's gaze towards Stuyvesant.

"He's right," the American said. "Those were copies. I kept the originals."

"Where are they?"

Grey spoke up again. "I imagine they're under the carpet."

"Tell him why you know that," Stuyvesant prompted.

"A line in the carpet shows where it has been folded back several times recently."

Stuyvesant raised his eyebrows at Doucet, who shook his head, but nonetheless walked over to where Grey was sitting. He knelt, bending down inches from the floor before sitting back on his heels. "Perhaps. But this is something M. Grey may know."

"He hasn't been to my room before."

"So you say." The *flic* tossed the carpet back against the purported line, revealing dusty floorboards.

Stuyvesant pulled out his folding knife and dropped to one knee across from Doucet. "Remember, you're not going to arrest me."

"Not until this is over, you said."

"Yeah."

When the loose board came up, Doucet made a sound of disapproval at the weapons, but he allowed Stuyvesant to pick up two of the three oversized envelopes in the cache, then to put the board back in place.

"I had three sets made. And before you start shouting, I stayed with the photographer while he worked—I didn't want him calling the police when he saw those torn-up faces, so I told him it was for a Surrealist art project. I had him keep his hands off the originals as much as possible. There's also a typed letter. The paper's too rough for prints, but you might be able to match the machine. Moreau's fingerprints will be on the photographs, I expect. Along with mine."

Doucet opened the top to glance at the originals, then pulled out the reproductions from the other envelope.

"Hmm," he said. "Yes. They're almost too realistic."

Grey had been staring out the window since the envelopes appeared, but the photographs might have been stuck up on the glass. "Look at their lips, their coated tongues. Look at the reflection off the eyeballs—particularly the gray-haired woman and the young brunette."

"I don't see a lot of reflection," Doucet replied.

"There is none. Even in reproduction, it is clear. These two women are so badly dehydrated, their eyes are drying up. That is not a thing you can fake."

Doucet studied Grey, still desperately focused on the rooftops.

"So," Doucet asked him, "what else do you see here?"

"Fear. Fear and exhaustion. The English woman is also in pain."

"Which one is English?"

"The older brunette. See the teeth? French women may have bad teeth—like the oldest woman, who is clearly working-class—but they're not tea-stained."

Stuyvesant and Doucet compared the faces for the nuances of horror.

"How can you tell she's in pain?" Doucet asked.

Grey turned away from the window at last. "How? I don't know. It's . . ." He paused. "Pain drags. Fear makes one pull away. That woman's face is doing both."

Like yours, Stuyvesant thought.

Doucet asked Stuyvesant, "Did you choose four that had had their heads turned the same way?"

"From what I could see, they were all like that."

Grey said, "I think you'd find that he tied them by their left wrist. They could move around, but not far."

"Anything else?" Doucet's question held considerably less skepticism.

With reluctance, Grey approached the desk. "May I see the originals?"

"Just don't touch them."

The *flic* eased the four pieced-together photographs from their envelope. Grey squinted at their edges, adjusting the desk lamp to throw light on the surfaces, then lowered his face to nearly touch the gray-haired woman. He drew in a deep breath through his nostrils.

When he straightened, his face was a study in indecision. "There's nothing I can pin down, but I get the impression that these are a few years old. Certainly the chemical smell has all but faded. And although I'm no expert in French hair-styles, this one"—he pointed to the young brunette—"looks like a cut that was fashionable in London two or three years ago."

"Great," Doucet muttered as he edged the originals back inside their envelope. "Now I'll have to extend the search back."

"You might begin with the summer—see how brown she is?—and with upper-class girls."

"Well, that would narrow—" Doucet stopped, then held the photo of the young brunette to the light.

"You recognize her?" Stuyvesant asked.

"It's hard to tell with that piece missing, but she looks a bit like a young Sorbonne student who disappeared in 1926, June it must have been. She wrote her parents in Lausanne to say that she was going to Bretagne with friends for a week. She never came home. Her heavy trunks were found in the baggage office at the Gare de l'Est. We arrested her boyfriend, but there was no evidence, so we let him go. Jacqueline-Celeste Delaurier, that was her name. She was nineteen."

The three men stared at the sweat-streaked, terrified young face, but as one, their eyes slid over to the blonde woman with dark roots and plucked eyebrows.

She looked nothing like Sarah. Nothing at all . . .

FIFTY-FIVE

"IF A STUDENT at the Sorbonne went missing," Stuyvesant said, "we really have to talk with Le Comte, no matter what your orders were."

Doucet gave a shake of impatience. "You will go nowhere near Le Comte."

"You can't be serious! I know the man's had half the ruling class of France drinking his champagne, but surely you can see—"

"M. Stuyvesant, *I* will see him, *I* will question him. But I will not take with me a man who has already attacked Le Comte once—yes, Sarah told me about that—and who has already made it clear that he is suspected of terrible crimes."

"Then take Bennett."

"This is a police matter, I cannot take along a civilian."

"It's not like you're questioning the man about Pip Crosby. You're just looking for your . . . your fiancée. Who was last seen at his party. What would be more natural than to take her brother? Hell, it would raise more suspicions if you *didn't* go talk to him. But please, I beg you, take Bennett. He'll know if your Count is lying."

It was a sign of Doucet's apprehension that he did not argue further, merely pulled a well-thumbed notebook from his breast pocket as he went out the door.

Grey put a hand on Stuyvesant's arm. "Who is Pip Crosby?"

"Pip's the reason I'm here. She's an American girl I was hired to find. That job led me to . . . all this."

"But she's more than a job. What was she to you?"

"Christ, don't you get tired of— Sorry, stupid question. Yes, Pip and I had a casual . . . thing, back in February. When she stopped writing to her mother a few weeks later, the girlfriend she'd been traveling with recommended me to Pip's uncle."

"More than casual."

"Five days is casual. It certainly was to her."

"And you think she's dead."

"As her roommate put it, she walked away from her life pretty thoroughly."

"Do you—"

"Look, maybe you and I could talk about this later?"

Doucet was in the room off the lobby with Mme. Benoit's telephone at his ear. When the ringing was answered, the *flic* identified himself and asked for M. Charmentier. He listened. "When will he return?" More listening. "No, that is not good enough. It is urgent that I see him today. Very well, then tonight. What time? Yes, let me give you a telephone number." He recited the Préfecture's number. "If I am not there, leave a message with my Sergeant. If I have not heard from you by midnight, I shall bring gendarmes to the door." He hung up.

"A threat," Stuyvesant noted.

"Butlers are too fond of their beds."

"You'll take Grey?"

"Do you wish to come?" the cop asked the small blond man.

"Now?"

"No. I'll be at the Préfecture until I hear from Le Comte's man. Shall I telephone you at your sister's house?"

"Fine."

"And M. Stuyvesant: I'll take those photographs, if you please."

"I'm keeping a set."

Doucet hesitated, but could think of no reason to object.

"Are you going to start an official search?" Stuyvesant asked as they descended the stairs for a second time. "For Sarah?"

"After I speak with Le Comte."

"*What?* Jesus, she's been gone since one yesterday morning and you don't—"

"Have you any idea, the consequences of calling off an official search? If it turns out I was premature and her employer knew where she was all the time? She would become . . . notorious."

The relationship made both public, and a laughingstock Stuyvesant nodded and let him leave. Without him, the lobby seemed considerably less crowded.

"So," Stuyvesant told Grey. "It's great to see you. In spite of . . ." His hand waved away the unspeakable.

"Yes. You've lost some weight."

"And you look about to drop." The small man looked as demon-haunted as the day Stuyvesant had met him. No need to ask if he had one of his headaches.

"It does seem a long time since your letter arrived," Grey agreed.

"Go back to Sarah's and get some sleep."

"I'm not sure I could."

"It won't help Sarah if you're dead on your feet."

"True. And I don't know what I can do anyway, short of knocking on doors. Why don't you come for dinner? Sarah's housekeeper always cooks for a platoon."

Harris Stuyvesant could hear a cry for companionship when it bit him on the nose.

"What's the address?"

Tucking the scrap of paper into his billfold, Stuyvesant said abruptly, "I don't suppose you have a photo? Of Sarah, I mean?"

Grey was silent. When Stuyvesant raised his eyes, the compassion on the small man's face looked like tears.

"Never mind," the American said, "I just thought that while I'm asking around—"

"Yes," Grey said. "I do have one."

It was not the photograph Sarah had given Stuyvesant three years earlier: this one showed the scars on her face. She was kneeling at a flower bed with a trowel in her hand, squinting into the brightness. She

looked so damned content, the impulse to joke—Sarah as *Hausfrau*—
nearly pushed past the desperate awareness of her absence.

He thrust the picture into his notebook. "Let's get you in a taxi before you collapse."

As they walked towards rue Vavin, Grey said, "I was sorry, that you
and Sarah . . . That she wouldn't see you."

"Well, if I'd taken more jobs in Paris, I'd have come across her myself."

"It was wrong of me, not to let you know."

"I'm not sure it was."

"Who is she?"

"Who is who?"

"Who is the reason you're wearing yesterday's shirt and you didn't
shave this morning?"

"I don't always shave," Stuyvesant protested.

"Harris, I can smell her perfume."

"That could've been— Oh, hell. Why do I bother? Pip Crosby's
roommate. A sweetheart of a girl named Nancy Berger."

"Miss Crosby was not one of the women in those pictures."

"No, thank God. She's— Look, it'll wait. Go sleep."

A taxi was perched impatiently at their toes. The two friends shook
hands, green eyes holding blue. "Do you think something has happened
to Sarah?"

"No. I don't know. But we'll find her. Doucet is good. Very good."

Grey listened to the truth in Stuyvesant's voice before turning to the
taxi door. Stuyvesant let his hand rest briefly on the small man's shoulder, then the gears clashed and Grey was away.

FIFTY-SIX

A SHIRT, A SHOWER, and a shave. With the photographs in his pocket, Stuyvesant went to lean on a few of Sarah's acquaintances.

He began with Cole Porter, the man Sarah had taken care to be standing beside at the strike of the full-moon bell. Porter lived with his wealthy wife in a garden mansion near Des Invalides—a marriage of convenience, since Porter's interests lay elsewhere. He was unlikely to be Sarah's lover, but he was certainly a friend.

Unfortunately, he was also an absent friend. The doorman who answered Stuyvesant's ring professed himself désolé but M. Porter was not at home, he was in the country writing songs, and would not return until the first of the week. Oh yes, certainly, with friends, but alas, it was impossible to say just who had gone with M. and Mme. Porter. Mais oui, there was a blonde Englishwoman—there had been, in fact, several English ladies with blonde hair here after Le Comte's party, but following breakfast, there had been a general dispersal and alas, he could not say which of the jeunes filles had gone in which direction: into Paris, or with M. Porter.

Stuyvesant figured a butler like this would have to know who went where, but he also figured that the only way to get more information out of the guy would be by fist. And there were too many footmen around for that.

So he tried Bricktop. Whose house-maid refused to wake her, although the woman did look at Sarah's picture and tell him that there was no one in the house who looked like that.

The routine at Josephine Baker's was remarkably similar.

He looked at the next name on his list, and decided that it required a dose of liquid courage. Down the boulevard Raspail, François-call-me-Frank was behind his zinc bar dispensing booze and wisdom. Both would be somewhat watered-down, but what was it they said about beggars and choosers?

Stuyvesant took his glass and laid out six of his seven photographs: Sarah in the garden, Man Ray's photo of Pip, and the four pieced-together faces from Didi Moreau's hidden room. "Know any of these girls?"

Frank dried his hands on his apron and picked them up. "She was in," he said at the top one: Sarah.

"When?" Stuyvesant said sharply.

"A month ago, maybe two," he replied. Stuyvesant's heart slowed. "She was looking for some artist with an interest in Africa. Matisse? No: Brancusi. Something to do with set design for a stage play."

"That's the only time?"

"So far as I remember. These others— Whoa." He had reached the third photograph, and stared at the woman's expression.

This might be a bad idea. "Looks realistic, doesn't it? It's an art project, for that same theater—the Grand-Guignol?"

"Yes, that would explain it."

"Qu'est-ce que ç'est?" Another customer sidled down to look, and in the end, a dozen or so men pawed over the pictures before they came back to Stuyvesant.

They'd all seen Pip's snapshot on his earlier visits, and the change to Man Ray's didn't affect their lack of recognition. Of the other photographs, only the blonde rang any bells, reminding three men of a singer who'd worked in the French bars, although come to think of it, they hadn't seen her much recently. The description stirred recognition in the back of Stuyvesant's mind.

"Name of Mimi?"

That was her, although the men were no more certain of the complete name than the women had been ten days earlier.

However, it was the picture of the youngest girl, the healthy-looking brunette with the missing segment in her face, that caused the most unease.

"This girl looks pretty beat up," said Frank.

"Great makeup department. But do you recognize her?"

"She looks a little like my sister." *Is your sister missing?* Stuyvesant tried to think of a gentle way to word the question, but Frank made it unnecessary. "At least, like she did until she had her second baby, she's ten kilos more than that now. Still, she's happy and her husband likes it, so who am I to complain? Who are these women?"

"They're all missing."

"What's that theater doing, eating them?"

Stuyvesant forced a smile. "It's probably a publicity stunt, but families worry."

"So you're setting up a missing persons agency. Any reward for finding them?"

"If I had the money to offer a reward, would I be drinking here?"

Frank's gale of laughter was a sore temptation, but Stuyvesant managed to walk out without hitting any of them.

One drink wasn't enough courage to face rue Jacob. Ten probably wouldn't be. He did not give himself a chance to chicken out, but marched up the street to the house and knocked. Softly. Maybe she'd be asleep, too.

She was not.

The housekeeper showed him into a room with dark pink walls and dark pink drapery, crowded with soft, multi-cushioned sofas, ornately carved chairs, vases of luxuriant flowers, and small tables strewn with books. Portraits of women lay along the walls, looking askance at his blunt masculinity.

When she returned, the gray-haired housekeeper seemed amused at his reaction to all this female décor. He turned away from a painting of a woman in man's clothing, and followed her through more pinkness until they came to Natalie Barney, nestled among settee cushions with a book.

"Mr. Stuyvesant," she said warmly. "So good to see you again. That *was* you at Le Comte's party the other night, wasn't it? I can't imagine you have too many lookalikes."

"That was me, in among the bones. Great music."

"And one of the odder assortment of guests. Will you have coffee? Wine? Do sit down. Berthe, this is Mr. Stuyvesant from New York, I met him a year or so ago at that mad party on the Île de la Grande Jatte. As I recall, Mr. Stuyvesant, you were working as a private investigator?"

"Still am," he said, accepting both chair and coffee.

"Dolly Wilde was saying I should write a murder mystery with a Sapphist detective. Detective stories seem all the thing."

"You'd sell a million," he said gamely.

"More to the point, I could have some fun with the clichés."

"That too."

"What can I do for you, Mr. Stuyvesant? Berthe said you were looking for a girl."

Putting down the cup, he chose two of the photographs, pushing all thoughts of death from his mind, and his voice. "Two girls, in fact. The first one's named Pip Crosby. She went missing in the spring, and her family's hired me to find her. The second is a friend—of mine, that is, not Pip's. Sarah Grey. She was at the party the other night, and hasn't been seen since."

Miss Barney put her feet on the floor to accept the pictures.

"Oh yes, Sarah. She works for Dominic."

"That's right."

"A sweet girl," said the lesbian.

Down, boy. "She is, yes. She and her fiancé had a little argument, and we both figure she's just gone off with friends for a day or two to let things cool off."

One eyebrow lifted. "And you were wondering if I might have been that friend?"

"It did occur to me that if she'd been feeling the urge to get away from the irritations of the male species for a while, she might have mentioned it to you. In passing."

Her lovely laugh went far to explain her reputation for conquest. "Mr. Stuyvesant, I *so* hope that one day I have need of a private investigator. However, no, Miss Grey did not express any specific dissatisfactions with the men in her life, and she is not taking shelter under my roof, although she would be welcome to do so."

"Well," he said, "thanks anyway. And thanks for the coffee."

Her gaze lingered on Pip. "Am I right to think this was taken by Man Ray?"

"That's right. Le Comte had it done. I understand he was thinking of putting her on the stage, and wanted it for publicity."

"Yes," she said.

Her drawled monosyllable caught his ear. "Is there something I ought to know about Man Ray?"

"'Ought to know,' Mr. Stuyvesant?"

"Pip Crosby was a good kid, and she's missing. He's one of the men she was in contact with."

"I'm sure it's nothing. But as you might imagine, people tell me things—gossip, yes, but also things that women feel other women ought to be told. One of those pieces of gossip concerned Mr. Ray. It seems he enjoys telling how he beat a former girlfriend with his belt. It is common knowledge that he prefers attractive young female assistants. They pose for him, and some of the poses are rather disturbing."

"Does any of this 'gossip' have him being an active threat?"

"No. And I'd have heard."

"I'd imagine that half the artists in Paris—half the male artists, that is—expect their women to be . . ."

"Submissive?"

"I was going to say 'agreeable,' but yeah, submissive."

"You are no doubt correct. And to be clear, Mr. Stuyvesant, I have no problem with submission, if given willingly." The meaning in her blue eyes was clear.

Stuyvesant rose to her playful challenge like a man. "Willing submission is the only kind that matters. Not the kind with a belt."

"Thus saith the knight in shining armor," Miss Barney pronounced. She handed him back the photos, watching him put them away. "You are welcome to stay, Mr. Stuyvesant. Friday afternoons I hold a salon, when we talk about everything from art to orgasms. You could show my friends your pictures. And, you might find the other guests entertaining."

"Not as entertaining as they'd find me, I expect."

She laughed again, and stood, taking his arm to steer him through the pink world and back onto the narrow gray street.

He went by the Hotel Benoit, to check for messages—none—and grab his overcoat, since dusk was falling.

The day awarded him one moment of bleak humor when Bennett Grey answered Sarah's door wearing a flowered apron, but it faded the moment Stuyvesant looked into his green eyes and saw their shared thought: *She's been gone forty-two hours.*

FIFTY-SEVEN

"Y OU'RE COOKING?" IT was obvious that the man in the apron
hadn't slept.

"Just rescuing some green beans from Sarah's garden. The housekeeper brought a cassoulet." *Rescuing Sarah's beans when you can't rescue
her,* thought Stuyvesant, and poured himself a drink.

Grey returned to his vegetables. "Tell me about your Miss Crosby."

"Not mine. She made that clear."

"You have a picture?"

Stuyvesant showed him the Man Ray portrait, then told him
about Pip in Nice: pretty girl in a bar, middle-aged man, unlikely but
promising—until she kissed him good-bye and left for Rome.

Grey snipped, sliced, listened as Stuyvesant described his fruitless
search through Montparnasse and Montmartre, and reluctantly, his despair over Pip's fate. The kitchen went still for a moment, muffled by a
blanket of dread.

"Miss Crosby sounds as wary of obligations as you are."

"What are you talking about? *I* wasn't the one to cut it off with
Sarah."

"Who said anything about Sarah?"

"Every conversation with you seems to be about Sarah."

"Yes, we've had so many conversations in the past few years."

"I've . . . been busy. Anyway, why would Pip be scared of something long-term? A twenty-two-year-old with someone my age is more likely to be bored."

"Those are not the eyes of a twenty-two-year-old," Grey said. He shoveled the beans into a steaming pot.

"Yeah. I know." Stuyvesant studied the man's profile. "Sarah said you came over in April?"

"I decided to try."

"It went all right?"

"It was hard. But I managed."

"Did she have really short hair then?"

"Not terribly. Does she now?"

"Yeah."

"It must make us look even more alike."

It's like he felt my thoughts against the side of his head. "It is a bit startling," Stuyvesant admitted.

"Harris, my sister is happy here," Grey said. "Her hand bothers her less each time I see her. And I like this Doucet chap."

"Yeah, I get it. She's fragile and I'm a threat. I'll leave Paris when . . . this is all finished."

The copper pan was taking forever to return to a boil.

Grey broke the silence. "I feel I would know, if . . . something . . . happened to Sarah. That Paris would go dark."

The forbidden topic—the two men's history, Stuyvesant's reason for avoiding Cornwall, the thing that had kept him wandering rootless across Europe for three years—stirred like a grizzly bear in the corner of the room.

"Look, I'm sure she's fine, we'll—"

The cutting board smashed into the sink, shattering amidst an explosion of bean-trimmings and soapy water. Grey stood, hands grasping his skull as if the easy lie had driven an ice-pick through it. "Don't. Please don't."

"Jesus. Bennett, I'm sorry. You said that your . . . abilities were fading."

"Not enough."

"So I guess the Project isn't leaving you alone?"

"Oh, they're still interested, all right. If I could just get them to stop spying on me, the arrangement would be almost bearable." He dropped his hands. "Look, this is about ready. Want to eat?"

Not really.

Grey served the food onto two plates and laid them on the kitchen table. Stuyvesant doggedly picked up knife and fork, casting around for a polite topic that wouldn't turn their stomachs. "I like this part of Paris. Almost like being in the country. Sarah said there was a blacksmith?"

"A self-educated philosopher who dispenses Plato along with his horse-shoes. I gave him a hand a few times, at the forge. Tell me about your girl."

"Nancy? She's . . . unexpected. Like your blacksmith."

"Not your usual blonde kitten?"

"Not blonde, no kitten. Nothing usual about her."

"I'm glad."

Stuyvesant glanced up. "I thought you approved of me and Sarah? In a big-brother kind of way."

"I did. At the time. But women have a way of making their own decisions." And before Stuyvesant could divert him with a question about Cornwall's weather or the health of his simpleton neighbor, Robbie, Grey walked right up to the conversational grizzly bear. "Whenever I see Sarah, it's like a knife in me. Her prosthetic, her scars, the way she shies at any loud noise—and now this insistence on facing down her demons with a nightmare job involving men like Didi Moreau. I look at all what she's going through and I think: *I did that.*

"You and I have both seen what men in the trenches can do. Incredible acts of courage. But I've never known anything like Sarah's everyday, long-term, soul-grinding bravery. And I'm to blame. I—"

"Not you. It was me, Bennett. I was slow and stupid and—"

"Shut up!" Grey snarled. "Harris, just . . . shut up. Look. I *see* things. I see everything, at every moment, smack in front of my eyes. But once—just once—three years ago, I let myself be distracted, by hope and by love, and my sister paid the price. God, what a price. You never told her, did you?"

Tell Sarah that her beloved brother had kept Stuyvesant from averting a catastrophe? "No."

"I've spent three years trying to convince myself that I couldn't have predicted Sarah's choice. But I know Sarah as well as I know my own body. I should have seen it coming."

"Bennett, you said it yourself: you're not a mind-reader. All you see is the tension. Even if Sarah planned what she was going to do—and I've always believed it was an impulse—would you have known? If she'd made a rational and, I don't know, *serene* choice, would you have been able to see through it?"

"I might have guessed."

"For Christ sake, man, *I* might have guessed. Quit killing yourself over it."

Grey's eyes rested on Stuyvesant's glass. "I do so want to drink myself senseless right now."

"But you won't, because Doucet needs your eyes."

Both men gazed down at their congealing food.

"Go see your Nancy," Grey said.

"I'll stay until Doucet phones."

"Have you even talked with her today?"

"No."

"You're a fool."

"I know."

Grey reached for the plates.

"Go ahead, call her. If Doucet finds it busy, he'll try again."

"I'll be quick."

The new number rang twice before Nancy answered.

"Harris! I hoped you would call."

"You mean you hoped I wasn't one of those men who . . . gets what he wants and then runs like hell?"

"I had little fear of that," she assured him.

If I were Bennett, I'd hear if that was a lie. "Good to know."

"Harris Stuyvesant, you're such a gentleman, I had to fling myself at you before you'd so much as kiss me."

"I—" He was suddenly aware of Bennett Grey, listening to every word of this coo-and-bill. "Honey, I can't talk, the fellow I'm with is waiting for a call. I just wanted to tell you I was thinking of you."

"Come and see me."

"It'll be late."

"It doesn't matter."

"Really late."

"Just ring the bell."

"Persistent, aren't you?"

"When it comes to what I want, yes."

Now, that was a heart-warming response. "I can't promise, but I'll try. And if not, I'll see you tomorrow."

"Bye," she said, and the line went dead.

Bennett Grey walked in to clear the last of the dishes.

"Don't say anything," Stuyvesant warned.

"Wouldn't think of it," Grey replied.

FIFTY-EIGHT

Two men in shirtsleeves, drinking coffee with the garden door standing ajar. As if waiting for a blonde-haired woman with emerald eyes to step inside, laughing at something she'd stumbled over in the dark.

"You think she's dead, too, don't you?" Stuyvesant said to the black rectangle. When there was no response, he glanced over and saw Grey's expression of horror.

"*Harris,* what—"

"No! Not Sarah! I'm sure she's—I mean, there's no reason—sorry! No, Jesus. I was talking about Pip."

Grey took a shaky breath and ran a hand over his face. "How the hell would I know?"

"Sure, I just—"

"Harris, don't make me into a bloody fortune-teller. Look: I see in the girl's face that she's been wounded. I see in your face that you tried like hell to find her. And that's all I see."

"Yeah. Sorry. It was a fire. Pip's injury. When she was ten she was badly burned. Broke her arm, too, but the scar was worse—big as my hand across. But she didn't seem sensitive about it—if anything, the opposite." *The most exquisite pleasure . . .*

"A physical wound wouldn't give her that look of mistrust."

"No? Then what?"

"If she posed for artists, I'd guess that was a way to flaunt the scar. Maybe she slept with middle-aged men as a way of facing the kind of injuries that don't show."

Stuyvesant stared at him.

"What?" Grey asked.

"No! You really don't need to know."

"All right."

Nancy, there in Luna Park: *The uncle. Maybe too close.*

The night air was growing cool, but neither of them moved to shut the door.

"How is your Miss Crosby tied to Doucet's investigation?"

"I don't *know* that she is. But when I brought her name to him, he started looking at his other missing persons and came up with a list of those with connections to the art world. There's thirty-one names, and he—"

"*Thirty-one?*"

"That's the names he and his sergeant haven't been able to clear, who didn't turn up in a morgue or at home. They can't all be related, but like I say, those are the ones who had something to do with art or music or acting. Whether that makes for a pattern, I don't know. You want to see my notes—see what you think?"

Grey shook his head, though not as a refusal. "It isn't the kind of seeing I'm good at, but I'll look if you like."

Stuyvesant tossed the notebook on the table. "These go back to the start of last year. Do you mind if I take a look at Sarah's things?"

"We went through her diary and letters this morning."

"Yes. Well . . ."

"Help yourself," Grey said.

A bedroom was where a person dreamed, where she kept her secrets, where she gave herself up to . . .

For once, Stuyvesant was grateful not to have Bennett Grey's skills: he really didn't want to see the hairs on the pillow, to breathe in the odors of their relationship. How many strange bedrooms had he stepped into, hoping for some clue to the person—the beloved, lively person who . . .

With a wrench, he forced his eyes to do their job.

Wide bed, tables on either side. English watercolors on the walls, English oak dresser on one side, English-looking dressing table on the other. Three hands stood on the dresser, painted tin with padded ends and complicated leather straps. Two were hardly worn, although the third was bent and chipped, with heavy marks of wear on the buckles.

One bed-side table held a small clock, tissues, a carafe and glass. Stuck into the lamp-shade was a small round lapel pin showing—he bent to see—an image of Bennett on a village street. On the other side of the bed, the table held an ash-tray, a pad with a pencil, and a brightly wrapped package the size of a small book. He pushed back its folded card:

Happy birthday, darling Émile!
—Your Sarah

Why hadn't the *flic* opened it?

In an abrupt decision, Stuyvesant yanked the ends of the ribbon. Not a book: the framed photograph of a woman with pale, close-cropped hair, her right hand clasping together a luxurious fox-fur collar. Her hair and the fur's highlights made sharp contrast against the dark background, as her unsmiling mouth was belied by the amusement pushing at her eyes.

Sarah had been photographed by Man Ray.

"Of course he saw the gift," Grey told him. "He said he'd wait until she was here. Why are you angry?"

"Look, I have no concrete reason to suspect the photographer of anything but a brutal imagination and a habit of slapping around his women. But—"

"All women?" Grey broke in.

"No. There was just one, that I know of. But when a name keeps cropping up during a mur—during an investigation, you pay attention. And his does."

Grey let the slip pass. "Montparnasse is a village. Don't the same names crop up all the time?"

"Of course."

"Like Man Ray."

"I *know*."

"You might as well suspect Fitzgerald, or Hemingway."

"Maybe not Scott. If he hasn't throttled Zelda by now, he's not the murdering kind."

"But Man Ray is all over the Quarter. Even I've met him, and I was here exactly three weeks."

"Where was that?"

"Sarah and I were feeding the ducks in Montsouris when we saw him and Kiki—you know Kiki?"

"Sure."

"—coming out of the park café. As out of place as bats in daylight."

"I can imagine. Do you know when he took this photograph?"

"Recently, judging by the hair. But Ray photographs everything from couture to perfume. One would expect him to be known all over Paris."

"Precisely. So will you go with me, while I question him?"

"Now?"

"Yes. No—Doucet needs you. But if nothing comes of tonight— and if Sarah doesn't return—then first thing tomorrow."

"If you say so. I think you'll find he's just another artistic oddball."

"Doucet thinks Ray is a flea in my ear."

"One might as well suspect Doucet," Grey commented.

Stuyvesant cocked an eyebrow. "Why do you say that?"

"He's all over Paris, too. You know how he and Sarah met?"

"He was questioning people about one of his missing persons."

"My point exactly. Even innocent people have all kinds of links, especially in Montparnasse."

"Yeah, but criminals leave patterns, if only you can see them. Speaking of which, anything jump out of my notes at you?"

Grey shook his head. "It's only facts." Stuyvesant hadn't really expected much—Grey's talents were more about producing information than processing it—but the Englishman wasn't finished. "I did wonder if Doucet shouldn't expand his search outside of missing persons. He could look at unsolved murders and assaults. In case the man tried, and failed."

He's talking about the missing, about assaults and abductions—and every other word in that speech was Sarah's name. "He may be working on that now—the art connection only cropped up when I came to him with Pip, ten days ago."

"What started him looking in that direction, do you know?"

"There were two women who went missing last—"

The telephone's jangle startled both men to their feet. Grey dove to answer, but it was not Sarah. The brief conversation consisted of, "Yes? What time? You want to come here? Fine." The telephone went back onto its cradle.

"Eleven-fifteen," Grey said. "Le Comte is going to his country house for the weekend, but he agreed to meet us on his way out of town."

Stuyvesant looked at the clock: 10:40.

"What about afterwards? Do you want me to wait here?"

"No, you go and spend some time with your young lady."

(Sarah . . .)

"Not while Man Ray's wandering the bars," Stuyvesant said. "I don't think I'll wait for you. I want to know where he's been, what he has to say about Sarah. It's Friday night, he's sure to be out there."

"Go, then. I'll ring you in the morning."

Grey glanced at the clock on the wall and started rolling down his shirtsleeves. He was looking positively haggard.

"You have one of your headaches, don't you?" Stuyvesant asked. "You should go to bed. Let Doucet meet the Count on his own."

"Well," Grey said, doing up his cuff buttons, "we may discover that

Sarah is being pampered in one of Le Comte's fifteen guest suites, and I'll be back for a blissful night's sleep."

"If so, have Doucet stick a note through Mme. Benoit's door and you can sleep in. Oh, that reminds me."

Stuyvesant found a piece of paper and wrote in capital letters:

SARAH

IF YOU COME HOME

CALL ME

He added the phone number of the Hotel Benoit, and was propping the card on the kitchen counter when the rattle of a car in the street heralded the *flic*'s arrival.

Stuyvesant looked down at Sarah's present to her lover. "Do you mind if I borrow that picture?"

"Go ahead."

The two men caught up their hats and stepped into the night. While Grey locked the door, Stuyvesant bent to rap on the taxi window. Doucet wound it down.

"Are you taking a gun?"

"M. Stuyvesant, please. American police may be in the habit of gunfire across a sitting room, but this is Paris."

The window rose, Grey got in, and the car moved off down the damp paving stones.

"So I'll take that for a 'no,'" Stuyvesant muttered.

He returned to the Hotel Benoit for his evening wear, then threw back the carpet to pry up the floorboard. When he went back down the stairs with thirty-six ounces of steel under his arm, he felt a little more cheerful about matters. But when he returned at 3:00 a.m., the only thing he felt cheerful about was that he hadn't actually used the revolver.

Although if pulling it had led to Man Ray, he wouldn't have hesitated.

FIFTY-NINE

"MADAME?" EARLY SATURDAY morning, Stuyvesant stood at Mme. Benoit's door. His third knock brought her response, if not her person. A sleep-thick voice replied: No, there had been no telephone calls for him, no visitors, no messages. So he fished through his pockets for some ten-centimes coins to phone the Préfecture. Doucet's sergeant answered.

The Milquetoast-Fortier was surprisingly brusque. "L'Inspecteur n'est pas ici."

"Don't hang up! Your boss said he'd phone me this morning with the results of a meeting. Have you heard from him at all?"

"No, but it is Saturday. His hours vary on Saturday." Fortier's English was good.

"Would you please phone him at home, and find out when he's coming in?"

"No."

"Sergeant Fortier, you and I met the other day. I have been helping Inspector Doucet with a case. You know me."

"I do not know you. I remember meeting you."

"And do you know Sarah Grey?"

"Je sais le nom." I know the name.

"Last night your boss went to see Sarah's employer, Dominic Charmentier, because Sarah has not been seen since a party Le Comte held Wednesday night. Doucet took Sarah's brother, Bennett Grey, with him. I expected to hear from one or the other of them before this. I have not." The silence went on. "Sergeant?"

"Come in and see me."

And the line went dead.

Doucet's loyal Sergeant was the sort of unimaginative and inexorable cop who could be a nightmare if he was set against you, and more valuable than a herd of informants if he was on your side. Things hadn't started out all that well between them, but Stuyvesant was willing to pant like a lap-dog to convince Sergeant Fortier that he could be helpful.

He started by leaving his revolver under the floorboards.

Fortier was at his desk next to Doucet's office, neat stacks of file folders on three corners. The man glowered over his half-glasses like a dyspeptic old woman.

"Any news?" Stuyvesant asked.

Deliberately, Fortier took off the glasses, placing them in the center of the page before him. "Inspector Doucet did not return home last night."

Stuyvesant sat down. "Well, he wasn't with Miss Grey. You see, her brother came over from England yesterday, and he and Doucet came to see me. I'd been out the night before, but when I got back . . ."

As Stuyvesant talked, he did not think the *flic* was hearing a word of it. When Fortier reached for his glasses, Stuyvesant stopped.

"Your presence," the sergeant pronounced, "coupled with l'Inspecteur's absence, make for an awkward decision. I am, in fact, required to hand an ongoing investigation over to another officer of his rank. And yet, the prospect of the inevitable delay . . . concerns me."

Stuyvesant made a sympathetic noise.

"L'Inspecteur was willing to bring you into his investigation, to an extent I personally would not have considered. He appeared to find your assistance worth the . . . unorthodoxy."

"How can I help?"

Fortier fiddled with papers. About two seconds before Stuyvesant stormed the desk, the cop placed two pages before him on the blotter: the two brunettes from the Moreau photographs. One was the young woman Doucet had tentatively identified as the missing Sorbonne student, Jacqueline-Celeste Delaurier; the other was the English woman with stained teeth.

"Yesterday afternoon, the Inspector gave me one set of pieced-together photographs and another set of reproductions, telling me to have the originals examined for fingerprints. We found many prints, although it is possible they belong to one individual." Now that the Sergeant's verbal pump had been primed, the words seemed to flow more freely.

"Didi Moreau?"

"So I understand."

"Is that the Delaurier girl?"

"I believe so. Because of the missing portion of the photograph, I cannot be certain, but the resemblance is striking. When it came to the other woman, l'Inspecteur had me take the photograph to the British Consulate-General. An hour ago, I received a telephone call. The woman's name is Joanna Williams. She was not on *our* books because she was not a missing person, but a murder victim. Her body was found on the twenty-second of June, 1927, near the Place de Montrouge, wearing little more than a torn chemise. Her hands were filthy and bleeding, looking, to quote the report, 'as if she had dug herself out of a grave.' Her left hand and wrist were broken and contused. She died without regaining consciousness. Cause of death was exhaustion and severe dehydration."

Stuyvesant looked at the Delaurier girl's photograph. "The list Doucet gave me only went back to the beginning of 1928."

Fortier picked up a sheet of paper. "My current task is a survey of missing persons dating back to the spring of 1927. This is the beginning."

Stuyvesant, astonished but grateful, ran his eyes over a dozen names and brief descriptions. "What's this question mark, on June 23?"

"An Italian woman left a bar late that night to use the facilities, and did not return. From the sounds of it, she was a femme de nuit who drank a lot of her client's champagne then stepped out, and he only reported her because he felt he'd been robbed."

"No name?"

"No names, of either the woman or the client. I imagine he had second thoughts, as he started to sober up. It was a bar up near Pigalle, I'm not sure it even has a— Yes, Massey?"

The uniformed man at the door gestured at the telephone. "Je pense que c'est important."

Fortier said to Stuyvesant, "Un moment," and spoke his name into the telephone.

Stuyvesant continued reading—until the weighty silence across the desk made him look up.

Fortier had the instrument pressed against his ear as if his very life depended on it. His eyes were staring straight across the desk.

Stuyvesant found it suddenly hard to breathe.

Nine days—nine very difficult and complicated days—after some gendarme had searched his room, Stuyvesant had by no means forgotten the episode, but it had been pushed to the back, fading from urgently bewildering to one more puzzling question. He no longer shot upright with every creak of the stairs.

Now, with Fortier's gaze fixed on him, Stuyvesant's gut went cold. If there weren't a hundred cops between him and the street, he'd have bolted for the door.

But since it was hopeless, he had to stay in his chair and bluff his way out—and since he stayed put, he quickly saw that the Sergeant was not staring at him, but through him.

"Où?" Fortier asked, then, "Quand?" A minute later he said, "Oui. Dix minutes." He hung up.

Where? When? Yes. Ten minutes.

"Je dois partir." Fortier sounded as if he was talking to himself.

"Where do you need to go?" Stuyvesant asked, but Fortier just stared at the telephone. When he raised his head to the man at the door, his face was as shocked as a soldier who looked down to discover that a blast had taken his leg. "L'Inspecteur," he said in wonder. "Il a été abattu."

The Inspector. He's been shot.

SIXTY

I T WAS NOT what Bennett Grey expected of an underground prison.

For one thing, the light. The photographs' flash had suggested darkness, but one tall ecclesiastical candle burned on a stone podium near the door.

For another, there was little stench of death. The floor had been scrubbed, the walls and shackle sluiced down—his nostrils could taste putrefaction in the air, but it was little more than a memory beneath the honey-smell of the candle and the mingling of wine and tobacco, perfume and sweat.

And there was sound. Beneath the minuscule hiss of wax being turned to smoke lay the bone-deep vibrations of life above—wheels and feet, machines and tools. The rhythm of two hammers occasionally coming together. A sewer main, with a half-second delay between the rush of water leaving the pipes and that water hitting the stones.

He even, bizarrely enough, knew what time it was. A clock-face protruded from the stone, the *tick, tick* of its moving hands almost comforting, a reminder of home.

However, the most unexpected feature of his prison was the people.

All around the wide room, figures danced. On this side, tapestry women in elaborately sleeved gowns lined up with tapestry men in velvet and lace, their merriment come from the looms three centuries ago. At the edges of the candle's light, slim girls in beads and sleek young men in black and white flung up their heels, brought to life so recently, he could smell turpentine. Some dancers were mere ghosts: two tapestry panels had been hung near a window, washing out their figures to pale outlines, while across the cavern, the ghosts of dancers-yet-to-be showed as charcoal lines on gessoed wood.

Two of the newer panels were by artists who could never have seen an actual human skeleton.

Here in the oldest section of the Danse where Grey was shackled, the tapestries had been pulled back from the stone like curtains from a stage. His left wrist was bound in steel, yet he sat with the shiny anchoring bolt to his right. The chain stretched across his chest like a sash of chivalry, heavy, cold, and uncomfortable, but he refused to stretch away from it in terror.

Eleven years since his first death in the trenches: plenty of time to consider the role of dignity when time came for the second.

SIXTY-ONE

THE COP IN the doorway and Harris Stuyvesant spoke simultaneously.

"Where is he?" asked the *flic.*

"Was there anyone with him?"

Fortier cocked an eye at the big American, but answered his colleague first.

"They took him to la Charité. Who would be with him?"

"Small Englishman, pale blond hair and green eyes."

"They didn't say, but—"

The other cop interrupted. "Is l'Inspecteur alive?"

"He was when they got to the hospital."

"Who shot him?"

"They don't know."

"Why not?"

"He's unconscious."

"Sergeant, do you—" But Fortier was moving, fast. He shouldered the other man out of the way and was gone. Stuyvesant reached for his hat, then stopped. Nobody would let him see Doucet. Bennett Grey didn't seem to be with him. And in no time at all, someone would come to throw Stuyvesant out.

He dropped his hat. He'd rather be tearing apart Man Ray's studio or Le Comte's house—or Didi Moreau's face—but he scribbled as fast as his pen would move: names, dates, and descriptions. He included the English murder victim and the alleged Italian prostitute from 1927. His notes were sketchy, but he was nearly at an end when a clerk came through the door. The fresh-faced young man stopped in surprise.

"Sorry, I was looking for Sergeant Fortier," he said in rapid-fire French.

"He's gone to the hospital to see Doucet. Something I can do for you?"

"Who are you?"

"I'm helping them with a missing persons case."

"Does he know you're looking at his files?"

"Mais oui." Sure.

The clerk was young, and gullible. "Oh, well, in that case." He dropped another file on the desk.

"You haven't heard anything, have you?" Stuyvesant asked, putting an inclusive emphasis on the *vous*.

The man shook his head, trying for gloom but betrayed by the thrill. "Just what everyone knows. That he's unconscious, and they're operating to remove the bullet."

"Anything further on where they found him?"

"Not yet—everyone's gone down to help with the search. Strange to have the place so empty, isn't it?"

"Sure is." Stuyvesant wondered how to ask *where* Doucet had been found without giving away the game. "Any idea what Doucet was doing there?" he tried. "Last I heard he was up in Montmartre."

"Maybe he was going to check in to St. Anne's," the clerk said, chuckling at his great wit—the mental hospital of St. Anne's was a stone's throw from Place Denfert-Rochereau. Then he realized that humor might be inappropriate, what with a shot policeman, and added, "Maybe he was looking at that shooting of the girl, last week? Someone told me it was the same place."

Stuyvesant felt that too-familiar cold rush: Lulu! *Quick, say something before the cop notices that your jaw's on your chest.* "So why'd they take him to la Charité?"

"They knew he was a police inspector, of course. They wanted him close to the Préfecture, so everyone could say . . . Well."

Could say good-bye. "Does he have family?"

"You haven't met his sister?"

"Oh, that's right, his sister. What about his fiancée?"

The man looked surprised. "L'Inspecteur is engaged?"

"Look," Stuyvesant said, "I should finish this. If you hear anything, let me know."

"D'accord."

Stuyvesant bent over his pages with increased vigor. With a gossip like that around, someone would hear of the stray American at Fortier's desk. And while he didn't care if they threw him out, he didn't want to lose his notes.

He trotted down the stairs four minutes later, notebook intact. Before he left, he scribbled a message with Bennett's suggestion:

Fortier—the presence of Joanna Williams among the missing persons suggests that you compare a list of all unsolved murders as well. If you need me, I'm at the Hotel Benoit.
Harris Stuyvesant

Out on the Pont Neuf, his hand raised for a taxi, he was hit by a sudden thought: *Nancy.*

He hadn't phoned her—hadn't even *thought* about phoning her. Like the kind of guy he'd told her he wasn't. He should have the cab take him there first. At least have it stop near a public telephone.

But what could he say? *Hi, sorry I can't come see you, I'm busy looking for an old girlfriend?*

And anyway, Nancy was a sport. She'd understand.

He hoped.

The Place Denfert-Rochereau was its usual bustling daytime self, with half a dozen musicians competing with twice that number of sheet-music sellers. None of the news-boys were shouting about a shot policeman, but when he neared St. Anne's, uniforms appeared. Pasting on an eager expression, he drifted over to a group of avid young men.

"What's going on?" he asked.

They told him. Several different stories, in fact, but all had to do with a cop who'd been found in that alleyway over there. In none of them did a blond foreigner play a part.

It was hard to feel that Grey's absence was a relief.

Experienced with the drawbacks of Sarah's rustic home, he had the taxi driver wait for him at her steps.

No one answered his knock, but the third flower-pot in the row hid a key. Inside, he felt the stillness.

"Bennett? Sarah? Either of you home?"

Silence replied. His note commanding Sarah to call him was untouched. There was no evidence that anyone had been there since last night.

He'd never been so glad for the absence of bloodstains in his life.

He added a line to the earlier message:

I WAS HERE AGAIN, SATURDAY NOON

Then he picked up Sarah's telephone. Nancy answered on the third ring.

"Hi, sweetheart," he said.

"Who is that?"

"Nancy, it's me, Harris."

"Do I know someone named Harris?"

"Yeah, I'm sorry, this case is getting a little—"

"Because if I did, it wouldn't be in a city like Paris with public telephone boxes and post offices and pneumatics about every ten feet. Not if he's said, 'Sure, I'll phone,' and then leaves a person twiddling her thumbs and feeling like a fool."

"Nancy, I'm sorry."

"Are lives at stake? Is the safety of the entire—"

"Yes."

"What?"

"I said, yes. Lives are at stake."

Silence, while she considered an appropriate response.

"Could you have called earlier?" she asked.

"Was it physically possible? Yes. Would you have wanted to talk to me? No."

After a minute, a sigh came down the line. "Harris, I'm not a demanding sort of person. I'm a grown-up. I realize that— No no, let me finish. I realize that adults have jobs to do. But I'll only tell you this once: I expect my friends to have manners. Any failure of communication in the future will require a first-rate reason. Like, you're unconscious in the hospital."

"Gotcha."

"So, does this phone call mean I'm free for the rest of the day?"

"I . . . Yes. I'll phone you tonight. If not, first thing tomorrow."

"I look forward to it. I hope you are well?"

"I actually don't know."

"Well, that is intriguing. Don't end up in the hospital, Harris."

"If I do, you'll be the first to know."

He returned the key to its pot and climbed into the taxi, giving the driver the address of the man who had last seen Grey and Doucet: "La maison de la Comte de Charmentier, s'il vous-plâit."

Le Comte was not at home. Or so the butler who answered the gate's bell claimed. The locked gates made Stuyvesant half believe that Le Comte was indeed out in the country, but in any case, he wouldn't have a lot of luck climbing over the gates in broad daylight.

He had the driver take him around the corner to Man Ray's studio.

Banging at the door of the pretty building brought Ray's upstairs neighbor to the window, cursing him soundly. No, he did not know when M. Ray would return, go away or the street would rain flower-pots.

Okay: Didi Moreau.

Rounding the corner to Moreau's street, Stuyvesant saw the activity.

"Pull over here. No, this is fine, just stop a minute."

The driver didn't care for this shifty behavior, and kneaded the steering wheel nervously as the *flics* swarmed the gate like flies around a dead rat.

After a minute, the small figure of Didi Moreau appeared, pushed in front of a sizable uniformed policeman. He was shut into a car; the car drove off.

Who next? Cole Porter? Natalie Barney? They all had his telephone number, if Sarah appeared. La Charité?

No: he might not have a chance at the Charmentier mansion until after dark, but Man Ray was still out there, somewhere.

He leaned forward. "Take me to the Dôme."

SIXTY-TWO

THE LIST OF missing:

1926:

6/?	f	brn	Jacqueline-Celeste Delaurier (F)

1927:

6/22	f	brn	Joanna Williams (UK)
6/23 ?	f	black?	[Italian woman]

1928

1/3	f	brn	Katrine Aguillard (F)
2/13?	f	blonde	Lotte Richter (Germ)
3/2	f	black?	Ethel Delaney (US)
3/22	f	blonde	Margot Jourdain (F)
3/26	f	blonde	Clara Klein (Germ)
3/30	f	brn	Holly LeClerc (F)
5/14	m	bald	Daniel La Plante (F)
6/1	f	blonde	Irma Matthieu (F)
6/19	f	brn	Alice Barnes (UK)
7/21?	f	brn	Elsa Werner (Germ)
8/7	f	blonde	Abigail Parker (US)
9/20	m	blond	Marc Dupont (F)

10/30	f	blonde	Ruth Anne Palowski (Poland)
10/31	f	brn	Eulalie Dambrose (F)
11/5(?)	m	gray	Joseph—? (F)
12/4	f	black	Fleur Villines (F)
12/17	f	blonde	Viviane Lapierre (F)
12/19	m	black	Eduardo Torres (Spain)

1929

2/15	f	red	Louise Hartman (UK)
2/20	f	black	Esmé Gasque (F)
3/1	m	brown	Raoul Bellamy (F)
3/21	f	blonde	Pip Crosby (US)
3/22	f	lt. brn	Isabelle Beauchamp (F)
5/20	f	black	Gisela Conti (It)
5/20	f	black	Norma Lombardi (It)
6/12	f	gray	Sylvia Davis (US)
6/21	f	brn	Nicole Karon (F)
6/24	f	blonde	Josette Achille (F)
7/19	f	brn?	Deanne Landry (US)
8/12	m	brn	Luc Tolbert (F)
9/11	f	brn	Gabriella Faulon (F)

SIXTY-THREE

S UCH SURPRISES, THOUGHT Grey: light, sound, dancers. And now, the icy fingers of dread.

He'd thought he was immune to a fear of death. Sarah worried about him—Harris Stuyvesant, too. That was why she'd chosen a house that might soothe him into visiting, why Stuyvesant continued to send him picture postcards: chain-links binding him to life.

They were right to worry. He yearned after the stones at the base of the cliff, brooded about one final swim out into the Channel. If he'd just been locked here without food or drink or light, he was pretty certain he'd have been content to curl up on the floor and welcome death.

Two pulls kept him from that.

One was hope.

That damned, inconvenient, pervasive, tantalizing demon that was hope. He could not decide if this prison had been deliberately constructed to make use of it, or if the hope was accidental.

On Friday night, he'd been forced at gunpoint to abandon Doucet, marched into the depths without explanation, chained to the wall, and left. He kept thinking about Stuyvesant's four photographs of women driven mad by terror. He tried to picture them left here as he was: with a blanket, some bread, and two full cups of water. He had no doubt that they'd been *here*: these stones were in all four photographs. Fear, exhaustion: yes. But was this the kind of horror that shattered a mind?

Dehydration suggested the women had not been given water; their staring madness suggested that light had been taken from them as well. Perhaps after a few encounters with uncontrollable prisoners driven insane by terror—one of whom, he thought, might be responsible for the newness of the bolt at the end of his chains—their captor had discovered the sedative effects of hope? Learned that a prisoner could be subdued by food and water, light and a blanket? Given those, surely the worst one could expect was a temporary, if bewildering, discomfort?

Hope.

But it was not the only thing that kept Bennett Grey from turning his face to the wall.

There was Sarah.

In his own part of the world—even in London—Grey would never have walked into that ambush. Not knowing Paris, and putting too much trust in Doucet's judgment, he had. Doucet paid the price: he'd dropped instantly, and before Grey could go to him, a third, warning shot had sparked along the stones. He had looked down the alleyway with Doucet at his feet and asked the gunman one question: "Where is Sarah?"

If the man had only answered—with "I don't know" or "Who?" or "She's fine" or *anything*—Grey would have known his sister's fate. If there'd been light on the man's face—but then they'd heard the gendarmes' approach, and the man had asked a question of his own: "Will I need to shoot them, too?"

Grey had dropped the man's sack over his own head and let himself be pushed into a narrow entranceway.

To sit, caught between the unasked-for hope and the unexpected dread.

SIXTY-FOUR

WHY A SATURDAY at the Dôme should be any different from a Wednesday, Stuyvesant didn't know—what did a weekend mean to artists and painters? But even at three in the afternoon, the cafés and bars of Montparnasse were thrumming like a beehive, frantically making honey before winter came.

The laughter and music grated on his nerves, the drinks went down his throat, and no one had seen Man Ray. At 5:00, Stuyvesant trotted down to Ray's address. He was back within twenty minutes, circulating like a shark.

At 6:00, he dropped three ten-centimes coins into a phone and listened to the ringing in Sarah's house. When the coins came back, he looked at them—Nancy?—then slid them back in his pocket.

By 7:00, Montparnasse was ablaze with light and life, music spilling from every door. Americans ebullient with fat wallets and the freedom of being two thousand miles from Prohibition shouted across the boulevard Montparnasse, summoning waiters and women, shoving past him on the terraces. Their blithe disregard of the shadows drove him mad.

A night like this had its ups and its downs, when it came to finding a man. Chances were good that Ray was here somewhere, but between the crowds and the smoke, he'd need to be within arm's reach before Stuyvesant saw him. All he could do was follow Ray's spoor, a delicate business that required more leisurely chat than his nerves would stand.

He finally spotted Kiki at the Coupole—not that he could ask her directly, but she and Ray moved in the same crowd.

On the edges of her group, he found someone who had been talking to someone who had seen Man Ray and his fiery new girl-assistant, going to the Lilas, or was it the Deux Magots? A waiter at the Lilas had seen M. Ray, but earlier in the day. Then back at the Coupole, a visiting Canadian Stuyvesant had met the week before detached himself from Kiki's crowd to head for the pissoir. Stuyvesant emptied his glass and moved to cut the man off.

"Hey, Morley—it is Morley, isn't it? How are you? You and the wife enjoying Paris?"

"We're having a fantastic time, and you? It's Stuyvesant, right?"

"That's me. Say, have you seen Man Ray? Couple of months ago I'd have asked Kiki, but she isn't too keen on him just now."

"Yeah, somebody told me he had a new girl. I haven't seen him, but— Hold on a minute. Francis! Hey, Francis! Stuyvesant, do you know Francis Picabia?"

They shook hands. "I don't think so, although you look familiar."

"You've seen a film called *Entr'acte*," Picabia suggested.

Stuyvesant bared his teeth in what he hoped looked like a grin. "The cannon on the roof? With the guy wearing a bowler?"

"Eric Satie."

"Great film. You're a painter, too, aren't you? I saw your stuff—where was it?"

"Theophile Briant's gallery?"

"Must've been." Stuyvesant had never seen one of the man's pieces, but Picabia's fingernails declared him a painter, and the question put him on the fellow's good side. "Say, I was trying to find Man Ray, he . . . he said he'd take some pictures of a friend who's headed back to New York in a few days. Any ideas?"

"Have you tried Le Boeuf sur le Toit?"

"Oh. Right! Of course that's where he'd be, if he didn't want Kiki underfoot."

"I don't know why he wouldn't, three-ways work just fine for some of us."

"Yeah, maybe he'd like it, but Kiki might feel otherway—otherwise." Stuyvesant blinked at the difficulty of that last word. "I'll go check there—it's still on the rue Pen—er, Penty—Penthièvre?"

"Unless they've moved it since last week."

"Ha! Thanks. Great to meet you, and Morley, great to see you, too, hope to see you again, sometime."

The city lights spun gently through the windows as the taxi drove him up to the VIII arrondissement. He straightened his tie, got a cigarette going on the third attempt, and wove his way inside.

Le Boeuf sur le Toit was, despite its Dada-esque name, a bar with hot jazz and a wide mix of patrons. The first person Stuyvesant saw through the smoke was Man Ray. The second was Lee Miller, a million-dollar baby draped across the artist like a five-and-dime rag doll.

He slipped into an empty chair at the back: if he waited and followed Mr. Ray home, he'd get some information out of him. One way or another.

But when he shifted the chair to see across the room, he found Lee Miller's big blue eyes looking straight at him.

She winked.

He instantly turned to the girl at his shoulder and said the first thing that came into his head. "That's a great pair of earrings you've got."

They were certainly great in size, golden triangles as big as a baby's head. She nodded with the amiability of the tipsy. Or maybe she was nodding to the music, it was impossible to tell. In either case, he threw a few more sentences at her until she leaned over and asked if she knew him.

"No, not yet, but anyone who likes jazz is a friend of mine."

"American?"

"Mais oui," he said in a bad accent. "From New York."

"Bienvenu à Paris, Monsieur. Got a light?"

He flicked his Ronson a couple of times and aimed it at the cigarette stuck onto ten inches of enameled holder. She thanked him carefully, and turned back to her table.

With a glance, he could see that Miss Miller was not fooled. *What about that girl in New York?* he wanted to ask her. *You think she considers your boyfriend a genius?*

At least the music was great, and the drinks were strong, and the friends of the earring-girl drew him into their sphere. Every so often, he half-rose to check on Ray's table; each time, the man was in place.

Until one time he wasn't.

It had been about five minutes since Stuyvesant's last glance, and he'd been distracted by a lively argument about New Orleans jazz. He idly glanced across the room and saw a quartet of Negroes settling down at the table. Stuyvesant shot to his feet—and found himself nose to hat with a belligerent Man Ray.

"Why the hell are you following me around!" the photographer demanded. "Do you have some kind of a fixation on me?"

"You could say that."

"Well, stop it, you damned pansy! You want me to have you arrested?" Half a dozen friends at his side lent Ray a lot of backbone.

"I'd like to see you try."

The Miller girl pushed in between them. "Please, let's go home, Man."

"Has he hit you yet?" Stuyvesant asked, his voice loud.

She gaped at him. "*What* did you say?"

"Your boyfriend here. Has he backhanded you yet? Beaten you with his belt? Maybe just turned you over his knee?"

"Jesus, Man," one of the others said, "this guy's plastered."

Ray's friends closed in to hustle the photographer towards the street. One of them stuck up his hand for a taxi, leaving Lee Miller to confront the big man with the angry face.

"Mr. Stuyvesant, you shouldn't go around making accusations like that."

He ignored her, talking in a loud voice to the man with the Valentino gaze. "When did you take Sarah Grey's photograph?"

"Who?"

"You heard me."

"Grey? English girl? Friend of Le Comte?" It dawned on Ray that this mattered to Stuyvesant. His dark eyes took on a gleam of triumph.

"Oh yes, I did her just the other day. The girl with the laugh that makes a man go all hard."

The night, the month—the year—rose up in the blood of Harris Stuyvesant. For two weeks, he'd been roaming Paris looking for an enemy, and finally, Ray's insult gave him what he needed. Righteous rage swept over him and he dove forward, getting in two solid punches before Ray's friends swarmed over them.

Sixty seconds later, he went down under a pile of *flics*.

SIXTY-FIVE

BENNETT GREY WAITED for the candle's flame to move.

Whenever he looked, it was perfectly still.

But why else would there be a chair?

Not that the flame didn't move at all: as the candle burned, the line of its light edged up the back of the chair. Once it had left the chair back, Grey estimated seven hours of wax before he was left in the dark with Death's pirouettes.

It didn't require a chair to shoot a man. And by the height of the five bullets that had hit the wall behind him, neither the gunman nor his victims were sitting.

He'd seen walls like that during the War, where deserters had been lined up for execution. But the only chairs during the War had been for soldiers too terrified to stand.

He waited for the flame to quiver. Surely his captor wanted something of him, some conversation long enough to require a seat?

Bennett Grey watched the dancers and the motionless flame, eked out his water and bread, and listened to the faint *tick* of the clock hands.

The vibrations of Saturday died away. A long night ticked past, waiting for his captor to return.

As Sunday grew above him, he began to wonder if the constructed hope was a vicious hoax. If food and light made just another layer of cruelty on top of torment . . .

No. The flame would move. Someone would come.

SIXTY-SIX

A DAY DIDN'T REALLY start in jail, it just grew louder, with the clanging of cell doors like the crack of doom. Stuyvesant groaned and pulled his arms more tightly over his throbbing head.

"Just fucking die, why don't you?" he muttered.

He was not talking to the jailers. *Jesus, what have I done now?*

"*Steevaysont!*" The nonsense syllables slowly assumed meaning. He raised his arm to squint at the door.

"Yeah?"

The cop jerked his head in command.

His neighbors in the drunk-tank cursed and kicked him as he waded through their legs. In the corridor, the cop pointed with his baton. Stuyvesant shuffled along, black and blue all over, stomach filled with battery acid, one hand on his trousers waistband since they'd taken pretty much everything, including his suspenders. *You stupid shit, here you are until Monday, and that sure does Sarah a whole lot of good. And Bennett. Jesus, you've done some really knucklehead things in your life, but this?* How could he get a message out? And who to: Nancy? Yeah, right.

He made a noise like a gargling crocodile and tried to speak. "Can I get a gl—"

A blow in the middle of his back sent him staggering against the wall. He looked up at the eager baton.

Yes, he could do without a glass of water.

A turn, some stairs, and at the end of the hallway, an open door. He slowed, but the baton delivered another shove and drove him expertly inside.

Instead of the gathered batons he'd been dreading, there was a single figure. "Fortier!" he said in relief. "I thought I'd have to wait till Mon—"

He was not prepared for the speed of the meek Sergeant's fist, or its force. Stuyvesant spun into the wall, rattling the window and ending up in a puddle on the floor while the cop bent over and assaulted him with words.

"You bastard!" his dizzy brain translated. "You fucking bastard, I thought I'd seen a lot in this life, but you honestly win it all."

"What the hell—"

"Stand up! Stand up, you son of a bitch."

Eyeing the furious Sergeant and the waiting guard, Stuyvesant warily obeyed. As he rose, the top of the table came into view, on it a familiar object: his pistol and shoulder holster. He'd left the rig beneath the floorboards last night, after he'd realized how much he wanted to use it.

Oh, Jesus. Had the various departments finally compared notes and fitted him up for Lulu's shooting? Or had somebody put a bullet into Man Ray after— *Oh, don't be thick-headed.*

"Look, what's going on? I haven't used that thing in months, and I always leave it in the room because I know guns are—"

"Ta gueule! I wanted to do this myself." Fortier's face was hard with pleasure as he crushed a pair of handcuffs onto the prisoner's wrists. "Harris Stuyvesant, you are under arrest for the attempted murder of Inspector Émile Doucet."

SIXTY-SEVEN

GREY'S CAPTOR DID not appear. The chair waited, the candle burned, the clock hands marched. Sunday evening, he licked the last of the water from the cup.

A few hours after Sunday's vibrations had died from the stones, a tapestried lady curtsied. His eyes snapped over to her, daring her to move again. She did not. She merely gave the same coy look over her fan that she'd been giving her dashing young lover for the past two days.

But while he watched her, a figure off to his right took a step.

He could not keep his eyes on them all. Soon, dancers whirled and leapt, musicians swayed, thread garments and painted faces rippled with motion. Panel after panel of Death waltzed with his scythe.

He shut his eyes.

Towards morning, the music began.

SIXTY-EIGHT

THE NURSES IN the Hôpital de la Charité stayed close to Émile Doucet, all of Saturday, Saturday night, on into Sunday. They eased teaspoons of water between his lips. They took his blood pressure, checking for signs of improvement, or failure.

Sunday evening, their heroic patient began to shift and mumble, indicating an approach either of consciousness, or of fever. At ten o'clock they tied his restless hands to keep him from pulling his bandages. At midnight, they were grateful when Sergeant Fortier arrived, taking up the bed-side watch to keep l'Inspecteur from damaging himself.

SIXTY-NINE

Accused murderers ranked higher than mere drunks in the Paris system of justice. Harris Stuyvesant had been given his own cell. And his own, almost-clean uniform, several sizes too small. There was even a cup of water.

He sat on the hard bunk staring at his bare, gnawed-looking shins. *Not murder: attempted murder.* Doucet was still alive, then. But what an incredibly, abysmally, *fatally* dim-witted ass he'd been. Would the cops even bother comparing his gun with Doucet's bullets? Or was he just too convenient a fall guy? Bennett and Sarah missing, Pip gone, Lulu murdered—and now Doucet. And what had Harris Stuyvesant done to help any of them?

He'd gotten smashed, blown up at an artist, and got himself thrown behind bars.

And for what? He'd been so sure about Man Ray. But in the harsh, sober light of a new day, could he honestly say the guy had killed Pip Crosby—or *anyone* on Doucet's list? Ray was the kind of man who liked to strut. He might talk big, might even use his belt on a girl, but a series of cold, deliberate killings? Deep in his queasy and somewhat tender gut, Stuyvesant didn't think the photographer had it in him.

He stiffly rose to lurch back and forth across the cell.

How about Didi Moreau?

He could see the little creep happily feeding body parts to his damned beetles, sure, but having the nerve and the wits to choose a series of victims, kill them, and conceal their bodies until they were reduced to bone? The man didn't have enough muscle to lift a medium-sized dog. He lacked the guts to stand up to his maid. And sure, any weakling could pull a trigger, and a man bullied by the help might harbor a built-up antagonism towards women, but any killer who'd managed to escape Doucet's attention for what looked to be years had to be either phenomenally lucky, or a clever and controlled man.

Which brought him to Le Comte. A decorated War hero who spent his life and his fortune helping his fellow soldiers and the people of Paris; a wealthy, middle-aged man with generations of aristocratic blood running through his veins; a man under whose influence Pip Crosby had learned self-respect.

Also Sarah's employer, Pip's lover, and—apparently—the last person to see Bennett Grey and Émile Doucet. Yes, Harris Stuyvesant was hardly an objective judge, having bone-deep misgivings about any man born with a Renaissance silver spoon in his mouth, but the Marquis de Sade wasn't the only rich bastard to get away with crimes that would throw a commoner to the gallows.

As for Doucet's list, well, the Comte had as much opportunity as the others to insinuate himself into the lives of any number of women and make them disappear. Hell, the man didn't even have to get his hands dirty if he didn't want to, since money like his could hire a cold-blooded assistant or six. Money like his could buy off . . .

Stuyvesant's feet shuffled to a stop. A cold draft trickled into the stuffy cell.

No! That was absurd. The man was near death in the hospital.

Or so Fortier said—and the *flic* hadn't lied. That kind of fury—rage enough to turn a Caspar Milquetoast Sergeant into a cop who beat a prisoner—couldn't be feigned, not if the man had all the skills of the Grand-Guignol. Sergeant Fortier honestly believed l'Inspecteur was dying.

So yes, Doucet had been wounded, probably to the head. But what if a man could summon the guts to lay a gun alongside his own skull and pull the trigger?

Would any doctor question that patient's lack of response? Would anyone in their right mind suggest that a police Inspector covered with blood had shot himself?

Only that chronic drunk and incompetent, Harris Stuyvesant.

On Friday, Grey had asked if Stuyvesant knew how Sarah and Doucet had met. Stuyvesant did: the Inspector was *questioning people about one of his missing persons* and got to talking with Sarah in the park. Grey asked in order to illustrate the unlikely links that bound the residents of Montparnasse.

But wasn't there another question behind his?

Yes, l'Inspecteur was all over Paris: meeting artists, rubbing shoulders with the upper crust, wandering through parks on sunny days showing pictures to pretty girls. Getting them into conversation. Getting them into bed.

But wasn't showing around the photographs of missing persons a job usually given to lesser cops?

No! *That's loony.* Stuyvesant resumed his pacing. A man with something to hide would never have welcomed an American private investigator. And damn it, *Bennett Grey* trusted Doucet!

Bennett: whose eyes were as blind as any man's when looking at someone comfortable with their madness.

From the start, Doucet's easy camaraderie had seemed unlikely from a cop—even a lily-white innocent cop. Stuyvesant might have reflected on that fact a little harder if he hadn't been so damned eager for the man's information.

But once that private investigator finally got around to wondering *why* Inspector Doucet was so cooperative . . .

It was too late. He was already in jail.

Charged with the attempted murder of that very Inspector.

Who any moment would conveniently wake up from his coma to point a shaky and grieving finger at the American busybody who had come to Paris to murder a former lover and her fiancé. And any evidence to the contrary—well, once on his feet, l'Inspecteur could easily tidy away such inconvenient matters as a bullet that didn't match a gun, or a suspect who had been seen elsewhere. He'd even have an explanation for Bennett Grey's absence. Or death . . .

Could France guillotine à foreign citizen? Or would they give Harris Stuyvesant over to the Americans to be hanged?

SEVENTY

SHORTLY AFTER 1:00 a.m., the heroic patient's eyelids flickered
open.

"Don't try to talk," Fortier urged, his voice low and close to his boss'
ear. "I'm not sure if you can, with that mummy-wrapping, but just in
case, the nurse said we weren't to let you and she's a ferocious little
thing, I wouldn't want her mad at me. So, you're in la Charité, lost some
blood but they got the bullet out and there's no infection. Not much,
anyway. Blink once if you understand."

Doucet blinked.

"Good," Fortier said. "Good. Well. The doctor said that if you woke,
I should tell you to go back to sleep, though it seems to me that a man
who's been out for two days might— Hey, no, wait, don't try to—okay,
I'll get the straps. Guess I shouldn't have let it slip how long you've been
out—don't tell the nurse, eh? Hah! There: better? Now, before you go to
sleep again, let me just say that we identified the fingerprints on the
photos and arrested Moreau, then we found the gun in Stuyvesant's
hotel room and picked him up for this. Tomorrow morning I'll go see
the American ambassador and— Wait—don't sit up! What? What was
that?"

The bandages kept the patient's jaw from opening, but the Sergeant
leaned down, hoping to hell the terrifying little nurse did not come in
and discover him permitting Doucet to speak.

SEVENTY-ONE

T HEY CAME FOR Harris Stuyvesant in the dark of the night. The door's crash hurled him off the bunk and upright, his back to the wall.

"Venez," a guard said.

Stuyvesant stayed where he was, knowing there was no way to defend himself, knowing he would try . . .

Venez, his brain whispered. The vous form, rather than tu. Politeness? No, a command was a command. But a single prisoner: no reason not to wade in, yet the guards just waited. Stuyvesant peeled his back off the stones and edged out of the cell.

He started down the silent corridor, skull and shoulders tense with apprehension, but the only blow that came was a prod, not a slam that left a man pissing blood. *Go here* rather than, *Go here or I'll beat you bloody.*

The corridor; the open door; Sergeant Fortier, again. If Doucet had died, wouldn't his sergeant look more hostile? The man's face gave nothing away.

The room's table held what remained of Stuyvesant's evening clothes. On top lay his shoulder holster, which he'd left under the hotel floorboards. No gun. Nor were the brass knuckles in the heap of things they'd taken from his pockets—notebook, cigarette case, Ronson, wallet—and from the hotel—folding knife and lock picks.

364 LAURIE R. KING

"Inspector Doucet is awake," Fortier said. "He ordered me to let you go."

Stuyvesant took a quick step to the side, as if the floor beneath him had shifted. "Well," he said. "Yes. Good. You mind if I sit down?"

He didn't wait, just dropped into a chair and reached out to disentangle the cigarette case and lighter from what had once been a bow tie. His hands were not very steady, he noticed, and scowled at them.

So: not Doucet, and not a setup.

"Who shot him?"

"The gunman had the light behind him. L'Inspecteur caught a glimpse of a man shorter than you before he was hit."

"Hit where?"

"Here, and here." Fortier drew his finger alongside his head above the ear, then jabbed the hollow of his shoulder, inches from his heart.

Stuyvesant's brain tried to operate through the sludge. *Shorter than me leaves most of France.* "Was Grey with him?"

"Yes."

"And he doesn't know what happened to Grey."

"No."

"Or Sarah? His . . . fiancée?"

"He asked about the young woman. He is not aware that she is missing."

"Am I free to go?"

"Until such time as we have evidence of your guilt."

"Does that mean you don't have any suspects? Other than me?"

"It means we will proceed with the case, Monsieur."

"You arrested Moreau?"

"Yes."

"And you're not giving me back my weapons?"

"You may apply in writing for the return of your possessions."

Stuyvesant put out his cigarette and got to his feet, more slowly than he'd sat down. "Where do I change?"

"The guard will take you to the men's room. And, Monsieur? I am ordered to apologize."

Stuyvesant looked at Fortier's outstretched hand. "What, for smacking me around? If I'd been in your place, I'd have done a lot worse."

"Nonetheless."

After a moment, the American shifted the bundle of clothing to his left arm and shook Fortier's hand. "Can I ask you a question?" Fortier didn't walk out, so Stuyvesant continued. "Saturday morning, I suggested that you take a look at unsolved murders. Did you have a—"

"I have been busy, Monsieur."

"I know. Well, it was just a thought. Tell your boss I hope he's feeling better."

"What will you do now, Monsieur?"

"I'm going to have a shave."

"And then?"

Stuyvesant fixed him with a bleak gaze. "I'm going out to look for my friends."

"Monsieur," the Sergeant said, "do not give me cause to arrest you again."

SEVENTY-TWO

NANCY BERGER WAS an early riser, by habit. Most mornings, she would spend an hour with coffee and a book before the day began.

Last night she'd finished the Agatha Christie (and dreamed about alarm clocks), so this morning, with her new coffeepot gurgling on the unfamiliar stove, she dug through the unpacked boxes in search of Stuyvesant's gift. Just because he was proving to be a louse didn't mean she should shun a writer recommended by Sylvia Beach.

She settled onto the settee, tugged at the ends of the endearingly amateurish ribbon, and lifted the book.

Something fell into her lap. A small booklet with a dark red cover, immediately recognizable. Nancy turned it over and saw the oval window in the front cover with the number: a US passport, but not hers.

She opened it, expecting Harris's name—or perhaps one of the poets who hung around Sylvia's shop. Dashiell Hammett's, even.

But the name caused her bemused smile to lock, then fade.

Philippa Anne Crosby.

Why would Harris give her Phil's passport? And do so by sticking it in a book?

More than that—where had he found it?

Her hand gave an involuntary jerk, sending Phil's passport flying.

What the *hell* kind of game was the man playing?

Stuyvesant stood beneath the streetlamps on the Pont Neuf, swaying with tiredness. He heard a voice: from a taxi, there at his toes. Gratefully, he fell inside, but before he could say "rue Colle," the driver rattled off a name: Les Halles. An American in battered evening wear could only be headed one place at five in the morning, right?

Bed? Or food?

"Yeah, sure," he said.

Minutes later, the smell of onion soup tugged him forward. The market was a reassuring bedlam of horse-drawn carts and blaring truck horns, and Stuyvesant lined up with the last of the night's drunks, the first of the day's market loaders, and the tiredest of the prostitutes for that most traditional of restoratives.

Afterwards, he set out through the maze of streets where only cats were awake, heading for the dingy little hotel that was his Paris home.

A conversation:

"Personnes Disparues."

"Oh good, there's someone there."

"Yes, Madame?"

"My name is Nancy Berger. Philippa Crosby's roommate? One of you left your card, the other day."

"That was I, Mademoiselle. How may I help you?"

"Well, it's about Phil—Miss Crosby."

"Yes?"

"Yes. I just opened a package and found her passport in it."

"Pardon?"

"I know—strange, right? It was in with a book that a . . . friend sent me, and I sort of wondered if it had got stuck in by accident. Or something."

"That is indeed remarkable. And the name of this friend?"

"Well . . . You see, he does have a reason to be looking for her. I mean, he was hired by her mother, after Phil disappeared, so he might well have found it somewhere, and then . . . It's just, I don't want to get him into—"

"Are we talking about M. Stuyvesant, Mademoiselle?"

"You know him?"

"That I do."

"Good, then you know what a good and responsible person he is. I just thought, well, it was odd."

"Indeed, Mademoiselle. I will send someone over immediately to take possession of the package. And I shall have a word with M. Stuyvesant. Please do not contact him yourself."

Nancy gave the man her new address and set the receiver onto its hook. She looked at the card Harris had left, with a phone number for the Hotel Benoit.

Do not contact him yourself could only mean one thing.

Should she warn him?

The florist's light was the only sign of life on rue Colle. Mme. Benoit's door was shut tight. A dozen snores followed Stuyvesant up the stairs.

He had to work at getting the key to turn. Inside, he left the lamp off: light from the hall told him that the place had been ransacked. He didn't need to see it.

He dropped his hat and overcoat on the table. His jacket followed and—with groans—the empty shoulder holster. He scratched his ribs and overgrown chin, then plodded down the hallway to the toilet. The minuterie had switched itself off when he came out; he didn't bother turning it back on.

Without sleep, he'd be useless. And anyway, Sarah's friends would slam the door on someone who looked as bad as he did. How many hours could he afford? He clicked on the desk light to scribble a note for the door:

Me réveiller à 11:00, SVP.

Five and a half hours of blissful oblivion before Mme. Benoit woke him.

He opened the door and tacked the note down. Stepping back inside, a slow, delicious wave of tiredness washed him. The bed whispered rumors of simple pleasures: crisp sheets to rub away the jail; a fluffed pillow to cradle his aching head; a blanket to bake away the stiffness in shoulders, arms, back . . .

He switched off the desk lamp: *click.*

And heard: *click.*

The echo stuck his shoes to the floor. Slowly, his spine straightened. He studied the light around the door, and waited for his brain to interpret.

The minuterie.

He turned the knob and put his head outside, expecting the careless feet and half-stifled giggles of drunken homecoming, but there was nothing, only Anouk's perpetual snore. He waited, shoulders leaning into the frame. His eyelids drooped. Must have been someone on the first floor, someone unusually thoughtful about noise . . . His head was pulling back when it came: the tell-tale creak of old wood. Once, twice—more than one man, surreptitiously climbing the stairs.

His body didn't wait for his brain to give the orders: step back, close the door, jam the chair under the knob; coat and hat, passport and wallet; ease up the window, throw out exhausted legs. The last time he'd tried this it had been broad daylight and the roof-tiles had been dry. He hadn't been stiff with a beating.

But he made it, across the rooftops to an external stairway. In two minutes he was on the boulevard Raspail with his hat brim pulled down.

———

The taxi pulled away from Sarah's address, leaving Stuyvesant half-stunned by the fresh dawn air. He forced leaden feet up the steps and gave a brief jab to the bell as he walked down to the third flower pot. The key was still there. Returning to the door, he tipped back his hat to see—

The door came open.

His hat flew off as he jerked upright. With a sharp cry, he stepped forward to fling his arms around an astounded Sarah Grey.

SEVENTY-THREE

A CONVERSATION:
"Sarah? Is that you?"
Yes, Bennett.
"I can't see you very well."
The candle's burning down, my dear.
"I'm going to be in the dark soon."
But not yet. And I'm here now.
"You should be with Doucet."

. . .

"Why aren't you? Is he dead?"
You said he wouldn't.
"I thought he had a chance. Can't you come closer?"
I will, soon.
"Can't you sit in the chair?"
That's not for me.
"Are you dead, sweetheart? Sarah? Has he killed you?"
I . . . do you think he did?
"No! I don't. I think if he'd killed you, I'd know. He'd have given it away, there in the alleyway. I think when I asked, he'd have gone tense, and he didn't."
Then I'm not dead.
"Oh, God, I hope not. Sarah, can't you come and talk over here?"

I'm dancing, Bennett. I love to dance, you know I do.

"So does Harris."

Yes.

"Does your policeman love to dance?"

Not like Harris.

"He's a good man."

Very.

"I meant Harris."

I know.

"He didn't mean to kill you."

He didn't kill me.

"Of course not. I meant, he didn't know . . . he tried, that morning. I stopped him, from going to help you."

Yes, I know.

"Do you forgive me?"

Dear heart, there is nothing to forgive.

"Stop dancing, please, Sarah. Those skeletons, they shouldn't be able to dance like that."

Bennett Grey took his eyes from the dancing, and saw the flame move.

SEVENTY-FOUR

"HARRIS! WHAT ON earth—?" Sarah pushed herself away from Stuyvesant's chest.

"Where the *hell* have you been?" he shouted.

"Visiting friends. Harris, what's happened to your face?"

"Jesus. We all thought— Oh my God, what a relief!"

"Come in—bring the paper. And your hat."

He picked up the newspaper from the mat and his fedora from a bush. Only when he turned again did he notice that she was wearing a dressing-gown and her boyish hair-cut was all on end. She looked so gorgeous he wanted to sink into her arms and stay there for a week.

Instead, he stepped inside. Followed her to the kitchen. Placed his coat over the newspaper. And watched, as Sarah walked and filled the kettle and lit the hob, talking the whole time. "What on earth are you doing out so early? Here, let me move those things. Do you know where Bennett is? He's been here, there's dishes in the sink and his valise in the guest-room, but . . ." She froze, then jerked around. "Harris, has something happened to Bennett? Is that why you're here?"

Bennett. Doucet.

He couldn't.

If he told her, she would fling herself out the door. And he desperately needed information—information only she could give.

He stuck a smile on his face. "Bennett? No, he's fine. Not sure where he is, though. Why didn't you phone me? I left you a note."

"I did phone you, about five minutes ago. I think I woke up your concierge. Harris, you really look terrible. Were you in a fight?"

He glanced at the wreck of his evening clothes. "That's where it started."

"Are the police after you?"

"Sort of."

"Well, sit down. You look like you could use some coffee."

She reached for the coffeepot, giving Stuyvesant his first glimpse of the stub on her left arm. He looked away. "Where were you?"

"Oh, I was *so* angry with the two of you at the party, squabbling over me like adolescent boys! Cole Porter told me that he and Linda were going to a friend's place in the country for a few days, and I said it sounded like a dream. He invited me along." She reached for cups, sugar. "And I thought, *He's right, Dominic's given me a few days off, why not go away?* I was going to come home to pick up some things, but they were leaving immediately the party was finished, and Cole swore there was no need, there'd be everything a last-minute guest could possibly require, from tooth-brush to rubber boots. I never do *anything* like that, so . . . I did."

"Thank God. You just disappeared."

Her green eyes blazed across the room at him. "Émile *did* watch, didn't he? I *knew* he would—so I went out through a little gate in the neighbor's garden. Oh, he treats me like a child!"

"We were worried. Both of us were."

"Good," she said tartly. "I hoped all this silliness would be over when I got back. If you and Émile are still at each other's throats, I shall be truly cross."

The clash between Sarah's half-flirtatious concerns and the grim realities of the past seventy-two hours felt like being drawn through the gears of a steam locomotive. Stuyvesant dry-washed his face, hearing three days of bristles: *Think! Ignore how furious she'll be, and think!*

"Harris, what is it? You weren't *really* worried?"

"Of course not. Did you have a good time? You look like you had some sun."

"It was glorious. There's a tennis court and a swimming pool and Cole played music half the day—he wrote a song for a stage revue in New York this November. And you'll think me shallow for having such a lighthearted holiday."

"Sweetheart, you deserve every minute of pleasure life can give you."

She went pink. "What about you? What have you been up to, other than fisticuffs?"

"Looking for Pip Crosby." *Looking for you.*

Her hand, in the act of setting out spoons, drifted to a halt. "How terrible. I'd forgotten. It seems a long time ago."

"You've been busy."

"Are you any nearer to finding her?"

"I think so."

"That sounds like, 'I'm afraid so.' Oh, Harris. I am sorry."

"Can I ask you a few questions?"

"I never met her, I told you."

"Sure, but you know a lot of people in Montparnasse. Finish making the coffee, your water's boiling."

She made the coffee and opened a cupboard. "Ah, the last of the biscuits. I wish Bennett had let me know he was coming, I'd have asked him to bring some. I know—he's gone somewhere with Émile! Émile was here, he found his birthday present. I had a picture done by Man Ray," she explained with a gesture at the wrapping paper. "For some reason he took the picture and not the frame. I guess for his wallet."

"What did you think of Ray?"

"Brilliant photographer, provocative film-maker. Not much of a painter, to my mind, although that's what he considers himself."

"He's popular with the ladies." *Lee Miller; Pip Crosby.*

"Some of them. It's those dark eyes. Makes him seem so intense."

"Isn't he?"

"Pablo Picasso is intense. Man Ray . . . looks intense. Don't tell him I said that—he has a short fuse. I saw him in a rage one time after some casual tourist sat down on the Dôme terrace and beat him at chess."

"Like Hemingway and his boxing."

"Of course, everyone had been drinking."

"That goes without saying. So, he's big on chess? I saw a really modernistic set in his studio, all circles and triangles."

"He and Marcel Duchamp play a lot."

"Funny he doesn't use more chess in his art—Man Ray, I mean. There was a film I saw the other day, started out with, um . . ."

"With what?"

"Dice. Played by a, er, wooden model hand."

She pointedly overlooked his embarrassment. "Yes, Man Ray has a bit of a 'thing' for hands. That's what he and Le Comte were talking about at Bricktop's the other night, a film project based on hands. He wanted an opening scene of . . . well, my hands playing chess. Ray had heard of that Terror game I told you about, the one in Le Comte's garden, and he wanted to re-enact it. Complete with decapitations and shots of Didi's hand collection."

"You didn't agree to it?"

"'Course not. However, there are plenty of amputees in Paris."

"And Le Comte liked the idea?"

"He loved it. Think how many people a Grand-Guignol film could reach, compared to that tiny theater."

"I'm trying to picture Le Comte and Man Ray working together."

"Wild, right? But you know, they do have a similar style. Meticulous preparation mixed with a dose of chaos. The Grand-Guignol's as tightly choreographed as a ballet, but Le Comte's favorite productions are when something goes wrong and the actors are forced to improvise. Like when he deliberately removed a key prop and no one noticed until halfway through."

"Hard on the actors."

"Or that party in the ballroom. I spent *weeks* planning every detail—the music, the food, the script for La Lune's interruption, all of it having to turn around his timing demands—but when it came to the guests, he wouldn't let me send RSVPs! I had absolutely no idea who was going to show up until they walked in."

"And six days later, he does it to you again. No wonder you took some time off."

"Life as theater, complete with disasters. He cherishes surprises, calls them 'the gift of the machine.' The curse of the machine, is more like it."

"What were his 'timing demands'?"

"For the party? He's a devoté of astrology, you know."

"Is he?"

"Sure—you've seen that clock. He adores making things coincide—like a danse that culminates at the moment the moon goes full. That's his 'machine.' The other side is the 'gift'—the random and uncontrolled element. So you have a precision timing of the clock linked to an arbitrary act of kissing whomever you happen to be standing beside."

"Or not so arbitrary, for those in the know."

This blush was not as heavy. "Yes, it's convenient to have a man like Cole around."

"So why isn't . . ."

Sarah didn't notice how Stuyvesant's voice trailed off, merely chattered about the modern marriage of Cole and Linda Porter, its freedoms and affections.

But to Stuyvesant, it was a distant buzz of words, farther away than the ticking of the great Charmentier clock.

Precise timing.

The four-faced clock at the center of the mansion. A drowned clockmaker. Dark and light; sun and moon; black-and-white tiles and a human chessboard in the garden. The stones and bones of Paris. A clock that struck the full moon.

No. That was—

A conversation: *a full moon event . . . underground . . . and with the equinox only five days later . . .*

Oh, sweet Jesus above: dark, and light, and the gifts of a machine.

"Harris!"

"Sorry?"

"I said, I'm going to get dressed. I decided to put Émile out of his misery by showing up for lunch."

He forced himself to stay in his chair until her feet hit the stairs. Then he leapt up to pat wildly through his pockets. If that damned Sergeant had done anything to his notes—

But no, here they were: the single sheet that began with the third day of 1928 and ended last Wednesday with Gabriella Faulon (f/brown/31). March, 1928—and, yes, March, 1929. June, 1928, and June, 1929.

September, 1928 . . . *oh sweet Jesus.*

Two coincidences aren't proof. They're little more than suspicion. But there was a piece of evidence that could prove it. Water began to run upstairs. He picked up the phone.

Fortier was in his office. He seemed to live there.

"Sorry I missed your men at the hotel this morning," he told the *flic.*

A moment passed. "M. Stuyvesant. Where are you?"

"Doesn't matter, since I won't be here long. I need a piece of information."

"We would like to clear up a couple of points regarding—"

"Sergeant Fortier, I'd like to propose a deal: I turn myself in tomorrow, if you give me one piece of information now."

"Turn yourself in for what, Monsieur?"

"Don't be cute. Do we agree? Or do I hang up and let you spend the next few weeks turning the city upside-down?"

Stuyvesant counted to six before the response came: "What piece of information would that be, Monsieur?"

"You were working on the missing persons list from 1927. I don't know how much you've done since Saturday, but I need to know if there's a man reported missing in September of that year?"

He reached eleven before Fortier admitted defeat. "You swear you will present yourself at the Préfecture no later than tomorrow noon?"

"I swear to you on—" He couldn't very well swear on his affection for l'Inspecteur's fiancée. "—on my American passport."

"Yes. Albert Gamache went missing on September the twentieth, 1927."

"Do you have his details?"

"Monsieur, I—"

"Was he blond?"

Stuyvesant listened to one word before hanging up on Fortier's squawking voice. He snatched Sarah's newspaper out from under his coat.

He ignored the screaming headlines, the French equivalent of which had hounded him across Montparnasse—POLICE DETECTIVE SHOT—and hunted for the page with odds and ends like the hour of sunrise and the stars in the sky.

He found it. The time jumped out at him: 12:52.

If he was wrong, Harris Stuyvesant was going to win the prize for idiocy. If he was wrong, he'd have to choose between turning himself in and running for the border . . .

But he did not think he was wrong.

Dark and light; men and women; summer and winter. All the machinery of the sun's progress.

He looked at his wrist-watch, and yelped with alarm. Hat on head, coat over his arm, he stopped.

He had to tell her.

Stuyvesant bounded up the stairs to the bathroom door, knocking lightly. Sarah's voice called a question.

"I have to go," he told her. "Will you be long?"

"Two minutes."

He eyed the doorknob. "Hurry," he whispered.

SEVENTY-FIVE

COUNT DOMINIC PIERRE-MARIE Arnaud Christophe de Charmentier entered the tapestried prison as he entered any room: calm, straight, and with the melancholy air that followed him like yesterday's perfume. He slid the bolt on the door, and picked up the wooden chair, carrying it across the floor to sit just out of his prisoner's reach.

"Good morning, Monsieur," he said.

"Do you have my sister?"

Le Comte looked surprised. "Your sister? Why would I want your sister?"

After a minute, the green eyes relaxed. "What about Doucet?"

"It appears the Inspector is still alive. Something of a relief, I admit."

Grey frowned at the reply.

"Your choice of position interests me," Le Comte said. "Most of my gifts take pains to sit as far as possible from the source of their imprisonment."

Gifts? "Most?"

"All."

"And when you take your photographs," Grey said, "you will find that I do not mimic their stance, either."

"You have seen the photographs?"

"The police are after you, Comte. It won't be long."

The man was either unconvinced, or unconcerned. "Your sister tells me— Ah, Monsieur, don't glare so, she is quite safe from me, certainly until the spring. Your sister tells me that you had a difficult time of it in the War."

"I doubt she told you anything more."

"No, she was most reticent. Perhaps you would like to tell me yourself?"

"Why would I?"

"Because the machinery is connected."

The clock *tick*ed, the candle whispered. *Machinery*, Grey thought. *Gifts*.

"Very well," Le Comte said. "Because if you do, I will refill your water."

"I'll have the drink first."

"You don't trust me?"

"Whose hand controls the key?"

The clock hands spoke: *tick, tick*.

Charmentier walked back over to the door to fetch the enamel jug that had sat at the foot of the chair for the past two and a half days. Grey had wondered about the jug—another element of hope? A cruel game? He discovered now that yes, it held water.

He gulped half the cup straight off, nursing the remainder against his chest. "What do you mean, 'The machinery is connected'?"

"You first."

Grey took another swallow, feeling the liquid push into his veins. "I was blown up in the spring of 1918. A shell landed in the mud under my feet, and went off. I died."

Le Comte considered that last word. "You were revived."

"I was reborn."

"Interesting distinction. What happened next?"

"The hospital; rehabilitation. I was too . . . damaged to go back to my men. Afterwards I went to Cornwall and became a farmer."

"You hid."

"What about you? You weren't too old for service."

"M. Grey, I have paid my country's blood tax in so many ways."

He wants to talk. Bennett could hear that, in the heaviness of the man's voice. *Talk, then. Tell me how to stop you.* "Was it the War?"

"It was the machine. One son died of a sniper's bullet on the winter solstice of 1917. My daughter died of the influenza, on March 21. After her funeral, my wife and our younger son stayed with her parents up in Saint-Gervais. They went to Good Friday services there."

"Should that mean something?"

"German's Paris gun?" Grey shook his head. "The Germans had a gun that could reach 120 kilometers. In the last spring's push, they threw shells at Paris. One of them hit the church of St. Gervais et St. Protais. One shell. Eighty-eight people died. Eighty-seven people, and my younger son."

Tick. Tick.

"And your wife?"

"My beloved wife. She had the most beautiful hair: dark brown, with threads of copper in the sun. It was her death that proved the machine, although it took me years to realize it. After the children died, despite being under close watch, my darling got her hands on a knife. And on the longest day of the year, she slit her lovely wrists."

"I am sorry for your loss. But how is that the machine?"

Le Comte gave his prisoner a quizzical look. "Do you know, you're the first one who has asked about any of this?"

"The first of how many?"

"Sixteen, Monsieur. You will make sixteen."

SEVENTY-SIX

S ARAH TROTTED DOWN the stairs. Her affectionate smile just broke Stuyvesant's heart. *Fresh, shiny—and about to be damaged, yet again.*

The smile began to fade when she saw him standing, hat in hands. "What's up?"

"Sarah, I have some bad news. Your friend Doucet was hurt—he'll be fine, but he's in the hospital. La Charité. You need to go see him."

A young eternity later, her starved lungs drew a gasping breath. "*Émile?*"

"He's going to be all right. He took a bullet in his left shoulder, and another grazed his head. Sarah, you hear me? Émile is going to be fine."

"And Bennett?"

"I . . . we can't be . . ."

She continued shakily down the stairs until she was before him, so close his neck bent and his arms yearned for her. "Harris. Was my brother with Émile?"

"They were together when they left here."

"I heard your voice—the phone, right? If this just happened, how can they be—"

"It happened Friday night. I . . . I've known since Saturday."

Her face crumpled. "And you just *sat* here? You sat and let me rattle on about Cole Porter and *tennis courts?*"

"Sarah, I'm so sorry. I needed to—"

He saw the blow coming, and made no move to avoid it. Her slap was full-handed, with all the power in her small body, and in his current state, it blinded him. When he'd blinked the tears from his eyes, he found her pulling on her hat.

"I'll find him," he promised.

Her eyes were bleak. "You'd better."

And she was gone.

Dear God, couldn't he just curl up on the floor and die for a while? He was so tired he was stupid. Look at the idea his feverish brain had come up with. Nuts, right? Impossible.

So, what if he was wrong?

If he was wrong with this cockamamie theory, Bennett Grey would walk in and present Harris Stuyvesant with a choice between giving himself to Fortier or heading for Germany.

And if he was right?

Then he had less than four hours to prevent Bennett's murder.

SEVENTY-SEVEN

"SIXTEEN DEAD MEN and women," Bennett Grey remarked, "and I'm the first who has talked with you? Perhaps you'd like to tell me about the machine."

"The universe is a mechanism, Monsieur. It requires maintenance, like any other."

"How?"

Le Comte hesitated. "If I tell you, you will think me mad."

"Sir, I already think you mad."

The older man's sad little sigh might have touched Bennett Grey, under other circumstances. "You may be right. Very well. Do you recall the dates of the tragedies in my life?"

"December, March, Good Friday, and June," Grey replied.

"Followed by my father's death in September. But as I say, it took me a shamefully long time to realize the pattern. For one thing . . . oh, but Monsieur, we lack the time, to tell the complete story. Had I known of your interest . . . Suffice to say that when I did see the pattern, and when I accepted my responsibilities as a member of the blood aristocracy of France, the machinery began to turn smoothly at last."

There was no arguing with the insane: Grey knew that. Still: "Monsieur Le Comte, soldiers have rituals; children avoid pavement cracks. My neighbor in Cornwall became a Spiritualist after losing her only son."

"You believe it is mad to find order in the universe?"

"I believe it is human to find order in the universe. But the reverse—to imagine that one's act might impose order—is . . . delusion."

"We are as gods, Monsieur. Those of us with the power to act have no choice."

No choice. The phrase rang through Bennett Grey's body like a blow to a tuning fork. Here lay Charmentier's truth, a truth that had waited too long to be heard: Le Comte prayed that he was wrong. His voice swam with regret and self-loathing—but until someone stopped him, he was driven to continue.

"Do I take your silence as skepticism, Monsieur?"

"You may take my silence as the manners imposed by chains."

"Monsieur, I take no pleasure in this."

"And the clocks?" Grey asked. "The one in your house, the one here."

Charmentier glanced up at the clock face. "Oh, but they are one and the same. The hands here are tied to the central mechanism that Olivier Lambert built for me."

"The clock sounds important."

"The clock is everything. Monsieur, my clock stands at the center of the house. It divides the room into four faces, reflecting all aspects of time's motion. Its faces alternate light and dark, its figures alternate male and female. As I, the owner, am required to do. Hence, the given lives that keep the machinery in motion, alternating and encircling the year."

The chill of revelation passed along Bennett Grey's spine.

Oh, you poor, mad, soul. If he hadn't been so desiccated, Bennett Grey might have wept.

SEVENTY-EIGHT

STUYVESANT WASTED SIX minutes in a frenzied search for something—anything—that might be useful. Not that he expected a gun, but couldn't the damned woman have a decent flashlight?

In the end, he shoved a stale roll into his pocket and added a third sentence to his note:

Sarah, I've gone to Le Comte's house to look for Bennett.

Stuyvesant shoved the key under the pot and threw himself in front of the nearest taxi, demanding that it take him to Montparnasse.

11:04.

SEVENTY-NINE

"Do you know what proved it, finally?" Le Comte asked his prisoner. "My clock?"

"Tell me."

"The machine itself."

"Olivier Lambert finished work in early December. We chose the night of the solstice as an appropriate time to start it up. I planned a dinner party. After the midnight ring, my guests left. I thought he would stay with me for the solstice ring—at 2:45—but to my surprise, he wished to go home, saying he had an early train to catch. I agreed to drive him.

"On the way we argued, over the . . . sanctity of the clock. He revealed that he had been offered a job, which might involve duplicating parts of its design. I forbade him. He swore he had the right to do what he wished.

"As we came to a bridge—the Pont Royal—he demanded to be let out of the car, saying he would walk. We both got out, continuing to argue. The champagne speaking, no doubt. In any event, I reached the end of my patience, and gave him a shove.

"I intended no harm, but he went over the side of the bridge into the river. I waited for the cries, but it was freezing cold and the shock must have killed him outright.

"When I looked at my pocket-watch, I saw that it was precisely

2:45. And that was when I understood: a gift would be given, that the machine might be served."

Grey felt the lie grate across his nerves. *It was not precisely 2:45.* Charmentier knew it, but chose not to. However, that was his only lie. *The poor bastard believes this demented conglomeration,* Grey thought. *Believes it to his bones.*

"And did M. Lambert have brown hair?" he asked.

"You do see it!" Le Comte was pleased. "Artists have known it forever: spring is a woman, the year's end is a man. The year begins with the light, and ends in the dark. September is when the year turns—with the light of the first half, but the masculinity of winter.

"You are quite right, Monsieur: September's gift is a light-haired man."

The Comte de Charmentier let his gaze run tenderly over Bennett Grey's pale head.

EIGHTY

S TUYVESANT KNEW OF three ways in and out of the Charmentier mansion. The front gate was too exposed for a daytime breach. The exit through the neighbor's garden that Sarah used to evade her cop fiancée meant two front gardens to cross. The third, used by Le Comte alone, was somewhere near a little-used alleyway—an alleyway where free-living blondes and too-trusting police inspectors could be drawn. Two shootings inside of a week guaranteed that entrance would be under police eyes.

However, no rich man wants the butcher pulling up to his front doorstep. There was sure to be a delivery lane behind the mansion.

He found it—blocked by five people and a horse-drawn grocer's van, who didn't look as if they'd be shifting any time soon. So he headed back to the main road, hoping an unshaven bum in the remains of an evening suit didn't attract too much attention. The front gates were locked tight—a pair of gardeners weeded the flower beds—but when he reached the other end of the lane, the only person facing his direction was the horse.

Halfway down the narrow alley, near a set of sagging gates, a trio of barrels waited for collection. He stole down the left-hand walls and, cursing his battered muscles, clambered on top of a barrel.

On the other side of this section of wall there had once been a garden, now a jungle of unpruned trees doubling as the neighborhood dump. He strained, kicked, cursed, and finally heaved his bulk over the wall, dropping onto the mold-stained carpet beyond. The stink of cat piss enveloped him, and he stifled coughs and groans as he fought his way across the woven hillocks.

Once on solid ground, the next Everest loomed: the wall separating him from the Charmentier garden was even higher. Next to it grew an ancient apple tree, but in his current state, he honestly didn't think he could climb the thing. His other option was a shed that had leaned against the wall since the Terror. So he crawled—up the remains of a gardener's barrow, onto the shed's cracking tiles, across its swaying roof. He seized the stone wall like a life-preserver, bracing himself for a second agonizing drop.

It took a while to get upright.

It was another world, orderly and fragrant. It was also part of the formal gardens rather than a service yard: soft ground instead of naked cobblestones, and mature shrubbery to conceal an intruder. He pushed his way forward until the shrubs ended.

The sun was overhead; the checkerboard and its terrace stood open to the house. If some house-maid chose today to shine the ballroom chandeliers, he'd be back in jail by noon.

But confidence was everything in an illegal entry. He assumed a bored look and set out across the checkerboard. No one tackled him; no one shouted. At the terrace doors he grasped the handle—and nearly fell into the billiards room beyond when the doors proved unlocked.

A table like an ocean liner held a neat triangle of balls. The room smelled of fresh wax; his shoes squeaked faintly as he moved.

He yanked them off and forced them into his coat pockets.

Outside the billiards room, the grand stairway ascended to his right, an invitation to the black-and-white clock-room. The front door was off to the left. And he needed to be on the other side of the stairs.

His sock-clad feet padded silently over the marble, but just as he cleared the bottom of the stairway, a door opened somewhere and heels began to tap their way towards him. He dropped behind the statue of a much-draped woman, every muscle screaming in protest. As the heels *tap, tap, tap*ped past, he risked a glance: the blond demon-footman. The front door opened, and Stuyvesant shambled towards the far side of the stairway.

The door was locked.

Shit. Stuyvesant fished out the lock picks—at least Fortier hadn't confiscated those—and bent over the mechanism. The servant would return any instant. He could hear voices: the man was talking to someone. The gardener? Yes, he heard the words *feuilles* and *pelouse,* something about—

Stuyvesant closed his eyes. Took a breath. *You have all the time in the world. It's a simple mechanism. Your hands are fine.*

The butler's shoes were *tap, tap*ping back across the tiles when the lock gave. The door opened and shut without a sound, leaving one beat-up American in the dark, sweating against the ancient stone walls.

EIGHTY-ONE

"How can you claim your victims are 'gifts'?" Grey asked. "You choose them. You knew several of them. One was even your lover."

"Philippa? Dear, shy, blossoming little Philippa? She was as much chance as any of them. You must understand, Monsieur, I merely receive what the machine brings me. I begin looking five days before the time of sacrifice. Some are given immediately, others at the last minute. Most, like you, are given a day or two before they are needed."

"*Objets trouvés.*"

"*Objets donnés.* Gifts from the universe."

"So the morning you needed a blonde woman, you woke up next to Miss Crosby and put a gun to her head?"

"No no, I had sent her away before that. I happened across her—that is, she was given—as I walked along the river. And what a special gift! Although I fear her bones are too distinctive for public eyes. You know, Monsieur, the world thinks of Didi Moreau as a bone artist, but his art is derivative of mine. I shall give him one or two of her bones, but the essential parts of Philippa Crosby—her life's story told in calcium—will be mine alone.

"Oh, Monsieur. It is not given to many men to free a young woman, first of her inhibitions, then of her flesh."

EIGHTY-TWO

S TUYVESANT THUMBED THE Ronson to life.
    Up the circular stairs lay the clock, and a ballroom smelling of death. Le Comte's story of using grave-soil to disconcert his guests felt like so much hooey: if there was a smell, it was more likely because the ballroom was near a decomposing body. That meant a door.

A door, and a man with a gun against a man with a jackknife and a cigarette lighter.

The house was sure to have an arsenal somewhere, given the touchy history of Parisians towards their aristocracy. But he had less than an hour before . . . God only knew. Leaving the stairway risked a fatal delay.

As he stood on the landing, torn between up and down, the stair-well came alive with sound: a bell, from the magnificent clock in the black-and-white room. Noon.

In fifty-two minutes, some bits of gear would reach a mark and the equinox would ring out, with the death of a blond-haired man to feed an obsession.

He glared up the stairway. *If I had a wrench, I'd jam it into your damned guts.*

He started down.

EIGHTY-THREE

1 2:01.

"Tell me about the bones," Bennett Grey asked. "You give them to Didi Moreau, he puts them in his boxes, and you hang the boxes on your wall. How does that serve the machine?"

"The bones are mere beauty—the gift's inner beauty, as the photographs record the outer beauty. At first, I simply took photographs and abandoned the gifts to the fate of all flesh. But some eighteen months ago, I happened to see one after the rats had finished with it, and found it beautiful. Shortly after that, I met Didi Moreau—your sister's doing, that introduction—and he taught me a better way to clean bones.

"My first attempt was with Philippa, and what a reward I had! Her bones—they are magnificent. It's a pity I can't let Didi have her photographs—it would be too great a risk—but most of her bones are anonymous enough. I shall treasure her, in my commemoration of gifts. As I will treasure you."

Grey blinked. Was he supposed to thank the man?

"You, Monsieur, like Philippa, are unique. Will the bones of a man twice dead reflect his difference? Oh, Monsieur, I fear I shall never have another such as you."

"Then maybe you should stop while you're ahead."

"There is no 'ahead,' Monsieur, there is merely maintenance."

"What about the other body parts I'm told Moreau had? The eye-balls, the skin."

A look of distaste passed over the patrician features. "Yes, he showed me his collection. Ghoulish. I've ordered him to get rid of them—to get rid of everything, in fact."

Grey gave a cough of disbelief. "Skin is ghoulish but bones are not?"

"Bones are eternal, Monsieur. Bones are what we give back to the world, when we are finished with them. These very walls are made of bones: millions upon millions of dead creatures, drifting to the bottom of a prehistoric sea." His eyes wandered across the rough-hewn stone, the smooth shearing and the tool-marks of the *carrièrs*, ending up on the instrument on the wall above.

12:07.

He sighed, and placed his hands on his knees. "I am grateful for this conversation, Monsieur, but my camera takes some time to set—"

EIGHTY-FOUR

OWN, AND DOWN, Stuyvesant's exhausted legs followed an endless descent. Fifty steps down, the lighter guttered. It came back up immediately, but it was clear warning.

Grimly, he flipped the cover over it, and instantly went blind. *The steps are even,* he told himself. *Even enough. You didn't fall before.*

His toes might have been at the edge of a bottomless cliff, so far as his grip on the iron railing was concerned. He forced his fingers a couple of inches down; his sock-clad foot gingerly felt its way. *One step—good. Now another. The step will be there.*

Why the hell hadn't he counted them the first time? Sherlock bloody Holmes would have. Fantômas would skip down them, Auguste Dupin would have figured everything out sitting before his fire—and any of those guys would've brought along a light better than a nearly-dry Ronson. *You want heroes? You got Harris Stuyvesant, blundering his way through the dark. In more ways than one.*

If this was a dead end and he got back to Sarah's house to find Bennett sitting in the garden, he would absolutely kill the little bastard.

Down, down. And down.

———

A faint flattening-out of the iron railing warned him of the stairway's end. Flame revealed two heavy doors—minus their pretty, black-gowned attendants.

He put the Ronson back in his pocket and felt his way to the crack, picturing what lay beyond: a dark corridor of bones—he'd be seeing if there were light—with long walls of tightly arranged skulls and tibias, running for some distance off to the left, and to the right for a lesser distance before turning a corner. Across and slightly to the left was the single heavy door that opened onto the cavern with the Danse Macabré.

Laying both hands on the latch, he turned, praying it was not locked.

It was not. With infinite care, he nursed his toe against the wood. It gave: an inch, two. A muffled voice came. Three inches; four—then a noise, the small stone scraping under the wood. He stopped, then continued even more slowly. The stone *click*ed when the door let it go, but by then the gap was wide enough to step through.

The door opposite was shut, a line of yellow light defining its lower edge: the church candle—he could smell it. As he could hear the voices, a murmur of speech: two men.

All the way down the stairs, Stuyvesant had picked up and discarded ideas: lights on? Draw Le Comte out somehow, and use the knife. Lights off? Thank God for the Ronson. But if he did bring the mad Comte out of his cavern, what was to keep the man from putting a bullet into Bennett Grey first?

His only hope was surprise. If he dove in and knocked over the candle, he'd have a chance. The idea of bullets in a stone room made his body want to pull up into itself, but at least he'd have a chance.

Unless the door was bolted. He'd be in deep shit then.

And what if there was a second candle? If he could find a rock—*Harris, you idiot, you're standing in a quarry.* He reached for the Ronson, to collect a handful of small stones—

Then the shouting began.

EIGHTY-FIVE

"... MY CAMERA TAKES some time to set—"
Le Comte's words nearly obscured the faint noise from outside the door—would have, even for Bennett Grey, had he not been waiting since the candle flame had danced, nine interminable minutes before.

He sucked air deep into his lungs, rallying his energies down to the dregs, and he shouted. The blare of his voice smashed the stillness, bouncing off the stones and startling Le Comte nearly backwards off his chair.

"HARRIS, HE'S ARMED! RUN! SMASH HIS CLOCK! RUN, UP THE STAIRS, YOU'VE GOT TO SMASH THE BLOODY CLOCK TO PIECES!"

Le Comte was on his feet, staring first at Grey, then at the door. Drawing a revolver from his pocket, he reached for the bolt.

When the door came open, Grey yelled all the louder, urging Stuyvesant to run faster, to smash, to hurry—and although the aristocrat had the sense to check first, snaking out an arm to flip a switch that beamed brightness through the doorway, Grey's racket covered any sound of an invader's feet rushing up the long circular stairs. Charmentier withdrew his head from the doorway, looking from prisoner to clock.

Grey could read the agony of indecision on Le Comte's face, then the choice: if Grey was creating a ruse, the chains rendered it pointless. But if that busybody American *was* out there . . .

His manifestation of order in the universe was at risk.

Le Comte ran for the stairway; Grey's exhortations followed him, until his dry throat strangled into coughs and ragged breathing.

Long seconds later, the faint sound of approaching feet. Grey watched the bright rectangle, panting . . .

Harris Stuyvesant filled the doorway, the grin on his face testimony to the size of his relief.

EIGHTY-SIX

S TUYVESANT SLAMMED THE door and ran the bolt at the top, re-
trieving the chair to wedge under the handle as insurance.

"Jesus, when you started shouting, I thought he'd shoot you for sure.
I nearly came for the door—didn't know it was bolted. I just squeaked
around the corner before the lights went on. Why didn't he? Shoot you,
I mean. Not that—"

"Timing," Grey croaked. "The point of equinox. Not sure when that
is."

"Twelve fifty-two." Stuyvesant spotted the enamel jug and splashed
the last of its water into the cup before easing down on his knees, lock
picks in hand.

"Sarah?" Grey asked.

"She's fine. Went off to the country with Cole Porter, if you can
believe that. And not only did she not apologize, she got royally pissed
at me because I sort of questioned her for a while before telling her
about Doucet. Can you shift so your wrist is in the light? Thanks."

"Doucet?"

"He's in the hospital, awake and talking."

"Good. He told me they were—Le Comte did—but I wasn't sure."

The picks explored the guts of the padlock. "Sorry," Stuyvesant
mumbled. "This is a better lock than I'd expect."

"Someone managed to get free. The wall bolt is new, too."

"Joanna Williams," Stuyvesant said. "English. June, 1927. Aha!"

He stuck out his hand to Grey, and the two kneeling men exchanged that heartfelt expression of male camaraderie, the handshake.

Stuyvesant used the wall to get to his feet. "He'll be back any second. I don't suppose he said anything about another door?"

Grey stared at his rescuer's laden pockets. "Aren't you armed?"

"Not really. I could set his sleeve on fire." He wrestled his shoes from his pockets and put them on.

"You came here without a gun?" Grey's voice rose in astonishment. "Then locked yourself in without knowing if you could get out?"

"I'd have brought a weapon if I had one—but yeah, that's about the picture."

"Any backup?"

"Not really. Fortier and Doucet know where I was going. Or, they will. Maybe not for a day or two. And we might be able to keep Le Comte out, but I'm not really keen on a diet of rats grilled over an altar candle. Oh—here."

He dug back through his pockets, handing Grey a smashed and filthy bread roll.

"Can you stand?" he asked.

Grey drank the last of the water and stuck the roll in his shirt pocket, freeing his hands to be pulled upright. Stuyvesant draped the blanket around his shoulders. "What do you think? Is there another door?"

"Sure to be."

"We need to either get it open, or figure how to shut it against Le Comte."

"I'm ready," Grey said.

But first, Stuyvesant went back to work the short puddle of soft wax free of the stone with his knife. With the stub flickering in his left hand and his right arm around Grey, they began to circle the room, two unlikely figures stepped down from the Danse.

"Here." Grey came to a halt before a dozen tapestry skeletons walking into graves. Stuyvesant stuck the burning wax stub on a lip of stone, and ripped the priceless weaving from the wall.

Behind it was a rectangular wooden door, black with age, its lower edge a foot above the floor. Stuyvesant got out his picks. "How'd you know it was here?"

"The smell."

"What smell is that?"

But when the hatch came open a crack, he knew: no veteran of the trenches would mistake that stench.

Stuyvesant leaned against the door, shutting out the smell of death. 12:15.

"D'you think he's waiting for us?"

Grey nodded at the candle. "If we put that out, can you get it going again?"

"God, I hope so." With a pinch of Stuyvesant's fingers, the cavern went black.

"Don't move," Grey whispered. The rustle of his trousers; the faint creak of the door. Neither man breathed until Grey drew back.

"He's not there."

"Say a prayer." Stuyvesant flicked the Ronson.

Once. Twice. The third time, the small flame persisted long enough to light the wick. Stuyvesant ran a hand over his face, and half-lifted Grey through the door.

On the other side was more catacomb, crumbling bones thick with dust. Only the *Inspection des Carrières* plaques suggested it was known to the daylight world. A narrow tunnel went for perhaps forty feet, then widened into another, smaller cavern.

This space was dominated by a new, stoutly built wooden box the size of a giant's coffin. The stench was almost overwhelming, with a mingling odor of sewage that seemed almost healthy in comparison. Even so, the smell of putrefaction was not fresh.

"I'd expect it to smell worse," Stuyvesant murmured.

"It must vent into the sewers," Grey replied. "It's how he hides the smell."

"Is that crate what I think it is?"

"Don't open it!"

Stuyvesant didn't have to. It could only be one thing: big brother to the corruption boxes of Didi Moreau. "What do you reckon we'd see in there?"

"At this point, not much but bones and beetles."

"She's been in there for three months. The bastard has it down to a science."

"It wouldn't be your Miss Crosby, would it?"

"Nicole Karon. A twenty-four-year-old brown-haired shop girl who vanished in June."

Stuyvesant moved, spilling candle-light across a stack of bones, neatly tucked in beside the corruption box.

The disjointed skeleton was fresh, soft-looking. Obscenely clean, although a few of the bones were still connected, their ligaments too tough for tiny jaws. The sternum and two ribs were smashed, probably from the bullet that had killed her. Most of the other bones were intact.

Next to the delicate skull lay the bones of a forearm. Its ulna showed the scar of a childhood break, where a ten-year-old had leapt from a fire.

"Oh, Pip," Stuyvesant moaned. "Oh, honey. God damn it all to hell."

Grey rested a hand on the other man's shoulder. *That would have been me.*

EIGHTY-SEVEN

A T 12:21, A FAINT noise echoed down the subterranean labyrinth; Stuyvesant blew out the light. They waited, but the noise did not repeat. The valiant Ronson produced a flicker on its sixth snap, and they went on.

He tried not to think of just how much catacomb there was down here. Three hundred kilometers, right? "Do you have any idea where we're going?" he asked Grey.

"I'm following the fresh air."

12:28, and the fresh air lay before them: on the other side of a massive, permanent iron grate. Reluctantly, they turned—and the candle blew out. This time, the Ronson would not light it. One of the greatest cities in the world over their heads, and they might have been in a skiff in mid-Atlantic.

Grey groped around for Stuyvesant's hand. He set it on his shoulder, and led the way into darkness.

Hours seemed to pass, a lifetime of staggering blindness before Stuyvesant's weary brain told him that the darkness had a shape: Grey's head. With a cry, he let his arm drop.

"Yes," Grey replied. "Should be just up here."

Another heavy grate. But this one had hinges, and a well-oiled padlock.

They stumbled into daylight, raising filthy faces to the sweet city air.

The cloudless sky was an azure bowl, the sound of children's voices like a caress from God. Taking two steps to the side, Stuyvesant recognized the Lion of Belfort.

"The Place Denfert-Rochereau!"

An accordion played nearby; Stuyvesant felt like grabbing his companion and dancing, but he merely grabbed Grey's hand and pumped it. "Thank God. Thank *you*. Christ, what time is . . ."

Both men goggled at Stuyvesant's watch: 12:45. He put it to his ear: was astonished to hear a steady *tickticktickick*.

"Jesus! I'd have sworn we were *hours* down there!"

Grey raised his eyes. "Harris, does Charmentier have a servant with light hair?"

The blond demon with the trident. "A footman. But, you don't think . . ."

"I do."

They stared at each other, then as one, turned and shuffled into a run. Two Bedlam escapees, hatless and unshaven, one with neither coat nor shoes. They plunged across the boulevard to the blare of taxis and the shouts of drivers, pounding towards the side road—just as one of the gardeners burst out of the Charmentier gates.

Leaving them wide open.

Stuyvesant, panting, looked at his wrist: 12:47. "He's going for the police. You're *sure* the timing matters?"

"Yes."

"And he really loves that clock?"

"It's his life."

"Okay, then."

Grey caught Stuyvesant's arm. "One other thing. He felt guilt over Doucet. Not about the others, but over Doucet, there was regret. Something we might be able to use."

They ran, with the nightmare sensation of too-slow muscles and syrupy air. Through the gates, across the forecourt, and in the open and unattended front door.

Straight into a tableau: servants, maids, footmen, and gardeners, gazing in horror up the great stairway.

The butler had reacted to threat, but only to a point: he'd fetched a shotgun, then remained at the foot of the stairs, frozen by the impossibility of turning a firearm on Le Comte de Charmentier.

Stuyvesant had never been so glad to see a fancy duck-gun in his entire life. He snatched it from the man's hand as he ran by, breaking it open on his way up the stairs to check: two shells.

The gorgeous stairs were a cliff-face, with two spent bodies pulling their weight up by the marble banisters. A young eternity later, they reached the upper floor. Stuyvesant hauled the small man to one side. "Stay here," he ordered.

He edged his head around the entranceway. Le Comte stood facing the magnificent clock. 12:50. He held a revolver, its barrel pressed into the blond scalp of the terrified young man kneeling at his feet.

Stuyvesant raised the shotgun and stepped onto the black-and-white tiles. "Mister, if you don't want me to put both barrels through that pretty timepiece of yours, I suggest you let that man go."

Le Comte gave a quick glance over his shoulder. "M. Stuyvesant, what a surprise. Is your English friend with you?"

"Him, and a shotgun."

"I will be with you in just a minute."

To Stuyvesant's dismay, Grey spoke, inches from his elbow. "You really should listen to him, Count."

"Get back," Stuyvesant ordered, but Grey ignored him.

"Monsieur Le Comte, we provide a wealth of choices here. Your man, Stuyvesant, me: three men with light hair. Which of us is to be the machine's gift?"

"Why not all?" Le Comte replied.

"Because you regret having shot Inspector Doucet."

Charmentier was silent.

"Jesus," Stuyvesant swore. "You kill Pip Crosby, and then you feel guilty over a *cop*?" If it weren't for the butler, he'd have pulled both triggers then and there. "Pip Crosby, Joanna Williams, Nicole Karon. Albert Gamache."

"Fifteen of them," Grey murmured.

"'Those were gifts, Monsieur Stuy—"

"And Lulu? Don't tell me Lulu was a goddamn 'gift'?"

The clock ticked a minute into the silence: 12:51. When Charmentier spoke, his voice was low. "Her, I regret. No, she was not a gift, although it was necessary to—"

Grey interrupted. "A woman. A police inspector. The pleasure you take in killing."

"I do *not*—"

"You do. Monsieur Le Comte, you cannot lie to me. You take pleasure in the killing. And because of that pleasure, you are here, open and in the light. This means that your 'gifts' are at an end. You know that. So, Monsieur, with three gifts at hand, which do you choose? Who shall be the very final sacrifice for your machine?"

For a long time, the only sound was the breathing of four men.

Then came the last *tick* of the great clock. 12:52. Somewhere in the depths of the machine, Olivier Lambert's exquisite gears began to turn.

Charmentier raised his head to look at Bennett Grey. As he gazed across the tiles, suddenly the years on his face and shoulders fell away, his burden of melancholy lifted.

Le Comte smiled. It was an expression his wife might have known, or his beloved son: tender and gracious and at peace.

An instant later, the black-and-white room was ripped by noise and smoke, its high mirrors lit up with the brilliance of blood. As the echoes of shot and falling trailed away, another sound came. The figure of Death atop the great clock grated, turned, and gave a single strike: the bell of equinox.

The final sacrifice lay at the foot of the great Lambert clock. Light from the dome windows shone bright on pale hair, a spread of blood, and the revolver, fallen from the dead hand of Le Comte Dominic de Charmentier.

EIGHTY-EIGHT

THE FOLLOWING AFTERNOON, Harris Stuyvesant went to the hospital. He found Doucet swathed in bandages but shaved and sitting up amidst a florist's shop of bouquets.

Sarah Grey was holding his hand.

"You look like you're going to live," Stuyvesant said.

"Do not be so disappointed, mon vieux," Doucet replied.

"Is my brother with you?" Sarah asked.

"I left him in your garden with the blacksmith, talking about Saint Augustine."

"Did I say thank you, Harris?"

"Only about twenty times."

"Well, make it twenty-one."

Stuyvesant crossed the room, hand outstretched. Doucet grasped it, then his eyes went sideways. "Sarah, go and get some fresh air."

She reached over to the nearest floral arrangement, plucking out a small white rose, then hopped off the bed to tuck the bloom into Stuyvesant's lapel. She rose on tip-toe to give his cheek a kiss—and to whisper, "If you send his blood pressure up, Harris Stuyvesant, I will hurt you."

She patted his lapel and walked out.

"I was sorry to hear about your Pip," Doucet said.

Stuyvesant pulled up a chair: his legs still felt like overcooked macaroni. "Her mother and uncle are coming over to claim her bones. The cable said they were grateful." Whether he took the uncle's money or bashed the man in the face would depend on what he saw there. *Just how "close" were you to your niece?*

Doucet continued. "I understand that you and Fortier worked out the details of what Le Comte was doing."

"Yeah, although your Sergeant seemed annoyed that he couldn't arrest anyone. Especially me. He'd already interviewed Bennett when I saw him, so he knew what Charmentier had said about 'the machine.' A hell of a reason to kill, fitting the victims to the time of the year. And it sounds like the man honestly felt he was doing it for the good of France."

"The War drove so many mad."

"I will say, Le Comte seemed almost relieved, at the end. Bennett says that's because he was ashamed, of Lulu and of you. I don't know. I'd say the bastard got a charge out of it."

"I suspect the urge was in his bones long before the War twisted him. There are generations of rumors about the Charmentier family."

Stuyvesant shook his head, but the privilege of money and status wasn't limited to France. "In any case, hiring Lulu to sneak Pip's passport into my hotel room and then getting rid of her was no 'gift,' any more than shooting you in order to take Grey was. Those two things were eating at him."

"Who can comprehend a mind like that?" Doucet mused.

"Speaking of nuts, what about Didi Moreau? What'll you do with him?"

"Fortier let him go for the moment. However, the search of his house turned up evidence that he has been making overtures to a mortuary. He wished to buy a dead body."

"What for?"

"To stuff it."

"*Stuff* it?"

"Taxidermy."

"Jesus. That's just . . . He's *got* to be tied up in this Charmentier business somehow."

"I agree. But there is no evidence that he did anything except receive the bones. As for the photographs, well, with no evidence other than fingerprints . . ."

"Yeah, and on photographs given to you by an *American* investigator . . ."

"According to M. Grey, Le Comte ordered Moreau to clear his secret room."

"Probably my fault. Charmentier might risk hiring a woman who turned out to be friends with a cop—might even have found it a thrill—but when another of her friends turns up with questions and a suspicious look, that may've been one threat too many. I wonder how long Moreau would have lasted before Charmentier decided he was too much of a risk."

"Or Sarah," Doucet said quietly, then changed the subject. "How is your Nancy?"

"Oh, fine. Although she seems to feel that all but accusing me of murdering her roommate might come between us. I'm trying to convince her it was just her way of playing hard to get."

Doucet gave him a crooked grin. "Forcing your *chérie* to turn you in to the police is certainly a *nouveau* method of wooing."

"Try it, if Sarah ever seems to be getting bored. Oh, before I go: Fortier wouldn't tell me if he'd identified the other two photographs."

"Aline David and Marie Michaud."

"Michaud? Known as Mimi, right? A singer? But she was, what, a couple of years ago? Not on your list."

"March, 1927. The David woman was a year before that. It would seem Le Comte only sent his early photographs to Moreau. Perhaps he thought the passage of time would render them less likely to be recognized."

"That and tearing the pictures into pieces. And none of the four had obvious scars or moles. You'll search Charmentier's house, for signs of the others?"

"Fortier tells me Le Comte had fifteen Displays on his bedroom wall. All had portions of photographs. He also found several typewriting machines, which he's comparing to the letter you took."

Stuyvesant got to his feet. "You look dog-tired. Get some sleep."

"I've done nothing but sleep," Doucet complained in a querulous voice.

"Yeah, losing a couple quarts of blood does that. However, your Sergeant told me not to leave Paris for a while, so when you get out, I'll buy you a drink and some oysters. Build up your stamina."

"I will hold you to it."

Stuyvesant put out his hand again, glad for the man's size. At the door, he discovered that Sarah had not gone for Doucet's suggested fresh air. She was curled into a chair across the hallway, fast asleep.

Stuyvesant studied her, his tired body swaying with the surge of conflicting emotions. Love and guilt, regret and loss and thanks, all of it boiling down to pure and simple affection. After a moment, he let go of the door frame to look back to the room, knowing it was all on his face, letting the man see it anyway.

"Oh, and Doucet? Make sure Sarah sends me an invitation to the wedding."

AFTERWORD

THIS IS A work of fiction. Some of its characters share the names
and general attributes of actual writers and artists of the early
twentieth century. However, it must be said that Ernest Hemingway
might well have bested Harris Stuyvesant in the boxing ring; the
Théâtre du Grand-Guignol had no patron named Charmentier; Cole
Porter does not appear to have been in Paris in September 1929; and
there is no reason to suspect Man Ray of anything but genius.

Similarly, travelers to Montparnasse need not search for the rue
Colle off the rue Vavin. It may have been there in 1929, but it is not
there today.

Background information may be found on the book page for *The
Bones of Paris* at LaurieRKing.com.

ABOUT THE AUTHOR

Laurie R. King is the *New York Times* bestselling author of thirteen Mary Russell mysteries, five contemporary novels featuring Kate Martinelli, and the acclaimed novels *A Darker Place*, *Folly*, *Keeping Watch*, and *Touchstone*. She lives in Northern California.

www.laurierking.com

ABOUT THE TYPE

This book was set in Caslon, a typeface first designed in 1722 by William Caslon. Its widespread use by most English printers in the early eighteenth century soon supplanted the Dutch typefaces that had formerly prevailed. The roman is considered a "workhorse" typeface due to its pleasant, open appearance, while the italic is exceedingly decorative.